Praise for the novels of
*New York Times* and *USA TODAY*
bestselling author BRENDA JOYCE

"In her inimitable style Joyce presents her unforgettable
de Warrenes in a mesmerizing new romance. Her
marvelous storytelling, combined with the high level of
emotion, makes for a non-stop delight of a read."
—*RT Book Reviews* on *An Impossible Attraction*

"Another first-rate Regency,
featuring multidimensional protagonists and
sweeping drama… Joyce's tight plot and vivid cast
combine for a romance that's just about perfect."
—*Publishers Weekly* Starred Review on *The Perfect Bride*

"Truly a stirring story with wonderfully etched
characters, Joyce's latest is Regency romance at its best."
—*Booklist* on *The Perfect Bride*

"Romance veteran Joyce brings her keen sense of humor
and storytelling prowess to bear on her witty,
fully formed characters."
—*Publishers Weekly* on *A Lady at Last*

"Joyce's characters carry considerable emotional weight,
which keeps this hefty entry absorbing, and her
fast-paced story keeps the pages turning."
—*Publishers Weekly* on *The Stolen Bride*

"Joyce excels at creating twists and turns
in her characters' personal lives."
—*Publishers Weekly*

# BRENDA JOYCE

# Seduction

HQN™

Recycling programs
for this product may
not exist in your area.

ISBN-13: 978-0-373-77655-9

SEDUCTION

For Sue and Laurent Teichman, with love and thanks!

# Seduction

# *PROLOGUE*

*July 1, 1793—near Brest, France*

"IS HE ALIVE?"

The voice surprised him. It sounded far away. And even as he heard the Englishman, pain stabbed through his back and shoulders, like nails being driven into his body, as if he were being crucified. The pain was so horrific he could not speak, but he cursed silently. What had happened?

He was on fire now. Even worse, he wondered if he was suffocating. He could hardly breathe. A terrible weight seemed to be pushing him down. And he was in absolute darkness....

But his mind was beginning to function. The man who had just spoken was English, but that was impossible. Where was he? What the hell had happened?

And the images began, rolling through his mind's eye with shocking speed, accompanied by horrific sounds— the bloodcurdling screams of the wounded and the dying amidst the racket of muskets and the boom of cannons, the river running red with the French blood of peasants, priests, nobles and soldiers....

He moaned. He could not quite recall how he had been wounded, and he was afraid he might be dying. What had happened to him?

Someone spoke, and the voice was familiar. "He is

barely alive, Lucas. He has lost a great deal of blood and has been unconscious since midnight. My surgeon does not know if he will live."

"What happened?" A second Englishman was speaking.

"We suffered a terrible defeat at Nantes, *messieurs,* a rout by the French under General Biron, but Dominic was not wounded in the battle. He was ambushed outside my apartments last night by an assassin."

And then he realized that his lifelong friend, Michel Jacquelyn, was speaking. *Someone had tried to murder him—because someone had known he was a spy.*

"Christ," the second Englishman said.

Dominic managed to open his eyes, a vast, prolonged effort of will. He lay on the beach on a pallet, under blankets—the surf beat the shore and the night above glinted with stars. Three men stood over him, in coats, breeches and boots. His vision was blurred, but he could distinguish them somewhat. Michel was short and dark, his clothes bloodstained, his hair pulled back in a queue. The Englishmen were tall and golden, their shoulder-length hair whipping in the wind. Everyone was heavily armed with pistols and daggers. Now, he heard the creaking of wood masts, the flap of canvas, the pounding of wind-whipped waves. And then he could no longer keep his eyes open. Exhausted, they closed.

He was going to faint, damn it....

"Were you followed?" Lucas asked sharply.

"*Non,* but *le gendarmerie* are everywhere, *mes amis.* We must make haste. The French blockade the coast— you will have to be careful to avoid their ships."

The other Englishman spoke, and he sounded cheerful. "Have no fear. No one can outrun the navy—or the revenue men—like me. Captain Jack Greystone, *mon-*

*sieur,* at your service on this highly interesting night. And I believe you already know my brother, Lucas."

"I do. You must get him to London, *messieurs,*" Michel said. *"Immédiatement."*

"He won't make it to London," Jack returned. "Not alive, anyway."

"We'll take him to Greystone," Lucas said flatly. "It's close—and safe. And if he's fortunate, he will live to fight another day."

"*Bien.* Keep him well—we at La Vendée need him back. God speed you all."

# CHAPTER ONE

*July 2, 1793—Penzance, Cornwall*

SHE WAS *VERY* LATE.

Julianne Greystone practically leapt from the curricle, having parked it before the milliner's shop. The Society's meeting was next door, in the public room of the White Hart Inn, but every space in front was taken up already. The inn always did a brisk business in the afternoon. She rechecked the curricle's brake, patted the old mare in the traces and quickly tied her to the post.

She hated being late. It wasn't her nature to dally. Julianne took life very seriously, unlike the other ladies she knew.

Those women enjoyed fashion and shopping, teas and social calls, dances and dinner parties, but they did not live in the same circumstances as she did. Julianne could not recall a time in her life when there had been days of leisure and frivolity; her father had abandoned the family before her third birthday, not that their straits hadn't already been dire. Father had been a younger son, without means, as well as a wastrel. She had grown up doing the kind of chores around the manor that her peers reserved for their servants. Cooking, washing dishes, carrying in firewood, ironing her brothers' shirts, feeding their two horses, mucking stalls.... There was always a chore awaiting her. There was always something left to do. There was simply not enough time in any given day, and she found tardiness inexcusable.

Of course, it was an hour's drive from her home on Sennen Cove to the city. Her older sister, Amelia, had taken the coach that day. Every Wednesday, come hell or high water, Amelia took Momma calling on their neighbors—never mind that Momma did not recognize anyone anymore. Momma wasn't well. She rarely had her wits about her, and sometimes failed to recognize her own daughters, but she loved to visit. No one was as adept at frivolity and gaiety as Momma. Momma often thought herself a debutante, surrounded by her merry girlfriends and chivalrous suitors. Julianne thought she knew what it had been like for her mother to grow up in a home filled with every luxury, where she was waited upon hand and foot, in a time before the Americans had sought their independence, a time of only occasional war—a time without fear, rancor and revolution. It had been a time of absolute splendor and indifferent and lavish ostentation, a time of blatant self-indulgence, a time when no one bothered to consider the misery of the common man next door.

Poor Momma. She had begun to fade away from them shortly after Father had left them for the gambling halls and loose women of London, Antwerp and Paris. But Julianne wasn't sure that a broken heart had caused Momma to lose her mind. She sometimes thought it far more simple and mundane: Momma simply could not manage in the dark, threatening circumstances of the modern world.

But their physician said it was important to keep her out and about. Everyone in the family agreed. So Julianne had been left with the curricle and their twenty-year-old mare. An hour's drive had become two.

She had never been more impatient. She lived for the monthly meetings in Penzance. She and her friend, Tom Treyton, who was as radical as she, had founded the society last year, after King Louis XVI had been deposed, and France had been declared a republic. They had both supported the French revolution from the moment it had become clear that great changes were afoot in that country, all in favor of easing the plight of the peasantry and middle class, but neither one had ever dreamed that the ancien régime would eventually fall.

Every week there was another twist and turn in France's crusade for freedom for the common man. Just last month, the Jacobin leaders in the National Assembly had staged a coup, arresting many of their opposition. A new constitution had resulted, giving every single man the vote! It was almost too good to be true. Recently the Committee of Public Safety had been established, and she was eager to learn what reforms it might soon bring about. And then there were the wars on the Continent. The new French Republic meant to bring liberty to all of Europe. France had declared war on the Hapsburg Empire in April of '92. But not everyone shared Julianne's and Tom's radical views and enthusiasm for France's new regime. Last February, Britain had joined Austria and Prussia and entered the war against France.

"Miss Greystone."

Julianne had been about to wave over the livery boy from across the street and ask him to water her mare. At the sound of the strident voice, she tensed and slowly turned.

Richard Colmes scowled at her. "You cannot park here."

She knew exactly why he meant to confront her. Julianne brushed a tendril of strawberry-blond hair away from her face. Very politely, she said, "It is a public street, Mr. Colmes. Oh, and good afternoon. How is Mrs. Colmes?"

The milliner was a short, pudgy man with gray whiskers. His wig was not powdered, but it was fine, indeed, and otherwise, his presence was impeccable, from his pale stockings and patent leather shoes to his embroidered coat. "I will not condone your society, Miss Greystone."

She wanted to bristle but she smiled sweetly instead. "It is hardly my society," she began.

"You *founded* it. You radicals are plotting the downfall of this great country!" he exclaimed. "You are all Jacobins, and you meet to exchange your terrible plots right next door. You should be ashamed of yourself, Miss Greystone!"

There was no point in smiling now. "This is a free country, sir, and we are all entitled to our views. And we can certainly meet next door, if John Fowey allows us to do so." Fowey was the innkeeper.

"Fowey is every bit as mad as you!" he cried. "We are at war, Miss Greystone, and you and your kind support the enemy. If they cross the Channel, you will no doubt welcome the French army with open arms!"

She held her head high. "You are simplifying a very complex issue, sir. I support the rights of every man— even the vagabonds who come to this town begging for a decent meal. Yes, I happen to support the revolution in France—but so do a great many of our countrymen! I am keeping company with Thomas Paine, Charles Fox, Lords Byron and Shelley, to name just a few of the distinguished minds who recognize that the changes in France are for the universal good of mankind. I am a radical, sir, but—"

He cut her off. "You are a traitor, Miss Greystone, and if you do not move your curricle, I will do so for you." He turned and stalked into his shop, slamming the door behind him. The glass pane rattled, the bells jingled.

She trembled, feeling sick inside her stomach. She had been about to tell the milliner just how much she loved her country. One could be a patriot and still support the new constitutional republic in France. One could be a patriot and still advocate for political reform and social change, both abroad and here at home.

"Come, Milly," she said to the mare. She led the horse and carriage across the street to the livery, hating the recent dispute. With every passing week, it was becoming harder and harder to associate with her neighbors—people she had known her entire life. Once, she had been welcomed into any shop or salon with open arms and warm smiles. It wasn't that way anymore.

The revolution in France and the subsequent wars on the Continent had divided the country.

And now she would have to pay for the privilege of leaving her mare at the livery, when they did not have change to spare. The wars had inflated the price of food stuffs, not to mention the cost of most other sundries. Greystone did have a thriving tin mine and an equally productive iron quarry, but Lucas invested most of the estate's profits, with an eye to the entire family's future. He was frugal, but they were all frugal—except for Jack, who was reckless in every possible way, which was probably why he was such an adept smuggler. Lucas was in London, or so she thought, although it was somewhat suspicious—he seemed to be in town all the time! And as for Jack, knowing her brother, he was probably at sea, running from a customs cutter.

She dismissed her worries about the unexpected ex-

pense, as there was no avoiding payment, and put aside
the recent and unpleasant conversation with the milliner,
although she might share it with her sister later.

Hurrying forward, she wiped dust from her freckled
nose, then slapped it off her muslin skirts. It hadn't rained
all week, and the roads were impossibly dry. Her gown
was now beige instead of ivory.

As she approached the sign posted beside the inn's
front door, excitement rose up, swift and hard. She had
painted it herself.

Society of Friends of the People, it read. Newcomers
Welcome. No Fees Required."

She was very proud of that last line. She had fought
her dear friend Tom Treyton tooth and nail to waive all
fees for memberships. Wasn't that what Thomas Hardy
was doing for the corresponding societies? Shouldn't
every man and woman be allowed to participate in an
assembly meant to promote the cause of equality, liberty and the rights of man? No one should be denied
their rights or the ability to participate in a cause that
would liberate them because he or she couldn't afford
the monthly dues!

Julianne entered the dark, cool public room of the inn
and immediately saw Tom. He was about her height, with
curly brown-blond hair and pleasant features. His father
was a well-to-do squire, and he had been sent to Oxford
for a university education. Julianne had thought he would
reside in London upon graduation; instead, he had come
home to set up a barrister's practice in town. Most of his
clients were smugglers caught by the preventive men. Unfortunately, he had not been able to successfully defend
his past two clients; both men been sentenced to two
years' hard labor. Of course, they had been guilty as
charged and everyone had known it.

Tom stood in the center of the public room, while everyone else was seated at tables and benches. Julianne instantly noticed that attendance was down yet again—even more than the last time. There were only two dozen men in the room, all of them miners, fishermen and smugglers. Since Britain had entered the Coalition against France in the war, there had been a resurgence of patriotism in the area. Men who had supported the revolution were now finding God and country. She supposed such a change of allegiance was inevitable.

Tom had seen her. His face lit up and he hurried over. "You are so late! I was afraid that something had happened, and that you would not make our assembly."

"I had to take Milly, and it was slow going." She lowered her voice. "Mr. Colmes would not let me park outside his shop."

Tom's blue eyes blazed. "Reactionary bastard."

She touched his arm. "He is frightened, Tom. Everyone is. And he doesn't understand what is happening in France."

"He is afraid we'll take his shop and his home and hand it over to the people. And maybe he should be afraid," Tom said.

They had disagreed on the method and means of reform for the past year, since they had first formed the society. "We can hardly march around dispossessing citizens of good standing like Richard Colmes," she rebuked softly.

He sighed. "I am being too radical, of course, but I wouldn't mind dispossessing the earl of Penrose and the baron of St. Just."

She knew he meant it. She smiled.

"Can we debate another time?"

"I know you agree that the rich have too much, and

simply because they inherited their means or were given the lands and titles," he said.

"I do agree, but you also know I do not condone a massive theft from the aristocracy. I want to know what debate I just walked in on. What has happened? What is the latest news?"

"You should join the reformers, Julianne. You are not really as radical as you like to think," he groused. "There has been a rout. The La Vendée royalists were defeated at Nantes."

"This is wonderful news," Julianne said, almost disbelieving. "The last we heard, those royalists had defeated us and had taken the area along the river in Saumur."

The gains made by the French revolutionaries within France were by no means secure, and there was internal opposition throughout the country. A very strong royalist rebellion had begun last spring in La Vendée.

"I know. It is a great reversal of fortune." He smiled and took her arm. "Hopefully the damned rebels in Toulon, Lyon, Marseilles and Bordeaux will soon fall. And those in Brittany, as well."

They shared a look. The extent of internal opposition to the revolution was frightening. "I should write to our friends in Paris immediately," Julianne decided. One of the goals of all corresponding societies was to keep in close contact with the Jacobin clubs in France, showing their full support for the cause of revolution. "Maybe there is something more we can do here in Britain, other than to meet and discuss the latest events."

"You could go to London and insert yourself in the proper Tory circles," Tom said, staring. "Your brother is a Tory. He pretends to be a simple Cornish miner, but Lucas is the great-grandson of a baron. He has many connections."

She felt an odd trepidation. "Lucas is really just a patriot," she began.

"He is a conservative and a Tory." Tom was firm. "He knows men with power, men with information, men close to Pitt and Windham. I am sure of it."

She folded her arms, feeling defensive. "He has the right to his opinions, even if they oppose our views."

"I didn't say he didn't. I merely said he is well connected. Better than you know."

"Are you suggesting I go to London and spy on my brother and his peers?" She was aghast.

"I did not say that, but it is hardly an idea without merit." He smiled. "You could go to London next month, since you cannot attend the convention in Edinburgh."

Thomas Hardy had organized a convention of corresponding societies, and just about every society in the country was sending delegates to Edinburgh. Tom would represent their society. But with Britain having entered the war against France on the Continent, the stakes had changed. Radicals and radical clubs were no longer looked upon with patronizing amusement. There was talk of governmental repression. Everyone knew that the prime minister was intolerant of all radicals, as were many of the ministers around him, and so was King George.

It was time to send a message to the entire British government, and especially Prime Minister Pitt: they would not be repressed or opposed by the government, not now and not ever. They would continue to propagate and espouse the rights of man, and support the revolution in France. They would continue to oppose war with the new French Republic, as well.

Another smaller convention had been organized to take place in London, under Whitehall's very nose. Julianne hoped she could find the means to attend, but a trip to London was costly. However, what was Tom really suggesting? "I am not spying on my brother, Tom. I hope you were in jest."

"I was," he assured her quickly. When she stared uncertainly, he added, "I was going to write our friends in Paris, but why don't you do that?" Tom touched her chin. His eyes had softened. "You are such a better wordsmith than I am."

She smiled at him, truly hoping that he hadn't asked her to spy on Lucas, who was *not* a Tory and *not* at all involved in the war. "Yes, I am," she said, hoping for levity.

"Let's sit. We still have a good hour of discussion ahead," he said, guiding her to a bench.

For the next hour, they discussed the recent events in France, motions in the House of Commons and Lords, and the latest political gossip in London. By the time the meeting had broken up, it was almost five o'clock in the evening. Tom walked her outside. "I know it's early, but can you have supper with me?"

She hesitated. They'd shared supper last month after a society meeting. But when he'd been about to help her into her carriage, he'd restrained her, and then he had looked at her as if he wished to kiss her.

She hadn't known what to do. He had kissed her once before, and it had been pleasant, but not earth-shattering. She loved him dearly, but she wasn't interested in kissing him. Yet she was fairly certain that Tom was in love with her, and they had so much in common that she wanted to fall in love with him. He was such a good man and a dear friend.

She'd known him since childhood, but they had not become truly acquainted until two years ago, when they'd both discovered one another attending the Falmouth meeting. That had been the real beginning of their friendship. It was becoming clear to her that her feelings were more sisterly and platonic than romantic.

Still, dining with Tom was very enjoyable—they always had stimulating discussions. She was about to accept his invitation, when she faltered at the sight of a man riding his chestnut gelding up the street.

"Is that Lucas?" Tom asked, as surprised as she was.

"It most certainly is," she said, beginning to smile. Lucas was seven years her senior, making him all of twenty-eight. He was a tall, muscular man with classically chiseled features, piercing gray eyes and golden hair. Women tried to catch his attention incessantly, but unlike Jack, who was a self-proclaimed rogue, Lucas was a gentleman. Rather aloof, he was a man of great discipline and greater duty, bent on maintaining the family and the estate.

Lucas had been more of a father figure for her than a brother, and she respected, admired and loved him dearly.

He halted his lathered mount in front of her and her delight in seeing him vanished. Lucas was grim. She suddenly thought of the bold sign just behind her back, welcoming newcomers to their meeting, and she hoped he wouldn't see it.

Clad in a brown coat, a burgundy waistcoat, a lawn shirt and pale breeches, his black boots brown with dust, Luke leapt from his red gelding. He wasn't wearing a wig and his hair was casually pulled back. "Hello, Tom." He shook hands, unsmiling. "I see you continue to peddle sedition."

Tom's smile vanished. "That isn't fair, Lucas."

"War is never fair." He turned a cold gray gaze on Julianne.

He had disapproved of her politics for several years

now, and he had made himself very clear when France had declared war on them. She smiled, hesitantly.

"You are home. We weren't expecting you."

"Obviously. I have galloped the entire distance from Greystone, Julianne." There was warning in his tone. Lucas had a fierce temper, when aroused. She saw he was very angry now.

She stiffened. "I take it you are looking for me?" *What was this about?* "Is there an emergency?" Her heart felt as if it had stopped. "Is it Momma? Or has Jack been caught?!"

"Momma is fine. So is Jack. I wish a private word and it cannot wait."

Tom's face fell. "Will you dine with me another time, Julianne?"

"Of course," Julianne assured him. Tom bowed at Lucas, who did not move. When Tom was gone, she faced her brother, absolutely perplexed. "Are you angry with *me?*"

"I could not believe it when Billy told me you had gone into town to attend a *meeting.* I instantly knew what he meant," he said, referring to the boy who came daily to help with the horses. "We have already discussed this, several times—and recently, since the King's May Proclamation!"

She crossed her arms. "Yes, we have discussed our difference of opinions. And you know that you have no right to force your Tory views upon me."

He colored, aware that she meant to insult him. "I hardly wish to change how you think," he exclaimed. "But I intend to protect you from yourself. My God! The May Proclamation explicitly prohibits seditious meetings, Julianne. It was one thing to engage in such activity prior to the proclamation, but you cannot continue to do so now."

In a way, he was right, she thought, and it had been childish to call him a Tory. "Why must you assume that our meeting was seditious?"

"Because I know you!" he exploded. "Crusading for the rights of every common man is a wonderful cause, Julianne, but we are at war, and you are supporting the government we are at war with. That is sedition—and it could even be construed as treason." His gray eyes flashed. "Thank God we are in St. Just, where no one really gives a damn about our affairs, outside the customs agents!"

She trembled, thinking of that horrid dispute with the milliner. "We meet to discuss the events of the war and the events in France, and to espouse the views of Thomas Paine. That is all." But she was well aware that, if the government ever wanted to bother with their small club, they would all be accused of sedition. Of course, Whitehall did not even know of their existence.

"You write to that damned club in Paris—and don't deny it. Amelia told me."

Julianne could not believe her sister had betrayed her trust.

"I took her into my confidence!"

"She wants to protect you from yourself, as well! You must stop attending these meetings. You must also stop all correspondence with that damned Jacobin club in France. This war is a very serious and dangerous business, Julianne. Men are dying every day—and not just on the battlefields of Flanders and the Rhine. They are dying in the streets of Paris and in the vineyards of the countryside!" His gaze on fire, he controlled his tone. "I have heard talk in London. Sedition will not be tolerated for much longer, not while our men are dying on the Continent, not while our friends are fleeing France in droves."

"They are your friends, not mine." And the moment she spoke, she couldn't believe what she had said.

He flushed. "You would never turn away any human being in need, not even a French aristocrat."

He was right. She drew herself even straighter. "I am sorry, Lucas, but you cannot order me about the way Jack does his sailors."

"Oh, yes, I can. You are my sister. You are twenty-one years old. You are under my roof and in my care. I am the head of this family. You will do as I say—for once in your excessively independent life."

She was uncertain. Should she continue on and simply—openly—defy him? What could he possibly do? He would never disown her and force her from Greystone.

"Are you thinking of defying me?" He was in disbelief. "After all I have done for you—all that I have promised to do for you?"

She flushed. Any other guardian would have forced her into wedlock by now. Lucas was hardly a romantic, but he seemed to want her to find a suitor she could be genuinely fond of. He had once told her that he couldn't imagine her shackled to some conventional old squire, who thought political discourse insane babble. Instead, he wanted her matched with someone who would appreciate her outspoken opinions and unusual character, not disparage her for them.

"I can hardly change my principles," she finally said. "Even if you are a wonderful brother—the most wonderful brother imaginable!"

"Do not try to flatter me now! I am not asking you to

change your principles. I am asking you to be discreet, to act with caution and common sense. I am asking you to desist from these radical associations, while we are at war."

She had a moral obligation to obey her older brother, yet she did not know if she was capable of doing as he had just asked. "You are putting me in a terrible position," she said.

"Good," he snapped. Then, "This is not why I have galloped my poor gelding across the entire parish to find you. We have a guest at Greystone."

All thoughts of radical meetings vanished. Under normal circumstances, she would be alarmed at the news of an unexpected guest. They hadn't been expecting Lucas, much less a guest. They had a single bottle of wine in the house. The guest room was unmade. The parlor had not been dusted. Neither had the front hall. Their cupboards were not full enough to support a dinner party. But Luke's expression was so dire now that she did not think she need worry about cleaning the house or filling the pantry. "Lucas?"

"Jack brought him home a few hours ago." He was grim. He turned to take up his horse's reins. His back to her, he said, "I don't know who he is. I am guessing that he must be a smuggler. In any case, I need you at home. Jack is already gone to get a surgeon. We must try to make the poor fellow comfortable, because he is at death's door."

GREYSTONE LOOMED AHEAD. It was a two-hundred-and-fifty-year-old manor house, cast in pale stone, with high sloping slate roofs. Set atop rugged, near-white, treeless cliffs, against barren, colorless moors, surrounded only by a gray, bleak sky, it seemed stark and desolate.

Sennen Cove was below. Its wild tales of the adventures, mishaps and victories of smugglers, customs agents and revenue men were partly myth and partly history. For generations, the Greystone family had actively smuggled with the best of them. As deliberately, the family had looked the other way as the cove was laden with illegal cases of whiskey, tobacco and teas by their friends and neighbors, feigning ignorance of any illegal activity. There were evenings when the customs agent stationed at Penzance would dine in the manor with his wife and daughters, drinking some of the best French wine to be had, sharing the latest gossip with their hosts, as if the best of friends; on other evenings, beacon fires blazed, warning the smugglers below that the authorities were on the way. Jack's ship would be at anchor, and the cove would explode with action as casks and cases were rushed into hiding in caves in the cliffs and Jack and his men fled the scene, the armed British authorities rushing down from the cliffs on foot, firing upon anyone who had been left behind.

Julianne had witnessed it all from the time she was a small child. No one in the parish thought smuggling a crime—it was a way of life.

Her legs ached terribly. So did her back. She rarely rode astride anymore, much less sidesaddle—her only option in her muslin dress. Keeping her balance at a brisk pace on the hired hack had been no easy task. Lucas had cast many concerned glances her way, and he had offered to pause for a moment so she could rest several times. Afraid that Amelia would linger with their neighbors and that the dying stranger was in the manor alone, she had refused.

The first thing she saw as she and Lucas trotted up the manor's crushed-shell drive was the pair of carriage horses turned out behind the stone stables, which were set back from the house. *Amelia was already home.*

They hurriedly dismounted. Lucas took her reins. "I'll take care of the horses." He smiled at her. "You will be sore tomorrow."

They were no longer arguing. "I am sore now."

He led the pair of geldings away.

Julianne lifted her pale skirts and rushed up the manor's two front steps. The house was a simple rectangle, longer than it was tall or wide, with three floors. The topmost floor contained attics and, once upon a time, living quarters for the servants they no longer had. The front hall remained in its original form. It was a large room, once used for dining and entertaining. The floors were dark gray stone, the walls a lighter version of the same stone. Two ancestral portraits and a pair of ancient swords decorated the walls; at one end of the hall there was a massive fireplace and two stately burgundy chairs. The ceilings were timbered.

Julianne rushed through the hall, past a small, quaint parlor with mostly modern furnishings; a small, dark library; and the dining room. She started up the narrow stairs.

Amelia was coming down. She held wet rags and a pitcher. Both women faltered as they saw one another. "Is he all right?" Julianne cried immediately.

Amelia was as petite as Julianne was tall. Her dark blond hair was pulled severely back, and her expression was characteristically serious, but her face lit up with relief now. "Thank the lord you are home! You know that Jack dropped off a dying man?" She was disbelieving.

"That is just like Jack!" Julianne snapped. Of course, by now, Jack was gone. "Lucas told me. He is outside with the horses. What can I do?"

Amelia turned abruptly and led the way up the stairs, her small body tight with tension. She marched quickly down the hall, which was dark, the wall sconces unlit, family portraits dating back two hundred years lining the corridor. Lucas had taken over the master suite long ago and Jack had his own bedchamber, but she and Amelia shared a room. Neither one cared, as the room was used only for sleeping. But the single guest chamber that remained had been left mostly untouched. Guests were rare at Greystone.

Glancing grimly at Julianne, she paused before the open door of the guest bedroom. "Doctor Eakins just left."

The guest room looked out over the rocky beaches of the cove and the Atlantic Ocean. The sun was setting, filling the small chamber with light. The room contained a small bed, a table and two chairs, a bureau and an armoire. Julianne faltered, her gaze going to the man on the bed.

Her heart lurched oddly.

The dying man was shirtless, a sheet loosely draped to his hips. She didn't mean to stare, but stretched out as he was, little was left to the imagination—the man was very big and very dark, a mass of sculpted muscle. She stared for one moment longer, hardly accustomed to the sight of a bare-chested man, much less one with such a powerful physique.

"He was on his abdomen a moment ago. He must have turned over when I left," Amelia said sharply. "He was shot at close range in the back. Doctor Eakins said he has lost a great deal of blood. He is in pain."

Julianne now saw that his breeches were bloodstained and dirty. She wondered if the bloodstains had come from his wound—or someone else's. She didn't want to look at his lean hips or his powerful thighs, so she quickly looked at his face.

Her heart slammed. Their guest was a very handsome man with swarthy skin, pitch-black hair, high cheekbones and a straight, patrician nose. Thick dark lashes were fanned out on his face.

She averted her eyes. Her heart seemed to be racing wildly, which was absurd.

Amelia thrust the wet cloth and pitcher into her arms and rushed forward. Julianne somehow looked up, aware of how hot her cheeks were. "Is he breathing?" she heard herself ask.

"I don't know." Amelia touched his forehead. "To make matters even worse, he has an infection, as the wound was not properly cared for. Doctor Eakins was not optimistic." She turned. "I am going to send Billy down for seawater."

"He should bring a full pail," Julianne said. "I'll sit with him."

"When Lucas comes in, we will turn him back over." Amelia hurried from the bedchamber.

Julianne hesitated, staring at the stranger, then pinched herself. The poor man was dying; he needed her help.

She set pitcher and cloth down on the table and approached. Very carefully, she sat beside him, her heart racing all over again. His chest wasn't moving. She lowered her cheek to his mouth, and it was a moment before she felt a small puff of his breath. Thank God he was alive.

*"Pour la victoire."*

She straightened as if shot. Her gaze slammed to his face. His eyes remained closed, but he had just spoken— *in French*—with the accent of a Frenchman! She was certain he had just said, "For victory."

It was a common cry amongst the French revolutionaries, but he resembled a nobleman, with his patrician features. She glanced at his hands—nobles had hands as soft as a babe's. His knuckles were cut open and crusted with blood, his palms calloused.

She bit her lip. Being this close made her uncomfortably aware of him. Perhaps it was of his near nudity, or his sheer masculinity. She inhaled, hoping to relieve some tension. *"Monsieur? Êtes-vous français?"*

He did not move as Lucas said, "Is he awake?"

Julianne half-turned as her brother entered the room. "No. But he spoke in his sleep. He spoke in French, Lucas."

"He isn't asleep. He is unconscious. Amelia said he is with fever now."

Julianne hesitated, then dared to lay her palm on his brow. "He is very hot, Lucas."

"Can you tend him, Julianne?"

She looked at her brother, wondering if his tone had been odd. "Of course I can. We'll keep him wrapped in wet sheets. Are you sure Jack didn't say anything about who he is? Is he French?"

"Jack doesn't know who he is." Lucas was firm. "I want to stay but I have to get back to London tomorrow."

"Is something wrong?"

"I'm examining a new contract for our iron ore. But I'm not sure I like leaving you and Amelia alone with him." His glance was on their guest again.

She stared, and finally Lucas stared back. When he chose to be impassive, it was impossible to know what he was thinking. "Surely you don't think he might be dangerous?"

"I don't know what to think."

Julianne nodded, turning back to her charge. There

was something odd about that exchange, she thought. She suddenly wondered if her brother knew who their guest was—but didn't want to say so. She turned to glance after him, but he was gone.

There was no earthly reason for him to withhold any information from her. If he knew who this man was, he would surely tell her. She was obviously wrong.

She stared at the dark stranger, hating not being able to help him. She pushed a hank of thick, dark hair out of his face. As she did, he thrashed so suddenly that his arm struck her thigh. She leapt up in alarm as he cried, *"Ou est-elle? Qui est responsible? Qu'est il arrivé?"*

*Where is she? Who has done this?* she silently translated. He thrashed again, even more forcefully, and Julianne was afraid he would hurt himself. He moaned loudly, in obvious pain.

She sat back down on the bed, by his hip. She stroked his hot shoulder. *"Monsieur, je m'appele Julianne. Il faut que vous reposiez maintenant."*

He was breathing hard now, she saw, but he wasn't moving and he felt warmer than before. Yet that had to be her imagination. And then he started to speak.

For one moment, she thought he was trying to speak to her. But he spoke so rapidly and furiously, so desperately, that she realized he was delirious.

"Please," she said softly, deciding to speak only in French. "You have a fever. Please, try to sleep."

*"Non! Nous ne pouvons pas nous retirer!"* It was hard to understand him, but she strained to make sense of the rapid-fire, jumbled words. *We cannot go back now,* he had said. There was no doubt in her mind that he was French. No Englishman could have such a perfect accent. No Englishman would speak in a second language while in a delirium.

Julianne crouched by his side, trying to understand him. But he was thrashing violently, enough so that he rolled onto his back, all the while shouting. He cursed. *They could not go back. They could not retreat!* Was he speaking about a battle? He shouted. *So many had died, but they had to hold this line! No, no,* he screamed. *Do not retreat! Hold the line! For liberty!*

Julianne clasped his hot shoulder, tears blurring her eyes. He was most definitely reliving a terrible battle that he and his men were losing. My God—could he be a French army officer?

*"Pour la liberté!"* he cried. "Go on, go on!"

She stroked his shoulder, trying to offer him comfort. *The river was filled with blood... Too many had died... The priest had died... They had to retreat. The day was lost!*

He wept.

She did not know what to do. She had never seen a grown man cry. "You are delirious, *monsieur,*" she tried. "But you are safe now, here, with me."

He lay panting, his cheeks wet with tears, his chest shining with perspiration.

"I am so sorry for what you have suffered," she told him. "We are not on the battlefield. We are in my home, in Britain. You will be safe here, even if you are a Jacobin. I will hide you and protect you—I promise you that!"

He suddenly seemed to relax. Julianne wondered if he was sleeping.

She inhaled, shaken to the core of her being. He was a French army officer, she was certain. He might even be a nobleman—some of the French nobility had supported the revolution and now supported the Republic. He had suffered a terrible defeat in which many of his men had died and it was haunting him. She ached for him. But how on earth had Jack found him? Jack did not support the revolution, yet he wasn't exactly a British patriot, either. He had told her once that the war suited him immensely—smuggling was even more profitable now than it had been before the revolution.

The man was so hot to the touch. She stroked his brow, suddenly angry—where was Amelia? Where was the ocean water? "You are burning up, *monsieur*," Julianne told him, continuing in his native tongue. "You must be still and get better."

They had to get his fever down. She re-wet the cloth, and this time, stroked it over his neck and shoulders. Then she laid the cloth there, picking up and wetting another one.

"At least you are resting now," she said softly, then realized she had lapsed into English. She repeated what she had said in French, sliding the cloth across his chest. Her pulse accelerated.

She had just laid the wet cloth on his chest again, where she meant to leave it, when he seized her wrist violently. She cried out, shocked, and her gaze flew to his face.

His green eyes were blazing with fury.

Frightened, she gasped, *"Êtes vous reveillé?"* Are you awake?

He did not release her, but his grasp gentled. So did his eyes. "Nadine?" he whispered hoarsely.

*Who was Nadine?* Of course, she knew—the woman was his lady love or his wife. It was hard to speak. She wet her lips. "*Monsieur,* you have been wounded in battle. I am Julianne. I am here to help you."

His stare was feverish, not lucid. And then suddenly he reached for her shoulder, still holding her wrist.

He winced, breathing hard, but his gaze did not waver. An odd light flickered there and she became breathless.

He slowly smiled. "Nadine." And his strong, powerful hand slid across her shoulder, to the back of her neck. Before she could protest or ask him what he was doing, he began to pull her face down toward his.

In shock, she realized he meant to kiss her!

His smile was infinitely seductive, confident and promising. And then his lips were plying hers.

Julianne gasped, but she did not try to move away from him. Instead, she went still, allowing him the shocking liberty, her heart lurching, her body tightening. Desire fisted, hard.

It was a desire she had never before felt.

Then she realized that he had stopped kissing her. She was breathing hard against his motionless mouth. She was acutely aware of the fire raging in her own body. It took her a moment to realize that he was unconscious again.

Julianne sat up straight, in shock. Her mind scrambled and raced. He had kissed her! He was with fever; he was delirious. He hadn't known what he was doing!

Did it even matter?

He had kissed her and she had responded as she hadn't dreamed possible.

And he was a French army officer—a revolutionary hero.

She looked at him. "Whoever you are, you are not going to die—I won't allow it," she said.

He was so still that he could have been a corpse.

# CHAPTER TWO

THERE WERE DOZENS of men in the mob, screaming in rage, fists shaking in the air, and he knew he must run… As he did, the cobblestones beneath his feet changed, turning red. He did not understand—and then he realized he was running in a river of blood!

He cried out, as the stately Parisian buildings vanished. Now, the river of blood was filled with screaming, dying men. Panic and fear consumed him.

And he knew he must wake up.

He felt cotton beneath his hands, not dirt, not blood. He fought the bloody river and saw Nadine smiling at him, her eyes shining, the moon full and bright behind her. He had kissed her—except, that wasn't right, because Nadine was dead….

Nadine was dead, and he was lying in a bed— Where was he?

Terribly drained, Dominic realized that he had been dreaming. His memories remained jumbled, and dread and fear filled him, but he fought the rising panic. He had to think clearly. It was a matter of life and death.

*It wasn't safe for him to remain in France now.*

*Someone knew who he really was.*

And he recalled being ambushed outside Michel's apartments. He tensed with more fear and alarm, fighting both emotions. And all of his memories of the past year and a half returned forcefully then. He had gone to

France to find his mother and fiancée and bring them home to England. He had never found Nadine, but he had found his mother, hiding above a bakery in Paris, her townhome destroyed. After seeing her safely aboard a Britain-bound ship at Le Havre, he had returned to Paris, hoping to find Nadine.

He had never meant to stay in France, gathering information for his country. Although his mother, Catherine Fortescue, was a Frenchwoman, his father was the earl of Bedford and he was an Englishman to the core. Dominic Paget had been born on the family estate at Bedford. An only child, he had been educated at Eton and Oxford. With William Paget's passing, he had inherited both the title and the earldom. Although he took up his seat in the Lords several times a year—he felt a duty to the country as a whole, for he must also look after Bedford's interests—politics had never interested him. In fact, several years ago he had turned down a position in Pitt's ministry. His responsibilities were clear—and they were to the earldom.

He hadn't discovered what had happened to Nadine. She had last been seen in the riot that had destroyed his mother's home. Catherine feared that she had been trampled to death by the mob. When he had returned to Britain, he had been concerned enough about the revolution in France to meet with several of his peers, including Edmund Burke, a man with great political connections. The information Dominic had gleaned while he was in France was so unsettling that Burke had introduced him to Prime Minister Pitt. But it was Sebastian Warlock who had persuaded him to return to France—this time with one single ambition: espionage.

It was impossible to determine who had learned the truth about Jean-Jacques Carre—the identity he had assumed. It could have been any one of dozens of Parisians, or even a mole planted amongst Michel's command. But someone had discovered that Carre was no print-shop owner and no Jacobin. Someone had learned that he was really an Englishman and an agent.

His tension escalated wildly now. He was frighteningly weak—and thus vulnerable. Pain stabbed through his back with every breath he took.

*Was he with friends—or foes?*

*Was he still in France?*

Afraid and fully alert, he noted that he was not shackled. Very carefully, he opened his eyes, just enough so he could peek out through his lashes.

He did not change the pattern of his breathing. He did not move a single muscle, other than his eyelids. He sensed he was not alone. He wanted whoever was with him—whoever was guarding him—to think he was asleep.

The vague outlines of a small bedroom came into his line of vision. He saw an armoire, a window. A moment later, he smelled the tang in the air, and tasted its salt.

He was near the coast, but what coast?

He fought fiercely to retrieve every possible memory. Had he dreamed of a long journey in the back of a wagon, mostly by night? Had he dreamed of the rocking of a ship, the creaking of masts, the whisper of canvas—and being in the throes of a terrible agony? What happened to him after he had been shot? Hazy images tried to form, and suddenly he thought he remembered a woman with titian hair, hovering over him, bathing him, caring for him.

And then a woman moved into his line of vision, bending over him. He glimpsed titian hair, her pale visage, an ivory dress.

She murmured, *"Monsieur?"*

Dominic recognized the sound of her voice. So she had cared for him; it had not been a dream.

He could not assume that she was a friend and an ally. Could he defend himself if necessary? Escape? He was so exhausted, so weak! Who was she and why had she nursed him through his illness? Was she a friend of Michel's? How had he come into her care? He debated waiting her out—sooner or later, she would leave him, and then he could decide what predicament he was in. His first order of business would be to search the room, then the house. He had to discern his location. And he needed a weapon with which to defend himself.

On the other hand, she could not be alone. She had to have comrades. When she left, someone else might be sent to guard him, and it might even be a man.

He opened his eyes fully and looked into the startled gray gaze of the woman.

She was seated in a chair, pulled up to his bedside, a writing tablet on her lap, a quill in her hand. She started and whispered, *"Monsieur, vous êtes reveillé?"*

He had no intention of answering her, not yet. Instead, he took a quick inventory of his surroundings. He saw that he lay in a narrow bed in a room he did not recognize. The chamber was a modest one, simply furnished, and it was hard to discern if he was in a bourgeois's or a nobleman's home. If the latter, they were impoverished.

One window let in the daylight—it was early afternoon. The sunlight was gray and weak, not at all like the bright summer sunshine in the Loire Valley.

How had he gotten to this bedchamber? Had he been taken in a wagon and then a ship—or had that been a dream? Damn it, he did not recall anything after being shot in the alley in Nantes! The only thing he was now certain of was that he was on the coast—but where? He could be in Le Havre or Brest, he thought, but he was uncertain. He could be in Dover, or Plymouth. Even if he was in England, he had to protect his identity. No one could ever guess that he was a British agent.

But she had spoken to him in French.

She spoke again. He became absolutely still, focusing on her, as the woman repeated what she had said before. "Sir, are you awake?"

Her color was high, a question in her eyes. Although she was speaking French, she had a slight accent. He felt certain she was English. And that should relieve him— except, he did not like the fact that she was speaking in French. Was she partly French, as he was? Or did she assume him to be a Frenchman, for whatever reason? Had she met him when he was undercover? Did she know the truth or any part of it? Where did her sympathies lie? If only he could remember more!

And why the hell was he stark naked beneath the thin sheets?

She suddenly got up. He watched her warily as she walked across the room, noticing that her figure was very pleasing, not that he really cared. She might be an ally— or she might be the enemy. And he would do whatever necessary to survive. Seducing her was not out of the question.

He now saw that she was putting the tablet and the parchment on the table, placing the quill into an inkwell there. She took up a cloth, dipping it in a basin of water. He did not relax. The hazy images became more focused, of this woman bending over him and bathing him with the cloth…of her face, close to his, as he prepared to kiss her.…

He had kissed her. He was certain of it.

His interest sharpened. What had happened between them? Surely this was to his advantage.

She returned, her face pale except for two bright splotches of pink on her cheeks. She sat, wringing out the cloth, as he watched her closely, waiting to see what she would do next. His body stirred.

In France, living on the verge of death every day, he had lost all the morality he had been raised with. There had been so many French women in his bed, some pretty, some not, very few whose names he had even known, much less recalled. Life was short—too short. He had realized that morality was a useless endeavor in a time of war and revolution.

The images he had awoken to were always there, in the back of his mind, haunting him. That enraged mob, the bloody street and then the bloody river in Saumur. The family he had seen guillotined, the priest who had died in his arms. His morality had died long ago, perhaps with Nadine. Sex was entertainment, an escape, because death was the only certainty in his life.

Tomorrow, someone could assassinate him.

Tomorrow, an enraged mob could drag him from this house and stone him to death, or he could be led in chains, past cheering crowds to the guillotine.

She smiled slightly and then she laid the cool cloth on his forehead.

He flinched, surprising them both. Then he seized her wrist. *"Qui êtes vous?"* Who are you? She had spoken to him in French, so he spoke back to her in that language, as well. Until he knew where he was and who she was— and if it was safe to reveal himself—he would simply follow her lead.

She gasped. "*Monsieur,* you are awake! I am so very glad!"

He did not release her. Instead, he pulled her closer, down toward him, his heart racing with his fear. He hated this vacuum of knowledge; he had to find out who she was and where he was. "Who are you? Where am I?"

She seemed frozen, mere inches between their faces now. "I am Julianne Greystone, *monsieur.* I have been caring for you. You are at my family home, and you are safe here."

He studied her, not willing to relax. The fact that she spoke of his being safe meant that she knew something of his activities. Why else would she suggest that he might otherwise be in danger? And who did she believe him to be in danger from? The Jacobins? Someone specific— like the assassin in Nantes?

Or did she think him in danger from his own allies? Did she think him a Frenchman in danger from the British?

Was her family home in England—or France? Why did she keep speaking in French?

She wet her lips and whispered hoarsely, "Are you feeling better? The fever has broken, but you remain so pale, *monsieur.*"

He fought a sudden wave of dizziness. *God, he was so weak.* He released her. But he did not regret intimidating her. He wanted her nervous and flustered and easily manipulated.

"I am sore, *mademoiselle.* My back aches, but yes, I am better."

"You were shot in the back, *monsieur.* It was very serious," she said softly. "You were very ill. We feared for your life."

"We?"

"My sister, my brothers and I."

There were men in the house, he thought. "Did you all care for me?"

"My brothers are not here. I cared for you mostly, *monsieur,* although my sister, Amelia, has helped, when she is not caring for Momma." Her color increased.

He was alone with three women.

He was relieved, but only slightly. Of course he would work this situation to his advantage. He might be terribly weak, but he would find a weapon, and three women would not be a match for him—they must not be a match for him, not if he meant to survive. "Then it seems, *mademoiselle,* that I am entirely in your debt."

Impossibly, she blushed another time and leapt to her feet. "Nonsense, *monsieur.*"

He studied her. She was very susceptible to seduction, he thought. "Do you fear me, mademoiselle?" he asked softly. She was *very* nervous.

"No! Of course not!"

"Good. There is nothing to fear, after all." He slowly smiled. They had kissed. She had undressed him. Was that why she was so nervous?

She bit her lip. "You have suffered through an ordeal. I am relieved you are well."

How much did she know? "Yes, I have." He was calm. He hoped she would continue and tell him how he had gotten to that house, and what had happened to him after Nantes.

She fell silent, but her gray gaze never wavered.

She would not enlighten him, he thought; he would have to draw her out. "I am sorry to have put you out. Surely there are servants to do your bidding?"

It was a moment before she spoke. "We have no servants, *monsieur*. There is a stable boy, but he comes for just a few hours every day."

There was more relief, but he remained wary.

"You are staring," she said hoarsely.

He glanced at her hands, which she clasped tightly against her white muslin skirts. There was no wedding band, no diamond ring—there were no rings at all. "You have saved my life, *mademoiselle,* so I am curious about you."

Her elegant hands lifted. She crossed them over her chest, defensively—or nervously. "You were in need. How could I not help?" Then, "You have not told me your name."

The lie came as naturally as breathing. "Charles Maurice. I am forever in your debt."

She finally smiled at him.

"You do not owe me," she said firmly. She hesitated. "You must be hungry. I will be right back."

The moment he heard her footsteps fading in the hall, he sat up and tossed the covers aside, about to stand. Pain shot through his back and chest. He froze, moaning.

And the room spun.

Damn it!

He refused to lie back down. It took him an endless moment to fight the pain, to will away the dizziness. He was in far worse condition than he had assumed. Then, slowly and carefully, he stood up.

He leaned against the wall, exhausted. It took a moment for the room to stop turning. But the minute the room was still, he staggered to the armoire. To his dismay, it was empty. *Where were his clothes?*

He cursed again. Then he moved to the window, his balance precarious enough that he knocked the chair over. There, he gripped the sill and stared past the barren cliffs at the ocean beyond them.

He had no doubt it was the Atlantic Ocean he gazed upon. He knew the steel-gray color of those often stormy waters. And then he stared at the pale rock cliffs, the desolate, flat landscape. In the distance, he saw the silhouette of a lone tower. He was not in Brest, he thought. The landscape looked very much like that of Cornwall.

Cornwall was renowned for its Jacobin sympathies. He turned, leaning against the sill for balance. The small table was before him, with her writing tablet, the inkwell, and the parchment page. He took two steps to the table, grunted hard and seized its edge to keep from falling down.

Dominic cursed again. He wasn't going to be able to run from anyone if he had to, not in the next few days. He wouldn't be able to even seduce her, for that matter.

His gaze found the parchment. *She had been writing the letter in French.*

Dread arose. He seized it and read the first line.

*My dear friends, I am writing to celebrate with you the recent victories in the National Assembly, and especially the triumph of establishing a new Constitution, giving every man the right to vote.*

She was a damned Jacobin.
*She was the enemy.*
And now, the words seemed to gray on the pale page. Somehow, he managed to read the next lines.

*Our Society is hoping that more victories over the Opposition will come. We want to ask you how we can further aid our cause of equality and liberty in France, and throughout the Continent.*

The words were now blurring rapidly, and becoming darker, and he could not make them out. He stared blindly at the vellum. *She was a Jacobin.*

Was she playing cat and mouse with him? he wondered. In France, everyone spied on their neighbors, looking for rebels and traitors. Was it now the same in Britain? As a Jacobin, was she hunting men like him? Hoping to identify British agents, and then intending to betray them?

Or did she think him a Frenchman? Now, he must make certain she never knew he was an Englishman. And how much did she know? Did she know he had just come from France? He needed information, damn it!

He was sweating and out of breath. Agitation was more than he could manage, in his state. Too late, he realized that the floor was undulating beneath him. He dropped the page, cursing.

Dark shadows were closing in on him.

It was hard to breathe. The room was spinning slowly, with all of its furnishings.

He must not faint now.

Dom finally sank to the floor. As he lay there, struggling to remain conscious, he heard the footsteps rushing at him. Fear stabbed through him.

*"Monsieur!"*

He fought to remain alert, so hard, sweat covered his entire body. His fists clenched and he inhaled, opening his eyes. The first thing he saw was her gray gaze, trained upon his face, as she knelt over him. Her expression seemed to be one of worry.

Miraculously, the room stopped swimming.

He stared up at her and she gaze down at him with great anxiety.

He was riddled with tension, lying prone beneath her. He was too weak to defend himself and he knew it. She must realize it, too.

But a weapon did not appear in her hand. Instead, she touched his bare shoulders, clasping them. "*Monsieur!* Did you faint?" Her tone was hoarse. And then he realized why.

He was naked; she was entirely clothed.

"I fell, *mademoiselle,*" he lied smoothly. He would never let her know how weak he was. She must believe him capable of self-defense—even aggression. Somehow, he lifted his hand and touched her cheek. "You remain my savior."

For one moment, their gazes collided. Then she leapt to her feet, turning her head away, to avoid looking at his body now. She was crimson.

He felt certain she had never seen a naked man before. Her inexperience would make her easy to manipulate. "I beg your pardon," he said, praying he would not collapse again as he sat up. "I cannot find my clothes."

"Your clothes," she said roughly, "were laundered."

He saw that she had her glance averted still, so he stood. He wanted to collapse upon the mattress; instead, he pulled the sheet from it and wrapped it around his waist. "Did you undress me?" He glanced at her.

"No." She refused to look at him. "My brother did—we had to give you a sea bath, to reduce the fever."

He sat on the bed. Pain exploded but he ignored it. Long ago, he had mastered the skill of keeping his expression frozen. "Then I thank you again."

"You came to us only in breeches and boots, *monsieur.* The breeches are not dry yet. It has rained since you came to us. But I will bring you a pair of my brother Lucas's breeches."

He now sought her gaze until she met it. *She remained undone by having glimpsed him unclothed.* If he were fortunate, she hadn't noticed how incapacitated he was. He smiled. "I would appreciate a shirt, as well."

She looked at him as if he had spoken a foreign language she did not understand. Nor did she find humor in his remark.

He sobered. "I am sorry if I have offended your sensibilities, *mademoiselle.*"

"What were you attempting to do, *monsieur?* Why would you arise without my help?"

He was about to respond when he saw her letter, lying on the floor behind her, where he had dropped it. He knew better than to try to avert his eyes; she had already turned, to look behind her.

He said softly, "When I fell, I knocked over the chair and I also bumped into the table. I apologize. I hope I have not broken the chair."

She swiftly retrieved the letter and placed it by the inkwell; as quickly, she lifted and righted the chair.

"I was thinking to open the window for some fresh air," he added.

Without turning, she hurried to the window, unlatched it and pressed it outward. A cool blast of Atlantic air rushed into the room.

He studied her very closely.

She suddenly turned and caught him staring.

And he knew he did not mistake the new tension that had arisen between them.

Finally, she smiled back slightly. "I am sorry. You must think me very foolish. I…did not expect to return to the chamber and find you on the floor."

She was a good liar—but not as good as he was. "No," he said, "I think you very beautiful."

She went still.

He lowered his gaze. A silence fell. To be safe, he thought, all he had to do was play her.

Unless, of course, she was the spy he feared, and her naiveté was theatrics. In that case, she was the one playing him.

"JULIANNE? WHY ARE YOU SO concerned?" Amelia said.

They stood on the threshold of the guest bedchamber, looking into the room. It was a starry night outside, and Julianne had lit the fire, illuminating the chamber. Charles remained asleep and his supper tray was on the table, untouched.

She was never going to forget the fear that had stabbed through her when she had found him lying on the floor; for one moment, she had been afraid that he had died! But he hadn't been dead, he had fallen. When he had slowly stood up—absolutely, magnificently, shockingly naked—she had pretended not to look, but she had been incapable of looking away. "It has been over twenty-four hours since he last awoke," she said.

"He is recovering from a terrible wound," Amelia pointed out, her tone hushed. "You are beginning to remind me of a mother hen."

Julianne flinched. Amelia was right, she was worried—she wanted him to wake up, so she could be reassured. But then what? "That is nonsense. I am merely concerned, as anyone would be."

Amelia stared, hands on her small hips. "Julianne, I may not have spoken with him as you have, but I am hardly blind. Even asleep, he is a very attractive man."

She fought to remain impassive. "Really? I hadn't noticed."

Amelia laughed, a rather rare sound for her. "Oh, please. I have noticed that when you are with him, you cannot keep your eyes to yourself. It is a good thing he has been sleeping, or he would have caught you ogling him! But I am glad. I had begun to wonder if you are immune to men."

Amelia might not sound so cheerful if she knew what Julianne knew about their guest—and Julianne would soon have to tell her, as they were all under one small roof. Amelia was apolitical. Still, she was a patriot, and the most rational person Julianne knew. She would be horrified to learn that they were harboring an enemy of the state.

"My, that sounds like the pot calling the kettle black," Julianne said quickly, changing the subject.

Amelia said softly, "I wasn't always immune to handsome men, Julianne."

Julianne immediately regretted having taken such a tack. She had been only twelve years old the summer Amelia had fallen in love with the earl of St. Just's younger son, but she recalled their brief, passionate courtship. She remembered standing at the window downstairs, watching the two of them gallop away from the house, Simon Grenville in pursuit of her sister. He had been so dashing, he had seemed to be a veritable black prince, and she had thought her sister terribly fortunate. She also recalled Amelia's shock when they had learned of his brother's death. He had been summoned to London, and Julianne remembered thinking that her sister shouldn't cry, for Simon loved her and he would be back. But she had been naive and foolish. He hadn't returned. Amelia had cried herself to sleep for weeks on end, her heart broken.

Apparently Simon had quickly forgotten Amelia. Julianne did not think he had ever written, not a single missive, and two years later he had married the daughter of a viscount. In the past nine years, he had not been to the seat of his earldom, just to the north of St. Just, even once.

Julianne knew that Amelia had never forgotten him. The year after St. Just left, Amelia had turned down two very good offers, from a young, well-off barrister and a handsome officer in the royal navy. And then there were no more offers....

"I am twenty five years old, and no beauty," she said, matter-of-fact now. "My dowry is sparse and I am committed to taking care of Momma. If I am immune to men, it is by choice."

"You are *very* attractive, but you seem to want to vanish in plain sight!" Julianne hesitated. "Maybe one day you will meet someone who makes your heart race." She blushed as she thought about Charles Maurice.

"I hope not!"

Julianne knew she must drop the sore subject. "Very well. I am not blind, so yes, Monsieur Maurice is rather handsome. And he was so grateful when he awoke. He was charming." Charles Maurice was very eloquent, indicating some education and perhaps a genteel background. And he was dangerously charming.

"Ah, if that last part is true, then clearly, he has won your fickle heart!"

Julianne knew she was being teased, but she could not smile. She had thought about their guest night and day, well before he had awoken. She hoped she wasn't as infatuated with the French stranger as she seemed to be. Maybe this was the right time to reveal his identity to her sister.

"Julianne?" Amelia asked.

Julianne pulled her out of the doorway. "There is something you should know."

Amelia stared. "Obviously I am not going to like it."

"No, I don't think you will. You know Monsieur Maurice is a Frenchman, as I told you, Amelia…but he is not an émigré."

Amelia blinked. "What are you saying? Surely he is a smuggler, like Jack."

She wet her lips and said, "He is a French army officer, Amelia. He has survived terrible battles and the loss of so many of his men!"

Amelia gasped. "And how did you reach such a conclusion? Did he tell you this when he was awake?"

"He was delirious," Julianne began.

Amelia turned; Julianne seized her.

"I have to notify the authorities!" her sister exclaimed.

"You can do no such thing!" Julianne stepped in front of her, barring her way. "He is seriously ill, Amelia, and he is a hero!"

"Only you would think such a thing!" Amelia cried. Then, lowering her voice, she continued. "I don't believe it is legal to have him here. I must tell Lucas."

"No, please! He is doing no harm—he is ill! For my sake, let us help him recuperate, and then he can go on his way," Julianne pleaded.

Amelia stared at her, aghast and very grim. She finally said, "Someone will find out."

"I am going to see Tom immediately. He will help us keep him here, in secret."

Displeasure was written all over Amelia's face. "I thought Tom was courting you."

Julianne smiled—the change in topic meant she had won. "Tom and I are always discussing politics, Amelia. We share the same views. But that is hardly a courtship."

"He is smitten. He might not approve of your guest." She glanced into the bedchamber—and paled.

Charles was watching them both, his expression oddly alert, even wary.

The moment he saw her looking at him, he smiled and began to sit up. The covers fell to his waist, revealing his muscular chest.

Julianne did not move. Had he just looked at her as if she was an adversary he did not trust?

Amelia hurried into the room, her face set. Julianne followed her into the bedchamber. Her tension escalated.

Had he overheard their argument?

If he had, he gave no sign. Instead, Charles exchanged an intimate, sidelong look with her. Her insides seemed to vanish—it was as if they shared a sinful secret.

But didn't they?

Images flashed through her mind of him standing up, stark naked, after falling; of his so casually wrapping the sheet around his waist, clearly not caring about his modesty; and of his slow, suggestive smile before he kissed her, when he had been delirious.

Her heart was rioting now.

She glanced at Amelia closely, but Amelia gave no sign that she was interested in his broad, sculpted chest. He was pulling the covers up modestly. As Amelia went to the table to retrieve the dinner tray, Charles looked at her again, a warm light in his eyes.

"Your sister, I presume?" he asked.

Amelia faced him, holding his supper tray, before Julianne could speak. Her French was excellent; she also spoke Spanish and some German and Portuguese. "Good evening, Monsieur Maurice. I hope you are feeling better. I am Amelia Greystone."

"I am pleased to make your acquaintance, Miss Greystone. I cannot thank you and your sister enough for your hospitality and your kindness in nursing me during my recovery from my wounds."

Amelia brought Charles his tray. "You are welcome. I see that you are as articulate as my sister has claimed. Do you speak English?"

Charles accepted the tray. In heavily accented English, he said, "Yes, I do." Then he looked at Julianne again. His smile faded. "Should my ears have been...burning?"

She knew she blushed. "You speak very well, *monsieur*. I mentioned it to my sister. That is all." His English, although accented, was also very impressive, she thought.

He seemed pleased. Turning to Amelia, who stood beside his bed, he said, "And what else has she said about me?"

Amelia's smile was brief and strained. "Perhaps you should ask her. Excuse me." She turned to Julianne. "Momma needs her supper. I will see you later, Julianne." She left.

"She doesn't like me," he said, some laughter in his tone, speaking in French again.

Julianne jerked and saw that he had lain his hand over his bare pectoral muscle. "Amelia has a very serious, sensible character, *monsieur*."

"*Vraiment?* I hadn't noticed."

She felt some of her tension ease. "You are in fine spirits."

"How could I not be? I have slept several hours, and I am with a beautiful woman—my very own angel of mercy." His gaze held hers.

She felt her heart turn over, hard. She reminded herself that all Frenchmen were flirts. To cover up her agitation, she said, "You have slept for more than an entire day, *monsieur*. And clearly, you are feeling better."

His eyes widened. "What is today's date, mademoiselle?"

"It is July 10," she said. "Is that important?"

"I have lost all sense of time. How long have I been here?"

She could not tell what he was thinking. "You have been here for eight days, *monsieur*."

His eyes widened.

"Does that fact disturb you?" She approached. Her sister had left his tray on a bedside table.

His smile came again. "I am simply surprised."

She pulled a chair over to his bedside. "Are you hungry?"

"Famished."

She sat in the chair beside him. "Do you need help?"

"Are you not tired of nursing me?"

Careful to keep her eyes on his face, she said, "Of course not."

He seemed pleased by her answer. She realized they were staring at one another—continuously—helplessly. Somehow, Julianne looked away. Her cheeks seemed to burn. So did her throat and chest.

She helped him settle the tray on his lap and sat back as he began to eat. A silence fell. He was ravenous. She stared openly, beginning to think that he found her as intriguing as she found him. All Frenchmen flirted…but what if he had the same feelings for her as she had for him?

Her heart leapt erratically. She became aware of the shadows in the room, the flames in the small hearth, the dark, moonlit night outside—and the fact that it was just the two of them together, alone in his bedchamber, at night.

When he was done, he lay back against his pillows, as if the effort of eating had cost him, but his gaze was serious and searching. Julianne removed the tray to the table, wondering what his intent regard meant.

It was very late, and it was improper for her to remain with him. But he had just awoken. Should she leave? If she stayed, would he kiss her again? He probably didn't even recall that kiss!

He said softly, "Am I making you uncomfortable?"

She colored, about to deny it. Then she changed her mind. "I am unaccustomed to spending so much time in a stranger's company."

"Yes, I imagine so. It is obviously late, but I have just awoken. I would like your company, *mademoiselle,* just for a bit."

"Of course." She trembled, pleased.

"Would it be possible to borrow your brother's clothes now?" His smile came and went, indolently.

That would certainly make her feel better, she thought. She went to retrieve the clothes, handed them to him and left the room. In the hall, she covered her warm cheeks with her hands. What was wrong with her? It was as if she was a young girl, when she was a grown woman! He had been delirious when he had kissed her. He seemed lonely now. That was all. And she had a dozen questions for him—even if she kept thinking of the pressure of his lips on hers.

Behind her, the door opened, revealing Charles, now clad in Lucas's breeches and a simple lawn shirt. He didn't speak, which increased her tension, and he waited for her to precede him into the chamber. He moved her chair back to the table, but held it out for her. The silence felt even more awkward now than before.

He was a gentleman, she thought, taking the seat. He would never take advantage of her and attempt another kiss.

He sat in the second chair. "I am starved for news, *mademoiselle*. What happens in France?"

She recalled his delirium and wanted to ask him about the battle he had spoken of. But she feared that might distress him. Very carefully, she said, "There has been good news and bad news, *monsieur*."

"Do tell." He leaned toward her.

She hesitated. "Since defeating the French in Flanders, Britain and her Allies continue to send troops to the front lines along the French–Belgian border, strengthening their position. Mainz remains under siege, and there are royalist rebellions in Toulon, Lyons and Marseilles."

He stared, his expression as hard as stone. "And the good news?"

She searched his gaze, but could not find a flicker of emotion now. "The royalists were crushed near Nantes. We do not know yet if their rebellion has been ended, once and for all, but it seems possible."

His expression never changed; it was almost as if he hadn't heard her.

*"Monsieur?"* Impulsively, she blurted, "When will you tell me the truth?"

"The truth, *mademoiselle?*"

She found herself incapable of drawing a breath. "You were delirious."

"I see."

"I know who you are."

"Was it a secret?"

She felt as if they were in the midst of some terrible

game. "*Monsieur,* you wept in my arms in your delirium, that you lost so many men—soldiers—*your* soldiers. I know that you are an officer in the French army!"

His stare never wavered.

She reached for his hand and gripped it. He did not move a muscle. "I have wept for you, Charles. Your losses are my losses. We are on the same side!"

And finally, he looked down at her hand. She could not see into his eyes. "Then I am relieved," he said softly. "To be amongst friends."

# *CHAPTER THREE*

HAD HE THOUGHT that he was amongst enemies? "I have cared for you for an entire week," Julianne said, removing her hand from his.

His green gaze was on her face now. "I feel certain you would care for any dying man, no matter his country or politics."

"Of course I would."

"I am a Frenchman—you are an Englishwoman. What should I have thought, upon awakening?"

She began to realize the predicament he might have thought himself to be in. "We are on the very same side, *monsieur*. Yes, our countries are at war. Yes, I am English and you are French. But I am proud to support the revolution in your country. I was thrilled to realize that you are an officer in the French army!"

"You are a radical, then."

"Yes." Their gazes remained locked. His eyes were not as hard as before, but still, she felt oddly uncomfortable, as if she had been pushed off balance, as if she were in an important—no, crucial—interview. "Here in Penzance, we have a Society for the Friends of Man. I am one of the founders."

He now sat back in his chair, seeming impressed. "You are an unusual woman."

She couldn't smile. "I will not be held back by my gender, *monsieur*."

"I can see that. So you are a true Jacobin sympathizer."

She hesitated. *Was* she being interviewed? Did she even blame him? "Did you think that you were in a household filled with enemies?"

His smile did not seem to reach his eyes. "Of course I did."

She hadn't had a clue as to his distress; he had been a master at hiding his thoughts and feelings. "You are amongst friends. I am your friend. In my eyes, you are a great hero of the revolution."

His brows lifted. And now she knew he had relaxed. "How much more fortunate could I be? To wind up in your care?" Suddenly, he reached for her hand. "Am I being too direct, Julianne?"

She went still. He had never called her by her name before; he hadn't even called her Miss Greystone. It had always been *"mademoiselle."* Yet she did not protest. "No."

And he knew that she had just allowed him an intimacy—and perhaps opened the door for even further intimacy.

He did not release her hand. It was late and dark and they were alone. "I hope you are not afraid of me," he said softly.

She slowly looked up from their clasped hands. "Why would I be afraid of you, *monsieur?*"

He met her gaze. "Hero or not, I am a stranger…and we are alone."

She didn't know what to say. His stare was unwavering, intense. "I enjoy our conversation, *monsieur,*" she finally said softly. "We have so much in common."

"Yes, we do." He was pleased. Then, "I am glad you think of me as you do, Julianne."

"What else could I possibly think?" She managed a fragile smile. "You are fighting for equality in France and the freedom of all men, everywhere. You have put your life in jeopardy for a great, universal cause. You almost *died* for the sake of freedom."

He finally let go of her hand. "You are a romantic."

"It is the truth."

He studied her. "Tell me what you are thinking."

He spoke in a murmur, but he had that tone of command again. She knew she flushed. She managed to look down at the table between them. "Some thoughts are meant to be privy."

"Yes, some are. I am thinking that I am fortunate to have been brought into your care. And not because you are a Jacobin."

She jerked to look up at him.

"When I first woke up, I remembered dreaming of a beautiful woman with titian hair, tending me, caring for me. And then I saw you and realized it was not a dream."

He had just walked through that open door....

"Am I being too forward? I am accustomed to speaking directly, Julianne. In war, one learns that time is precious and no moment should go to waste."

"No. You are not being too forward. " She trembled. He was feeling the same pull toward her that she felt toward him. Amelia would be shocked if she knew what was unfolding; her brothers would be furious.

"And does your sister think of me as you do?"

She was so off balance that, for one absurd moment, she thought he was asking her if Amelia also found him attractive.

"I do not have the impression that she thinks of me as a war hero," he said.

It was hard to think about Amelia just then. But he

was waiting for her to respond. She inhaled. The change of topic had been so abrupt. "No, she does not," Julianne breathed.

"She is not as radical as you are?" he supplied.

She took a breath, finding her composure. "She isn't radical at all, *monsieur*." She could not tell what he was thinking or feeling. She did not want to worry him. "But she is not political, and she would never turn you over to the authorities, I promise you that."

For another moment, he stared, considering her words. Then he rubbed his neck, as if it ached. Before she could ask him if he was all right, he said, "And have you been able to aid our Jacobin allies in France? Is it easy to send word to them?"

"It isn't easy, but there are couriers these days. One must merely pay handsomely to get a message across the Channel." Did he wish to send word to France? She tensed. Wouldn't he want Nadine to know he was alive?

"What's wrong?"

The French woman had to be a lover—he could not possibly be married, not when he'd flirted with her as he had. But she hated ruining the evening by asking about her. She was afraid she would learn that he still loved her. She smiled quickly. "I was just thinking that I wish I could be of more help to our allies in Paris. Thus far, we have merely exchanged a few letters and ideas."

He smiled at her. "And what is your brother, Lucas, like? I will have to eventually find a way to repay him for my use of his clothes."

She looked closely at him, sensing he wished to ask far more. "Lucas will not mind you wearing his clothes. He is a generous man."

"Would he turn me over to the authorities?"

He was worried, and rightly so, she thought. She hesitated. Hadn't she feared that Lucas would do just that? Charles was most definitely interviewing her.

"No," she finally said. "He would not." She would not allow it.

"Is he a radical, then, as you are?"

She was grim. "No."

"Julianne?"

"I am afraid that my brother Lucas is a patriot," she said carefully. "He is a conservative. But he has no time for politics. He manages this estate, *monsieur,* providing for this family, and that occupies all of his time. He is rarely here—and I would never tell him who you are, if he suddenly appeared."

"So you would withhold the truth about me from your own brother in order to protect me?"

She smiled weakly. "Yes, I would."

"You believe that he would turn me in."

"No! He could not do any such thing, anyway, because we would never tell him who you are."

"Are you expecting him in the near future?"

"He always sends word when he is returning. You do not have to worry about him." But Lucas hadn't sent word a week ago; he had simply appeared. She decided not to tell Charles that.

He scrutinized her and said, "And your other brother?"

"Jack doesn't care about this war, not one way or another."

"Really?" He was mildly disbelieving.

"He is a smuggler, *monsieur.* The war has raised the price of whiskey, tobacco and tea—indeed, it has raised the price of many items—and he says it is good for his business."

He rubbed his neck again, and sighed. "Good."

She didn't blame him for his questions. Of course he

would want to know who the members of her family were—and what their politics were, as well. He would want to know if he was safe. She watched him massage his neck. Was his tension that great? How could it not be? "I have been wondering why Jack brought you here."

He looked at her.

When he did not respond, when she could not decipher his direct regard, she said, "I haven't seen Jack since he brought you here—he comes and goes very erratically, and he was gone when I arrived at the manor and found you here in a terrible state. I have been wondering about it. Lucas only said that Jack found you bleeding to death on the wharf in Brest."

He hesitated. "I have a confession to make, Julianne. I do not remember how I got here."

She was stunned. "Why didn't you say anything?" she cried, concerned.

"We have just barely become acquainted."

She could not absorb that explanation. Why hadn't he asked her how he had gotten to the manor, if he couldn't recall it? How odd! But she felt terribly for him. "What do you remember? Are there other memory lapses?"

"I recall being wounded in battle," he said. "We were fighting the La Vendée royalists. The moment I felt that ball in my back, I knew I was in dire jeopardy. Everything became a haze of pain—and then it was simply darkness."

He had been in that great battle against the La Vendée royalists! When she had told him the news of the rout, he hadn't even blinked. She wondered why he hadn't revealed how pleased he was—for surely their defeat had thrilled him. It seemed odd that he would receive news of his last battle with such an impassive demeanor. "Isn't Nantes inland?"

He studied the table. "I suppose my men brought me to Brest. I wish I could remember. They might have been looking for a surgeon—we are always short on surgeons. Perhaps we got separated and cut off from our troops. Perhaps they were deserters." He now looked up at her. "There are a number of possible scenarios. They may have even decided to leave me behind and let me die when they reached Brest."

She was shaken. How could his men have left him to die? Had they been such cowards? He was staring closely at her now. She trembled. "Thank God Jack found you! I didn't understand why he brought you to Cornwall," she said, their gazes locked, "but maybe he mistook you for a fellow smuggler. Knowing my brother, he might have been in a rush to disembark. He is usually on the run from one navy or another, or the revenue men. I am guessing that instead of leaving you to die, he simply brought you on board his ship and cast off. Lucas must also have thought you were a smuggler."

"No matter what happened, I am fortunate, am I not? Had Jack not rescued me, I would not be here now, with you."

His regard was filled with significance. "I am so glad he rescued you," she said softly. "Jack will be back, sooner or later, and then we can find out what really happened."

He reached across the table and took her hand and enclosed it in his larger one. "Fate put me in your hands," he said. "Isn't that enough, for now? You have saved my life."

His soft tone washed through her, causing so much tension.

As she watched him, he sighed, releasing her hand

and rubbing his neck again. "Thank God," he said softly, "for Jack."

She watched him rub his neck.

He caught her watching him and grimaced. "I have been in bed for far too long, I think. My neck is terribly stiff."

The tension within her thickened. She could help him—if she dared. "Are you in pain?"

"Some."

Her heart went out to him. She wanted to comfort him. But there was more. She wanted to touch him.

She had bathed him while he was unconscious. She knew what his skin felt like, what his muscles felt like. In the space of seconds, she was breathless.

She slowly stood up, barely able to believe herself. She felt like a different woman, someone older, wiser and experienced. The Julianne she knew—that her family and friends knew—would never do what she meant to do now.

His eyes became languid and watchful.

She whispered, "Can I help ease you, *monsieur?*"

He was looking up at her. *"Oui."*

She walked around the table, toward him. She moved behind him, almost dazed. She began kneading his neck.

He made a deep, guttural sound. It was terribly male and terribly sensual.

Desire renewed itself, instantly. All other thoughts vanished and she began to increase the pressure on the knotted muscles of his neck with her thumbs, trying not to tremble, trying not to breathe. And as she did so, she felt the muscles there soften slightly; his head tilted back.

If he knew he had lain his head against her breasts, he gave no sign.

JULIANNE HAD ALREADY CHECKED upon Charles several times that morning, but he had been asleep. Still, he was recovering from being shot and the resulting infection—and she hadn't left his bedchamber till half past ten last night.

She bit her lip. It was noon now. Her heart was racing like a schoolgirl's, she thought, pausing in the corridor outside his door. Had she imagined it, or was something wonderful happening? He found her beautiful—he had said so, several times. He seemed as aware of her as she was of him. And they were both passionate revolutionaries. What if they were falling in love?

If only she were more experienced. She had never been as interested in anyone before. The feelings she had could not be one-sided!

But she was going to have to ask him about Nadine. She had to know about his relationship with the other woman.

She looked inside, smiling nervously. Charles was standing at the window. He was shirtless, staring outside. For one moment, she stared at his broad shoulders, his muscular chest and his narrow waist. Her mouth dry, her pulse pounding, she whispered, *"Monsieur? Bonjour."*

He turned slowly, smiling at her. "Good morning, Julianne." Clearly, he had known she was there.

Her heart turned over, hard. The way he was looking at her told her that he had to be thinking about the evening they had shared last night. It told her that he was as interested in her as she was in him.

He moved his gaze over her carefully, taking in the fact that she had curled her hair where it framed her face. Her hair was loose and hanging straight down her back, as was fashionable. She wore another ivory muslin dress, this one with a rounded neckline and fuller skirts. His gaze skidded across her bosom before he lowered his eyes and walked over to the chair where his shirt was hanging. He picked it up.

Julianne meant to look away, but she watched as he shrugged it on. The muscles in his chest and arms rippled. He looked up and caught her staring. He didn't smile now.

Desire made her feel faint. She prayed she wasn't blushing. She forced a smile. "How are you feeling today, *monsieur?*" She realized she was clinging to the doorknob, as if that would keep her standing upright.

"Better." He spoke as softly as before. He paused, and then said, "You have changed your hair."

"I might have to go into Penzance this afternoon," she lied.

He said, "You did not change it for me?"

She became still. "Yes, I changed it for you."

"I am glad." He said, "I believe I am well enough to go downstairs, if you do not mind. Walking would be beneficial."

She started. "Of course I don't mind." But she wondered if he would be able to make it down the stairs, which were rather steep and narrow.

"These four walls might madden me," he added, buttoning up the rest of his shirt.

She watched his long, blunt fingers sliding the buttons into the buttonholes. Last night, his hands had been on the arms of his chair as she had rubbed his neck. Eventually, she had seen his knuckles turn white. She still could not believe her audacity—or how touching him had affected her.

He sat and began to pull his stockings on.

She wanted to ask him about his family, but she said, "Can I be of help?"

"Haven't you helped enough already?" He seemed wry.

He knew she was as nervous and anxious as a debutante, she thought, flushing. She watched him pull both boots on. "Where does your family live?"

He stood up. "My family is from le Loire. My father's shop was in Nantes." He smiled, extending his arm. "Will you walk with me, Julianne? I can think of nothing I wish to do more."

Julianne took his arm. "You are so very gallant. Of course I will walk with you. I just hope we are not rushing your recovery."

"I enjoy your concern." His gaze slid over her features, lingering on her mouth.

She forgot to be worried about his welfare. *He was thinking about kissing her.*

"I would be rather dismayed," he added softly, "if you were not concerned about me."

Her smile failed her. He gestured and they traversed the corridor in a new silence. She felt his thoughts racing. She wished she knew exactly what he was thinking, certain he was thinking about her.

Suddenly she realized his breathing was becoming labored. *"Monsieur?"*

He paused, leaning against the wall. "I am fine."

She gripped his arm more tightly, to steady him, and his biceps pressed against her breast. Their gazes locked.

Her heart slammed.

And then he sagged, as if his knees had buckled. Julianne leapt forward, wrapping both of her arms around his waist, afraid he would fall entirely over and down the stairs. She embraced him, her face pressed against his chest.

"You are far too weak for this," she accused breathlessly. She could hear his heart pounding beneath her ear.

He was silent, breathing hard, and she felt his frustration change. He grasped her waist loosely, his chin pressing against her temple, and she felt his breath against her cheek.

They were in one another's arms.

Breathing became impossible. Her heart thundered. And his entire body began stiffening against hers.

Julianne went still. She looked up; his eyes were heated now.

"Julianne," he said. "You are far too tempting like this."

His tone had been rough. She wet her lips. *"Monsieur."* Did she dare confess that she was as tempted by him?

"Charles," he said softly, tightening his embrace. "You are so beautiful… You are so kind."

She could barely think. Most of her body remained pressed against his. Her breasts were crushed by his chest. Her skirts covered his legs. She felt his knees against her thighs. He was stirring against her, a sensation she had never before experienced. She wanted to tell him that she would not mind, if he thought to kiss her. She wanted him to kiss her—she wanted, desperately, to kiss him back.

Suddenly he shifted and she was the one with her back against the wall. His gaze moved to her mouth but he released her, stepping backward. "I do not want to take advantage of you."

She wasn't sure she had ever been so disappointed. "You cannot take advantage of me."

One brow cocked upward, skeptically. "You are a woman without experience."

"I have had a great many experiences," she tried.

"I am not referring to assemblies and debates, Julianne." His gaze was searching.

She did not know what to say. "I have been courted. Tom Treyton is smitten with me."

He stared. "Let us go downstairs. I am determined, now."

Dismay consumed her. Why hadn't he kissed her? And didn't he care about Tom? It was a moment before she could speak. "Are you certain? You are obviously weaker than either of us realized."

"I am certain," he said softly, "that I must regain my strength, which I will not be able to do lying in bed with your tending to my every whim." He suddenly pulled away from her, seized the banister and started downstairs, giving her no choice but to follow.

In the hall below, he paused, lightly holding on to the banister, glancing carefully around.

For one moment, Julianne almost had the feeling that he was memorizing the details of her home. "Perhaps we should sit before the hearth," she said, indicating the two burgundy chairs there.

"Is that the parlor?" he asked, glancing at a pair of closed doors.

"That is the library. The parlor is the room closest to the front door."

He stared past the library doors, which were closed.

"That is the dining room." She answered his unspoken question. He was pale. He should not have come downstairs yet.

He faced her. "Where are your mother and sister?"

Did he want to know if they were alone? "Amelia took

Momma outside for her daily ambulatory. They will be back shortly, as Momma cannot go far."

"I was hoping for a tour of the premises." He finally smiled at her, but it did not reach his eyes, and she found that odd, until she realized that he was unusually pale. Perspiration was beaded upon his brow.

"You cannot go far, either. Your tour will have to wait."

His brow lifted at her tone.

"We are going back upstairs," she said, meaning it. "You are not the only one capable of giving orders. You are still ill!"

He looked at her. Some amusement began to shimmer in his eyes. "You are so worried about me. I will miss your anxious concern when I leave."

She started. She had almost forgotten that, one day, he would return to France. But surely that was weeks away, or even months! "You almost fell down the stairs," she managed.

He slowly smiled. "And if I had? I would hardly suffer from your attentions after such a fall, Julianne."

"Your hurting yourself again isn't amusing—not at all. Have you forgotten how ill you were?"

His smile faded. "Actually, I have not."

She took his arm, guiding him back to the stairs, glancing at him uncertainly. "Am I being too shrewish?"

"You could never be shrewish. I think I rather like being ordered about by you."

She smiled. "I thought pale, fainting, compliant females were in vogue."

He chuckled. They started up the stairs, this time going up them while abreast. Julianne had no intention of releasing him, and he leaned on her again. "I don't care for vogues. And I have never cared for women who swoon."

She was fiercely glad she had never fainted, not once in her life. They traversed the hall in silence. As they entered the bedchamber, he said, "And will you order me to bed?"

She saw the humor in his eyes. But she also thought there was another innuendo in his words. Now, she was afraid to look at the bed.

She wet her lips and managed to sound brisk. "You may sit at the table, if you wish, and I will bring us both a light luncheon."

"Maybe," he said, stumbling slightly, "I had better lie down."

Julianne rushed to help him.

A FEW HOURS LATER, Julianne hesitated outside Charles's door. When she had brought him a light luncheon earlier, she had found him soundly asleep. She had placed his lunch tray on the table, covered him with a thin blanket and left.

His door was ajar, and in case he was still sleeping, she did not knock. She peered into the bedchamber and was rewarded by the sight of him at the table, eating the stew she had left for him earlier. "Hello," she said, stepping inside.

"I fell asleep," he exclaimed, setting down his fork, his plate empty.

"Yes, you did. Obviously our small outing was far too strenuous for you. And I can see that you have enjoyed your late lunch."

"You are an excellent cook."

"Charles, I burn everything I touch—I am not allowed to cook. It is a rule in this house."

He laughed.

"You are feeling better," she remarked, pleased.

"Yes, I am. Come, sit and join me." As she did so, he said, "I hope I was not as difficult as I recall, in demanding to go downstairs earlier."

"You were not *too* difficult," she teased. "Are you in a rush to recuperate fully?" She hesitated, reminded that he would leave Greystone Manor and return to France when he was well.

"As much as I enjoy your hovering over me—" he smiled "—I prefer being able to see to my own needs. I am not accustomed to being weak. And I am used to taking care of those around me. I can hardly take care of anything right now."

She absorbed that. "This must be awkward for you."

"It is. We must repeat our attempted outing tomorrow." His tone was one of command, and she knew she would not refuse. He smiled. "However, you are the one bright light in this difficult circumstance. I like being here with you, Julianne. I have no regrets." His gaze locked with hers.

She wanted to tell him that she was so glad he was there, in her care, and that she had no regrets, either. Instead, she hesitated.

"When you worry, you bite your lip." He spoke softly. "Am I a terrible burden? It must be maddening, to have to care for a stranger day in and day out. I am taking up all of your time."

Impulsively she seized his hand. "You could never be a burden. I am pleased to care for you. I do not mind, not at all." And she felt as if she had admitted all of her feelings for him.

His green eyes darkened and he returned her grasp. "That is what I wanted to hear."

She stared into his eyes, which were smoldering. Breathlessly, she whispered, "Sometimes, I think you deliberately guide me into making admissions and confessions."

"Our conversations flow freely. That is your imagination, Julianne."

"Yes, I suppose it is."

"I wonder if I will ever be able to repay you for all you have done and are doing for me."

When he looked at her that way, she felt as if she were melting. "I would never take any kind of repayment from you. When you are well again, you will take up arms for the revolution. Why, that is all the repayment I will ever need!" She touched his hand again.

He took her hand and suddenly clasped it firmly against his chest. She went still. For one moment, she was certain he meant to kiss her palm. Instead, he looked up at her from beneath his heavy dark lashes. She felt his heart beating, thickly, a bit swiftly. "What would your neighbors do, if they knew I was here?"

"They must never learn that you are here!" She added, "You have a disconcerting habit of changing subjects so suddenly."

"I suppose I do. Your neighbors do not share your sympathies, I fear." He released her.

"No, they do not." She was grim. "There are a few radicals in the parish, but since Britain joined the war against France, patriotism has swept most of Cornwall. It is best if my neighbors never know that you are here— or were here."

It was as if he hadn't heard her. "And may I ask who your neighbors are and how close they are to this manor house?"

He was interviewing her again, she thought, but

she did not blame him. If she were in his position, she would be asking him the same questions. "The village of Sennen is just a short walk from the manor, and it is much closer than the farms that border Greystone. We are rather isolated."

He absorbed that. "And just how far is the closest farm?"

Did he truly think that he was in jeopardy from their neighbors? "Squire Jones leases his lands from Lord Rutledge, and he is about a two hours' ride from us. Two other farmers lease their lands from the earl of St. Just, but they are perhaps fifty kilometers away. Penrose has a great deal of land to the east, but it is barren and deserted. The Greystone lands here are also barren—we have no tenants."

"Does the squire call? Or Rutledge?"

"The only times Squire Jones has ever called was when his wife was terribly ill. Rutledge is a boor and a recluse."

He nodded. "And St. Just?"

"St. Just has not been in residence in years. He runs in very high Tory circles in London, as does Penrose—who is rarely in the parish. I believe they are friends. Neither man would ever call, even if they were here."

"How far away is St. Just? Penrose?"

"The manor at St. Just is an hour from here, by horseback—in good weather. Penrose's estate is farther away." Attempting levity, she added, "And the weather is rarely good, here in the southwest." She reached across the table to take his hand. "I don't blame you for asking so many questions. But I don't want you to worry. I want you to rest and heal from your ordeal."

His gaze held hers. "I am exercising caution. Where are we, exactly, Julianne?" He glanced down at her hand, as if he did not want her to touch him now, and then he slid his hand away from hers. "Is it possible to have some maps?"

Almost hurt, she said, "We are above Sennen Cove. You are more worried than you have let on!"

He didn't respond to that. "How far is Sennen Cove from Penzance?"

"It is an hour's drive by coach."

"And the Channel? We are on the Atlantic, are we not? How far is it on foot to the closest point of departure?"

He was already thinking about returning to France, she thought, stunned. But he was weak—he could hardly leave anytime soon! "If you walk down to Land's End, which I can do in fifteen minutes, you are, for all intents and purposes, facing the southernmost portion of the Channel."

"We are that close to Land's End?" He seemed surprised, and pleased. "And where is the closest naval station?"

She folded her arms across her chest. This was undoubtedly how he was when in command of his troops. He was so authoritative, it would be hard to refuse him—not that she had any reason not to answer him. "There is usually a naval gunship at St. Ives or Penzance, to help the customs men. Since the war began, our navy has been diverted to the Channel. From time to time, however, a gunship will cruise into one port or another."

He steepled his hands and leaned his forehead there, deep in thought.

"When will you leave?" she heard herself ask, her tone strained.

He looked up at her. "I am in no condition to go anywhere, obviously. Have you told the Jacobins in Paris about me?"

She started. "No, not yet."

"I ask that you do not mention me. I do not want word of my having been wounded to get back to my family. I do not want to worry them."

"Of course not," she said, instantly understanding.

Finally, he softened. He took her hand and shocked her by kissing it. "I am sorry. You have been nothing but kind, and I have just rudely interrogated you. But I need to know where my enemies are, Julianne, just as I need to know where I am, if I ever have to escape."

"I understand." Her heart beat so wildly now she could hardly think. Such a simple kiss—and she was undone!

"No, Julianne, you can't possibly understand what it is like to be surrounded by one's enemies—and to fear discovery with every breath one takes."

He still held her hand to his chest. She tried to breathe, she tried to think. "I will protect you."

"And how will you do that?" He was openly amused. But his grasp on her hand tightened. Somehow, her knuckles were pressed against the bare skin exposed by the top and open buttons of his shirt. "You are such a tiny woman."

"By making sure that no one knows about you."

His eyes darkened. His smile vanished. "Amelia knows. Lucas knows. Jack knows."

"Only Amelia knows who you are and she would never betray me."

"Never," he said, "is a dangerous concept."

"If a neighbor called, they would not realize you are upstairs in this room," she insisted.

"I trust you," he said.

"Good," she cried fervently, their gazes locked.

He lifted her hand to his lips, but slowly. Now Julianne froze. His gaze on hers, he pressed his mouth to the back of her hand, below her knuckles. This time, the kiss was entirely different. It wasn't light, innocent or brief. His mouth drifted over her knuckles and the vee between her thumb and forefinger. And then his eyes closed and his mouth firmed. He kissed her hand again and again.

As he kissed her, her heart exploded. His mouth moved over her skin another time, with more fervor, and her entire body tightened—her own eyes closed. His mouth became insistent and fierce, as if he enjoyed the taste of her skin, as if so much more was to come. She finally allowed her mouth to part. She heard a small moan escape her lips. He separated her fingers and nuzzled the soft flesh there. She felt his tongue.

"Are there weapons in the house?"

Her eyes flew open, meeting his hot yet hard green gaze.

"Julianne?"

She was trembling. Desire made it almost impossible to breathe, to speak. "Yes." She wet her lips. She inhaled. Her body was throbbing, the need acute.

"Where?"

She exhaled. "There is a gun closet in the library."

He continued to stare. Then he lifted her hand, kissed it and released it. Abruptly, he stood.

If he ever truly kissed her, with the passion that raged between them, she might lose all of her good sense, she thought.

He glanced at her. "Do you know how to use a pistol? A musket?"

She must find her composure, she thought. "Of course I do. I am a good markswoman."

She added, "You do not feel safe."

His gaze moved over her features, then met her eyes. "I do not feel safe here, no."

Julianne slowly stood up. He watched her, and she wasn't sure she trusted herself to speak now. So she turned and left the room. She went downstairs, her body on fire, wondering if she should kiss him. She was certain he would allow it.

In the library, she paused, finding herself staring through the glass doors of the gun closet.

Three pistols and three muskets were racked within. It wasn't locked. It never was. When there were revenue men descending on the cove, those guns were instantly needed. Julianne took out a pistol, then closed the glass door. She retrieved powder and flint from the desk before going back upstairs.

Charles was standing by the window, staring at the threshold, clearly waiting for her to return. His eyes widened when he saw her with the pistol, powder and flint.

Their gazes locked. Still tight with desire, Julianne crossed the room. She handed him the pistol. She managed, "I doubt you will need to use it."

He put the pistol in the waistband of his breeches. She handed him the flint and powder. He slipped the powder bag's strap over one shoulder. He put the flint in his pocket. Then, slowly, he reached for her.

She went into his arms.

But he did not kiss her. "I hope not."

Trembling, she slipped her hands up his heavy biceps, which flexed beneath her palms.

He did not smile. He slid his fingertips over her cheek, then tucked a tendril of hair behind her ears. "Thank you."

Somehow, Julianne nodded—and he released her.

# CHAPTER FOUR

HE HEARD HER before she appeared in the open doorway. Dominic pushed the maps she had brought him aside, already having entirely familiarized himself with the southernmost part of Cornwall. He picked up his quill to resume the letter he was writing to his "family" in France. After all, that was surely what Charles Maurice would do, and if Julianne ever thought to spy, she would read the reassuring letter he was writing to the family he did not have. He had learned long ago to take elaborate precautions to guarantee than no one ever suspected he was using an alias.

Julianne arrived on the threshold, smiling. He slowly smiled back, meeting her gaze. Some guilt nagged at him. He owed her greatly; she had saved his life. He now knew she would not be very enamored with Dominic Paget—a titled, powerful Tory. It almost amazed him that his life had come down to this constant game of deception, of plot and counterplot.

He still didn't know her well, but he knew that she was genuinely kind, as well as intelligent, educated and opinionated. She was also terribly beautiful and completely unaware of it.

He stared openly, aware that she noticed his obvious admiration for her. His body stirred. He was recovering more swiftly now and his body had begun to make demands—urgently.

He knew he shouldn't seduce her. She was a gentle-woman, without experience, and in love with his alias—not him. She was already clay in his hands. The problem was, he wasn't interested in being moral. He was fairly certain that his time in London would be brief. His assignment was to ensure that the British resupplied Michel Jacquelyn's army. Once he had arranged that and was assured that the correct quantity of troops, weapons and other sorely needed supplies were being routed to La Vendée, he would be sent back to the Loire Valley or Paris.

His entire body tightened. He refused to allow his memories of the wars or the mobs to form. He was sick of dreaming of death, of being afraid, and he was sick of how a small gesture or word could cause those memories to come flooding vividly back.

"I have brought tea," she said softly. "Am I interrupting?"

He had been anticipating her company. She was an interesting woman and their conversation was never mundane. Sometimes, though, he felt like shaking some common sense into her.

She should not trust him!

He took his time answering, considering her carefully. He wondered how she would feel if she ever knew the truth about France—or about him.

Sometimes, he wanted to tell her. Usually that was when she spouted her nonsense about liberty and equality in France, and for all. His anger was instant, but he would hide it. He wanted to tell her that the ends did not justify the means, that France was a bloodbath, that innocent men and women died every day, that he hated the tyranny being inflicted on the country—that it was tyranny, not freedom!

Sometimes, he wanted to shout at her that he was a nobleman, not some damned revolutionary—that his mother was a French viscountess, and that he was the earl of Bedford!

But there was more. Sometimes, when she looked at him with those shining gray eyes, he felt a terrible stabbing of guilt, which surprised him. And then he felt like shouting at her that he was no hero. There was nothing heroic about running a print shop in Paris and fawning over the local gendarmes so they would never suspect the truth about him, or about flattering and befriending the Jacobins so they would truly think him one of them.

Writing ciphers by candlelight, then smuggling them through a network of couriers to the coast, to be transferred to London, was not heroic—it was terrifying. It was not heroic to pretend to be that Frenchman or to pretend to be a French army officer—it was not heroic to take up a musket and march off into battle, fighting to defend one's birthright against one's countrymen. It was all a great necessity, a matter of survival.

It was all madness.

How shocked and horrified she would be by it all.

But she would never hear any such nonsense from him. He was too deep in this alias to get out. If anyone at Greystone learned that he was an Englishman, much less that he was Paget, there was but one obvious conclusion to draw—that he was a British agent. After all, he had been transported from France, he'd been speaking French and he now posed as a Frenchman. The leap would be a simple one to make.

Her sister and two brothers could be managed, certainly—they were patriots. He did not worry about their mother; he had eavesdropped and learned that she was mentally incapacitated.

But it was preferable that they never learned of his identity. Only five men knew that Dominic Paget, the earl of Bedford, was a British agent working under an alias in France. Those men were Windham, the War Secretary; Sebastian Warlock, whom he assumed was his spymaster; Edmund Burke, who was highly influential in governing circles; his old friend, the earl of St. Just; and of course, Michel Jacquelyn.

That circle must never be expanded. The more people who knew the truth, the more likely it was that he would be unmasked.

But Julianne was a different matter entirely. She was not a patriot. Her friends in Paris would soon recruit her to actively work on their behalf—it was how the Jacobin clubs operated. Even now, he did not trust her entirely. If she ever learned he was Dominic Paget, he would not trust her at all.

Sooner or later, he would return to France and continue the fight for his land and his people. He had spent summers at his mother's chateau as a boy. It was his chateau now. The men and boys who had died at Nantes so recently had been his neighbors, his friends and his relations. He had known Michel Jacquelyn since childhood. Jacquelyn had already lost his estate—it had been burned to the ground by the revolutionaries. They couldn't burn his title, though—they couldn't burn his birthright—or his patriotism.

If Julianne ever learned who he was and exposed him to her French friends, he would be in even greater jeopardy. The spy networks inside France were vast. Men he thought mere commoners and men he knew to be gendarmerie would have his description and seek to uncover him. No one in Paris could trust the kindly matron next door, or the elderly bookseller down the street. Neighbor spied on neighbor, friend upon friend. Agents of the state were everywhere, seeking traitors. Enemies of the revolution were decapitated now. In Paris, they called it Le Terroir. There was nothing like the sight of the gendarmerie leading the accused in shackles to the guillotine, the crowds in the street cheering. There was nothing like the sight of that street running red with blood. He would never survive discovery and arrest.

But he was being very careful. If all went according to plan, he would recover from his wound and simply leave. He would be journeying to London to plan for the resupplying of La Vendée by the War Office, but Julianne would assume he had gone back to France, to resume his command in the French army.

It was so ironic.

She *was* interrupting him, he thought. She was interrupting because this was a game, not a real flirtation. He was not her French army officer, eager to share tea, but a British agent who needed to get to London—and then return to France. He estimated it would be another week before he was ready to leave the manor and travel to London. It was at least a two-day carriage ride. But in a few more days or even a week, he could steal a horse or a carriage and go to St. Just. Even if Grenville were not in residence, as he most likely would not be, his staff would leap to obey his every command once he made it clear who he was.

Their time together was very limited now. He would leave on the pretext that he was returning to France. His cover would not be compromised; Julianne would remember him as her war hero, while her brothers would assume him to be a smuggler whose life they had saved.

The solution was ideal.

"You are staring," she said softly.

He smiled at her. "I am sorry. You are easy to stare at." It was the truth, so he softly added, "I enjoy looking at you, Julianne, very much so."

She no longer blushed at his every word, but he knew his flattery pleased her. "You can be impossible, Charles." Her stare was direct. "I also enjoy looking at you."

Julianne sat opposite him and began to pour the tea, trembling. He wanted her, but she was so innocent. Yet he wouldn't think twice about taking that innocence if she were infatuated with the man he actually was. He would enjoy having such a woman as his mistress, both on his arm and in his bed. He would like showing her the finer things in life or taking her about London. But that would never happen.

"You are so thoughtful today," she said, handing him a cup and saucer. "Are you thinking about your family?"

"You are very astute," he lied.

"You must miss them," she added, her gaze on his. "Do you realize that you have asked me dozens of questions, while I have not asked you anything at all?"

"Really?" He feigned surprise. "You can ask me anything you desire, Julianne." Outwardly he was casual, but inwardly he was entirely alert.

"Who is Nadine?"

He started. How did she know about Nadine? What had he said in his delirium? He avoided thinking about his fiancée. He would never forget the months he had spent frantically trying to locate her—and then, eventually, his only choice had been to conclude what had been her fate. "Did I speak of her when I was delirious?"

She nodded. "You mistook me for her, Charles."

It was always best to stay as close to the truth as possible. "Nadine was my fiancée," he said. "She got caught up in a riot in Paris and she did not survive it."

Julianne cried out. "I am so sorry!"

"Paris isn't even safe for the *sans-culottes,*" he said, referring to the unemployed and the homeless. "Unfortunately, the mobs are incited to violence more often than not." He spoke calmly. "Nadine was knocked down when she tried to navigate the crowd." That was true. He had known Nadine since childhood and their engagement had not surprised anyone. Nadine's ancestral home was outside Nantes, just down the road from his mother's chateau. Her family had fled France shortly after her death.

He had imagined her death in the riot many times; he was careful not to do so now. He was careful not to really think about what he was saying. He was careful not to feel. "You do not want to know the rest."

It was a long moment before Julianne spoke. When she did, her gray eyes glistened with unshed tears. "I thought that the mobs were protesting the lack of employment and the high prices. Everyone deserves employment, a good wage and a decent price of bread. The poor cannot feed their families or even shelter them!"

Spoken like a true radical, he thought grimly. "Their distress is inflamed by the politicians," he said, meaning it. "Yes, everyone should have employment and a wage, but the radicals—the Jacobins—deliberately incite crowds to violence. Fear rules the streets—the people. There is power for those who can cause the fear. And the innocent like Nadine are caught up in the violence and are its victims." He knew he must stop, but he hadn't actually said anything amiss. After all, any man would speak as he just had if his beloved fiancée had been murdered in a mob.

Julianne hesitated. "What happened to your fiancée

is terrible, Charles. But really, if you were starving and without means, or if your employer paid you pennies for your labor while living in the lap of luxury, wouldn't you take to the streets to protest? I would not need direction. And why would the Jacobins or anyone incite such extreme violence? I know they cherish human life—they hardly wish to cause innocent bystanders to die."

She was so wrong, he thought grimly. She did not understand how power corrupted even the greatest cause. "I'm afraid I am not fond of politicians, not even radical ones." He managed to soften, thinking it time to withdraw from the conversation.

But she was taken aback. "You almost sound like my brother Lucas. He favors reform, not revolution. He despises the mobs. He has accused the radicals in Paris of the same kinds of actions as you have. And Lucas fears violence here, at home."

"Reform can be kinder and violence should always be feared."

Her eyes widened. "The French nobility—the French king—would have never given the country a constitution without great pressure, Charles. The kind that comes from the rising up of hundreds of oppressed people."

He smiled at her, knowing that she truly believed her words. But the pressure she spoke of had caused the execution of King Louis. Because of "pressure," there was no constitutional monarchy now. Thousands of French noblemen had fled—and they would never return. Their lands had been taken away, or even destroyed. Why couldn't she see the terrible loss that this was? Why didn't she realize how savage and murderous the mobs were—and how many innocent men, women and children had died because of them? Would she still insist that this was liberty? Equality?

"I am against oppression. Who isn't? But the violence in France is not justifiable. There are different ways one can achieve the same end, Julianne," he finally said.

She stared at him, shocked. "Were you conscripted?" she finally asked.

He knew he must backtrack now. "I volunteered," he said flatly. "There is no conscription in France. I am not against the revolution, Julianne, obviously. But I would have preferred a different means—a different beginning. But the convening of the Third Assembly has led us to this point in time, and there is no going back. Innocent men have died in my arms. Innocent men—and boys— will continue to die. I suppose I am glad you do not understand the reality."

"I do understand," she whispered, covering his hand with hers. "And I am so sorry for those you have lost. I am so sorry you have suffered so much pain."

She did not understand at all, he thought. "I will fight to the death for my cause—the cause of freedom." For him, freedom meant being able to live in the Loire Valley without fear of reprisal—without fear of having his home taken from him. Just then, his family and friends were fighting for that very freedom in le Loire, yet they were running out of arms and food.

"You are frightening me."

He looked at her. The urge to take her in his arms was stunning. "That is not my intention."

She had saved his life and he owed her a great debt that did not include this deception. It did not include seduction. But he could not deny the urgent attraction he felt. "You are afraid for me."

"Yes," she whispered.

"Death is a part of war, Julianne. Even you know that."

"How can you be so casual about it?" she cried.

He almost told her that he did not feel casually about the subject at all. But he would never tell her any such thing. "Everyone dies sooner or later, whether in war or from sickness or from old age."

She stared, stricken. "I must ask you something, Charles, and it is difficult for me."

Although wary, he looked calmly at her.

"How long has it been since you lost Nadine?"

He instantly understood. "It has been a year and a half, Julianne." He saw the flicker of relief in her eyes, and that twinge of guilt came again. Was she truly in love with her revolutionary war hero? "There has been so much death, in these past few years. One learns how to accept it rather quickly."

She stood up and walked over to him and lay her shaking hand on his shoulder. "Do you still love her?"

"No."

"I'm sorry." She turned partially away. "I shouldn't have asked. That was selfish of me."

He stood, pulling her into his arms, and her soft, voluptuous body inflamed him. It was becoming hard to think clearly. "You had every right to ask."

She was trembling. He could feel the same insane urgency in her. He turned up her face. "I have become very fond of you, Julianne."

"So have I," she gasped. "I am so glad…Jack brought you here. I am so glad…that we are friends."

He looked at her parted lips, very carefully. It was becoming hard to think coherently. "But we are more than friends, no?" he asked softly.

"We are more than friends," she whispered hoarsely.

"Soon, I will return to France." Finally, he was speaking the truth.

The tears brimmed. "And I will miss you."

And as they stared at one another, he heard a door downstairs slam.

He could not believe her sister's timing. It would not serve him or his deception to have Amelia walk in on them now. But there was no turning back now. Surely, one kiss would not hurt either one of them.

Dominic bent over her, touching his mouth to hers. And very carefully, he feathered her lips with his. As he did, he was blinded by a flood of hot desire.

She gasped, seizing his shoulders, opening for him.

The desire brought a shocking anguish. And as he claimed her mouth, hard, the memories of blood and death, of rage and hatred, of distress and despair engulfed him. A part of him was in France, in agony, another part of him was with her, in ecstasy. He could not pull away. He could not check himself now. Nor did he want to.

He deepened the kiss, demanding everything from her, and she mated fiercely with his tongue.

And he thought, she should know better than to trust a stranger.


AMELIA AND JULIANNE had gone into the town of St. Just together for some groceries. Dominic stood at the top of the stairs, unbeknownst to them, and watched the sisters exit the house.

Julianne had been concerned about leaving him alone for an hour or two but he had reassured her.

She had accepted his promise that he would rest. He had appeared stoic, but inwardly, he had been thrilled.

Spying was inherent in his nature now. Everything he had learned about Greystone, the family and the area and its denizens, he had learned from Julianne. He was eager to go through the house, prying into the family's lives and affairs. He didn't expect to find very much, but one never knew. Jack Greystone held the most promise. He might claim not to care about the war, and be a simple smuggler, but he could be actively involved.

He entered a woman's bedroom. He saw the two beds, the two small bed stands, each with its own candle, the clothes hanging from the wall pegs, and knew the sisters shared the chamber. Julianne wore white muslin, exclusively, while Amelia favored gray frocks as if to make herself drabber than she actually was.

Within ten minutes, Dominic had made a thorough search of the room. He found some old journals, a few toiletries, spare candles and a sheath of letters, hidden in the armoire, under a pile of shirtwaists.

He paused, taken aback. The stack was tied with a blue ribbon, and his immediate assumption was that the letters belonged to Julianne.

He glanced at the top one—and realized he was looking at love letters written to Amelia. Oddly relieved, he put the letters back where he had found them.

The next room belonged to Jack. He was certain of it. It smelled like ships and the sea.

He began a rapid, thorough search. He found nothing of interest until he looked under the mattress, where he found a dozen navigational charts. The charts had been meticulously sketched. He was getting the inkling that Jack Greystone had made them himself. He sat on the bed, looking closely at the first chart, which detailed a cove at Land's End, right down to hidden reefs and rocks. He went through them quickly then. The man had charted the entire Cornish peninsula, from Cape Cornwall, just above St. Just, to Penzance.

And there were maps of the coves and beaches near Brest, too.

He looked back at one of the Cornish charts. Here and there Jack had marked the coast with X's. Dominic wondered what the marks stood for.

Jack had starred an area above St. Just, writing the word, *navy,* above the star.

"What a good man," Dom murmured.

And he heard a horse whinny outside.

He leapt up, ran to the window, and saw Amelia and Julianne alighting from the carriage, both women carrying large baskets. He turned, unperturbed, and carefully began rolling up every chart. It would take the women a few minutes to unload, he thought, and he intended to put every chart back in the same order as they had been when he had discovered them.

As he adjusted the sequence of the charts, all now rolled and tied, he heard the front door slam. He now lifted the mattress and replaced the charts, then carefully adjusted the bedcovers. He was fairly certain that a successful smuggler would be astute enough to realize if anything in his private chamber had been touched.

The front door slammed again.

Satisfied that the bedchamber was exactly as he had found it, he went to the window and looked out. He became mildly alarmed when he saw Julianne alone at the carriage, retrieving more parcels. Where was her sister?

Julianne was very susceptible to his deceptions but he had no delusions about Amelia. She was blind to his appeal. She had a great deal of common sense. Although they were actually allies, in a way, just then they were enemies—he had an alias to maintain. He did not want to have to deceive the older sister, who had made it clear that she did not care for Charles Maurice at all.

Dominic was crossing the hall when Amelia appeared at the top of the stairs. Her eyes widened when she saw him.

His heart leapt but then quieted. He smiled at her. "I thought I heard a horse."

"Were you in Jack's chamber?" she asked.

"I went to the window so I could look out on the drive. Can I help with the packages?" he asked pleasantly.

Amelia stared at him. It was certainly unacceptable for a guest to walk, uninvited, into someone else's private chamber. Amelia walked past him and opened up the door to Jack's bedroom, as if she expected something to have been disturbed.

"I apologize," he said amiably. "The door was ajar and I know your brother is not at home."

Amelia shut the door, rather forcefully. "Yes. You have been spending a lot of time with my sister, and she speaks freely, does she not?"

"She is an unusual woman. I am grateful to have had her company while I convalesce."

Amelia gave him a sharp look. "I am not a fool, sir. You may have worked your wiles on my sister, but I do not approve of who and what you are."

Before he could reply, Julianne gasped, "Amelia!"

They both turned to find her on the landing. She hurried toward them.

"He was in Jack's bedchamber," Amelia said.

Julianne looked at him in surprise.

"I heard the horse," he said calmly. "I went to the window to see who was calling." He gave her a significant look.

And she understood, immediately, the implication he intended. Julianne faced her sister. "Amelia, no one can know who he is or that he is here. I knew we shouldn't have left him alone! Of course he would go to see who was calling. Our friends are *not* his friends."

Amelia looked back and forth between Dominic and Julianne. "I hope you are right."

"You don't trust him because he reminds you of St. Just," Julianne said.

What was this? Dominic wondered.

Amelia started. "That is very rude, Julianne. Your Frenchman has nothing in common with St. Just—they don't even look alike."

"They both have that same air, that same tone," Julianne said. She turned to Dominic. "It is all right, *monsieur,* There is no harm done."

Amelia took her arm. "I'd like to talk to you downstairs." She faced Dominic. "You need not come down to help with the groceries. You are ill, after all."

He smiled at her. "I should like to help."

"Absolutely not." Amelia turned and marched down the hall and downstairs.

"I am sorry," Julianne said.

"She is concerned about you. I hardly blame her." He approached, recalling their very heated kiss of that morning. "You shouldn't discuss me with her."

"You're right. But she is a mother hen. She is always asking about the time we spend together."

"Divert her," he suggested. He reached out to stroke her jaw with his thumb, the gesture unintentional. Realizing he had simply wanted to touch her, he dropped his hand.

She hesitated, then cupped his cheek, her gaze heating.

His entire body stiffened. "We don't have much time, Julianne."

"I know."

He kissed her hand. "Come to me tonight." He could hardly believe himself. But he knew that if she came, he would not send her away.

Her eyes widened.

A heavy silence fell. From downstairs, Amelia called, "Julianne!"

"You had better go."

She bit her lip, turned and rushed to the stairs. He waited for ten seconds, and then followed. As he did, he closed his chamber door loudly, so they would think he had gone inside.

He did not want to make a sound as he went downstairs. But Amelia's voice was raised and he realized they were just below the stairs. He did not have to go down them, after all. He knelt, straining to hear.

"In the past few days, I have become suspicious of him," Amelia cried. "In fact, the more you speak of him, as highly as you do, the more suspicious I become."

"Why? He is a kind, sincere man who has suffered greatly. And he is a hero!"

"My God, listen to yourself. He has charmed you senseless," Amelia accused.

"I have hardly lost my wits."

"You are at his bedside constantly."

"He is recovering—where else should I be?"

"Has he seduced you?"

"What?" Julianne gasped.

"Well, I take it he has not, and thank God for that," Amelia said harshly. "I do not trust him, and you shouldn't, either."

It was a moment before Julianne spoke. "Amelia, I won't dissemble, I like him very much. But you are jumping to false conclusions!"

Another pause ensued. "Can you deny that you are infatuated?"

Julianne gasped.

"I didn't think so. I am sorry, Julianne, I disapprove. The sooner he is gone from Greystone, the better. Hopefully Jack will return at any moment and we can send Monsieur Maurice on his way! I wonder what Jack would think if he learned that our guest was in his bedchamber."

"He had cause to be there. Our neighbors are his enemies," Julianne said softly.

"I just want him gone," Amelia said, sounding distressed.

"He is going back to France, soon," Julianne reassured her.

He had heard enough. Dominic went back to his room.

JULIANNE LAY MOTIONLESS in her white cotton nightgown. She was almost afraid to breathe. Yet she was trembling wildly. Tension riddled her entire body. Very slowly, as if moving her head might awaken Amelia, she turned so she could look at her sister. Amelia slept just an arm's length from her, in the other bed.

She expected to find Amelia watching her, an expression of accusation on her face.

Instead, she saw her sister curled up on her side, soundly asleep.

She inhaled, and the sound was loud in the quiet night. Julianne glanced at Amelia again. But her sister kept breathing evenly and deeply. Amelia worked herself to the bone by day, and fortunately, she slept deeply at night.

But Julianne had many restless nights. When she couldn't sleep, she had the habit of going downstairs to the library, where she would read. If Amelia awoke in the middle of the night, she would surely assume that Julianne was reading, even if she had been suspicious of her and Charles earlier.

Her heart leapt. Very slowly, praying her bed would not creak, Julianne sat up. It was probably close to midnight. Outside, a few stars twinkled. A crescent moon hung in a partially cloudy night. Their window was cracked open—they both slept better if it was cool in the chamber—and a strong breeze was coming from the ocean. A shutter was banging against the side of the house. As she sat up, she heard the buoy bell that was outside the cove.

Amelia never moved.

Was she really going to get up and go to Charles's room? Was she really going to make love to a man she had known for only two weeks—and when he had been conscious for only half of that time? Was she really going to give him her virginity? In a week or two, he would return to France.

And he had said he would die for the cause of freedom.

Sitting up, she hugged her knees to her chest. He had frightened her terribly when he had said he would die for their cause, but she had never respected or admired him more. And her heart was singing wildly— Julianne had little doubt that she had fallen deeply in love with him.

She hadn't ever realized how much a woman could desire a man. She had thought him terribly handsome before he'd ever opened his eyes; it was so much worse now. Their every conversation—their every encounter—fueled her desire. She hadn't ever felt desire before, not like this. Touching him and being with him was all she could think about.

She felt tears arise. He was going to go back to France and the war. She hated even thinking about the possibility that she might never see him again, or that he might even die. They had so little time left in which to be together!

She flung off the bedcovers. She slid slowly to the floor, aware of the floorboard groaning, watching Amelia, who never moved.

Julianne left the room quickly, closing the door quietly behind her. Her heart was rioting in her chest now.

His fierce kiss had been haunting her since that morning. How could she not go to him?

Julianne crossed the corridor, barefoot. The floors were cold, but she didn't shiver—her skin felt feverishly hot.

His door was closed, but not entirely shut. She raised her hand to knock, and realized how absurd that was.

Julianne pushed open the door. As she stepped inside, she saw that the chamber remained slightly illuminated. Embers glowed in the hearth from the fire that had been made at supper time. Charles stood by the hearth, clad only in his knee-length drawers. He was staring over his shoulder at the door.

"Julianne," he said softly.

She closed the door behind her, trembling. She was suddenly uncertain, insecure and oddly afraid. He was a stranger, but she loved him and he could die in France....

He came forward, toward her. She hugged herself, gazing at his bare, sculpted chest, his concave, rippling belly, and then at the bulge pressing against thin cotton.

He quickly crossed the small room, unsmiling, his eyes ablaze. "I wasn't sure you would come." He caught her shoulder with one hand, her chin with the other. "I want you to be sure."

"How could I refuse you now?" she whispered.

He kissed her.

She moved into the powerful circle of his arms, as his

mouth opened hers. She forgot her doubts, her fears. This was Charles. She was in love.

Julianne found his hard, muscular back, and helplessly, she began exploring the rigid tendons there, as he softened his kiss, finally pausing to breathe hard against her cheek.

Every inch of him was aroused.

"I don't want to hurt you," he said harshly. "Not now—or ever."

"You won't hurt me," she said, grasping his shoulders. His words somehow seemed odd, but it was so hard to think coherently.

His green gaze was burning. "I want you, Julianne. God, I have wanted you—needed you—from the start."

He embraced her again, his mouth on hers. She felt herself become pliant, yielding to him, pressing against him, kissing him back. She felt so faint with need now. He tore his mouth from hers, but only to press his mouth against her throat and then into the vee of her nightgown. She moaned.

He began pulling up her nightgown. Julianne went still as her knees and thighs were bared. "You are beautiful," he whispered, pulling it up and over her head, then tossing it aside. And before she could think about the fact that she was unclothed, with firelight washing over her, he cupped her breasts and kissed her nipples, then slid his hand low over her belly. She gasped with pleasure.

And then her heart began a wild pounding, as did every pulse point in her body.

She could not move. She did not want to. His tongue moved over her nipple. His hands moved between her thighs. He began to stroke her, deftly. Julianne cried out, stunned by the building crescendo of pleasure.

He moved his hand there, his fingers featherlike now.

Julianne began to tremble violently. She wanted to tell him that she could not stand the pleasure he was bringing her—it was pleasure and agony, at once.

And he suddenly lifted her up and seated her on his hips, wrapping her legs around him. Julianne somehow opened her eyes in real surprise, her back against the door as he surged up into her.

The pressure was blinding, the pleasure shocking, the explosion instantaneous.

She clung. She clawed. She wept. And vaguely, she heard him moaning her name.

"Julianne."

# CHAPTER FIVE

OUTSIDE CHARLES'S BEDROOM, Julianne hesitated, holding a breakfast tray. Her heart was racing and her knees felt weak. She was ridiculously nervous about seeing him.

*Charles had made love to her last night.*

Her heart leapt in her chest. She recalled his kisses, his touch, how he felt beneath her hands, and she felt faint all over again. There was a delirious joy in her heart and a maddening urgency in her body. *They were lovers now.*

And she had no regrets.

She was deeply, irrevocably, in love.

Balancing the tray, she knocked gently on the door. "Charles?"

"Julianne?" he said, sounding hoarse and sleepy. As she came in, he slowly smiled at her, pulling the covers up past his naval. "Apparently I have overslept."

"Apparently," she breathed, stealing a glance at his bare chest. She was shocked that she would be so aroused by his mere presence again. She wondered if she would ever be able to look at him, without thinking terribly sinful thoughts—without wanting to be in his arms. She set the tray down on the table, images of his lovemaking last night flooding her mind. "I will leave you to give you some time to properly attire."

"Prude," he said softly.

She jumped.

"Are you afraid to look at me?"

Flushing, she slowly met his gaze. Humor filled it. "Of course not." Some of her tension faded.

"Good. I prefer to have your company," he said, staring. "There is no reason to feel embarrassed, Julianne."

"I am not embarrassed."

He glanced at the open door.

She always left the door open when they were in his chamber together. It would be inappropriate to do otherwise. "I think it better to go on as usual." She kept her voice low.

He smiled as he got up, and she averted her eyes from his powerful body. Her mind went oddly blank. There were only those stunning, passionate memories—and her uncertainty about their relationship.

"How is Amelia today?" he asked, shrugging on his shirt.

"She remains ignorant. I hate deceiving my sister."

"I know. I have already realized how honest and open you are." And suddenly he touched her from behind, startling her, enough so that she whirled to face him. His green gaze steady, he said, "Why are you afraid to look at me today? Do not deny it. You are avoiding me—and you are so terribly tense. Do you regret last night?"

She met his intense, searching gaze. "No." Her heart was pounding with frightening force. She was so acutely aware of the desire they had shared and how explosive that passion could be, again.

"Good. I have no regrets, either." He became very serious. "How do you feel this morning? I am worried that I was rougher than I should have been."

She glanced behind her, at the open door. He said, "We are alone," tucking some hair behind her ear.

The tender gesture thrilled her. "You did not hurt me. Not at all. But I have never felt this way before." When he didn't comment, she explained, feeling shy, "I am aching and warm—in a terribly wonderful way—even in my heart."

He smiled and pulled out a chair for her. She took it, gazing expectantly at him. He sat, allowing her to pour his tea as he began to eat from his plate of eggs and sausage. Julianne stared. Where did they go from there?

He looked up at her. "You are never so quiet. Should I worry?"

This was the second time he had asked her what was wrong. She felt her smile fade. Hadn't he told her that he liked to know what she was thinking? "I am afraid of discovery."

"I thought so." He laid his knife and fork down. "It was foolish to linger together for as long as we did. It was entirely my fault. You should have left well before sunrise."

"I knew better, also," she said shyly. "I did not want to leave."

"You will come to me tonight, won't you?"

Her heart leapt in excitement. Of course she would come; they were lovers now.

But how did she ask him about his feelings? And why did she even think it necessary? He had made *love* to her.

"Do you think you will go into St. Just or Penzance today?"

In a way, the change of subject was welcome. "I hadn't planned on it. Why?"

"I am anxious for news, especially of the war and the latest edicts in Paris," he said, taking a sip of tea.

"I didn't have time yesterday to ask for news," she said. "Amelia is always in a rush."

"Would you go into Penzance today, just for the purpose of soliciting news—perhaps from that friend of yours, Treyton?"

"Of course," she said, surprised that he would recall Tom. She had mentioned him only that one time.

"I would appreciate it."

His stare was piercing—as if he wished to know her most personal secrets. She had a moment of discomfort. She felt that she wore her feelings rather openly; he, on the other hand, was very guarded. She never knew what he was truly thinking. "What is it?"

"Why me, Julianne?"

So he wanted to have a serious discussion about their affair. Alarmed, she hesitated. "We have become good friends—close friends," she said carefully.

He was silent. Then, "Yes, we have."

"We crusade for the same great cause."

It was a moment before he spoke. "Yes, we both cherish freedom."

"I respect and admire you very much." She finally met his gaze. It remained intent.

It was a moment before he said, "I am flattered. But you have put your reputation in jeopardy."

"I don't care about my reputation, Charles," she said, meaning it.

"All women care about their reputations." He smiled.

And she smiled back. "With one exception."

His gaze sparkled. "And why, pray tell, have you no regard for your reputation?"

She didn't mind sharing her feelings with him. "I am not like other women. And not just because I am so radical. Before the war, when I was welcome in my neighbors' homes, I was called odd behind my back—I have even been called mannish, all because I am educated, well-read and I have opinions. I believe I was twelve or thirteen when a neighbor told Momma that I had opinions, and didn't she seek to repair that?" Julianne smiled, although at the time, she had been hurt by the Lady Delaware's criticism. "That lady told my mother I would never catch a husband if I was not silenced." His gaze was riveted upon her. She shrugged. "I don't know why I am so different. I don't know why I don't care at all about fine silks, pearls and handsome suitors, but I do not."

He finally smiled. "I cannot imagine you lusting for a silk ball gown—although you would be lovely in one."

She flushed. "I have no use for ball gowns, obviously."

"You have never been to a ball?"

"No. It would be rather hypocritical, don't you think?" But secretly, she imagined that a ball must be glorious, indeed. And attending a ball or two would hardly be the crux of evil, not if one crusaded constantly for freedom for the common man—not that she would ever have such an opportunity.

"No one would ever accuse you of being a hypocrite."

She smiled. "Thank you."

He was considering for a moment. "I am sorry that your neighbors do not appreciate your character and integrity."

She hesitated. "Many doors that were once open to me are closed to me now." Of course it saddened her—and it even hurt, at times—as she knew the entire parish so well. But she could not pretend to be someone she wasn't.

"It cannot be easy, being a pariah," he said softly, touching her cheek.

"Well, I am hardly a pariah!" She sighed. "Some in the parish are more hateful than others. Those who are the rudest are the very same people who are most afraid of the changes in France. I understand, and that helps. I am not hateful in return."

"No, you would never be hateful, not to anyone, not even your political enemies."

She cocked her head, gazing at him. "You have come to know me well."

"I think so." He touched her cheek again. "But you still haven't answered my original question—why me?"

She went still. Her heart thundered. What should she say?

"Why me?" he asked again, firmly.

"I have come to care about you, Charles," she said, trembling. He seemed to sit up straighter; his gaze now sharp. "I care enough to want to be with you—no matter the circumstance. But you already know that."

"If there is one thing I truly admire about you, it is your candor," he said. That wasn't what she wanted to hear, but he added, "And you know how much I have wanted you, from the moment I awoke from that fever, practically in your arms."

"Actually, although you flirted with me, I didn't know how much you wanted me, not then." She smiled at the memories of his first waking moments at Greystone.

He smiled back. "Because you have so little experience."

She dared, "Not anymore."

He gave her a look which said that a great deal more experience was to come. Then, reflectively, he said, "You saved my life. I will always owe you. It is not unusual for a wounded man to become uncommonly attracted to his savior, Julianne."

She was dismayed. "I do not believe this attraction common, not at all."

"That is not exactly what I meant." His smile flitted across his face. "You are a well-bred young woman. I realize your family has fallen on hard times, as many fine families have, but there are expectations in your circles, aren't there? You must be expected to marry well one day, no matter how eccentric you might be. How will you do that now?"

Did he expect her to consider marriage to another man, after what had just happened? Or was he asking her about her intentions because of what had happened? "My upbringing hasn't been usual," she said hesitantly. "Lucas has always hoped to find me a husband who appreciates my intellect, and that is no easy task." She thought to herself that Charles appreciated her intellect.

He was surprised. "Your brother must truly care for you."

She rubbed her own arms, wondering if he might harbor matrimonial intentions toward her. "He has always been more of a father to me than a brother. My father left us when I was three."

"I see," was all that he said.

"I don't even remember him, although there is a portrait of him somewhere in the attics. He was the black sheep of his family, disowned for his gaming and wenching. All he inherited was this estate. Lucas took over the family's affairs when he was sixteen.

"When did your mother lose her wits?"

The question surprised her. "Shortly after Papa left us."

"You have had an unusual upbringing," he said. "And it has made you a very interesting and original woman." He leaned across the table and kissed her, directly on the mouth.

HE NEEDED HER SO MUCH. Dominic thought he could not control his explosive desire for much longer, as he looked down at Julianne. She writhed beneath him. He moved deeply, urgently, raining kisses on her throat and breasts. His heart thundered; he felt faint. And now, knowing her a bit better, he was quick to cover her mouth with his, kissing her as she cried out in her climax. Moving deeply, he held her tightly, and found his own, shocking release.

When some time had passed, when his mind began to function again, he was aware that he still held her tightly. For one more moment, he allowed himself oblivion, kissing her shoulder. They were spooned together and she smiled at him.

But in that moment, he saw Nadine, not Julianne, lying dead in the street on her stomach, one white cheek upturned, her skirts crusted with dirt and blood. He shoved the horrid image aside, but it was too late—vague, ugly shadowy memories of blood, death and destruction were roiling in his mind. He embraced her even more tightly, just for a moment, his heart surging oddly in his chest. Then he kissed Julianne's neck and released her, rolling onto his back.

He stared up at the ceiling, one arm around Julianne. He focused on the white paint and plaster, remarking places were the paint was splotched and peeling. He did not want to think about Nadine or her murder; he did not want to think about France or the war, the revolution or death.

"Charles?" she whispered, recognizing the new tension in him.

He looked at her. Had the circumstances been different, he might have allowed himself to become fond of her. But the circumstances weren't different.

He pulled her close and held her against his chest, stroking her hair. And suddenly his gut was hollow, his loins hard and he needed to be with her again.

But pale gray light was filtering through the window. It was dawn.

He would hate it if they were discovered. It was bad enough that he had taken her innocence, while maintaining his deception. He kissed her temple absently.

His heart lurched. If he didn't know better, he would think that he had already become fond of her. But only a fool would harbor feelings for her. He was about to leave. They would never see one another again—and that was for the best.

"You should go, *ma chere*," he said softly, "so we do not tempt fate again." He was reluctant to release her.

She smiled at him, gazing into his eyes, her fingertips on his chest. "That was wonderful," she whispered. "And I hate leaving you."

His heart skipped oddly and he couldn't deny it. But that did not mean he had feelings for her. Even if he did, he would dismiss them. She had no place in his world.

He wished that she weren't so transparent. He wished she weren't head over heels in love with Charles Maurice. But he had been very aware of her feelings for him before he had seduced her. He had ignored the twinges of guilt. He had deliberately played upon her affections, all for the sake of maintaining his alias. And he had chosen to treat her like any other passing lover. He was experienced enough to know that her feelings would blossom, once they made love—yet he hadn't cared about that, either.

He had cared only about using her for his own ends, and the desire raging between them. He had lied when he said he had no regrets.

"You are brooding. What's wrong?" She kissed his chest.

He smiled slightly at her. "Nothing is wrong. You are perfect."

"I will see you at eight," she said, smiling.

He lay still as she got up. She expected him to return to France. She would never learn that he wasn't her beloved hero, Charles Maurice.

He watched her slip on the white, virginal nightgown. He said, "Walk with me today on the cliffs."

She brightened. "That is a lovely idea."

He warned, "My motives are rather base."

She laughed. "I know exactly what your motives are, Charles." And she turned and slipped from the room.

His smile faded. It was time to leave. Prior to their affair, it hadn't ever occurred to him to discuss it with her—he had envisioned simply vanishing one day, perhaps leaving a note of gratitude behind. Unfortunately he would not be able to reimburse her and her family for their care, as that would threaten his alias. Now, he wasn't so sure he felt comfortable simply walking out without a word, or leaving a simple note behind.

And that made him a fool.

"I THINK THAT AMELIA is suspicious," Julianne said, but she was smiling. It was a gorgeous summer afternoon, the sun high and bright. Below the cliffs where they strolled, the ocean was an unusual shade of sapphire-blue. A slight, cool ocean breeze whipped her skirts against his legs as they walked. A pair of shaggy herding dogs had followed them from the stables and were hunting grouse amidst the gorse, tails wagging.

"She doesn't like me, which is different from being suspicious," he said, smiling. The manor remained behind them and in sight. As he glanced back, he knew that they could be seen with the naked eye, and Jack had a spyglass in his bedroom. Amelia could be watching them as they spoke. "Does she dislike most men, or is it only me?"

Julianne reached for his arm and he tucked her hand firmly against his side. "She was heartbroken years ago. I didn't realize it until you came into our care, but I think she still has feelings for that man—and you are somewhat like him. I believe that is why she is so mistrustful of you."

"She was involved with the nobleman you mentioned, St. Just?"

"You have an excessively good memory, Charles."

"You said he was a patriot—making him my enemy. Of course I recall him," he said amiably. But what was this? He knew Grenville well, and while no ladies' man, Grenville always kept a beautiful mistress. Dominic could not imagine him courting Amelia Greystone. Surely the petite, dour Amelia had misconstrued whatever interactions had occurred. "Your sister was casting about for an earl?"

"He wasn't the earl then, or even an heir," she said. "And my sister does not cast about, fishing for men! St. Just discovered her at the market. He called on her many times, but he obviously had no genuine interest, because when his brother died, he simply left the parish and never called again." She glowered. "He did not even write a letter."

Dominic could not imagine Simon Grenville behaving like a besotted fool, but Simon's older brother had died nine or ten years ago. People could change, he supposed.

"Look," Julianne said.

A pair of huge boulders was ahead. They were as tall as towers, and Dom felt his entire body tighten. Julia slipped her hand into his. Grinning, she pulled him forward and around the corner, until they were safely out of sight.

Instantly he embraced her, his heart slamming. Her smile was gone and he saw the hunger in her eyes, which had to match his. It had been only a few hours since she had left his bed, but he pulled her close. He wanted her with a maddening urgency.

Why not linger for a few more days? When he left, he was never returning. When he left, his life would be reduced to a few moments in London, and then nothing but war and espionage, revolution and death.

"Charles," she whispered roughly. "Make love to me."

He inhaled. She knew he was well enough to leave; she knew that day was coming, even if they hadn't discussed it.

Dominic kissed her, hard, before pulling her down to the ground with him.

"I HAVE NEVER SEEN you in such good spirits," Tom Treyton said, his gaze sharp.

Julianne smiled warmly at Tom as they drove up the rocky road toward Greystone, sharing the front seat of the carriage together, his horse tied behind the rear fender. Several days had passed since she and Charles made love by the ocean. She had gone into Penzance for badly needed supplies, and had bumped into Tom outside the candle maker's. She hadn't had a chance to speak with him since Charles had awoken from his delirium, almost three weeks ago. And as eager as she was to return to her lover, Tom always had the latest news. She not only wanted information for herself, she wanted it for Charles.

*Her lover.*

As she thought about him, her heart lurched with so much love and desire. For almost two weeks—it had

been twelve days, to be precise—she had been stealing into his bedchamber every night, or walking with
him on the cliffs, or in the cove—which meant that they
were making wild, frantic love in the afternoons. Julianne knew she could no longer think straight—not when
with Charles. She was deeply in love.

And Julianne was certain he loved her as she loved
him. His passion was greater now than it had been at
first. He seemed as aware as she was of the ever-tick-
ing clock, as their time together ran out. And he was
always asking her personal questions about her life at
Greystone, both her past and her future. Julianne thought
that if he ever wanted to, he could probably write a biog-
raphy about her.

She was terrified of his leaving her.

Of course, they never spoke of his pending departure
for France. It was as if they had reached a silent accord
to live in the moment—dangerously, passionately, fortu-
itously.

That morning, she had reluctantly told him that she
had to go into the city. To her surprise, he had encouraged
her—as if he did not mind missing their afternoon tryst.
It was then that he had stressed how badly he needed the
London newspapers. She had seen the dark urgency in
his eyes—and it had been like a dash of ice water, thrown
into her face. They were carrying on as if two lovers
without a care in the world. They had forgotten about
the war, the revolution, and even the government's war
policies there at home—and it was inexcusable.

Of course she would bring him news.

And Tom's news was not particularly good. Lyon,
Marseilles and Toulon were now in the hands of antirepublican leaders. There were continuing riots in Paris,
mostly because of the high prices of bread and the spec-

tacular shortage of foodstuffs, and the city was in a state of near anarchy. Mobs ruled, except when the police were present. According to Tom, the riots were occurring throughout the rest of the country, as well.

Until then, they had spent the entire drive catching up on the war. They had not had a chance to discuss their personal affairs.

"I am always in good spirits," she now told Tom. "But you do not seem happy. Is anything wrong, Tom?"

"I have heard rumors that Pitt has erected a ministry to deal with French espionage in Britain." He rolled his eyes. "It is called the Alien Office."

"Are there French agents in Britain?"

"I imagine so. Those damned émigrés are everywhere, hatching up all kinds of royalist plots against the Republic." He added, "But the real gossip is that Pitt wishes to use this new agency to hunt down Jacobin sympathizers like you and me."

She was stabbed with fear. "That is absurd! Surely our government will not persecute its own citizens."

"I don't know if it is absurd or not. I do know that Pitt hates us—the king hates us—and the Tories hate us."

She shivered.

"Just be careful. We haven't spoken in weeks, Julianne. I received a letter from Marcel," he said, referring to their contact at the Parisian Jacobin Club they corresponded with. "He claims an émigré family has settled in south Cornwall or will do so. He wishes for me to locate the Comte D'Archand and his two children. Have you heard of this man?"

"No, I have not," she said, taken aback. "Why do they wish to know of this man's whereabouts?"

"I have no idea, but I said we would help."

"Of course we will help," she said, patting his forearm.

Tom looked at her. "I have missed you."

She tensed.

"What is wrong, Julianne? Why are you looking at me like that?" he asked. "I know you are aware of my affection for you."

"Of course," she managed, in dismay. The manor was finally visible, standing out starkly against the sky and the ocean. She inhaled. "I told you about Maurice." She had sent Tom a note weeks ago. "I have had a very ill guest to care for. I haven't had a moment to think of myself." She turned away, blushing at the shameful lie. All she had done these past two weeks was think of herself and her need to be with Charles.

"I would think you put out by having a guest for so long, especially one who's convalescing, impinging upon your interests and passions."

Oh, this was terrible, she thought, her heart lurching now. "Fortunately, Charles is a very interesting man. I have been entertained, not put out. You will like him immensely, Tom. He is very articulate and very charming."

Tom's eyes sharpened. "It is Charles?"

Not quite looking him in the eye, she said, "He has become my friend."

Tom sighed. "Of course he has. He is a French army officer, so of course I like him already. Has he been regaling you with war stories, Julianne? It seems unlikely that an army officer would be so articulate."

"He is the son of a jeweler, but he owns a print shop in Paris, and he is very well read, as you shall see," she said eagerly. Charles had told her all about his family and his life in France. She couldn't wait for the two men to meet. They would like one another instantly—they had so much in common.

Tom stared at her. They were traveling up the drive,

his fine gelding trotting briskly in the traces. "How unusual, for a jeweler's son to be literate."

"It is very unusual," Julianne said, "but Charles is hardly average, as you will see."

"You almost sound smitten."

She said carefully, "I am hardly smitten."

They fell into silence now, approaching the house. Tom halted the carriage, setting the brake. Julianne got down without his help, and was about to walk with him to the front door, when a sense made her turn. She glanced over her shoulder and saw Charles sauntering out of the stables.

What on earth? she thought, but she smiled.

He did not smile back, as he slowly approached.

Tom said harshly, "That is Maurice?" Displeasure was in his tone.

She glanced at him and saw how dark his expression was. "Of course it is. Who else would it be?"

"You failed to mention that he is a big, handsome fellow."

Her heart skipped in alarm. "That is hardly a topic of conversation," she began.

"The man looks like a damned rake," Tom said flatly.

Julianne glanced back and forth between both men, realizing that Charles was staring at Tom, a half-smile on his face now, as Tom glowered back. Tom said, "What was he doing in the stables? Maybe he was going to ride off to... What? Spy?"

"We're on the same side," she said tersely. "So if he did mean to spy on our neighbors, what difference would it make?"

Charles was now in earshot. He smiled casually at her. She quickly introduced both men.

"I am very pleased to finally make your acquaintance," Charles said politely to Tom. "And I apologize for my poor use of your language."

Tom shook hands. "Julianne told me about you, as well. I see you are fully recovered."

"I am improving on a daily basis, and I owe my life to Mademoiselle Greystone." He turned to Julianne. "Did you enjoy your afternoon in the city?"

"Yes, of course, and I have two newspapers for you."

"Thank you." He hesitated. "I appreciate what you are doing for my country, *monsieur.*"

"I am a man of great principle," Tom said. "I abhor despotism and tyranny. Of course I am supportive of the great revolution in France." He added, grimly, "I also appreciate the sacrifices you have made."

Charles smiled and glanced at Julianne. "I am going to leave you to your conversation."

As they all started toward the house, Tom restrained her, so that they fell behind Charles. He halted, and Julianne had no choice but to do so, too. "What is it?"

"I do not trust him," Tom said in a low voice.

"Tom!" Julianne gasped.

"A jeweler's son?" he scoffed. "That man is as patrician as St. Just."

AFTER TOM HAD LEFT, Julianne hurried upstairs. Charles was sitting at the table, reading the newspapers she had brought him. For one moment, her heart turned over hard, as she watched him. He glanced up and smiled.

She smiled back, but then became grim, entering. "Tom is suspicious of you."

His brows lifted and he was amused. "How so?"

"He doesn't think you a French army officer!"

"He doesn't like me, Julianne." Charles calmly laid his newspaper aside.

"He took an instant dislike to you. And he seems suspicious of our relationship, too." She walked over to the table and sat.

Charles took her hand. "He is in love with you, so of course he dislikes me. But we hardly spoke to one another. If he has suspicions, they are not of our making."

"Should we worry?" she asked.

Charles was indifferent. "I have been through too much to worry about what Treyton thinks of me. Is there war news?"

Of course he needed the latest news. She would not even consider Tom's suspicions. "It isn't very good, Charles. Lyon, Toulon and Marseilles are in rebel hands." She rubbed her arms, suddenly cold. One day, he would be in France, facing those rebels or the allied armies. She did not want to think about it—not now, not yet.

But his expression never changed. If he was as dismayed as she was, he did not show it.

Then she recalled that odd request from Marcel. "We have heard from our friends in Paris, as well. Apparently we can help the revolution. An émigré has moved to Cornwall and we have been asked to locate him, although I don't know why that would be useful to the cause."

"They undoubtedly wish to infiltrate his household, to uncover any royalist plots against the Republic," Charles said evenly. "They might even wish to send assassins. Will you do as you have been asked?"

She started. "Of course I must help, but surely no one means to assassinate an émigré!"

"If he is plotting against the Republic, as most émigrés are, he will be disposed of."

She was aghast.

"Do not involve yourself," Charles said flatly, as if giving a command. "It is too dangerous an assignment.

If you succeed, they might ask you to infiltrate the household and actively spy. As intelligent as you are, you are too honest to be adept at spying. Stay out of it, Julianne."

"I would be a terrible spy, but I don't think I will be asked to spy on anyone."

"You are naive. It is a part of your charm." Charles dropped his hand. "You are fond of Tom."

She went still. "We are friends."

"He seems well heeled. Does he come from a good family?"

"Yes, he does. Why on earth are you asking?"

"Is he a suitor?"

She was taken aback. "How can you even ask such a thing?"

His stare intensified. A pregnant pause ensued. "I can suggest it because we have both been avoiding the subject of my departure from Greystone."

Her heart lurched. "Don't."

He slowly stood. "Don't what? Bring up a subject we both wish to avoid?"

"Don't go," she whispered. "Not yet."

"Julianne." He moved past her and closed the door. Julianne did not protest—but if Amelia came upstairs, there would be a huge explanation to make. "I must leave. We both know I could have left days ago. We both know why I have lingered here."

She got to her feet, sick with dread now. She had spent the past weeks dreaming of his smile, of being in his arms, of his laugh and of their next rendezvous. She had very deliberately avoided thinking of the future. She had deliberately avoided thinking of his returning to France to rejoin the war.

It did not feel as if she could let him go. She was so deeply in love. "Can you stay a little longer?"

He hesitated. "It will probably take me a few days to make my travel plans."

She took his hand. She knew she should tell him that all he had to do was walk into the tavern in Sennen and he would find a half a dozen young men, all smugglers, eager to cross the Channel, if they were well paid.

"Will you go back to the front lines?" she heard herself ask harshly.

"Undoubtedly."

She felt fear then. "How will I know if you are alive and well?"

"It would be best if, when we said goodbye, we cut all ties."

She was shocked speechless.

He was silent and grim.

"Surely you mean to write to me!" she finally cried.

His expression never changed. "Yes, I could write to you," he said flatly, unsmiling. "But what would be the point? I will be in France, while you are here pining for me. When you should be thinking of other men—suitors who can offer you marriage. Should I then allow myself to miss you? To want you? To what end, Julianne? It would be better for us both to say goodbye and sever all ties."

"I could wait for you. All wars end."

He came around the table and clasped both of her shoulders. "I know this is hard for you. I don't want you waiting for me. I don't want you pining for me. I have many regrets, but Julianne, damn it, I do not regret our affair." He was harsh, his eyes hard. "You do not deserve to be a war widow here in Cornwall. You deserve far more than I can give you."

"You are not going to die in France." Somehow, she looked up at him, fighting tears.

"I am sorry," he said.

She felt her heart turn over with dread. "How much time do we have?"

His grasp on her shoulders tightened. "A few days."

They had been living in the moment for weeks. Julianne went into his arms and he embraced her. Somehow, she must stay in the moment now, for the little time they had left.

# CHAPTER SIX

JULIANNE LAY IN Charles's arms, refusing to move away. He held her tightly as the pale dawn crept into the bed-chamber.

She fought the tears seeping out of her closed eyes. She was trying not to think about his leaving in a few days, but it was impossible after the conversation they'd had last night. He kissed her neck, her shoulder. "You had better go."

She didn't move. "We should make the most of this day. Let's picnic in the cove."

He smiled. "I can hardly object. But, Julianne, discovery at this point is as dangerous as at any other time."

He was right, except she was so acutely aware of their time running out. He was leaving her, and he meant to sever all contact. She knew she would find a way to write to him, whether he wished it or not. But even worse, he could die.

She turned and kissed him, before sliding from the bed. As she put on her nightgown, she wished she could see some sign of anguish on his face, but his expression was so controlled, so contained. Once, she had admired his stoic nature. Now, she wanted a sign from him—an outburst! Yet she knew him so well now. He would never allow himself an emotional outpouring of any kind.

"I will see you at breakfast," he said.

At the door, she faltered. She did not want to question

his feelings for her, but doubt nagged at her. *If he loved her, could he walk away like this?*

He was a hero. He was going to war. Of course he could walk away. It was a matter of patriotism.

She hurried from his room, reminding herself that she must find her composure and enjoy the time they had left. Every minute was precious now.

"Where have you been?" Amelia asked sharply.

Julianne froze on the threshold of the chamber they shared. Amelia was fully dressed, which meant she had been up for some time, and she was clearly waiting for her. Her sister's expression was tense and unhappy, and Julianne also thought it was accusing.

*She had been discovered.*

"Julianne? I have been up for a half an hour. I looked for you in the library. Where have you been?"

"I have been ill," she said quickly, her pulse accelerating. She hated lying to her sister. "I have been sick for most of the night… It must have been something I ate." She held her belly and stared breathlessly at her sister. It crossed her mind if she claimed she was too sick, she would not be able to see Charles at breakfast—Amelia wouldn't let her go.

Amelia stared, her gaze searching. "Perhaps you had better go back to bed," she finally said.

"I think the sickness has passed," she said. "I'm going to get dressed and come downstairs."

Amelia picked up her shawl, wrapped it around Julianne's shoulders, and left the room they shared without saying another word.

DOMINIC HAD THE HOUSE to himself. Amelia had taken Mrs. Greystone out for a drive, but not before sending Julianne to the village of St. Just on an errand. Julianne had promised him she would be back within two hours, in time to tryst that afternoon in the cove.

He had nothing to do but read. He had already gone through the entire house on several occasions, and his most interesting discovery remained Jack's charts. He had already ascertained that the Xs on those charts were caves. He'd discovered several on another occasion, earlier in the week, when left to his own devices. Two of the caves had contained smuggled cases of brandy.

Yesterday, he had checked out the horses in the barn. Neither the gelding nor the mare stabled within was young or fit enough to make the journey to London. When he left, he would take the gelding to St. Just, and get a better mount from his friend's extensive stables. That way, he could have the horse returned to the Greystone family. Julianne, of course, would think he had disembarked for France.

He decided to admit it—he would miss the times they had shared.

She had asked him to stay a few more days. He had intended to refuse. He had healed completely. If not for her, he would be entirely bored in the countryside. In fact, he looked forward to a round of clandestine meetings in London with men in the know, like Warlock and Windham. He also looked forward to the finer things in life which did not exist for him in France—extravagant restaurants and hotel bars, lavish meals and elegant wines, his custom-made clothing, and of course, the luxurious accommodations of his Mayfair home.

Home. He could barely wait. He hadn't been home in a year and a half.

But he hadn't refused her. He had meant to, but instead, the words that had come out of his mouth were *Yes, I will stay a few more days.*

There were many rules to espionage. They were all rules of survival, and most he had learned the hard way, through narrow escapes with death. Some rules had been taught to him by Warlock. The most basic was to remain unattached. Attachments made one vulnerable.

And he knew that firsthand. When Catherine and Nadine had been in France, out of all communication with him, he had been near panic. He was amazed that he had successfully located his mother and gotten her out of the country, considering his state of mind.

He had become somewhat attached to Julianne. He looked forward to the times they spent together. He certainly looked forward to making love to her. But he hoped, very much, that his attachment was due more to the relief she provided him than any genuine affection on his part.

But it didn't matter, because when he left, he would sever all ties, and it would be over. And even though he had told her he would not allow her to wait for him, maybe, when the war was over, if he was alive, he would call on her, just to make sure she had survived the affair and that she was married with children.

Dominic opened the terrace doors and for one moment stared out at the sight of the Atlantic Ocean, stretching away as far as the eye could see. It was a sunny but hazy day, making the ocean that dull shade of monotonous gray that he was now accustomed to. It was impossible to decide where the sea and sky met.

Some might consider the view majestic; he found it unbearably bleak.

Dominic poured himself a glass of brandy—Greystone kept a very fine French brandy, perhaps the best he'd ever had—and sat down to read from a new publication, which he happened to know was government sponsored,

*The British Sun.* He had just become engrossed in an article about the successes of the Association for Preserving Liberty and Property Against Republicans and Levelers—pure Tory propaganda—when he heard the front door slam.

He had the library door wide open, and he glanced up, expecting to see Julianne, even if only an hour had passed since she had left. But before anyone emerged into his field of vision, he heard brisk, booted footsteps. Dominic stood, alarmed, his gaze now trained on the part of the front hall that he could see. He was acutely aware of the gun closet, half a room away. There was a dagger in the desk near that closet, but even as he contemplated quickly crossing the room and taking up the dagger, he realized that only Lucas or Jack Greystone would walk into the house without knocking.

The footsteps approached. A tall, broad-shouldered man with golden hair and cool gray eyes, in a frock coat, breeches and boots, appeared in the library doorway. He locked his stare on Dominic as he pulled off his leather gloves. He then looked beyond Dominic, scanning the rest of the room, before returning to him. "I see that you have discovered my brandy, Paget," he said. "Lucas Greystone, my lord."

Dominic's alarm was instantaneous. How would her brother know the truth about his identity? "I believe you have made a mistake, *monsieur,*" he said smoothly in his heavily accented English.

"You can give up the cover," Lucas said flatly, closing the door behind them. "I take it no one is home?"

Dominic dropped the accent. "No one is home."

"Good." His smile was flitting, and without mirth. He was, Dom saw, a cool, controlled man. "Sebastian sent me to France to retrieve you last month, and he has sent me to Greystone to retrieve you now. His exact words were "You have been on holiday long enough." You are sorely wanted at the War Office, my lord."

Some tension abated, but not all of it. He smiled, for that most definitely sounded like Warlock. But if Sebastian Warlock had sent Lucas Greystone to France to rescue him, then Juliann's brother was hardly the usual country gentleman. "Good to meet you, Greystone. And I am glad to replace the brandy. I have been enjoying it for about a week."

"It's my pleasure," Lucas said, coming forward. He extended his hand and Dom took it. "I hear you have rather charmed Julianne."

Amelia had written to him, Dom thought. Amelia had not approved of all the time Julianne had been spending with him. He did not change his expression, and he could not tell what the other man was thinking.

"When I first awoke from the fever, I did not recall anything after being shot in Nantes," Dom said carefully. "I did not remember being brought here, nor did I know whether I was in France or England. Your sister was speaking in French to me, but I knew she was English, so my confusion was even greater. The truth is that she had heard me shouting in my delirium and she jumped to the assumption that I was an officer in the French army."

Lucas's eyes widened. "Ah, and now I see." He smiled slightly. "My radical little sister must have been thrilled to think you a French officer. You instantly became a hero in her eyes."

How well he knew his sister, Dom thought. "She was very thrilled. I also saw that she was writing a letter to the Jacobins in Paris, and I quickly concluded that she was a Jacobin sympathizer. A few questions confirmed that. And while it became clear that I was in Cornwall, I thought that I was in a nest of Jacobins. So I played along. Once I was into the alias, I obviously could not shed it without her realizing what I was doing in France. I did very little to charm her. She was charmed by the mere notion that I was an officer in the French army. And she still believes me to be Charles Maurice."

Lucas walked over to the magnificent carved sideboard and poured his own brandy. "And Amelia believes it, as well."

"She has been in correspondence with you."

"Of course she has." Lucas sipped. "When I left you here, my instructions were precise. I wanted to know the moment you were out of all danger and on the way to recovery."

"I believe I began recovering a week after I was first brought here. And I have been here for three weeks."

"It has been three and a half weeks," Lucas corrected, watching him as he sipped. "Amelia felt concerned enough to write me a few days ago. As it happened, Sebastian had just ordered me to return and fetch you."

Dom took a sip of the brandy and had to admit he still could not read the other man. He set his glass down and sat on the sofa, crossing his legs. He preferred not to discuss Amelia's concerns. "Tell me how I got here, precisely."

Lucas started. Dominic's tone had been one of command; he meant to remind the other man who was the one in authority. Lucas settled his hip against the sideboard. "I was given orders on July 1, just after dawn, to make haste to Brest to pick up a wounded man and convey him directly to Sebastian. I was in London. I recruited Jack, who happened to be in town, carousing. No one is as adept at avoiding the navy, any navy, as he is. Sebastian arranged for a small gunship and a crew. We left that night and arrived in Brest the evening of the first. We had been given very precise directions—we were looking for a beacon fire five kilometers south of the main harbor. It was easy to find. You, my friend, were more dead than alive, and we decided that the sooner we got you to dry land, the better. And so we brought you to Greystone, not London." He added drily, "Sebastian was not pleased. I did explain that he would have been even less pleased if we brought a corpse to London."

The Greystone brothers had defied the French navy and the French army to rescue him, not to mention any gendarmes, and he had repaid them by seducing their sister, Dominic thought. He was a good judge of character and knew this man would try to kill him if he ever learned of the affair. It was certainly unfair. But he had learned long ago that life was unjust, and filled with surprising twists and turns that no one wanted. After all, he also owed Julianne, and he had repaid her with a seduction.

The now-familiar guilt returned. "I owe you, Greystone, and your brother, as well. I intend to repay you—and the entire family." He would settle a generous payment upon the family. And if ever a Greystone needed a word from him, or a push in high places, they would have it. "I can always be reached in London at my home. When I am not there, the Dowager Countess manages my affairs. I always repay my debts."

"You don't owe us anything. I am a patriot, and I was glad to be of help."

Dom knew he meant it. He watched him, while Lucas paced restlessly, and Dom was certain he was going to return to the subject of his relationship with Julianne. But then he had a comment or two of his own to make. He said flatly, "You need to watch your sister."

Lucas started.

"For an intellectual woman, her naiveté is shocking. She has no clue what is happening in France, she has no clue as to what war means, and she has glorified the revolution and the republicans. We are at war and she supports the enemy. No good can come of that."

"I am well aware of Julianne's views," Lucas said sharply. "I have tolerated them, but I do not approve, and she knows it. But what, pray tell, concern is this of yours?"

"She saved my life. In this way, I am saving hers. She should not be open about her radical leanings, not in such a dangerous time."

Lucas stared very closely. "I still do not understand your concern, Paget."

Dom shook his head. "You do not need to understand it, then. Did you know she is thinking of aiding and abetting the Jacobins in Paris by hunting down an émigré family that has settled in Cornwall?"

Lucas said grimly, "No, I did not."

"Treyton is in love with her. He is dangerously radical."

"I do not approve of Treyton. She can do better. How do you know about this Jacobin mission?"

He did not approve of Treyton, either, so that satisfied him. "She told me. I have warned her not to go after this émigré family that her Jacobin friends are hunting. She will never survive such games of espionage."

"I have chastised her over and over. I have forbidden her from attending radical assemblies. And I agree with you—Julianne can hardly survive games of espionage! But my sister is stubborn, and very hard to control. I can hardly put her under lock and key."

"She must be controlled, or she might wind up in a

predicament she cannot get out of. Her views are seditious, if not treasonous, and she might find herself in serious jeopardy. Our people could decide to prosecute her, and the Jacobins would destroy her the moment they were done with her."

"Is it that bad in France?" Lucas asked.

"It is that bad in France," Dominic said. He chose his words with care. "Your sister has her own charm. I have become fond of her in the past few weeks. I do not want to see her pay a terrible price for her inexperience." The men locked stares. "She should mind her own affairs, stay out of politics and marry well."

Lucas laughed without mirth. "You know, Paget, I respect you, and not because you are Bedford, but for what you are doing for our country. And as much as I agree with you about Julianne, if you think I could force a marriage on her, you do not know her as well as you claim to. I am loath to force her into anything, for that matter."

"But you are head of this household, Greystone, and you decide what is in her best interest. Clearly, someone must look out for her. I am prepared to help in this matter," he added.

Lucas was surprised. "What does that mean?"

"Again, I always repay my debts. I owe you and your brother and sisters. I can help with her dowry."

Lucas looked shocked. Then he said, harshly, "Why the hell would you do that? Amelia wrote me that she was very concerned by Julianne's susceptibility to your persuasion. She told me she was alarmed because Julianne had gone from nurse to companion. She elaborated that the two of you were constantly together. I, of course, knew who you were when I received her letter, so I was not alarmed, although I was surprised, knowing my sister as I do. But I am alarmed now. *What is the extent of your relationship?*"

He controlled his facial muscles. "You do not need to be alarmed. You already know the extent of our relationship—she has been my savior, my nurse and my companion. I have appreciated her companionship while I have been confined. And that is the end of it. Surely you are not suggesting an inappropriate connection?"

Lucas stared. After a moment, he said, "No, of course not. You are an honorable man."

He almost flinched. He knew that the motto *War with Honor* existed, but anyone who believed it was a fool who would not live for long. "Consider my offer, Greystone."

"You are not helping with my sister's dowry." Lucas was flat.

He realized he would not be allowed to contribute even a penny. The other man impressed him. "I am also afraid that Julianne will be manipulated by her radical Parisian friends. If I were you, I would intercept her correspondence."

He flushed. "The truth is, I have considered it. But I despise the notion of spying upon my sister. It goes against my sense of honor."

"She needs your protection. You will regret it if you do not."

Lucas took a draught of the brandy.

Dom knew an opening when he saw one and he barreled on. "She saved my life and I do not want her life endangered by her foolish views. Did you know she is having difficulty with your neighbors? That she is shunned by some of them? That doors which used to be open to her are now closed?"

"Yes, I do know," Lucas said grimly. "But if you think the solution is for me to marry her off, so her husband can be her gaoler, then you are mistaken. Even if I got her to the altar, she would still maintain her radical principles—even more strongly, I believe." Lucas picked up his drink, but he only stared at it while rotating the glass in his hands.

Dom realized he had made the strongest case that he could. He was surprised at how important it had been to do so. But Julianne was her own worst enemy. Someone had to look out for her.

He reminded himself that she was not his affair, not any longer. The reminder felt hollow. And he knew Julianne well enough to know that in the end, she would stubbornly do as she wished.

There was, however, one more thing. "I have made the points I wish to make, with one exception."

Lucas looked up.

"I cannot be unmasked, even now."

"Julianne would never betray you to your enemies, Paget. Surely you know that?"

He knew no such thing. "Only five men have known of my activities, Greystone, and now, it is six. The women in this house are not to discover who I am, or that I am English, or that I am Bedford. I cannot have such information in their hands. That information is highly classified."

Lucas stared. "Sebastian has already made this case for you. I have told no one—not even Jack—about you."

"Good." Dom smiled for the first time that morning, and picked up his glass. "So I will remain Charles Maurice, and you can pretend to apprehend me."

THE MOMENT JULIANNE led the carriage horse into the stables, she saw Lucas's red gelding in its stall.

*Lucas was home.*

*He would discover that Charles was a French soldier and turn him over to the authorities.*

She rushed the startled mare into her box, shut the door and latched it and ran from the barn, her pulse pounding with fear. She must prevent Lucas from interfering; she must not let him arrest Charles! She lifted her skirts and raced across the drive, tripping several times. By the time she reached the front entrance, she was panting and breathless. She rushed inside, not bothering to close the door. The house seemed strangely silent. *Where were they?* All she could hear was her own heavy, labored breathing.

She started for the stairs, passing the closed library door. And then she faltered, detecting the murmur of male voices from behind the entry.

She froze, still out of breath. The tone of the conversation sounded low key and ordinary—as if a quiet discussion was taking place.

Lucas must be within, but he could not be with Charles. They must have another guest. For Lucas would not have an ordinary discussion with an enemy of the state! Voices would be raised—she would detect the tones of alarm or anger. Julianne reached for the doorknob. But she was so agitated that her hand slipped off the knob instead of turning it, and as she grasped it again, she heard Lucas speaking, very clearly, with some amusement in his tone.

She closed her eyes in relief—perhaps Charles had fled the house.

And then she heard the perfectly cultured tones of an Englishman speaking back to him.

Disbelief began.

*That could not be Charles speaking.*

Without thinking, she laid her ear against the door.

"Apparently he will have my head if we are not at Whitehall within forty-eight hours," Lucas was saying.

"That is the republican way, and I must admit, I find that jest in rather bad taste."

The disbelief intensified. *It was not possible*. The Englishman almost sounded like Charles! She would have thought it Charles, except he did not have a French accent. Instead, his tones were cultured and upper class.

"We will leave this afternoon, if that suits you, Paget. We can hire a coach with fresh horses in Penzance, and that way you will be at the War Office as commanded."

"It suits me," the Englishman said. "I debated trying to get a letter off to London, but I was afraid to put any intelligence in the post."

"I can imagine you are eager to leave Cornwall."

"Frankly, I am very eager to get back to London. I can't quite imagine walking down a city street without the fear of coming across a crazed mob, intent on violence, brutality and murder. And I am very eager to return to my home. It has been well over a year—a year and a half, actually."

Disbelief had become shock. *No*. That was not Charles, because Charles was a Frenchman, with an accent, and he did not have a home in London!

"Julianne will fight our ruse tooth and nail," Lucas said. "She will be furious when I apprehend you to take you to the London authorities."

"She can never know who I really am."

She realized she was paralyzed. *She can never know...*.

Somehow she pushed open the door—and saw Charles and Lucas standing before the dark hearth.

*Oh my God.*

As one, both men turned to look at her. Lucas smiled;

Charles did not. "Hello, Julianne. I have met your friend, Maurice."

Julianne did not even see Lucas. She saw only Charles—who was not a Frenchman at all.

The shock intensified; she stared, absolutely speechless.

*He was a lie. Everything was a lie.*

In French, he said, "I'm afraid our picnic has been canceled. Your brother has other plans for me."

"Before you start shouting, I must take him to London. The authorities will wish to interview him," Lucas said.

She began to tremble wildly, her gaze locked with Paget's. *"Liar."*

His green eyes flickered.

Lucas walked over to her, laying a hand on her arm. She flung it off, not looking at him. "Liar! I heard you— speaking English perfectly—without an accent! You aren't a Frenchman—you are English!"

His expression never changed. He stared, not saying a word, but she felt his mind racing.

"There is no way out of your lies. You are no Frenchman!" Where, she thought, was her beloved Charles Maurice? How could this be happening?

Lucas said calmly, "How long were you standing at the door, Julianne?"

She could not stop shaking. She continued to stare at the *Englishman.* "Long enough to hear you call him Paget—a very fine, old, revered English name. Long enough to hear him speaking in English, without the slightest accent. Long enough to know he lives in London, not France. That he has a home there that he misses!" she cried. "Long enough to have heard you say you must be at Whitehall in forty-eight hours." She gasped, the horror complete now. "Tom was right! He said I must not trust you!"

And she had trusted him completely—with her body and her heart.

Finally, his expression changed. "I am sorry," he said.

How could this be happening? The library was tilting, spinning. She could not think clearly—this was impossible!

And then her stunned mind understood exactly who she was looking at. He had been wounded in France, but he was an Englishman, which meant one thing. He was a British agent, and he had been in France to undermine the revolution. "You are a spy!"

He was firm. "I am very sorry, Julianne, that I found it necessary to lie to you. But I am not a spy. My mother is French, and I was visiting her properties in France when I got caught up in the violence there."

She almost laughed at him. As if she would ever again believe a word he uttered!

*Where was her beloved Charles—the revolutionary hero who loved her?*

"Julianne, you must be calm. It was a matter of survival for Paget to go along with your misconception that he was a Frenchman and an officer in the army."

She finally looked at her brother. "Did you know, too?"

"No."

She didn't believe him, either. "My God, are you a spy, too? Is that why you are always in London these days? Maybe you are gallivanting around Paris, as well!"

"I don't have time to spy, Julianne," Lucas said. "And you know it."

She looked back at Paget, not knowing any such thing. As he stood there, he looked arrogant, patronizing and wealthy, every inch the British noble. Did he have a title? The disbelief, horror and shock had become one mass of confusion. This was a nightmare. This could not be happening.

"I don't believe either of you." She whirled and ran from the room.

JULIANNE DID NOT KNOW how long she stood at the window in her bedroom, gazing blindly out at the driveway and stables below. She couldn't move. She couldn't breathe. It was impossible to think clearly. The shock was too debilitating, and it overwhelmed her.

Everything was a lie.

She was consumed with her memories of Charles and all the times they had spent together—sharing meals, reading the newspapers, strolling along the cliffs, making love. His smile flashed, his green gaze turned warm and then it smoldered....

She loved Charles Maurice, and Charles had loved her—she was certain! She wanted him back, desperately!

But Charles Maurice did not exist. Her heroic French army officer was a lie. The month that they had spent together, first as an invalid and nurse, then becoming friends and lovers, was a lie. That man downstairs, that cold-eyed patrician stranger, was an Englishman and a spy!

She had spent weeks in the bed of a British spy!

And in spite of the shock, hurt began, as did the very beginnings of anger.

"Would you care to have a reasonable conversation?"

She froze at the sound of *his* voice. And slowly, Julianne turned.

The Englishman—Paget—stood on the threshold

of her bedchamber, his face grim, his gaze intent and searching.

She fought to breathe, trembling wildly. "Get out!"

He came forward. "We are leaving for London very shortly and I wish to have a discussion with you." He closed the door behind him, then faced her.

Rage blinded her. Julianne strode forward and struck him viciously across the face. The slap sounded like the crack of a whip in the small room.

His cheek turned red, but he did not even flinch. "I probably deserved that."

"Probably?" she gasped.

"I had hoped to leave with your memories of Charles Maurice intact."

She tried to strike him again; this time he intercepted the blow, seizing her wrist. "I don't blame you for wanting to hurt me, Julianne, but slapping me will not solve anything."

She wrenched free. "You meant to leave without my ever knowing the truth about you?"

"Yes, I did. Julianne, you are a Jacobin, in contact with the Parisians. I have survived for as long as I have by trusting my instincts, and my instinct was to play along with your assumption that I was an officer in the army. Obviously I was afraid you would relay my real identity to my enemies."

"You lied to me! I nursed you, read to you, made you meals—and you lied! I brought you the news—and leapt into your bed! And all you did was play on my sympathies—and lie!"

He said, "It was too dangerous to reveal myself. Keep your voice down."

She wanted to strike him again—and then claw out his eyes. But she lowered her voice. "We have been lovers for weeks! At any time, before, during or after making love, you could have told me the truth!"

"Actually, I could not."

"Oh, God! All those smiles, all those shared looks, the tenderness and affection—it was all lies."

He hesitated. "I am very fond of you."

She hit him again and he let her. Then she backed away, finally crying. "I fell in love with you!"

"You fell in love with the man you wanted me to be."

"I fell in love with the man you claimed to be—the man you pretended to be! And that suited you, didn't it?" Horror consumed her now as she realized how she had played into his hands. "Oh, you meant to seduce me, you meant for me to love you! You ruthless, unfeeling, lying bastard! Get out! Get away from me! Go back to France! I hope you die there!" She wept.

He flinched.

When he didn't move or speak, she finally brought the tears under control, turning to find a handkerchief in the pocket of another dress hanging on a wall peg. When she turned, he said quietly, "I never meant to hurt you. I meant only to protect myself. Maybe, one day, when you are calmer, you will understand why I acted as I did."

"I will never understand."

"I will be in London for several weeks, if you need me."

She choked. "You disgust me. I would never turn to you for anything."

"You need only send word to me at my Mayfair home. Ask for Bedford."

Her addled wits tried to comprehend this. His name was Paget—who was Bedford?

"Julianne. You saved my life. I know you will not be

receptive to anything I say today, but I am very grateful and I am in your debt."

"If I had known that you were a spy, I'd have let you die."

"We both know you do not mean that."

The tears arose again, but she fought them.

"I have to go. Your brother is outside with a hired coach. I am very sorry it had to end this way."

*He was leaving.* And strangely, her heart suddenly shrieked in protest. Julianne hugged herself, ignoring the sudden dismay. "Good riddance."

He stood there, his gaze on her face, as if there were more that he wished to say.

And Julianne suddenly wished that Charles would come forward, take her in his arms, and tell her that he loved her. But Charles did not exist! A stranger would be doing so....

She hated him!

He sighed and walked to the door, but paused there. "There is one more thing. You will forget you have ever heard of me, much less that we were acquainted."

Hadn't he wanted to sever all ties? Now, she knew why.

"I have enemies, Julianne, but I am confident you are not one of them."

Julianne seethed, fists clenched. "Go to hell, where you belong." And then, "Charles was a hero! You, Paget? You are a coward!"

His expression unreadable, he turned and left.

# *CHAPTER SEVEN*

JULIANNE FALTERED AS SHE was passing the guest chamber. Amelia had left the door open after changing the bed. She stared into the empty room, stricken.

Three days had passed since the Englishman had left Greystone, and the shock was gone. In its place was a terrific, raw hurt.

She stared into the room that had been Charles's for almost an entire month. She fought not to allow a single memory to come to mind. She kept seeing his dashing dark looks, his intent green eyes. She had loved him so deeply, so completely, but she was a fool—she had loved someone who did not exist.

Abruptly, she shut the door. She could not have a broken heart. It was impossible. Being heartbroken was only possible if Charles had truly existed.

Charles Maurice had been an alias. His real name was Dominic Paget.

She shivered. How could she have been so blind? Tom had become suspicious instantly. Hadn't she wondered time and time again about his tone of voice, his bearing, his eloquence, his education?

But he had always had an explanation, and she had eagerly soaked up his every word.

She trembled. How long would she hurt this way? Paget had held her in his arms, looking at her with smoldering heat while bringing her to the heights of passion;

he had held her hand, smiled tenderly at her and gazed on her with warmth and affection. And it had all been lies.

Maybe she would feel better if, at least, that damned Tory spy had loved her, instead of using her for his own ends.

And did he really expect her to forget who he was?

Julianne grimly faced the stairs, aware that she could have her revenge if she really wanted it. Dominic Paget was a spy. How her Parisian friends would love to receive such information.

She faced the stairs, hearing Amelia and their mother in the parlor, struggling for composure. She had told Amelia the bare facts about Dominic Paget, but she had desperately tried to hide her feelings from her sister. She wanted to cry herself to sleep at night, but she refrained. She had allowed herself the luxury of tears only when Amelia was gone and she was alone in the house.

She was also grateful that Lucas was gone, otherwise he might notice her bleak mood—her grief—as well. Not that she owed him anything now. He could interview her endlessly and she would maintain a stony silence! She was furious with him for his failure to alert her to the truth about Paget from the start. But as angry as she was, she was worried, too. Lucas was obviously involved in the war somehow, and she didn't like it. As a family, they could not survive without him. And she loved him in spite of his deception.

Julianne went downstairs. She noticed for the first time that there was a fine drizzle outside. How perfect, she thought, for the day was as gloomy as she felt.

Was he in London now?

Thinking of him that way made her furious, with herself! What was wrong with her? If he was in London, he was at the War Office, giving intelligence to the war secretary!

Amelia stepped out of the parlor, holding a finger to her lips. "Momma has just fallen asleep."

Julianne forced a smile. "It is the perfect day for an afternoon nap."

"It isn't yet noon, Julianne."

Julianne felt her smile fade. Amelia took her hand. "Help me prepare lunch."

Julianne allowed herself to be led into the kitchen, suddenly thinking of carrying Charles his meals on a tray. Pain stabbed through her heart and she was angry with herself again.

In the kitchen, Amelia handed her a bowl of string beans to wash and clean. Julianne moved over to the sink. As she filled the bowl with water, Amelia said, "You seem better rested today."

Julianne supposed she had slept a few hours last night. "Yes."

"What will you do this afternoon?"

"Read, I suppose."

"Why don't you call on Tom?"

Julianne drained the bowl of beans. She turned and looked at Amelia. She was going to have to face Tom sooner or later. In a way, she was eager to rush to tell him what had happened. When he heard about Paget, he would be outraged. He would also write Paris immediately.

But that made her hesitate. On the other hand, this was *war*.

Amelia said softly, "I think it would do you good to have one of your radical discussions."

She had shared so many political discussions with Paget. And now she knew why he feared the mobs and accused the Jacobins of inciting violence—why he had regretted the execution of the King, the purging of the National Assembly—why he seemed to mourn the flood of émigrés to Britain. He had been *pretending* to support the revolution. He was a *royalist*.

"Julianne, when will we talk about what happened?" Amelia came over to her, her gaze kind but worried.

"There is nothing to talk about. I believed him a hero. But Charles Maurice was an alias." She sounded so calm!

Amelia seized her hands. "I know how infatuated with him you were. I know how crushed you are now! Let me help you, dear."

She trembled. "I am fine, Amelia. Truly. I must simply come to grips with the truth."

"How can you be fine? You nursed him to health, you became close friends and you were his constant companion. You saved his life, and his repayment was a terrible deception. He betrayed us both, Julianne, but I didn't care for him as you did. I am angry—but I can only imagine how you feel."

"I despise him."

Amelia nodded. "In time, you will forget."

He had ordered her to forget he had ever existed, or that they had ever been "acquainted." Suddenly Julianne felt sick.

He was the coldest, most unfeeling human being she had ever met. How could he have deceived her as he had? How could he have walked away, with no feeling, no heartbreak? He deserved whatever fate the war handed him!

Amelia wrapped her in an embrace.

"I fell in love with him," Julianne confessed in a whisper. "I loved him so! This hurts so much. And the worst part is, I keep wondering where he is now—and if he cared at all—if that damned Tory cared!"

"I am sure he cared—you were friends—and you did save his life. But you will forget him, Julianne." Yet her words somehow sounded like a question, and doubt laced her tone.

"How can I ever forget what he has done? Amelia, I saw his lack of expression—his lack of emotion." She was a fool to hope that he had cared, she thought with another huge pang. He couldn't have deceived her as he had if he had cared at all.

Amelia stared, her gaze searching. "Julianne, the morning you were ill—when I asked you where you had been." She stopped. "Were you really ill?"

Julianne turned away.

Amelia seized her arm. "Please tell me you weren't with him."

Julianne trembled, intending to deny it, but she met her sister's eyes and desperately needed her love, her kindness, her support. She heard herself say, "I was with him, Amelia."

"Oh, God!"

Julianne turned and saw that her sister was as white as a ghost. "It really doesn't matter now."

"It matters!" Amelia cried, suddenly turning red with anger.

"You are to tell no one!" Julianne realized the jeopardy her confession had placed her in. "Amelia!"

"He wasn't some commoner. He is a gentleman and a man of honor!" Her sister was horrified.

Julianne wanted to laugh. She could not. "I am sorry, he might be a nobleman, but obviously he is not a man of honor."

Amelia whispered, "Bedford should be held to a higher standard."

Julianne was confused. "He mentioned something about my asking for Bedford if I ever needed him." The only Bedford she knew of was an earl, a very high-ranking peer. "Please don't tell me he is related to the earl of Bedford, for I might truly die."

Amelia said softly, "He *is* the earl of Bedford."

TOM LOOKED UP from the desk in his High Street office, surprised. Then his surprise became concern. "Julianne?"

She had left Amelia standing in the kitchen, for the moment she had learned that Dominic Paget was the earl of Bedford, anger had consumed her. She had thought of nothing but the extent of his deception for the past hour. "I have news," she said harshly, trembling.

Tom was on his feet and sliding on his handsomely embroidered olive-green coat. He quickly came toward her. "You seem very distraught. I am very afraid to ask what has happened."

She somehow smiled tightly at him, but inwardly, she was seething. Dominic Paget had played her for a fool, claiming to be an officer in the republican army, when he was not just any noble but an earl, seated in Britain's House of Lords! Everyone knew how wealthy Bedford was. Worse, Bedford was a renowned Tory! Pitt offered him the ministry of the Exchequer in a previous year. "A lot has happened in the past few days." She inhaled, meeting his worried gaze.

He was clearly alarmed. "You are frighteningly pale. You should sit. I can make tea."

"You are my friend and I need you, Tom."

"What happened?"

She shook her head. "You were right about Maurice.

He was pretending to be an officer in the French army. He is actually…Bedford." She waited for a reaction, the need to hurt Paget now savage.

Tom's eyes widened. He was stunned. "Wait a moment. The earl of Bedford is a British agent?"

Suddenly Julianne felt a tingling of dismay, followed by the slightest sense of shame. *She had just unmasked Paget.* Tom was no fool and he had instantly understood the implications of his deception. Did she really want to destroy Bedford? Did she really want him to return to France and be uncovered—and guillotined? So many memories flooded her that she could not speak—and in every one, she was in Paget's arms.

"That entire time—a month—you were nursing the earl of Bedford, not some common soldier?" Tom was incredulous.

When she did not answer—she could not—he cried, "God! I knew something was wrong. I could smell the deceit all over him!"

Julianne shoved the painful memories away, hugging herself. Paget was a liar. He had used her miserably. He did not deserve any concern on her part. He would get what he deserved. "You were right and I was wrong. I am a fool."

Tom clasped her shoulder. "Julianne, you are the most intelligent woman I know. This is not your fault. It is his fault. He is a good-looking, charming man—and he knows it. Where is he now?"

She hesitated, reluctant to say any more. She would never tell Tom that Lucas was also involved in the war against France, and that he had taken Paget back to London. But should she tell Tom that Paget had returned to London? "He left." She suddenly wanted to hedge.

What was wrong with her? Didn't she want Paget brought to the justice he deserved?

*I will be in London for several weeks, if you need me. I am very fond of you.*

She wanted to scream aloud, *Liar!* Instead, she stared at Tom.

"I am going to write Marcel immediately," Tom decided. He started for his desk, and then whirled. "Julianne, did he say where he was going? Did he return to France?"

The hesitation within her grew. She was confused. Did she truly want him to die?

"Julianne?"

If she told Tom that Paget had gone to London, would he bother to write to the club in Paris? Wouldn't it be better to wait and carefully decide what to do next, when she was calmer? "He went to London, I think. But he will never use the same alias if he does go back."

Tom stared at her, studying her. "If he is in London, we can find out easily enough. I'm sure half the town knows where his residence is."

"What are you going to do?" she asked, filled with unease.

"Locate him, if I can. And of course, relay the information to Marcel."

She became terribly uncertain—and frightened. She wished she hadn't told Tom about Paget. She had never believed in vengeance, but she was simply so hurt. A course of vengeance was a decision that should be made carefully—not in a fit of anger. "What will they do? Will they…send an assassin?" She trembled.

"I doubt that. But they probably have agents in town, and they will watch him closely. That is what I would do, at least, and I would be prepared to continue the surveillance once he returns to France." He grinned. "This information is a godsend!"

Julianne felt like crying. She turned away so Tom would not see.

"Are you all right?" he asked softly, from behind.

If she wasn't careful, she'd go into his arms. She fought to recover some calm. "Yes."

He studied her. "What happened, exactly? How did you uncover him? He certainly did not volunteer a confession."

She had put Paget in jeopardy; she would never endanger Lucas. "I overheard him speaking with our stable boy—in perfect English," she lied. "I was so upset that I confronted him and he could not deny the truth."

"But how did you ever learn he was Bedford?" Tom demanded instantly.

Julianne froze. And she recalled their last conversation. "He admitted it," she said, trembling. "He admitted it and then ordered me to keep his secret."

Tom accepted that and said, "Do you know how long he was in France, spying for Pitt?"

"No." She walked over to one of the chairs in front of his desk and slumped down in it. She realized she was exhausted. But then, she had told Amelia that they were lovers, and now, she had told Tom that Bedford was an agent.

Tom came over to the desk and lay his hand on her shoulder. She smiled up at him, gratefully. "I can't answer any more questions, not today."

"You were very fond of him," he said slowly. "I have been so carried away with the fact that he is an agent that I have overlooked how you must be feeling."

"Please, don't. I am fine."

"How can you be fine? It is one thing to betray a cause—it is another to betray a person."

"I am angry…and hurt. I thought we were friends. But I will recover."

Tom was silent. He finally said, very carefully, "You didn't look at him as if he were a mere friend. You looked at him as if he were the prince of all your dreams."

She jerked.

"You fell for him, didn't you?"

Julianne hugged herself, tears arising. "Yes."

"Damn him," Tom said savagely. "I knew it! Well, I will make sure Bedford gets what he deserves and he will rue the day he revealed himself to you."

Julianne leapt up. "Maybe we shouldn't interfere. Maybe we should leave these war games to the spies and agents who know how to play them!"

Tom was incredulous. "Surely you wish for him to meet his just deserts?"

"I don't know what I want!" Julianne cried.

DOMINIC SMILED TO HIMSELF as they passed the tall, Gothic spires of Westminster Abbey, inhaling the rather noxious odors of London in the summertime. "God, I have missed the city."

Lucas held a handkerchief over his nose. "A year and a half is a very long time."

The coach they shared continued on, the ride rather jarring and bumpy. Dominic had not discussed his activities in France with Lucas. But they had been traveling for two entire days, stopping only to change horses and drivers and partake of a quick meal, and they had come to know one another rather well. They had spoken of the war, the revolution and the latest news at home. Greystone knew every pertinent detail about the wars

on the Continent and quite a few details about the state
of French politics. It had become very clear to Dominic
that Lucas Greystone was involved in the war effort, although how, he did not know, did not ask, and Lucas did
not say. He was clearly as conservative as Dominic was,
and dead set against the revolution reaching the shores of
Britain. Dominic liked him, but that made him somewhat
uncomfortable—he felt as if he had betrayed Greystone
by carrying on with his sister.

They had not discussed Julianne. Aware that the journey to London would take them two or three days, de-
pending upon both the coaches they acquired and the
weather, Dominic had been careful to keep their conversation impersonal.

Their coach turned north onto Parliament Street, and
Dominic glanced briefly at the river, which was filled
with ferries and barges of all shapes and sizes, the traffic heavy, as it always was. Dominic's last confrontation
with Julianne bothered him still. So did the moment she
had learned the truth about him and his deception. He
would never forget her absolute disbelief, nor would he
forget her justifiable anger. He was very sorry the affair
had ended as it had; he was even sorrier that she had ever
learned that her hero did not exist.

A few minutes later they arrived at the Admiralty, and
were climbing out of the coach. Lucas advised the driver
to wait.

Dominic was silent as they walked up the broad, pale
stone steps and crossed the spacious lobby. Naval officers and diplomats, peers and government officials, were
coming and going.

"Bedford!"

Dominic turned to find the earl of St. Just crossing
the lobby. Grenville was a tall, dark-haired man with a

brooding air about him that made many accuse him of being aloof, while others took it for arrogance. He was very well dressed in a dark brown velvet coat, lace cuffs, pale breeches and white stockings. Characteristically, he did not wear a wig, his dark hair pulled back into a queue. Dominic let Greystone go on to the reception as St. Just halted, unsmiling. "I wondered when I'd see you again. Or even if I would." He clasped Dom's shoulder. "Glad that you are back, Bedford."

Dominic smiled. "You are in town—in late July? I can only imagine why." He was fairly certain that, in spite of having two small children, Grenville spent most of his time on the Continent—he was fluent in several languages. Like Dominic, he adamantly opposed the French revolution.

"We will have to catch a drink together, and share our secrets," St. Just said, lifting his brows as he took in his appearance. "You need a new tailor, my friend."

"What I need is my own closet. It is a long story. One I might think to share."

"I will only be in town a few more days." St. Just's smile faded.

Dominic felt his own smile fade. "I will not be here very long, myself."

They shared a look and St. Just walked off. Dom turned and saw Greystone at the reception, speaking with a pale, lanky clerk with pale blond hair. He strode toward them, the clerk coming forward. "My lord, I am Edmund Duke, the secretary's assistant. He is delighted that you are here. It is my pleasure to escort you to him."

Dominic shook the young man's hand. "Duke."

"Mr. Greystone? Secretary Windham would like to see you, as well." Duke gestured that they should follow him inside the Admiralty.

They left the lobby. Inside, numerous offices were occupied, mostly by naval officers and clerks. Following Duke, Dom nodded at two admirals he happened to know. He had never met Windham personally, and he was curious. Windham's office was at the far end of the corridor, the two teakwood doors wide open.

Duke knocked politely on the open door.

Dominic saw past him into a very spacious room. One wall of windows looked out onto Whitehall, a luxurious seating area before it. A vast desk was at the chamber's other end, with several chairs before it. One wall contained bookcases. A large table was against the last wall, with several chairs, and piles of paperwork. Clearly numerous clerks assisting Windham worked there.

Two men stood up, having been seated on the sofa. Dom was not surprised to see Sebastian Warlock, nor was he surprised to see Edmund Burke. Both men were his mentors, even if no one knew it except for the parties involved.

Windham was a heavyset fellow in a green velvet coat, his wig white and powdered. He came forward, smiling, but the smile never reached his eyes. "Bedford, at last. It is a pleasure."

Dominic shook the war secretary's hand. "The honor is mine, sir."

Windham turned and smiled at Lucas. "Greystone."

"Sir."

So they already knew one another, Dominic thought.

"I believe you know Warlock and Burke."

Dom nodded. "Yes, I do."

Sebastian came forward. He was a tall, dark-haired man, exceedingly good-looking, with piercing eyes that never missed a trick. "And have you thoroughly enjoyed the sandy beaches of Cornwall? You seem to have caught a bit of sun."

"A well-deserved reward, don't you think?"

"Actually, I do." He extended his hand and Dom took it, as their gazes locked. He instantly knew Sebastian had dozens of questions, and that he would wish to speak to him privately when Windham was done with them.

Burke was not as aloof. He embraced Dom as he would a brother or a son. "I am glad to see you so well, Dom." He slapped his back now, once. "I am glad you are safe and sound, and back."

Dom glanced at Lucas. "I owe Greystone and his entire family. Otherwise, I would not be standing here right now."

"Edmund, pour everyone a scotch. My best, if you please," Windham said. "There is some good news for you, Bedford. Jacquelyn defeated an entire division of Biron's troops on July 17."

He felt his entire body flood with relief. "Thank God. We were routed at the end of June, outside Nantes. We were outnumbered and outgunned."

"We know," Burke said.

Dom faced the war secretary. "Sir, we are in dire need of guns, powder, cannon, other munitions, not to mention bread and other foods. And we need surgeons. We have no way of caring for the wounded, not if we suffer another rout as we did then." He accepted a glass of scotch from Duke.

Windham turned. "Thank you, Edmund."

The assistant backed out of the room, closing both doors.

Windham said, "We are very aware of your needs. Jacquelyn has sent us several missives. But we have logistical problems."

Surely, they would not deny aid to the rebels in the Loire Valley, Dom thought, disbelieving. "Sir, I am here to ask you for supplies, and to arrange a rendezvous between your convoy and Jacquelyn. La Vendée must be supported if you wish to defeat the French republicans."

Burke clasped his shoulder. "Even as we now speak, Toulon, Lyon and Marseilles are in our hands. Bordeaux is in the throes of a counter insurgency. There are pockets of rebellion in Brittany, as well."

Dom started. "That is damned good news." He glanced at Sebastian. "Is the road to Paris still open?" If the Allies took Paris, the French republicans would be crushed. They could not withstand such a defeat.

Windham said, "Yes, it is. General Kellerman is marching on Lyon with eight thousand troops but we believe he faces fifteen or twenty thousand rabidly antirepublican citizens. The French have sent a very young, inexperienced army officer to take Toulon, a man by the name of Napoleon Bonaparte. He will never succeed. And Coburg is consolidating the Coalition's positions in Flanders, the Rhine and the Pyrennees. The war is going well."

Dom wet his lips. Coburg was not marching on Paris? "What about our supplies, sir?"

"There are French Islands in the West Indies that interest us. Pitt has sent several divisions to the Caribbean to take them," Windham said. "We are damned short of men, ships and supplies."

Dom wanted to curse. "Is that why Coburg is sitting on his ass along the front lines?"

"Coburg believes it vital to secure our position," Windham said, disapproval in his tone.

"Will the Duke of York march on Paris?" Dominic asked, in growing disbelief.

"He is joining Coburg. Eventually, in a month or so, they will march on Paris."

"In a month or two," Dom muttered. His frustration made him drain his scotch. How could such an opportunity be missed? "The road to Paris has been open since April, when Dumouriez defected, but we will not march on the city and take it? The La Vendée rebels need troops, guns and bread, but those supplies are going to the West Indies?"

"We can resupply La Vendée in the fall," Windham said, "but not sooner."

"I doubt we can wait that long!" Dom cried. "I came to London to beg for aid, while we remain viable enough to fight the French. Sir, I am begging you now. Divert the aid to us, immediately."

"You cannot allow the Loire Valley to fall," Sebastian said softly.

Windham said firmly, "We will send a convoy in the fall, and I will keep you apprised of the situation."

Dominic knew that it would be a miracle if Jacquelyn and his men survived the summer. But there was no persuading Windham. "Sir, if I may?"

The war secretary nodded.

"The war news sounds promising—even certain, for us. But I promise you, victory is not certain in France." He paused. "France is in anarchy. There are chronic food shortages everywhere. Mobs control the street, easily incited by the Jacobins and the National Assembly. The Commune now links the street with the countryside, and it is run by the city's most radical elements. The Jacobins have formed a new Central Revolutionary Council to raise armed bands throughout the country, to instill fear in everyone, should anyone think to support an insurgency! France is consumed with two elements—fear and passion. Even those on the side of the revolution fear being labeled an enemy of the republic. The passion of the radicals to spread their world of equality and liberty—or mayhem and death—is like nothing I have ever seen. That passion infuses the officers and soldiers of the French army. You believe the French army a ragged group of conscripts? Oh, they are ragged, indeed—and they are rabidly determined to destroy the Powers of Europe, to free the common man there from tyranny and injustice, and to see the revolution in France to its inglorious end—a republic without elites, without nobility, without prosperity. A republic of the people, and for the people, where no one can have anything that someone else doesn't have." Dom halted. "Those conscripts will gladly die for *La Liberté!*"

Dom realized he was trembling. A grim silence followed his diatribe. It was Greystone who handed him another drink. Dom took a gulp of whiskey, and said, "This will not be a short war."

Windham said grimly, "I hope you are wrong." Then, "I want a letter from you, Bedford. Detail your needs. And I want a second letter, telling me in writing what you have just told me in person. I have a meeting, so I am afraid this concludes our affairs for today. Bedford, thank you. And thank you, as well, Greystone."

Dominic filed out with the others. In the lobby, Sebastian said, "I'd like a word."

Dom nodded, not surprised, and quickly said goodbye to Burke and Greystone. He glanced at Sebastian as they walked outside. "Do you know Greystone?"

"Yes. In fact, I know him rather well."

Dominic waited for an explanation, but none came. Instead, Sebastian pointed at a black coach with the shades drawn over the windows. Dominic smiled as they got in. "Do we really need to have the shades down?"

Sebastian rapped on the glass behind the driver. "St. James Park," he said. He looked at Dom. "Who shot you?"

Dom sobered as the carriage moved off. "I believe that I was spied upon in Paris. The radicals are in an excessive state of paranoia, spying on everyone. If I was followed to Nantes, I was uncovered when I joined up with Jacquelyn."

"It is fortunate that you lived."

"Very fortunate—I can see how moved you are." Dom was wry.

Sebastian said, "Didn't I teach you never to attach yourself to your associates?"

Dom smiled tightly, without mirth. He thought of Julianne. "Yes, you did. And it is fortunate—for us both—as I am as invested in taking back France from the radicals as you are. Did Jacquelyn send word that I was hurt?"

"Indeed, he did. I was afraid to allow you to recover in France, in case another attempt was made on your life," Sebastian said. "That said, I need you to go back immediately."

"How immediately?"

"Within a month, at the latest. Do you have the will to do so?"

Dom nodded. "Oh, I have the will. I could never turn my back on my friends and family there."

Sebastian said, "Good."

Dom turned to stare out of the window. They were in St. James Park now, which was lush and green, a few carriages and hacks upon the park's trails. But he didn't see the pretty park. "I have held dying men in my arms, men who were my neighbors, my friends and my distant relations. We need aid, Sebastian, desperately." He lifted his gaze.

"Pitt is making a huge mistake, going after a few trophy islands in the West Indies. I will urge Windham to find something to divert to Jacquelyn. You are attached, my friend."

He thought of Michel, whom he'd known since childhood   and of Julianne. "I am attached."

"France was never safe for you. It is even less safe now. Get rid of your attachments."

Dom stared at Sebastian. "That is easier said than done."

"You are one of my best agents. You are as collected as an agent can be. Yet you feel passionately for France, le Loire, your friend Jacquelyn... It worries me." He was blunt.

"The good news is," he said slowly, thinking of Julianne again, "I am adept at keeping those passions in check."

"Are you?"

"Yes."

Sebastian studied him. "What happened at Greystone? You seem fully recovered. It's been a month. Why didn't you come to London a week ago—even two weeks ago?"

He had been expecting the question. "I was enjoying the holiday."

Sebastian seemed to accept that. "What do the two women know?"

He hesitated. "Both sisters know I am Bedford—and it is worse than that."

Sebastian darkened. "How much worse?"

He hesitated, wanting to protect Julianne now, not just from herself but from Sebastian. "What do you know about the family?"

"Everything."

Could Sebastian possibly know that Julianne was a radical? He hoped not. "Unfortunately, the women assumed I was a Frenchman—and I played along. They now have guessed what I was doing in France."

Sebastian looked out the window. "I'll manage them."

He did not like the sound of that. "Is that necessary?" he asked "They are at the end of the land, Warlock. Neither woman gets out of the parish, much less Cornwall." But even as he spoke, he thought about Julianne, writing to her Jacobin friends in France.

"Would you leave the fact that they know who you are, and what you have been doing, in their hands? Do you trust them with such information? Would you leave the possibility it would be conveyed into the wrong hands to chance?"

"What are you intending to do?" Dom asked coldly.

"Why haven't you mentioned that Julianne Greystone is an active radical?"

He was startled. "Because she is probably harmless, and she saved my life."

"Is that what you believe? That she is harmless?"

He hesitated. He did not want to pit Sebastian against her. And she wasn't harmless, she was too easily manipulated. "She means no harm. She has grandiose ideas about the common man—and don't we all? She is naive, Warlock. She has vast ideas about universal equality and faith that this is what is happening in France. Yes, she could be used by our enemies—but I owe her a vast debt. I won't have her on your watch list."

Sebastian looked at him oddly. "She not only has radical inclinations, she is in correspondence with the Rue de la Seine Jacobin Club. She has been in contact with them for well over a year."

He froze. "She is already on your watch list."

Sebastian was grim. "Actually, she is not officially on any list."

Thank God, he thought. "Then why do you know so much about her?"

Rather wryly, Warlock said, "She is my niece."

# CHAPTER EIGHT

DOMINIC APPROACHED the front hall of Bedford House as Warlock's coach pulled away. His home had been built centuries ago, but had been renovated and added on to during his father's lifetime. Rather square and three stories tall, it boasted three round medieval towers, the central tower housing the entry hall. A circular drive had been placed in front of the house, and carefully kept gardens were in the back. Roses and ivy crept along the front walls, and lush lawns slid away to the street beyond the driveway.

Suddenly the images flashed through his mind—wounded and dying men, the chaos on the front lines, and Nadine, lifeless, a corpse on a cobbled bloody street....

With difficulty, he jerked back to the present. Why had he just been swept back in time? My God, he was home!

He blinked and now saw two doormen in royal-blue-and-gold livery standing before the ebony front door, gaping at him. He took a moment to compose himself. He had never needed to be home more. Damn the war.

He approached, smiling slightly at them, as he bounded up the front steps. Opening the door, they both swept him bows.

And the vivid memories were gone now. Instead, he paused inside his front hall, glancing around. Little had changed. Gilded chairs in red damask lined the walls. The floors were black-and-white marble, the walls white stucco and the vaulted ceiling above his head was three stories high. Several portraits and landscapes adorned the walls, including an oil of him and his parents, painted when he was a small child. He was *home.* It was incredible—almost beyond belief.

His butler came rushing into the hall from its opposite end.

Shock covered Gerard's features. "My lord!" he cried, hurrying forward. "We were not expecting you!"

Dominic smiled. For the next month, he wanted all the comforts—all the peace—his life in London could offer him.

"Good day, Gerard. You do not have to run. Yes, I am home. Is the Dowager Countess in?"

Gerard reached him, flushing. "My lord, welcome home! Lady Paget is in the gold room, my lord, with callers." Gerard was a middle-aged Frenchman who had been with his mother's family since she was an adolescent. He was slim and gray haired, devoted to Dominic and even more devoted to Catherine. Now he ogled Dominic's clothes.

"They are borrowed." He smiled and strode past the butler, who followed.

"My lord, what can I get you?"

"Where is Jean?" he asked, referring to his valet, as he stepped to the threshold of a large salon with sunny golden walls and gilded furniture. His mother was seated at one end of the room with two other ladies, resplendent as always in green silk and emeralds. She saw him immediately. No one, of course, had a clue that he had been anywhere other than in the country, where he had several fine estates, or that he hadn't had any contact with Catherine in months. "Good afternoon, Mother."

To her credit, she did not gasp or cry out, when he

knew she was stunned. Instead, her expression hardly changed, although she blanched. Slowly, she stood.

"I will summon Jean immediately," Gerard said.

"I wish to bathe and change," Dom directed. "Have him draw a hot bath. And, Gerard? Open my best pinot noir. The '87." He strode forward.

Catherine Fortescue Paget was a petite woman with dark blond hair and an exceptional figure. She was tiny, but she carried herself with such a bearing that one did not notice it until he stood close to her. She remained terribly beautiful and very charming—she had turned down a dozen serious offers of marriage in the past five years since William had died. Now, she slowly smiled at him, and he saw how hard she was controlling herself. "You are looking very well," he said, meaning it. She was stunning in the green ensemble she wore, and she did not look old enough to be his mother.

"Dominic," she said, sounding hoarse. He knew she was close to tears. "You have been in the country for far too long."

Dominic reached her and took her hands. "Yes, I have, and I am very glad to be home." He kissed each cheek in turn and then allowed her to introduce him to her callers. Both women greeted him enthusiastically, then told Catherine they would return later in the week, as she clearly needed a moment with her son. Dominic waited, hands in the pockets of his frock coat, as Catherine walked them to the salon doors, thanking them for coming and promising them that she would call on them in several days. "You must bring Lord Bedford," Lady Hatfield said.

"I will do my best," Catherine promised. When they were gone, she turned, and she was ashen.

"I am fine," he said softly.

Tears filled her green eyes. "Oh, Dominic!" She

rushed to him and hugged him, hard. Then she stepped back. "What happened to you? Three weeks ago, Sebastian Warlock told me that you had been shot. He said that you would be returning to London when you could travel. But that bastard did not tell me another thing!" She flushed now. When angry, sparks shot from Catherine's eyes. "I was so furious when he would not tell me anything else!"

He took her arm and guided her back to the sofa. He would not lie to his mother—but he would not alarm her and tell her that he had been unmasked in France and had been the target of an assassin. "As you know, I joined Michel Jacquelyn and his rebels in le Loire." He had managed to get a letter to his mother after first meeting up with Michel. "We engaged the French army in May and June, several times. Our first two engagements were very successful—we sent the French troops fleeing. But we were not successful in the third battle. The fighting was vicious. I was shot." He shrugged, despising the lie he had just told. But it was necessary. Catherine would never recover if she learned that an assassin had been sent after him. "Warlock sent some men to extract me from France. I hardly recall crossing the Channel, but in the end, I survived. As you can see, I am fine."

She gave him a disbelieving look. "How badly were you hurt?"

He smiled at her. "It was a flesh wound." He would never tell her he had been at death's door.

She stared unhappily at him, clearly unconvinced. "Why didn't you write? Warlock said you'd been taken to Britain, but he would not tell me where you were! I became frightened when I did not hear from you."

He hesitated. "I was in south Cornwall, in the hands of a Jacobin sympathizer." She gasped. He sobered, thinking of Julianne. "But she was very kind and she cared for me. Actually, she assumed I was French army," he added, and his mother's eyes went wide. "Obviously I could not reveal myself and one thing led to another." He thought of their heated affair, no longer smiling. Not for the first time, he wondered if she remained furious with him. "I was not about to write and have my letter intercepted by her or her friends."

"God," she said harshly, "the Jacobins are everywhere! I cannot believe a Jacobin nursed you back to health!" She took his face in her hands and kissed his cheeks, in turn.

"She was pleasant company," he supplied.

Catherine sighed. "Ah, so she was beautiful, and helped to pass the time."

He decided not to comment.

"Sit with me," she said, moving to the sofa, where she sat.

He joined her. "When I left, the radicals here in Britain were a tiny fraction of the literate population."

She sent him a dark look. "They remain a small group, Dominic, but they are vociferous—as rabid as the Jacobins in Paris. They are holding a convention here in London next week. And that awful radical, Thomas Hardy, is holding a convention in Edinburgh. They would welcome the French army if it ever came to our shores."

He looked at her. He hated thinking that she remained as affected by her time in France as he was by his time there, but he was fairly certain that her memories tormented her. When he had found her in France almost two years ago, they had spent several nights in various inns, their rooms adjoining, as they made their way to Brest to escape. He knew she had had nightmares and insomnia.

He had returned to France within weeks of bringing

her safely to London, to search for Nadine. They had not had a decent conversation in the very long year and a half since. "How have you been?" he asked.

"Worried, of course."

"That isn't what I meant. How has London treated you?"

She smiled, but it was fleeting. "The revolution has changed this town. Everyone speaks of the atrocities in France on a daily basis, not to mention the war. And now there is even talk of an invasion. Can you imagine? Could the French invade Great Britain? Would they dare?"

He was calm. "Certainly not in the near future. And if they ever invaded, they would do so far to the north, perhaps in Scotland, or in the south, where there is so much Jacobin sympathy for them." He thought of Julianne again.

She stared tersely at him, then took both of his hands in hers. "I go back and forth between London and Bedford Hall. I go to teas and supper parties, the theatre and balls, and once in a while, there is a suitor whom I encourage. Not because I am interested in going to the country, or going to a ball, or having a courtship, but because I am still alive, and it is what a woman must do."

His heart lurched. "I am sorry I was gone for so long." Catherine needed to remarry, he thought, and he wondered why he hadn't thought about that before.

"I know you won't speak of it, but I am glad you are a patriot, Dominic," she said softly. "I am glad you stayed in France." She did not finish her thoughts, which relieved him, as he would never speak openly about his activities with her.

"I am worried about you. You aren't happy."

"I am happy that you are home!" she cried. "But how can I be happy when my country is being destroyed,

piece by piece, day by day, week by week? It sickens me."
Tears filled her eyes.

"There are rebellions everywhere," he said, "in Lyon,
in Toulon, in Marseilles—"

She cut him off. "I know. Maybe this will end well,
after all."

He glanced away.

"You don't have to pretend," she said softly. "I am
trying to be optimistic, but I do not feel optimistic. Not
at all. Have you been back to the flat? Is anything left?"

"Nothing remains," he said firmly, without emotion.
"But the chateau is intact. The vineyards are doing well."

"Intact," she echoed. "They will rape our home, Dominic."

He took her hand. She had been born in the chateau.
"Maybe not. La Vendée is strong right now."

She faced him, a strange expression on her face, her
grasp on his hand tightening. "Dominic. You haven't
heard, have you?"

"Heard what?" He had not a clue as to what she was
referring to.

"I have news—good news." She wet her lips, then
smiled. The smile reached her eyes. "Nadine is alive."

"I AM SO GLAD you are taking this holiday," Amelia said
with a soft smile, seated on her bed across from Julianne's.

Julianne paused in the act of folding another gown,
before placing it in her valise, which lay open on the bed.
"I am excited," she admitted with a small but genuine
smile. "It's been an entire year since I was in town."

"And I am excited for you," Amelia said.

Julianne smiled. She had always loved London, even
if it was a city of great contradictions. She loved the

crowds, the noise, the bustle; she even loved the traffic. She loved the libraries and museums and, mostly, she loved the clubs.

While every class of society abounded in the city, from the poorest of the poor to the wealthiest of peers, London was a magnet for intellectuals. The city was filled with poets, writers and artists, philosophers and professors—and radicals. On any given day, she could find an assembly of like-minded men and women, arguing for the improvement of society, for the liberation of the common man. Debates would be waged over the Corn Laws and free trade; over the minimum wage and the conditions of labor. Pamphlets were to be found on every street corner espousing universal suffrage, decrying conditions in the mills and mines, protesting the war against France, supporting the reform of boroughs. On one block, she would walk by mansion after stately mansion, staring after women in their silk gowns and diamonds, the noblemen in their velvet coats frothing French lace cuff and collars, yet on the next street, the unwashed and the homeless would crowd tight doorways in abject misery, while their children grabbed her skirts, begging for a penny.

London was the most exciting place she had ever been.

"How fortunate it is that Tom is off to that meeting of his in Edinburgh, so you can travel to London with him," Amelia said.

Julianne thought that it was very fortunate that the London convention she was attending was a week prior to the convention in Edinburgh. Amelia did not know that was the reason Julianne was going to London. But Julianne thought her sister would have encouraged her to go even if she had known the truth. Amelia remained that concerned about her.

It had been a week since Paget had been exposed as a liar and a spy and had left for town. Julianne thought that it had been the most difficult week of her life. She had had to face the fact that her heart was broken. She had been in love. She had been lied to and even, in a way, jilted. The pain was bone deep.

She would always be angry with Paget for his deception. She had begun to feel terribly used and abused.

But the facts were the facts and she could not change them. What she could do was fight her memories of the affair and get on with her life. She was not going to let that bastard inflict any more damage than he had already done.

But sometimes, she would awaken in the middle of the night, aching for Charles—missing him impossibly. And in those moments, she had to repeatedly remind herself that the man she loved didn't exist.

She desperately needed to get away. Traveling with Tom would be very enjoyable. They would spend the entire two- or three-day journey discussing war and politics. There was nothing better than that! With Tom—and while attending the convention—she would not be as likely to allow her mind to drift into painful memories of Charles, or hateful memories of Paget.

"It's also fortunate that Lucas has room in his flat for you," Amelia said. "But I am surprised you don't want to go to Edinburgh with Tom."

Julianne laid her folded dress in her valise. "He asked me, Amelia, but we cannot afford such a trip. It is double the cost of going to London!"

"Do you want to go?" Amelia asked softly.

Julianne straightened. Tom had invited her to join him at Thomas Hardy's convention again. He had bluntly told her he would pay for her expenses, including her hotel room. He had reminded her that he could afford it, and it would be his pleasure. Julianne had refused.

A month ago, she would have been thrilled to accept his offer—and have the opportunity to meet Thomas Hardy—but she would have considered acceptance of such an invitation highly improper.

But nothing was as improper as her affair with Paget. She had to admit to herself that she didn't want to go to Edinburgh now. She had lost interest in that assembly. She wanted to go to London....

And that was frightening. Even though she would never forgive that damned Tory for what he had done, she knew he might still be in London now. Dominic Paget was still on her mind.

Julianne smiled grimly at Amelia and sat on her bed, across from her sister. "I know what you are thinking. You are intending to cut back on your expenses so I can go to Edinburgh."

"I want you to be happy," Amelia said, reaching for her hand.

Julianne was dismayed. "I am not as distraught as I was," she began.

Amelia interrupted. "Misery is written all over your face most of the time."

Her heart *was* broken. She had loved Charles so much. But she would not do as Amelia was suggesting. "You spend nothing on yourself. You are the most self-sacrificing person I know! I won't have you cutting back even further, so I can go attend radical debates in Edinburgh! Besides—" she smiled "—you dislike my politics and you do not want to encourage me."

Amelia became teary. "Right now, if your politics would brighten your eyes, I would very much encourage you! I feel like writing Bedford and setting him straight."

Julianne stiffened, horrified. "Don't you dare even think such a thing."

"Why not? He is a cad. He owed us both, and this is how we were repaid—with your seduction. If you are with child, I am telling Lucas."

Julianne stood up. "I am certain I am not with child!"

Amelia stood, as well. "He ruined you, Julianne. You are young and beautiful, and Lucas could make you a wonderful match, if only you let him!"

She felt herself flush. "You know how I feel about matrimony." She thought of Paget and how his green gaze smoldered. Had he felt *anything* for her? "But you deserve a good husband and children, Amelia—we both know you adore children. You would be a wonderful mother!"

"We are talking about you!" Amelia cried.

"Yes, we are—because you are always selfless. So let's talk about you." Julianne sat down hard on her bed. "*You* should be the one going to London. You are the one who is always caring for Momma, who cares for us all, really. You cook and clean, and I run off to my meetings—or wind up lost in a book."

"No one would allow you to cook, as you burn everything," Amelia said. "And you clean as much as I do."

Julianne did try to keep up with her chores; once in a while, though, she would become so engrossed in a debate or a journal that she would forget. She had been entirely wrapped up in Paget while he was convalescing, and then in their affair. And now she had been consumed with her hurt and misery. She was rushing off to London—but it was Amelia who deserved the holiday.

She asked softly, "Was this how you felt when St. Just failed to come back to the parish?"

Amelia paled. Then, she spoke briskly. "Yes, my heart

was broken, but I was a fool, Julianne. You were too young to remember, but everyone warned me about him and I did not listen. After all, he was a wealthy nobleman when we met, and we are impoverished gentry. When his brother died, I should have realized that it was over, that he would turn to a debutante as blue blooded and privileged as he. You were not a fool, as I was. You were taken advantage of. You were lied to and deceived deliberately—unconscientiously."

"You should go to London in my place."

Amelia shook her head. "I am staying here and taking care of Momma. I have nothing to do in London, Julianne, but you do. I want Lucas to take you to teas, to stroll with you in the park, to introduce you to handsome gentlemen. I want him to take you to supper parties, where you will be asked to dance—where you will be flirted with."

*"What?"* Julianne gasped, shocked.

"You are young and beautiful!" Amelia cried. "Life must not pass you by!"

"Lucas doesn't run in such circles!" But Julianne was aghast, for wasn't life passing her sister by?

"He does when he wants to. Our uncle Sebastian can open any door for us."

Julianne hugged herself. "I barely recall him. I haven't seen him in years."

"He and Lucas are on good terms."

"Are you suggesting that I go to London so Lucas can find a suitor for me?"

"Why not?"

Julianne cried out. "I don't want to marry—"

Amelia cut her off. "And what if you met someone who turned your head the way Paget did? What if you had a suitor who could arouse your interest as Paget did?"

Julianne simply stared, her heart thundering. She would have done anything for Paget—had he asked her to marry, before his exposure, she would have said yes.

"I thought so," Amelia said, sounding satisfied.

Julianne wet her lips. "Amelia. I will never feel that way about someone else. You need a suitor—not I."

"You will meet someone else. I am resigned to spinsterhood. Someone must take care of Momma and this house."

"You have been caring for this family for a decade, at least. When you should have been a carefree child, you were this family's matriarch."

"Momma fell ill when we were children. She hardly did so deliberately. And even if I decided to look for a suitor, no one will have me, in case you haven't noticed. I am too serious and too plain."

"You aren't plain," Julianne said. "However, I agree, you are so serious, overly so. I don't know, Amelia. I feel horrible about going to London now."

"I want you to go." Amelia came over and hugged her, hard. "I am insisting that you go! And if you want to go to Edinburgh—"

"No!" Julianne cut her off. "I don't want to encourage Tom," she said, and it was a part of the truth.

Amelia studied her very carefully. And Julianne had the notion that Amelia knew why she was so eager to go to London—and it had nothing to do with the Convention in Favor of the Universal Rights of Man.

"My lord, the Dowager Countess asked me to tell you that she will be a few more minutes. Can I bring you anything while you await Lady Paget?"

Dominic shook his head, pacing impatiently in the front hall. He was wearing black velvet that day, chosen by his valet with his approval, with very pale breeches, white stockings and black patent shoes with silver buckles. "No, thank you."

Gerard left. Dominic stared after him. Nadine had arrived in town last night, and he was about to call on her.

*Nadine was alive.*

He had had an entire week to come to grips with the news that Nadine was alive. It was a goddamned miracle. He was still in some shock. But he was overjoyed

She hadn't been trampled to death by that mob, as Catherine had erroneously concluded. But she had been badly hurt in the riot, and rescued by a kindly Parisian family. It had taken her months to heal. Apparently there had been some temporary memory loss. By the time she was completely cognizant of her situation, her family had already fled France. She had then struggled to get word to her father, now in Britain. Once she had done so, the Comte D'Archand had brought Warlock into the loop. He had sent his people to extract her. She had arrived in London in the spring, but the Comte had already taken up a residence in Cornwall and they had immediately retired to the country.

While he was recovering at Greystone Manor, Nadine had been somewhere in that part of the country. While he had been in Julianne's arms, his fiancée had been very much alive.

Of course there was guilt. Reminding himself that he hadn't known that Nadine was alive did not alleviate it.

But now what? His affair with Julianne *was* over, even if it did not feel over. Even if he wished he could speak with her again, and perhaps convince her that he wasn't completely rotten and conscienceless. As for Nadine, two years had passed since their engagement, and he was a very changed man.

He stared grimly out of a tall window in the tower room, but he didn't see the gardens outside or his waiting coach. He had known Nadine ever since he could remember. Catherine had brought him to France every summer, from the time he was a toddler. They had practically grown up together—her family had been frequent visitors in London. They had played together, done their reading together, ridden their ponies together and played hide-and-seek and tag in the vineyards with their friends and cousins. He would always love her.

He thought of the passion he had shared with Julianne. His body stirred instantly. He still wanted her—of that there was no doubt—in a way that was almost maddening. He had held and kissed Nadine after their engagement, but he couldn't recall ever being blinded with desire for her.

Maybe when he came face-to-face with Nadine again, those terrible urges for Julianne would disappear. He supposed he hoped so. But it really didn't matter.

Because two years was a very long time. And while two years couldn't change his affection and loyalty, it had changed his commitments. He was committed to stopping the revolution in France. He was committed to preserving the French way of life. He was committed to aiding the royalists in the Loire—and throughout the rest of the country.

He had told Julianne once that she must not wait for him.

He had no choice but to tell Nadine the very same thing. She deserved far more than what he could offer her—she deserved a loving husband and an ordinary life.

"Dominic?"

He turned at the sound of his mother's voice. He managed to smile as Catherine glided into the hall, wearing red silk, rubies and a very ornate, bejeweled wig. She was smiling as she approached him. "You are very dashing, but black?" She raised a penciled brow. "You are calling on your fiancée after two long years. This is a celebratory occasion."

"I'm afraid Jean insisted and I chose to indulge him."

She clasped his cheek. "Then Jean must have his way, even with Bedford, as he is a most invaluable valet." She added, "It has been a long week, waiting for D'Archand to bring Nadine to town so you could finally have your reunion with her." Her regard was searching.

He took her arm and they started for the door. "It has been two years. Two years is a very long time without the additional circumstances of surviving both war and revolution—for both of us. You know how I feel about Nadine. But I am experiencing some trepidation."

Two liveried doormen leapt to open the massive front door for them. "You have known Nadine your entire life. She loves you and you love her. The moment you see one another, I am sure all discomfort and strangeness will vanish."

His mother adored Nadine. She would not be pleased to learn that a wife no longer fit into his plans; she would not be pleased when he returned to France. He helped Catherine up into his luxurious black coach, a six in hand.

"I am sure you are right," he said noncommittally, climbing into the coach beside her.

Catherine grasped his forearm. "Dominic, there is something I must tell you." She was grim.

He felt dread arise, and he waited.

"Nadine is not the same."

DOMINIC FALTERED on the threshold of the D'Archand's salon. As he did, Nadine, who had been seated on the sofa, slowly stood up.

And he felt warmth steal through him. Thank God she was alive.

She smiled a little at him.

He smiled back. Physically, Nadine hadn't changed at all. She was very petite with dark hair, dark eyes and an olive complexion. She wasn't wearing a wig, and her heavy dark hair was down. With her heart-shaped face, her full rosebud mouth, her dark eyes framed by thick black lashes and her hourglass figure, she was a strikingly beautiful woman.

Now she stared, the small smile fading. For a single moment, he saw the apprehension in her eyes as they searched his.

"Dominic!" her two younger sisters screeched, in unison.

He hadn't noticed Veronique or Angelina, or even the Comte D'Archand. Now, he saw the rest of the family. As both girls charged across the salon toward him, Catherine stepped aside, as did the butler. He had to smile, as he was leapt unfashionably upon.

"Why have you stayed away for so long?" one of the girls cried in French.

"We have missed you so, as has Nadine," the other cried in English.

Veronique was twelve, Angelina thirteen, but they were almost identical, as if twins. They took after D'Archand's deceased wife, blond and amber-eyed. "I have missed you, as well," he said, kissing each on both cheeks, in turn. "But for one moment, I almost thought I was being trampled by American savages!" He finally looked at Nadine again, still smiling.

"You have forgotten your manners, the both of you," Nadine said softly to her sisters, but she never took her gaze from his. "Hello, Dominic."

She had always been one of the most graceful and gracious women he knew. There was something about her movements, her gestures, her tone and bearing that beckoned those around her like an offered hand, yet also indicated a vast and reassuring sense of nobility. She would have made an exceptional countess.

But he instantly realized that while her innate grace remained, she was filled with sadness. The sparkle in her eyes was gone. He released Veronique and walked over to her, taking both of her hands in his. "How are you?"

She hesitated. "I am well." Moisture arose.

He did not hesitate. He bent to kiss each cheek, then opened his arms. She stepped into them and he held her, comforting her for all that she had been through.

She was so very familiar, for he had held her many times, intimately but casually, as he was doing now. But as he held her, he thought of Julianne. He was shocked, not just because his thoughts were errant, but because when he held Julianne, there was nothing casual about it. And then he was uneasy. In his arms, Nadine felt like a sister, not a fiancée. He loved her dearly, he would always protect her and provide for her, but he suddenly knew he would never be able to make love to her.

He released her and managed a smile. "I am so glad you are alive. I spent months searching for you in France."

The tears shimmered, unshed. Yet Nadine was not the kind of woman to cry easily. "I know. I heard. Please, Dominic, do not blame yourself for failing to find me. I was in hiding."

He touched her cheek. Nadine was a very strong

woman, but she had to have been afraid, and she had been alone. "I wish I had been with you."

"I know you do, but there is no point in lamenting what cannot be changed."

"No, there is no point," he agreed. He turned to her father and they shook hands, warmly. "So you have settled in Cornwall?"

"Yes. We were guided to an estate that had been neglected for years and I purchased it," D'Archand said. He was a tall, dark, good-looking man who had married an older woman at a very young age, the marriage arranged by both of their families. He had been widowed for many years now. He had lost two vast estates in France, one in le Loire, the other in the south, near Marseilles. "It seems like a secure place to raise Veronique and Angelina." He was firm and, before either girl could protest, he sent them quelling looks.

Dominic turned back to Nadine, aware that the girls detested the country. "How do you like Cornwall?"

"It is quiet, isolated...but we are together now." She smiled briefly, and he wondered what she really thought. "You have changed, Dominic."

He hesitated. "I am older."

"We are both older. You have changed a great deal," she said, very thoughtful now. "But then, I suppose we have both changed."

"You are even more beautiful than when we last were together."

She finally smiled, brushed away the moisture in her eyes and cocked a brow. "Dare you play the gallant with me?"

"I mean it."

"I don't care, and you know it."

"Yes, I do know it." Nadine had never cared about her

looks, and unlike every other Frenchwoman he knew, she had not been a flirt. "Do you want to take a stroll?"

"Of course." She gave him her arm and he looked carefully at her. Why was there so much tension between them? Once, they had been as close as a young man and a woman who were not lovers but good friends could be. He knew her so well, and she had never been so self-contained. It was as if she had erected an invisible wall between them. Or had he done that?

D'Archand opened the door to the terrace and the back gardens. He smiled at them as they went out. Nadine seemed to watch where she was going, and he studied her classic profile. "I am very glad you are home." He paused at the edge of the slate terrace, a small garden and fountain just beyond the low terrace walls.

She released his arm and met his regard. "But this isn't my home, not really."

He touched her cheek. "How do you really like Cornwall?"

She inhaled. "So you can still read my mind, like a Gypsy?"

"No, I cannot."

She started, their gazes holding. "I used to be able to sense your thoughts, and I can't sense them now, either. I only know there is something different with you, or with us."

He wanted to tell her that he had spent the past year and a half in France, spying for Pitt. He knew he must not. And how should he respond to her comment? "You never answered my question."

She shrugged, the gesture so European. "I suppose I will become accustomed to my new circumstances, but I will always miss my home in the Loire Valley."

"You need some time to recover and adjust. That is all."

She smiled a little at him. "Yes, in time I will adjust to this new life."

He finally said, softly, "Have we both changed so much that we have become strangers to one another?"

Tears filled her eyes. "I hope not! I love you, Dom."

He knew she did not mean it passionately, and he reached for her. She came again into his arms. "Have you been in France this entire time?" she asked, her face against his chest.

He tensed. He did not want to lie to her. "It is better," he said slowly, "if we discuss the future, not the past."

She looked up at him. "So we will not talk about what we have both endured, these past years? It has been two years, Dominic, since we last saw one another."

His heart lurched. He recalled the last time he had seen her—at a ball, the night before she'd left for Paris.

They had kissed with feeling, with passion, and suddenly he was saddened. How innocent they had been. How naive—and they had been so prepared to love one another for an entire lifetime.

"There are things I cannot discuss, not even with you," he said.

She detached herself from him and looked up at him. "Then I will assume you have survived a very difficult time, as I have."

"Yes, we have both managed to survive two very difficult years." He took her hand and held it, wishing he could be honest with her—wishing he had been honest with Julianne. But he had a duty to the state. And his duty required duplicity and caution and distrust. "And isn't that a feat?"

"You are one of the strongest men I know. I would

expect you to survive a hurricane—even if on a raft in the ocean."

He finally, genuinely, smiled. "No one could survive that!"

And she also smiled. A long moment passed as they studied one another. "This is awkward, isn't it?"

"Yes, it is."

"I am not as strong as you," she said.

He was alarmed. "What does that mean? I can see that you have suffered. I can see that you are saddened."

"It means that I have changed. I have lost my innocence, Dominic, my naiveté." She did not smile now. "The woman you wished to marry no longer exists."

"No," he said sharply. "You do exist—but you have changed, just as I have. I am not a reckless boy anymore, just as you are not a naive girl."

"You were never a reckless boy," she said softly. "You were always a young man of honor, pride, courage and duty. And I can see that those traits have been strengthened, not diminished."

How wrong she was, he thought grimly. "Do you know what hasn't changed?"

She jerked slightly, as if with alarm.

"My loyalty."

"I knew that was what you would say…" She trailed off.

"And you are dismayed? I will always care for you and I will always protect you, if I can."

"But?" she supplied.

He was silent, not wanting to open up an especially intimate subject.

She smiled. "*But* we aren't two barefoot children now. We aren't even a rich French heiress and a powerful English earl, dancing the night away or attending lawn parties."

Very carefully, he said, "Maybe we will have to discuss the past two years."

"Yes, maybe we will—at another time."

He was relieved that they would delay the discussion. He hesitated. "War changes everyone. I hate that it has affected you at all. I wish I could have spared you, Nadine. I spent five months looking for you. I would have never given up if I had thought you were alive. And I will not allow the past years to destroy our relationship."

"But there is a hurricane in France. The war—the anarchy—the mobs—the Jacobins—have they not destroyed everything in their path?"

He was silent again, letting every bloody memory he had flow over him, and he also let in every memory he had of Julianne. And in that horrific moment, he realized that the damned revolution had already destroyed two of the most important relationships in his life.

"Nothing is the same, is it?" Nadine finally said. *"Nothing."*

His heart thundered. "No. Nothing is the same, Nadine."

# CHAPTER NINE

"THAT MUST BE THE HOUSE," Julianne said, surprised.

She was seated in the backseat of Tom's carriage, facing a very pleasant two-story home on Cavendish Square in London. It was in a well-to-do neighborhood filled with other stately two- and three-story homes. Shady elm trees lined the street, as did fine curricles and carriages. Oxford Street, with its luxury shops, was but a block away. The house was much larger and far more upscale than she had expected.

"I am guessing that the mine and quarry are doing better than Lucas has said," Tom remarked, sounding amused.

"How can we afford this?" she asked. Lucas could not possibly manage such a house by himself. He would have to have a housekeeper and a maid.

"I suppose you will ask your brother," Tom said with a smile. "Ah, I see that there is a stable boy."

Julianne saw a young man approaching from the back of the house, a carriage house and stable visible at the end of the short driveway. She got out of the carriage, as did Tom, who spoke briefly with his driver. Tom was to spend the night before he went on to Edinburgh in the morning.

She watched a very elegant brougham approaching, a pair of high-stepping bays in the traces. When it came close enough, she saw two stunning young ladies in the back, dressed in pale silks and towering headdresses. The ladies waved their gloved hands at her as they passed.

It was a rare moment, but Julianne felt poor and gauche.

Tom came to stand beside her, scowling. "They are absolutely indifferent to the suffering that is right around the corner," he said.

She sighed. "Yes, they are. But you must admit, they were beautiful."

He gave her an odd look, and it was partly reproving. "No, they were not. You are the beautiful one."

Julianne managed a smile. The drive from Cornwall had taken three days—they had spent each night at a public inn. It had been a pleasant trip, as she enjoyed Tom's company, as well as that of the widow who was traveling with them. Julianne could hardly travel alone with Tom, and Mrs. Reston had been meaning to visit her children in the city for some time now. They had spent the entire time reading newspapers, writing letters and discussing politics, Mrs. Reston napping. Fortunately, he had been kind enough not to bring up the still-sensitive subject of Paget. Tom had found numerous moments in which to admire her wit, her intelligence and her traveling outfits. Was he making his feelings clear? Or was he being kind?

Her heart remained bruised and raw. She still thought about Paget on a daily basis, with hurt, anger and confusion. She hoped Tom did not have serious intentions.

On the very first day of travel, she had dared to bring up the subject of his writing to their Jacobin allies in Paris—which she had been constantly worrying about. "Have you written to Marcel yet?"

"Yes, I have."

She had felt a distinct stabbing of dismay. "Did you identify Bedford?"

"I most certainly did, Julianne. Surely you are not having second thoughts about disclosing his activities, are you?"

She was very certain then that she did not want his activities known by his enemies in France, but she had fallen silent. Tom had taken her silence as acquiescence, and the conversation had ended.

Now, she said, still uncomfortable by his flattery, "Let's go inside and rest a bit. You still have a long journey ahead of you." She took his arm.

As they turned toward the house, the front door opened.

Lucas came out, smiling at her. "I see you have made it to London in fine form. Hello, Julianne." He strode forward, wearing a dark green frock coat and a silver waistcoat over his pale breeches. He was not wearing a wig and his tawny hair was pulled back into a queue, but he was very dashing anyway.

Julianne embraced him, aware that his smile was fleeting and his gaze searching. She wasn't really angry with him now, and she looked forward to having a sincere conversation with him, as soon as possible. "We have survived some very bad roads," she said lightly. She watched Lucas turn to Tom and shake his hand. The last time she had seen them interact, they had been in Penzance. That had been over a month ago—on the day of the last Society meeting she had attended. The day Jack had brought Paget to Greystone.

Lucas had been disapproving of Tom then. He was cool and formal now. "Thank you for escorting Julianne to town, Thomas."

"It is my pleasure," Tom said.

"Tom will stay the night, if you do not mind," Julianne said quickly.

"He is only staying for a single night?" Lucas asked calmly.

Julianne realized she could not get a sense of his thoughts. Just then, he reminded her of Paget. But wasn't he deceiving her—and Amelia and Jack? It had been obvious when she had discovered Lucas with Paget that he was somehow involved in the war against France. Hadn't he said something about orders from Whitehall?

"I am off to Scotland," Tom said.

"Ah, yes, that radical assembly of Tom Hardy's." Lucas's face was impassive. His tone however, was just slightly mocking. But before Julianne could become alarmed, he said, "It is hardly a secret. So do come inside. I have planned a supper for us." He looked at Julianne. "I am amazed you haven't tried to convince me to allow you to go to Edinburgh with him."

Julianne thought about her London convention. She simply smiled.

His stare sharpened.

JULIANNE PAUSED BEFORE the open door of the salon, where Lucas sat alone with a brandy and the *London Times*. Supper had been over for some time, and he had changed into a paisley dressing gown and his slippers. He saw her and stood, a dark brow cocking upward.

Julianne hadn't changed out of the gown she'd worn to supper. It was the best dress she owned, a rose-colored floral silk with a square neckline and three-quarter-length sleeves, the full skirts ruched to reveal the darker rose-patterned underskirts. Amelia had insisted she take her mother's pearl pendant and earrings, which she had yet to remove. She smiled, coming into the salon, but closing the door behind her as she did so.

"Supper was pleasant enough," Lucas said, pulling out a small pale blue chair with carved and white-washed arms and legs. "I am glad you have come to town Julianne, but I must leave in the morning. It is rather unexpected, but it is just for a few days."

Julianne thought about the convention, which was only a two-day assembly, and she felt relief. Lucas would never find out the real reason she had come to London now. "I will be fine." She hesitated. Once again, he was traveling. Hadn't she wondered if he was always in London when he said he was? "Where are you going?"

"Manchester. I have found a new foundry for our ore."

She couldn't help doubting him. "You made a vast effort to get on with Tom, Lucas, which I appreciate." She sat down.

He sat, too, on the sofa, and stretched out his long legs. He was blunt. "I don't like his leanings. And I worry he will urge you into actions you might not otherwise consider."

"I am hardly meek and mindless," she said, surprised.

"But you are often malleable." His gray gaze did to waver.

Was he referring to her foolish infatuation for Paget? She did not know where to start—whether to ask him about the house or Paget or his wartime activities. "Why didn't you tell me who he was?"

Lucas hesitated. "There didn't seem to be a point, Julianne."

She stiffened. "I believe you are lying to me now!"

He actually flushed.

"What are you involved in? You are never at Greystone, but are always in London—or so you claim! And how can we afford this house? Are you also a spy?" she cried.

"I am not a spy. However, I am a patriot. If, in some small way, I can help my country, I will." His tone was hard, and so were his eyes. "The house belongs to our uncle, and he never uses it. I am renting my room here for a very small sum."

That explained the house, she thought, shocked by his tone and expression. "And how are you helping our country? By helping Paget survive? I am beginning to think that you brought him home, not Jack." She no longer knew what to believe.

"I was sent for Paget. I recruited Jack. Julianne, you are the last person I am comfortable disclosing this information to."

She was dismayed. Her mind raced. "You are my brother—I love you."

"I know you do. You are not to tell anyone, and by anyone I am including Tom and Amelia, that I was sent to France to help Paget return home."

She hugged herself, aware of her heart racing. Of course she would never tell Tom. "How well do you know him?" she finally asked.

"I don't know him well at all. We became acquainted for the first time when I arrived at the manor, and then I became somewhat better acquainted during our journey to London. Why?" He was sharp.

She supposed she was relieved. "Shouldn't I be curious? He was our guest for many weeks, yet I don't have a clue as to who he really is."

"He is the earl of Bedford. What else do you need to know?"

She had been Paget's lover. She felt as if she needed to know far more than that single fact. But did it matter?

She hesitated and felt her cheeks burn. "Is he still in London?"

Lucas's eyes narrowed. "I believe so. Again, why?"

She didn't know how to respond. Why did she care where he was? She wasn't going to call on him. He had betrayed her in every possible way. She despised him and their affair was over; she had nothing to say to him. Or did she?

How could he have loved her as he had—while deceiving her so deliberately?

"I don't know. Will he go back to France?" If he did return, what about Tom's letter to Marcel?

A headache began. If she learned he was returning to France, she might have to warn him that his enemies were aware of his activities and his identity.

Lucas stood. "I am not discussing Paget with you." Then he hardened. "Let me amend that. I am not discussing his plans with you, not in any way. Not that I know them." He added, "But I do wish to discuss the relationship you had with him. You both went to great ends to tell me that you had become more than a nurse and the injured. Like you, he said you had become friends. But it was an odd friendship, was it not?"

He was suspicious, she thought warily. "He is an intelligent, educated man. And he was very well informed on the war. We had a great deal to discuss. How could we have not become friendly? Especially when I thought we were allies in the great cause of freedom."

"I know you, Julianne. You became friendly with him because you thought him a war hero. But was it more than that? He is an erudite and handsome fellow. He is charming. I can see that he might have caught your romantic interest."

She wanted to dissemble, she did, but she felt frozen instead.

"You have feelings for him." He was grim.

"I cared for Charles Maurice. So yes, I suppose you are right. I am hurt by his deception. I am angered by it. But I have no feelings for Paget." And as she spoke, her heart shrieked at her. It was as if Maurice could not be separated from Paget, as if they were one and the same.

Grimly he stood and walked to the salon's elegant sideboard. Julianne watched him pour a sherry, which he handed to her. Lucas studied her. "I suggest you stay away from Mayfair," he said. "And from Bedford House."

JULIANNE WALKED DOWN Newgate, aware that she was late. It was her second day in London. Two small, thin children in rags stepped in front of her, barring her way. Julianne handed them each a coin without breaking stride; they grinned and galloped off. She smiled, even though she shouldn't be giving away her funds.

She sobered. It was an hour walk, at the very least, from her uncle's Cavendish Square house to the inn where the convention was being held. She had not considered taking a hansom—she would not waste the money. But last night on her way home, as tired as she had been, she had been outrageously tempted to veer away from Marylebone and into Mayfair.

She had been so tempted to see where he lived. What on earth was wrong with her?

She had actually wondered what would happen if their paths did cross.

But their paths were not going to cross. She wasn't going to wander into Mayfair, even if a part of her wanted to, and he would not happen upon Cavendish Square or

Newgate. In fact, she felt certain that he had never set foot in London's downtrodden and destitute East End.

Newgate was as different from Mayfair as the night from day. The streets were narrow and dirty and littered with refuse; shabby shops lined them, offering penny wares, all crowding in on one another. Above them were small flats, with laundry hanging out of the windows like pennants, crisscrossing the street below. Cobblers, carpenters, prostitutes and laundresses had their shingles set out. Door stoops were filled with the homeless and the hungry, and beggars abounded.

No one was starving uptown, yet in the East End, destitution was everywhere. It enraged Julianne, and made her cherish her cause. And she was outraged when she glimpsed gentlemen on their fine Thoroughbreds or in their lacquer carriages, cruising the slums while trying to decide which prostitute met their fancy. How disgusted the sight made her!

If Paget had ever bothered to traverse the slums of London, he would surely understand why she supported the political and social changes in France that she did, and why she yearned for justice and equality in Great Britain. He might not change his Tory views, but surely he would yearn for some degree of social justice, too.

She didn't even know what his real views were. She almost wished she'd had the foresight to ask him why he'd thought it necessary to go to France and spy on the French republicans.

The inn was now in sight. She was grim. She had been too hurt and angry to even think of demanding some basic truths from him before he'd left Cornwall. She had spent weeks with a man, and she didn't know anything about him. Lucas had not filled in any of the blanks. She decided that, if there was one thing she wished to know, it was how he had been wounded. He had claimed to have been wounded while fighting against the La Vendée royalists. She was afraid he had been fighting the French republican army!

Julianne sidestepped some garbage and pushed open the door to the inn. She was in town to attend debates and discussions, to promote the cause of the French revolution and the rights of the common man, not to brood about the past or imagine an encounter with Paget. Paget stood for everything she was fighting against—he stood for indifference, ostentation, inequality and injustice. She had to remind herself of his deception and their differences. She had to get him out of her mind.

One of the convention organizers stood just within the front door at a small table. George Nesbitt held a list of names of everyone attending, but when he saw her, he smiled. "You are late, Miss Greystone. Go right in."

She smiled back. Of course he remembered her. About seventy-five people were attending the convention. She had glimpsed only five other women. Most of those in attendance were factory workers, artisans and domestics, but a few gentry were present, as well. As she entered the public room, she saw it was entirely filled, as it had been yesterday. But she found a bare space on one long bench and sat. The young man there smiled at her. "Hello. John Hardy," he said, holding out his hand. He had dark, curly hair and fair skin.

She took it. "Julianne Greystone. Are you a relation?"

"I wish." He grinned. Then he whispered, "That is Jerome Butler."

Her interest was piqued. Yesterday the convention had consisted of a morning introduction, then lectures from two relatively well-known radical thinkers. But everyone had been anticipating the lecture from Butler—a little-known but highly controversial barrister. Butler stood on the podium, a dark, heavy man with a magnetic manner. Julianne listened, and realized Butler was dismissing the concept of reform within Britain. He began to tick the most anticipated reforms off the list—such as the disposal of rotten boroughs and the widening of the franchise—and he stated all the reasons why these actions would be meaningless. Reform would not sever the cozy relations between the wealthy and Parliament. Reform would not advance wages and employment, because those in power conspired against such advancement. Only a revolution like that in France could truly dislodge the landed interests from the control they welded in the government and the economy! Only revolution, with an absolute dissolution of all landed wealth and a subsequent redistribution to everyone who was landless, would bring justice!

"In closing," Butler cried, his face florid and flushed, "I will say this—we must welcome the French armies when they land upon the beaches of Dover and Cornwall, the rocky shores of Ireland! Yes, we will follow the example of the French republicans here in our own country and we will hunt down those who oppose and repress us! Yes, we will espouse liberty and equality for every man, no matter the policy of the current minister, no matter the law à la Français!"

The assembly burst into loud, raucous applause. Cheers began. Julianne glanced at the faces around her, taken aback. The men she glimpsed were rapt. But Julianne hardly wished to steal from the rich to give to the poor. That was illegal! Butler hadn't even suggested other means of instituting social justice, such as implementing the controversial income tax on the wealthy, or repealing the Corn Laws.

"He is good, isn't he?" The young man seated beside her said, flushed with excitement.

They were giving Butler a standing ovation now. Julianne managed a smile when a commotion by the room's doors made her glance back over her shoulder. She, too, stood up, somewhat reluctantly. She noticed a handful of men, holding their hands to their mouths. She was fairly certain they were booing Butler, but there was pandemonium within and she could not hear. A young man in a blue coat moved through the crowd, his strides hurried—Julianne thought he meant to leave the assembly. He opened the door that she had entered from, but he did not leave. Instead he stood back.

A dozen men, maybe more, swarmed into the hall, waving sticks and clubs.

Julianne froze.

The men rushing into the assembly began to shout, as if giving orders, but Julianne could not hear what they were saying, as everyone continued to cheer and applaud Butler. From the corner of her eye, she saw the man in blue take up the list of attendees. Shocked, she stared.

He suddenly glanced up and their gazes met. He sent her a mocking smile as he folded up the list, apparently in no rush, and put it in his interior breast pocket.

He sauntered down the aisle as the armed men began pushing the attendees to the walls and threatening them with their sticks. Some of the attendees were pushing back at the armed men. She saw one of the invaders slam the butt of his pistol across an attendee's face. She saw another punch a man who was trying to shove him back.

*They were being attacked.*

*She needed to leave, now.*

But she was surrounded by fisticuffs and violence.

She backed up, into two struggling men, and leapt away from them. She saw that Butler had been grabbed and was being wrestled to the floor by four men below the podium. In horror, she watched as he was kicked repeatedly. She was afraid they would kill him.

Julianne meant to rush forward to help Butler. But someone slammed his elbow into her ribs as she tried to reach the podium.

It was an accident, but the blow was like a cannonball, and she was shoved backward, hard. For one moment, she could not breathe.

Then, gasping for breath, she straightened and shoved past three men in a wrestling match, dodging someone else's fist. She straightened and saw that the devil in the blue coat was standing at the podium. Their gazes met.

"Stop this," she screamed at him. Behind him, Butler lay unmoving on the floor, and she did not know if he was unconscious or dead.

He raised a speaking trumpet, his handsome face hard. "Sedition will not be tolerated in Britain," he said to the crowd. "We are from the Reeves Society! We will fight the radicals and levelers here. There will not be sedition and treason in Britain! Suffer the consequences of your treason now!"

Julianne glanced around and saw that the attendees who were not fighting back were being pushed to the wall, with their hands held high in the air. A dozen of her fellow radicals were on the ground, all battered and bloody. A number of vicious fights continued, but her friends were unarmed. A few of the men were refusing to go forward, and they were simply hit with the clubs or pushed to the ground. Her heart slammed with fear.

Of course she knew all about the damned reactionary Reeves societies. She had read about these vicious and brutal groups, who would disrupt radical meetings whenever they could, any way that they could.

She was too frightened to be furious.

"Even ladies have to go to the wall, if that is what you are," a man sneered behind her.

Julianne whirled to meet the enraged gaze of a huge Reeves man, about to protest. Before she could speak, he shoved her toward those already at the wall.

It was the same as being hit. She was propelled backward, into a pair of battling men. An elbow hooked her in the jaw.

She gasped in pain as light exploded in her vision. Before she fell, she was hauled upright by the big, burly Reeves man, who jerked her hard against his side. "Got me a pretty little wench."

Fear became alarm and then panic. Julianne tried to twist violently away, but he refused to let her go. Without thinking, she clawed at his face.

He released her instantly.

She jerked back, shocked to see red lines on his cheeks.

"You bitch!" he cried, in disbelief. Then rage filled his eyes.

He was going to kill her, Julianne thought.

The man in blue stepped between them.

She turned, desperate to flee. She was snagged by an arm or a leg and she fell, hard, to the floor. Someone tripped on her and she knew she had to get up.

She would be trampled in the riot if she did not stand! And just when she tried to arise and was knocked down again, she was pulled to her feet.

She looked into the Reeves leader's blazing blue eyes.

He dragged her through the fighting crowd and flung her at the door. "Go home," he said.

She wanted to strike him. Julianne fled.

IT WAS A VERY BEAUTIFUL day, Dom thought.

He trotted his black Thoroughbred across the riding path in Hyde Park, passing several handsome carriages, a coach and a curricle. Most of the vehicles contained beautiful women, many of whom he knew. He nodded and tipped his top hat to everyone. They all, apparently, knew him, for the women smiled, welcoming him warmly back to London. He also received several supper invitations.

The sky was robin's-egg-blue, with a handful of fluffy white clouds, the sun bright. The grass was green, the foliage lush and daisies dotted the lawns. He inhaled deeply, and realized he had missed the simpler moments in life. There hadn't been any simple moments like this in France, and he knew that he had taken his life in Britain for granted in the past. He would never do so again.

A walking path was adjacent the riding path, and two young women were strolling, hand in hand. A servant followed them, a pair of dancing cocker spaniels on a leash. They were Nadine's sisters' age, and he smiled at them, causing them to giggle and blush.

He sobered. Nadine had clearly suffered during the past two years. He did not want to hurt her, but he could not imagine going through with the marriage they had planned. He could hardly marry her and then abandon her, practically at the altar, to carry on his wartime activities in France—perhaps never to return.

A rider drew up beside him on a handsome chestnut stallion. "Ogling the ladies, Dom?" Sebastian asked, clad in a dark green frock coat, a darker green waistcoat and tan breeches. He was amused.

"Why not?" Dom smiled at him. "When I cease to appreciate the fair sex, I will surely be dead."

"They are very young."

"I was enjoying the view, just as I am enjoying this delightful day." He urged his gelding into a walk, and Sebastian had his mount walk alongside him.

"And I hope that you are also enjoying your time in town," Warlock said, his meaning clear. Dominic's time in London was but a brief respite.

"Did you ask me here for small talk?" Dom returned evenly.

"No, I did not." He withdrew a dirty, rumpled envelope from his breast pocket. Halting his horse, he said, "Friends arrived in town yesterday. This is for you."

Dom took the envelope, instantly recognizing Michel Jacquelyn's handwriting. His heart skipped. "Did you open it?"

"Is it not sealed?"

It looked resealed, Dom thought. "Thank you." He wondered if the friends who had come from France were émigrés or agents. He nudged his mount forward, as did Sebastian.

"Did you enjoy your reunion with Lady Nadine?" he asked.

Slowly, Dom smiled, without mirth. "If I didn't know better, I might think you had spies in my household."

"Why would I do that?"

"Because you are obsessed and have nothing better to do than play chess with human pieces." He had little doubt that Warlock was up all night, plotting and counterplotting.

The spymaster said, "You remain affianced. It was inevitable that you would call on her, sooner or later."

"Do you also spy on her?" Dom asked, not quite lightly.

"Gossip is as valuable to me as letters like the one you hold. I heard the Comte had come to town. The reason for such a return, especially in this heat, was obvious."

Dom met his near-black stare. "Is this why you wished to rendezvous? To discuss my fiancée?"

"I have news."

Dominic's heart lurched.

"The convoy for La Vendée will leave Dover on October the fifth."

JULIANNE STUMBLED into Sebastian Warlock's house, closing and locking the door, and then leaned against it. She choked on the sobs she had been fighting as she had half walked, half run all the way back to the West End from the Newgate inn.

She started to cry, whimpering as she did so. God, she had been so afraid!

She had been pushed, elbowed, struck and nearly trampled to death. And she wasn't ever going to forget being on that floor, pain exploding into bright lights, knowing she must get up, and also knowing she couldn't stand quickly enough. That damned ringleader of the Reeves men had hauled her up, and much as she hated him, she was thankful for that.

She moved to the stairs and collapsed on the bottom step, pulling off her shoes. Her feet were so badly blistered two of her toes were bleeding.

She started to cry again. She wished Lucas were home!

And then she thought of Dominic, his power, his strength, and how wonderful it would be to hide in his arms. Oddly, she felt certain he would never let anyone hurt her.

Except, he had hurt her terribly.

She began to cry again. She kept seeing the men she had attended the conference with being clubbed, being pushed, being shoved and beaten; she saw Butler, being dragged to the floor and being repeatedly kicked.

Julianne stood, trembling wildly, her knees almost buckling. Somehow she staggered into the salon. She almost fell down as she reached the sideboard; instead, she clung to the counter. She wept harder now.

The images of the riot and the beatings whirled through her mind, for a long, long time. When her mind finally quieted, when she could hear harsh breathing— her own—instead of her sobs, she was in a heap on the floor.

She curled up and lay there, trying not to think.

But she had one single thought. If she wasn't so exhausted, if her feet weren't so blistered, she would go to Dominic.

Instead, she got to her hands and knees and managed to stand. She took the sherry from the sideboard, uncorked it and took a swig. Then, bottle in hand, she stumbled to the stairs. Taking them up to her bedroom was the longest walk of her life.

She put the bottle down on the bedside table and fell onto the bed, beyond exhaustion, and sleep came immediately.

"OPEN UP! JULIANNE GREYSTONE!"

She blinked as she awoke, so tired that she had to drag her eyes open. Then she stared at a night-darkened ceiling she did not recognize. Where was she?

"Open up! Julianne Greystone!"

And instantly she was awake. She remembered that she was in the house Lucas had let from Warlock and recalled the terrible attack upon the convention, the ensuing riot, the beatings.

A man was banging on the front door, shouting angrily for her.

She sat up, horrified.

And she heard the door being forced open, wood splintering as it slammed loudly against the wall.

*She had to hide.*

The instinct was an animal one. She did not know who was running into the house and up the stairs, but she heard the steps of several pairs of boots!

"Julianne Greystone!"

Julianne dove from the bed onto the floor. Their booted steps were louder now—almost at the top of the stairs. Oh, God! She would never get out of the room in time. She crawled under the bed, in sheer, mindless panic.

And a moment later, she heard them on the threshold of the bedchamber. She saw a small portion of the room become illuminated—someone held a candle. She trembled in terror.

Steps sounded. She saw a hand—and it touched her shoulder. She screamed.

She was seized by her hair and dragged out from her bed. Then she was hauled to stand—and she came face-to-face with a British army officer.

"What do you want?" she gasped.

Two men stood behind him, but they were not in crimson uniforms.

"You are under arrest," the officer said. "Sedition is a crime against the King."

# CHAPTER TEN

THE GUARD ESCORTING her down the dark stone corridor tightened his grip on her arm. She cried out, but not because he'd hurt her. Her feet hurt terribly. Every step caused pain. But what was even worse was that her hands were manacled behind her back, so if she fell, she could not protect herself.

She was shocked and disbelieving. She had been taken to the Tower of London—as a political prisoner.

Barred cells lined each side of the corridor. Torches glowed from the sconces there. The shadows cast were eerie—but not as eerie as the prisoners they were passing. The men came to the front of their cells to leer at her.

Her heart lurched so forcefully she was sick. "What are you going to do with me?" she gasped.

The guard jerked on her arm, not answering. The officer who had arrested her an hour ago had refused to answer her, as well. She'd been tossed in the back of a carriage and she had been told to remain silent. She had asked about the charges, about proof, about a barrister, but she had been ignored. In shock and more exhaustion, she had collapsed in the corner of the carriage, too frightened to cry. Her breathing had been ragged with fear.

"Cell sixteen—this is for you."

She saw an empty cell and relief flooded her. At least she would not be incarcerated with other prisoners, all of whom seemed to be male. Five men were in the cell next to hers. They were staring as she and her guard approached her cell door. Julianne looked away.

"Let's go," the guard said grimly, opening the cell door and removing her shackles.

Julianne stumbled inside, seizing the bars as she tripped again. "When will I be charged? When will I be able to speak with an attorney?" If she could get word to Tom, he would help her.

The cell door slammed. The lock clicked loudly—ominously. The guard didn't look at her again as he walked back down the corridor, disappearing from her view. Finally, tears welled.

No one knew where she was. She could be in that cell for weeks, even months, before being charged or tried. She'd heard so many horrifying stories about what happened to prisoners. She began to shake violently. She could not breathe properly.

"Miss Greystone?"

The voice was familiar. She jerked in more disbelief and saw George Nesbitt standing in the adjacent cell, with four men she recognized from the convention. She cried out. Maybe there was hope! She wasn't alone!

"Are you all right, Miss Greystone?" he asked.

His face was bruised, one eye black-and-blue. "Are *you* all right?" she gasped in return.

"I'll live—if we're only tried for sedition."

Julianne had been holding so tightly to the bars that her fingers ached. She eased her grip. Comprehension failed her. But then, she was so tired, and at the end of her wits. "What are you trying to say, Mr. Nesbitt?"

"I'm saying that I've heard the rumors for months now. It's Windham, not Pitt," he said referring to the war secretary, who was notorious for being a very hard-nosed and impatient war hawk. "The Alien Office was his idea.

And it's all about cracking down on sedition, about stalking and arresting radicals like us."

She swallowed hard. The King had outlawed sedition in May with his Royal Proclamation, and a royal edict was the law. "We are not guilty of sedition, Mr. Nesbitt. And this is a land of laws. Our government cannot stalk its own citizens, much less falsely accuse them."

"No? So why are we all in here?"

"Laws are ignored all of the time, and especially in times of war," one of Nesbitt's cell mates said. He was a tall, thin fellow. He introduced himself as Paul Adams.

She closed her eyes tightly against more fear. Her stomach churned and she thought about the leader of the Reeves men. He had deliberately disrupted their peaceful assembly. When his men had begun to brutalize the attendees, he hadn't ordered them to stop. He had also taken the registration list—she had seen him. Did he secretly work for the Alien Office? Or had he decided to simply help the Alien Office of his own volition?

Could they actually be charged with sedition? Could they be found guilty?

She shivered, suddenly cold. She was wearing only a summer dress—dirty and bloodstained—and she hadn't thought to ask if she could bring a shawl. Was he right? "The leader of the Reeves men—who was he?"

"Rob Lawton," Nesbitt spat. "He's a fanatic and a reactionary."

She shivered again. "Have you been charged?"

"No. But I'm wondering if we'll be charged for sedition—or treason." He stared at her.

She stared back, her heart slamming. Treason was a hanging offense. "Perhaps it can be argued that our assembly contained seditious speech, but there is a vast difference between treason and sedition, sir." But then she recalled Jerome Butler and she cringed. He *had* been advocating treason.

"They might also decide to forget we're here, until the war is over." Adams spoke up harshly.

"We have laws," Julianne managed. "We cannot be detained without being charged. At some point, we must be charged."

"Men like Windham don't care about the law. Surely you realize that now?" Adams cried. "They mean to stop the revolution—no matter what it takes."

Julianne wanted to argue but was too tired to do so now. She was a radical, but she did not believe that men like Pitt and Windham would subvert the rule of law to attain their own ends. They were Englishmen!

"You should not be here, Miss Greystone," Nesbitt said, suddenly sounding tired. He walked away to sit down on a pallet.

"None of us should be in here. We have done nothing wrong," Julianne said firmly. But she wanted to cry again. No one knew where she was, or that she was in such dire straits.

This was a terrible mistake! Couldn't she find a way to convince the authorities to release her, without charging her? God, if only that damned Rob Lawton hadn't appeared at their convention! Julianne knew that wishing the night had never happened would not solve anything, but she was so exhausted and frightened that it was hard to think clearly. Her mind was spinning uselessly.

There were several pallets in the small cell. She limped over to one, sat down and began removing her shoes. Her blisters were bleeding again. She needed soap and water and bandages. Obviously, no one would bring her any of those things.

She hugged her knees to her chest and gave in to the

flood tide of despair. How had this happened? Tears rose up against her closed lids. She fought them. She had to think of a way out of this predicament.

Lucas would arrive home tomorrow. At some point, perhaps late tomorrow night, he would realize that she was missing. He would turn London upside down to find her.

But how would he ever locate her? Had a neighbor seen her being taken from the house in shackles in the middle of the night? Julianne tried to remember exactly what had happened when she had been escorted from the house to the carriage waiting outside, but she couldn't recall anything. The moment was a blur, filled with panic, disbelief and shock. She prayed someone had seen the episode, but she couldn't count on it.

Had she left any clues behind? And even if he found her, how would Lucas get her out? Once, hundreds of years ago, the Greystone name was revered and distinguished. But the family was clinging by a thread to respectability now. He didn't have the means or the power to get her released.

Sebastian Warlock, her uncle whom she hadn't seen in years, had means. Did he have power? Surely he would help, even if he barely knew her. Hadn't Amelia said that he and Lucas were fairly close?

Julianne rocked against her knees, sick to her stomach. What was she going to do? If only her headache would go away, if only the fear would abate so she could think clearly!

*Power...*

Green eyes assailed her mind's eye.

Julianne sat up, her eyes opening. But she didn't see her cell or the cell across the corridor. She saw Dominic Paget.

*"You saved my life. I owe you... If you are ever in need, Julianne, send word to me."*

*Dominic would help her.* Somehow, in spite of all that had happened between them, she believed it.

Julianne stood. Barefoot, she ran to the front of her cell. "Guard! Guard!" she cried.

"They won't answer you," Adams said.

She looked almost blindly at him. Hope had replaced despair. She had to get word to Dominic! "Guard! Guard!"

But there was no response.

JULIANNE HAD BEEN AFRAID to fall asleep, afraid she would miss the guards bringing the prisoners their breakfast. As a result, she lay on her side on the pallet, hugging herself to ward off the cold, wishing for a blanket, refusing to let her eyes drift closed.

Eventually all conversation died in the gaol. Eventually the only sounds to be heard were snores and the scurrying of rodents. And eventually, the light within her cell began to pale.

Julianne lay still as dawn's first light filtered into the cell from the small window high above her head. The cell became brighter and brighter. The other prisoners stirred. Conversation began. She heard someone using a chamber pot. She ignored it.

Footsteps sounded, and she heard the sound of rusty wheels.

Julianne sat up as a pair of guards came into view, wheeling a cart filled with bowls. Every cell had small barred windows and these were lifted, the bowls handed over to the eager prisoners. Julianne realized that her cell mates were eating with their fingers. Her stomach churned.

"Well, well, if it isn't the pretty traitor," the guard said, pausing by her cell. "Come an' get it, darling."

Julianne stood up. "I'm not hungry. I need your help."

He gave her a lewd look, laughing. "Let me guess. You'll take care of me if I take care of you?"

She was so tired, at first she did not understand. Then she flushed when he stared directly at her breasts. "I need to get a message to the earl of Bedford. Surely you can bring me a quill and parchment?"

The guard sauntered up to her cell door. "Oh, I will gladly bring you diamonds, yer Highness, if you do me first." He winked.

She knew that color flooded her face. "I must get word to Bedford. And there will be a handsome reward if you help me! Please!" Surely Dominic would help her reward this man. And if he would not, then she would find another way.

He eyed her rudely. "As if Bedford would have anything to do with the likes of you. But you invite me in, say, tonight, and I will get you a 'quill and parchment,' *my lady*." He mimicked her genteel manner of speech.

"Tonight?" she gasped. "I can't wait until tonight. I must get word to Bedford—"

He cut her off. "You want the gruel or not?"

"No!"

He walked past her cell, pausing by Nesbitt's cell to give the men within their bowls.

Julianne was in disbelief. Then she seized the bars of her cell. "Who is in charge here? Damn it! Bedford will have your head, guard, when he learns how you have spoken to me and that you have refused to help me!" She was becoming enraged now. "Who is in charge? What is your name?"

The guard turned to look at her, scowling. "The constable is in charge of all the prisoners, lady. And I know you're not an earl's wife or sister. The earl of Bedford ain't gonna care. This is a trick!"

"He will care—I am his mistress!" she cried.

A dozen men turned to look at her, including her comrades in the next cell. She inhaled and spoke firmly. "He will care. He will care very much. You can help me now, or you can suffer the consequences of your apathy later. Because eventually Bedford will learn that I am here. And you do not want to be the one he directs his wrath at."

The guard seemed uncertain now. He looked at the other guard, who was wide-eyed, and said, "Maybe you should get the constable. I'll finish here."

Julianne almost sagged against the bars in relief, but she didn't dare show weakness now. The one guard left. The other continued down the corridor, dispensing bowls. Nesbitt said softly, "You should eat."

She glanced at him and saw the gray matter in his bowl. She felt fairly certain it contained all kinds of bugs. "I will help you, too."

He said, "Bedford is a Tory."

She faced the corridor, grimly.

Time passed with agonizing slowness. Julianne didn't know if five minutes or fifty passed. But eventually the other guard returned. "What happened?" she cried.

"The constable isn't in yet."

Julianne cried, "Then go back and wait for him!"

The guard simply shrugged and walked away, clearly indifferent.

Julianne paced. Surely that guard would speak with the constable when he arrived? But the morning and the afternoon passed with agonizing slowness. The constable did not come. Different guards had brought their noon meals. They had entirely ignored her requests to speak with the constable. Julianne finally fell asleep, choking on fear and tears. When she awoke, it was dark outside the Tower windows.

In a few more hours, she would have been incarcerated for an entire day, she thought miserably. By now, the constable would have left the Tower. She imagined him at his home in a cozy parlor with his wife and children.

"You missed supper," Nesbitt said.

Julianne tried to smile at him and failed. Her stomach hurt too much from anxiety for her to have an appetite. She paced the cell, slowly.

How many times had Lucas begged her to be careful of voicing her opinions? How many times had he forbidden her from attending radical assemblies? He had only wanted to protect her—and he had been right. It was too dangerous now to be open about her positions and her views. But she hadn't listened.

Had Lucas returned to London? Was he even now at the house? Was he worried about her? Was he speaking to the neighbors? Even if they had seen her being hustled into that carriage, Lucas wouldn't have a clue as to where she had been taken.

Maybe, just maybe, he would enlist Paget's help.

Suddenly a wave of dizziness swept her. Julianne hurried to her pallet to lie down. Once on her back, she simply lay there, fighting how heavy her eyes were, how exhausted her body was. Choking on despair, she curled into a ball, closing her eyes, thinking about her life at Greystone Manor, the affair with Paget and the riot. Eventually, near dawn, sleep claimed her another time.

Bright morning light awoke her. The jail was filled with conversation. She immediately recognized the sound of the wheeled food cart. Julianne sat up slowly, with dread.

She was still in the Tower.

The same two guards were approaching with the food cart. She got up—and a wave of dizziness made her sit back down. She waited for it to pass.

Then she got up more slowly and walked over to the front of her cell. The guard she'd spoken to yesterday looked at her and she said, "The constable never came."

"He wasn't here yesterday when I got off duty."

"Bedford must know that I am here." She spoke quietly. She did not have the energy to shout or make demands. "You will be rewarded."

"I'll see if I can speak to him when I am done in here," he said. He picked up a bowl and held it near her cell's food door, lifting it.

There was no dread now. Julianne took the bowl, sat on the pallet and ate the gruel with her fingers. She ignored the black specks she saw in it.

Then she used the chamber pot, as discreetly as possible, and sat back down, praying that the damned guard would speak with the constable. Minutes turned into an hour, then two. She stared at the end of the corridor, refusing to allow herself to think about an eternity spent in the Tower, with no way out.

The door opened. The man approaching was well dressed in a brown velvet coat, a copper waistcoat, pale breeches and stocking. His wig was even powdered.

She slowly stood up. "Constable."

He looked her up and down, very skeptically.

Julianne knew she looked like the homeless in the East End. "I am Julianne Greystone," she said. "My brother is Lucas Greystone, my uncle Sebastian Warlock. And my friend is Bedford. Please tell him I am here."

The constable stared at her. "You speak very well."

She fought her desperation. "Bedford will not be happy when he learns I am here and that my pleas have fallen on deaf ears."

The constable stared and she knew he was trying to weigh the pitfalls of approaching a peer like Bedford with what might possibly be a con.

"I am telling you the truth. You must tell Bedford that I am here. Sir—what could I possibly gain by sending you on a wild-goose chase?"

"That is precisely what I am trying to decide," he said.

"GOOD MORNING, darling," Catherine said, walking into the breakfast chamber, which was a corner tower room with bright yellow walls.

Dominic laid down his newspaper and arose, moving to her to kiss her cheek. She was clad in a riding ensemble, and her cheeks were flushed, meaning she was just getting back from an early morning ride. "Good morning." He was surprised that she had cut her ride short to join him for breakfast. "This is a pleasant surprise."

"We haven't had a private moment in days." She smiled and took the chair he had pulled out for her.

"That is because you are the height of fashion, and you are on a constant whirl," he said with affection, meaning it. Catherine was always being called on, and her calendar was full.

"Should I stay at home by myself? Hmm, how dull would that be?"

"God knows, you are never dull."

A servant appeared, pouring Catherine her favorite tea. She thanked him and said, "Did you enjoy the fête Lady Davis gave last night?"

He looked inquiringly at her. "I was rather bored."

"I thought so. I saw Nadine did not attend, although she was invited."

Dominic hadn't seen Nadine since their reunion, and he had expected to see her at the soirée. D'Archand had been present, and while he had seemed in good spirits, he hadn't wanted to discuss Nadine with Dom, beyond saying she had a bit of a cough.

Dom hadn't believed him. He suspected Nadine had as much use for society now as he did.

They had more in common now than they had had before the revolution began, he thought. "I will see her later today. I have already sent a note."

"Good." She smiled at him. "You are the perfect diplomat, Dominic, and the perfect gentleman. Have I ever told you that? Nadine is a fortunate young woman."

Suddenly he thought of Julianne, screaming at him that he was a liar. Julianne would very much disagree, he thought. "Being diplomatic is usually the practical solution to a conflict," he said evasively. Catherine would be horrified if she ever realized that he had sacrificed his gentility to the cause of survival long ago.

"Well, if you are calling on her this afternoon, I will wait and do so tomorrow." She smiled, clearly pleased. Then, softly, "I am sure the awkwardness will pass, Dominic."

He sipped his tea. Catherine would not be pleased when he broke off the engagement, he thought. She would have to adjust to that event, just as she would adjust to his leaving shortly for France. Before he could summon up a bland response, Gerard entered the room. "My lord, you have a caller."

Dom frowned. "It is 9:00 a.m. No one calls at this hour."

"He claims to be the Constable of the Tower."

Dom started. "The constable of *what* tower, pray tell?"

"The Tower of London, my lord." Gerard waited.

Dom did not know the Constable of the Tower of London. Rather intrigued, he stood. "Where is he?"

"In the entry hall."

"Excuse me," he said to Catherine, who was as surprised as he was. He walked past Gerard, who followed him from the breakfast room into the corridor outside. The Tower served as a prison, an armory and a storehouse for royal treasures and monies. The Constable could have any number of responsibilities, but none to do with him. "Did he say why he wishes to see me?"

"He said he has a message for you from one of his prisoners."

Dominic could not imagine knowing someone currently imprisoned in the Tower. Those sent for incarceration there were often high-ranking figures, mostly political prisoners of some sort. But he had been away for a long time. He might have an acquaintance who was imprisoned there. Aware that Catherine had followed them into the hall, he looked over his shoulder at her. "Has anyone we know been recently imprisoned?"

"Not that I can think of," she said.

These days, no one really knew who might be an enemy of the state, he thought. But those against the war—and in favor of the French Republic—hid their views.

And then Julianne's image came to mind.

Julianne—an open Jacobin sympathizer.

His heart felt as if it had briefly stopped. He shoved the alarm aside. Julianne was in Cornwall. No one cared about her Society of Friends of the People. No one, other than Treyton and himself, knew that she had been asked to locate an émigré family by the Parisian Jacobins. No one in London would even know of her existence.

He calmed slightly as he entered the grand, high-ceilinged foyer of the house. The constable turned, smiling. Dom saw that he did not know him. Portly and elegant, the man bowed. "My lord, I am Edward Thompson. I am very sorry to call at this hour, but I was given a message to relay to you from one of my prisoners. It is highly unusual, of course, but she insisted. I only pray there is no treachery here, and I am not the victim of a small conspiracy."

*She* insisted... .

Somehow, he kept the utter shock from his face. No, it could not be Julianne! "Who wishes to contact me?"

"Miss Julianne Greystone, my lord. She insisted I come to you directly and inform you of the fact that she has been incarcerated. I pray I have not made a grave error."

*Julianne was in the Tower.*

The anger began. "Take me to Miss Greystone."


SURELY DOMINIC WOULD come for her.

She prayed he was a man of his word.

Julianne sat on her pallet, hugging her knees to her chest, staring toward the end of the corridor. The door was too far away for her to see it, and the end of the hall was cloaked in shadows. But she knew the door was there. Dominic would have to walk through it if he came for her. He would come, wouldn't he?

She thought she saw a movement at the corridor's end. Afraid to hope, she froze. And then she heard the heavy iron door closing. She heard faint footsteps.

Please, let it be Dominic, she prayed.

The footsteps were clearly audible now. They grew louder, approaching.

She was so afraid that a pair of guards would be walking toward her. Her heart slammed wildly, making it impossible to breathe.

And Dominic emerged from the shadows....

He saw her at the exact moment that she saw him. Their gazes met; he halted. His green eyes widened in shock.

Slowly, Julianne stood, trembling and faint from exhaustion and relief. And she wondered how she had ever thought him a mere army officer. He was the epitome of wealth, power and authority, every inch the nobleman. She had never seen him in his own clothes before, and he wore a navy blue velvet coat, a pale, silvery blue silk waistcoat, fine white breeches, white stockings and black buckled shoes. He even had on a dark, elegant wig and a black tricorn hat.

His gaze slammed down her bloodstained, blackened skirts. He turned. Julianne saw that he was wearing several rings. "Release her at once." His voice was filled with dangerous warning. It was a tone that no one would dare disobey.

"Yes, my lord." The Constable nodded, and a guard rushed to obey.

Julianne fought the terrific urge to break down and weep. He had come. He was getting her released.

And she met his gaze again. She wondered if he was angry. His green gaze was dark.

"Are you all right?" He spoke calmly as the guard turned the key in the lock.

She hesitated. She wasn't all right, and she didn't think she would ever be all right again.

"Whose blood is that, Julianne?" he asked as calmly.

"I am not hurt." She inhaled as the door was opened. "I don't know."

His brow slashed upward.

The guard gestured for her to come out, but she turned and looked at Nesbitt, Adams and the other three men in the cell. They stared back. She had already told them that if she were released she would help them get out, while Nesbitt had urged her to expose the atrocious despotism of Pitt's government. She had promised him she would.

"Julianne," Dominic said, as quietly. Nevertheless, it was an order.

She smiled weakly at her friends and turned, starting forward. As she did, the cell tilted wildly. She watched the bars spinning.

He cried out.

Julianne saw his horror as he rushed toward her—and that was the last thing that she saw.

JULIANNE BECAME AWARE of light pressing against her closed eyelids—and a solid, familiar wall of muscle behind her back, equally familiar male arms around her. "Charles." She murmured, the cloud lifting.

"You have fainted. Be still."

She opened her eyes and looked at Charles's beloved face. But it wasn't Charles who held her in his arms, as she lay in the back of a coach with red velvet seats. It was Dominic Paget.

Recollection returned instantly. "Dominic."

"Yes."

"You came." Relief flooded her. She wasn't in the Tower. She was with Paget—she was safe.

"Of course I came." His expression was bland, his tone utterly collected.

She struggled to sit up and he released her. Her weary

mind raced. He was a man of his word; the horror of the past few days was over. "I was afraid you would not come."

His green eyes searched hers. "I told you to send word if you ever needed me, Julianne. I meant it when I said I owed you." His mouth firmed ever so slightly. "We are probably even."

He was so devoid of emotion. Had she really seen anger in his eyes a moment ago? "I was afraid that you had left London."

"As you can see, I have remained in town." His gaze moved slowly over her face.

Her heart skipped a beat. She remained prone upon the bench, in a near state of collapse, their bodies touching. She had no wish to move away from him now, when she knew she should put some distance between them. His stare remained intent upon her face. It was searching.

He had rescued her from the Tower.

She hadn't ever expected to see him again.

"You are staring," she managed. She added, on a breath, "You don't look very republican now."

He looked away immediately.

Could he possibly feel guilty for his past deception? she wondered.

"Where are we?" The coach was traveling at a moderate speed, but the shades were partially drawn and she couldn't really see outside.

"In my coach. The Constable wanted me to take you to his office but I refused. I wanted to get you out of there—and to my physician—as quickly as possible. Are you ill?"

"I am weak. I haven't eaten in days," she added, by way of explanation. She now really looked at the stunningly luxurious coach they were in. The sconces were gilded, and gold tassels were hanging from the crimson window shades. The seats were velvet, the wood lacquered. Then she looked at him—at the silk waistcoat he wore, at the lace cuffs spilling from his velvet coat sleeves, at the two rings he wore. The signet ring was sapphire, the other a large ruby. Then her gaze lifted to his steady, unwavering green regard.

"Thank you, Paget."

"You're welcome." He touched her chin and she winced. "Your jaw is black-and-blue."

She hesitated. How much did he know? "I was caught in a terrible mêlée. Someone hit me in the face."

He frowned, his gaze even darker now. She wondered if she would ever forget the horror of that brawl—or the greater horror of being imprisoned in the Tower. She almost wished to be held and comforted, but she knew she must fight such urges. She must not forget why they were at this abysmal place in time.

But what did his stare mean?

Obviously she was a sight. She was bruised, her clothing dirty and stained. She intended to burn her gown. It was unfortunate that she couldn't dispose of her memories the same way.

"Do you think you will faint again? You are very white."

She looked at him, wondering if concern was reflected in his regard. "I am still light-headed." Without thinking, she told him, "I have never been so afraid."

Something flickered in his eyes and he pulled her close, tucking her chin to his broad chest. She closed her eyes, fighting the sudden surge if tears. He lay his chin on the top of her head. As if sensing her distress, he said, "You do not need to be afraid anymore."

The tears began, trickling slowly down her face. He

tightened his embrace and she turned her face onto his chest. She had been struck in the jaw and knocked to the ground. She had been dragged from her bed and thrown into the Tower. She had never been so frightened, and she had truly understood what it was to be powerless, without rights, without protections.

"Do you know how brave you are?"

"I am not brave at all."

"I beg to differ with you." And to her surprise, his gaze moved to her mouth.

Even though his eyes instantly lifted and he moved away from her, she knew what that look meant. Charles had looked at her that way a hundred times when he was about to kiss her.

She tensed. Her heart thundered of its own volition. Did he want to kiss her?

"I want to know what happened."

She hesitated, studying him. He was so grim, and she was almost certain that he was angry. She hoped he was angry because she had been incarcerated and mistreated—and not because he knew about the convention and disapproved. "I came to London to attend a two-day assembly of radicals. I couldn't afford to go to Thomas Hardy's convention in Edinburgh, and Tom suggested I go to London. Of course, neither Amelia nor Lucas knows why I came to town. They believe I came to town to—" She stopped. She wasn't sure she should be honest now. "They believe I came to London to lift my spirits."

"In the wake of my deception?" he asked.

"Yes," she said grimly, "in the wake of your deception."

He eyed her. "What happened, Julianne? Precisely?"

"Reeves men broke into the assembly and attacked us.

A brawl erupted. I was caught up in it. That is how my jaw got bruised."

His expression hardened.

"Have you ever heard of Rob Lawton? He was their leader, his men had sticks and clubs. He condoned the assault!" she cried. "I was knocked down and I thought I would be trampled to death!"

He pulled her close, stunning her. "I know Lawton. He is fervently set against republicans, Julianne."

She jerked away. "He is a vile brute, using violence and intimidation to achieve his reactionary ends." Then she thought of how he had dragged her to her feet and gotten her out of the assembly. She dismissed the recollection. "Those Reeves men should have been rounded up, not me."

"I am not going to condone vigilantism, Julianne, just as I do not condone the use of violence to achieve any ends. But we are at war and you support the enemy. Was there seditious speech at that assembly?"

She stiffened.

"You cannot go around London or Cornwall or any part of Britain, openly espousing the defeat of the British Army and the triumph of the French Republic."

She had already reached that conclusion, but she did not feel like admitting it. "I am a British citizen, with rights. Lawton took the list of delegates, I saw him. I was dragged from my own bed that night by a British officer."

"I am sorry," he said grimly. His eyes were very hard—almost ruthlessly so.

"Are you angry?"

"I am very angry."

"With me?"

"With you—with Lawton—with the officer who arrested you." And he embraced her, holding her tightly against his chest.

Her heart picked up a new, swift, pounding beat. What was he doing? She had to protest—didn't she?

Then he kissed her temple.

It was a tiny, feathery kiss. Desire surged. Her thoughts became completely blank. Her attraction to him hadn't faded, not at all.

He feathered her ear with his lips and she shivered, becoming so hollow, so faint.

She inhaled, trembling, on fire. If only she could think clearly. She should not be in his arms like this. But he would protect her. Just then, she felt as if she needed protection.

And he caught her chin, tilted her face up, eyes blazing—and he looked at her mouth.

More desire slammed. "Kiss me, Paget," she heard herself whisper.

And before she had even finished the sentence, his mouth covered hers, firm and determinedly. There was no escape—Julianne didn't care. She cried out, opening eagerly for him. His tongue thrust deep. She slid her hands under his jacket, over his waistcoat, wanting to feel his naked skin. He tore his mouth from hers and rained kisses down her throat and on the bare skin of her collarbone and chest, above the edge of her bodice. She moaned, reaching for the front of his breeches. A massive, rock-hard bulge was there.

"Promise me, Julianne, you will never tempt fate again."

"I want you," she whispered, barely hearing him. "God help me, I do."

"Good." He pushed her down on the plush squabs. Their mouths mated again. And as their lips fused and their tongues sparred, a shocking need raced up and down her legs and through her entire body. The coach halted. She didn't care. He kissed her for another moment, deeply, and she kissed him back as fiercely. He finally broke the kiss. Lifting his head, breathing hard, he looked down at her.

She stared up, stunned that the raging desire between them hadn't changed. If anything, it had intensified.

"We will finish this later."

And she realized she wanted nothing more than to leap into his bed. But sanity was rapidly returning now. She could not resume their affair. It was impossible.

He sat up, holding out his hand.

Julianne hesitated, then sat up without giving her hand to him. He gave her an indecipherable look, and yanked down his waistcoat and jacket. As he did, the coach door opened.

Julianne started. A footman in royal-blue-and-gold livery and a tricorn hat stood there. Then she looked past the footman at the water fountain in the center of the shell drive, and her shock began. Beyond the magnificent fountain was an ancient mansion with three towers, perfect red roses creeping up its ancestral walls.

"Welcome to my home, Julianne."

## CHAPTER ELEVEN

DOM HANDED HER down from his coach and Julianne faltered, staring at the imposing facade of his house. The house was very old, very well kempt and very daunting. Of course she knew that Paget was an aristocrat with lands, a title and some amount of wealth. But she hadn't expected this.

He had stepped down from the coach and he took her elbow. "Are you all right?" hc asked softly.

She jerked to look up at him. "I don't know." She had fallen in love with a common Frenchman who believed in social justice the way that she did. But there was nothing common about Paget, and they were on opposite sides of both a war and a revolution.

"This house has been in my family for centuries, Julianne."

Of course it had. He had inherited his home, his title, his wealth. He represented the social injustice she was fighting against. Yet she did not want to fight him, and she was hardly hypocritical enough to be against inherited wealth. Lucas had inherited the Greystone estate.

She trembled. Without his wealth and power, she would still be in the Tower.

"You're cold," he said sharply, his expression distraught.

"I'm fine," she lied, her teeth chattering slightly. She

was ill; it was a warm August day, yet she was cold enough to be shivering.

He wrapped his arm around her and guided her across the shining white drive and up a set of broad stone steps. Julianne felt as if the coachman and the two footmen were watching them—as if they knew of their affair.

Liveried doormen had already opened a tall, wide ebony door for them, and now, they swept bows at them. Julianne felt her heart lurch. So many differences remained between them—an even better reason to remain set against him.

She stumbled as she took the top step. As if sensing her distress, he tightened his grasp on her. "You are ill."

"I shouldn't be here."

"Nonsense. I am summoning the physician, Julianne."

She could not answer, because he guided her across the threshold and into the entry hall.

As she took in the size of the circular chamber, the height of the ceiling, the beauty of the floors and the furnishings, she heard him speaking quietly to the manservant who had materialized before them. She wondered if she could collapse in the closest chair. Her knees felt terribly weak.

"Julianne," he said, interrupting her thoughts, "this is Gerard. Anything you wish for, you must only ask and he will provide it for you."

"I hope you are in jest," she said, now aware that he had kept his arm around her.

"You have suffered a terrible ordeal. You are here to recover and rest. I am being earnest," he said flatly. "Gerard, summon the Moorish physician, Al Taqur."

"And if I ask for diamonds and pearls?" Tears suddenly welled. Whatever had made her say such a thing? She was not a mistress, to be showered with such gifts.

His face hardened. "You would never ask for either."

She was very close to weeping again, but not because of the horror of her recent ordeal. Her heartbreak felt recent, raw and fresh. Somehow, she shook her head now, trying to signal him that this was unbearable and impossible.

Soft, feminine footsteps sounded, high heels clicking on the marble floors.

Julianne tensed and turned. A shockingly beautiful woman had just entered the hall from its opposite end. The lady stopped when she saw them, her expression stunned.

"My mother, Lady Catherine Paget, the Dowager Countess," Dominic said softly.

Julianne realized she was very much in Dom's embrace, and any fool would guess at their relationship. She wanted to twist free, but she couldn't move, for Lady Catherine was now approaching.

The Dowager Countess was the most elegant woman she had ever seen. She had never seen as many jewels, or such a splendid headdress and white wig. The ladies passing her by in Cavendish Square, who had made her feel impoverished and gauche, were nothing in comparison to this magnificent, obviously wealthy woman. Her gaze—the exact same shade of green as Dominic's— never wavered from them. As Catherine paused before them, her face hard and set, Julianne realized that what was most striking about her was her air of absolute confidence and authority. She was certain that Lady Catherine would never miss a thing.

"So this is the radical you have rescued from the Tower," she said.

"Mother." His tone was filled with warning. "Julianne Greystone saved my life. She spent weeks nursing me back to health in Cornwall, without a single servant to aid her."

Catherine looked at Julianne. Her smile was cold and controlled and it did not reach her eyes. "Then I am indebted to you, Miss Greystone. Welcome to my home."

Julianne fought for composure. Dominic had said the exact same thing, but his words had had a hint of warmth in them. Catherine clearly did not mean a word she had said. Julianne was almost certain that the other woman hated her on sight. "Thank you."

Catherine gave her a condescending look, as if she was very gauche and had said the wrong thing.

Julianne did not want to face this woman just then, when she was at her worst in every possible way. She felt so faint now, and she was so cold and so tired. As the chamber tilted, images flashed, so quickly, she could barely decipher them. Being dragged out from under her own bed, the guards leering at her and asking her for her favors, hanging on the bars of her cell, begging for the constable....

"You are going to faint again!" Dominic exclaimed, and he lifted her into his arms.

She clung to his shoulders to balance herself, terribly dizzy, but not enough to miss his mother's hard, disapproving expression. "I can walk. I must go. I should not be here," she gasped.

"I am not letting you go anywhere," Dom returned, striding from the hall. Over his shoulder, he said, "Send me a maid with a dressing gown, a dinner tray and a bottle of brandy."

Julianne closed her eyes, but not before she glimpsed astonishment on the faces of the doormen. She pressed her cheek into his chest. "Everyone knows."

"No one knows. You are very ill and I am very concerned. You took care of me once. I will take care of you now." He began striding up a staircase.

The dizziness refusing to recede, she opened her eyes anyway, glimpsing a winding staircase with a red runner. Shivering, she stared downstairs as he went up, noting several salons, their doors open, all magnificently furnished. One contained a grand piano. She hadn't played in years.

He had reached the second landing. "What is it?"

"We sold our piano when I was thirteen. I cried that day." *Am I delirious?* she wondered. Why would she ever tell him such a thing?

He pushed open a whitewashed door and entered a beautiful pink-and-white bedroom. Julianne glanced around as he laid her down in the middle of a four-poster, canopied bed, taking in the pin-striped silk sofa, the red floral chairs, the Aubusson rug, the marble mantel over the hearth. He sat beside her, moving hair out of her face, and she jerked to look at him.

His smile was tender, but he said gravely, "You have a fever, Julianne."

She was very cold. She realized he was removing her shoes. "What are you doing?"

"I want to get you under the covers," he said, "but not in that gown." He tossed both shoes onto the floor, and then began unrolling her torn and dirty stockings.

She wanted to protest. She did not have the strength. She sank back against the dozen pillows on the bed, absolutely exhausted, as her stockings were also tossed aside. She realized they were not the only ones in the bedchamber. A young maid stood there, her eyes wide, as did Lady Paget, who was coldly observing them. The Dowager said, "I believe Nancy can undress her, Dominic."

*He is ruining my reputation,* she thought. Then, feeling oddly drunk, she realized she had no reputation left to ruin.

"Help me with this gown," he ordered.

Julianne sat up as the maid and Dominic divested her of the bloodstained dress. His mother turned and left the room, her face taut with anger. Julianne looked at Dominic as her stays were removed, shivering and trying to keep her eyes open. "She doesn't like me."

"No, she does not." He was calm, handing off each item to the maid. He then helped her out of the plain cambric under petticoat she was wearing.

"I can keep my chemise," she managed.

His gaze locked with hers. "It needs to be laundered."

She would be starkly naked without it.

He stood and gestured at the maid. "Remove it."

Julianne trembled, relieved, as Nancy helped her out of the filthy garment. Dominic kept his head turned away as the maid helped her into a beautiful silk caftan.

Julianne could not sit up for another moment and she collapsed, but he caught her and laid her gently down. "I think I am ill," she began.

"Julianne!"

She gave up. Darkness claimed her and she welcomed it.


"ARE YOU IN LOVE with her?"

Julianne trembled, on fire. She tried to recall the identity of the woman who was speaking, certain that she knew her. Charles said calmly, "That is a highly impertinent question."

"I have never seen you so concerned about anyone, not even Nadine!"

Julianne kicked layers upon layers of blankets off. His fiancée was Nadine, she thought somehow, but Nadine was dead.

"She saved my life. I will do whatever I can to save hers."

"The physician has said she is young and healthy—she will hardly die. She has a fever, that is all."

"You did not see that place. It was infested."

"She is a Jacobin, Dominic. She is the enemy. You cannot trust her!"

"I owe her. She is awakening."

"You are in love!"

"Julianne? It is all right. You are with me, Dominic. You are in my home—you are ill."

Julianne somehow looked up at him. Dominic? No, it was Charles, her beloved revolutionary hero. She smiled at him and reached for his face. His green eyes widened. She pulled him close and tried to kiss him. "I love you," she said, and then it occurred to her that Charles did not exist, that everything was a lie, and her hero was Dominic. He had rescued her, taking her from the Tower....

His mouth feathered hers. Then he said softly, "You have a fever. You are delirious."

*I love him,* she thought. And she realized she had spoken aloud.

He stared, his face grim. "Who?"

Her mind swam. She saw Charles, no, Dominic, a question blazing in his eyes. Dominic, Charles…

A cool cloth was placed on her forehead, another on her chest. He stroked her hair. "Close your eyes. Go to sleep. Your fever has broken."

"Charles." She sighed.

Julianne awoke and froze for one instant, not recognizing the lavish bedchamber she was in. She stared in shock at the pleated rose canopy over her head. *Where am I?*

Her memory returned with stunning clarity and force.

Dominic Paget had rescued her from the Tower and brought her to his home.

As she slowly sat up, aware of the exquisite sensation of silk sliding across her naked skin—she was wearing a beautiful rose-and-gold-striped caftan, with nothing underneath—she saw Dominic sprawled in a small red floral bergère, long legs crossed, a quill in hand, a tray upon his lap. He was rapidly writing upon parchment laid out there.

Her heart turned over hard. If she was remembering correctly, he had taken care of her. She stared, entirely surprised, recalling his carrying her into the bedroom, helping her to undress, and even laying wet compresses upon her.

*Are you in love with her?*

Had she been dreaming, or had his mother really asked him that? What had he answered? And was she mad, to even wonder about his response?

Of course he did not love her.

But she bit her lip, trembling.

"You almost look frightened. Good morning." She jerked as Dominic spoke, amusement in his tone. She met his gaze, which was warm. He stood, clad in a men's dressing gown and slippers, his robe an exquisite shade of green that reminded her of his eyes.

She would never forget her first glimpse of him as he strode into the prison and the flood of relief that had accompanied that sight. She had needed him desperately and he had come.

*I think I am in love with him,* she thought helplessly. *Yet he is an absolute stranger—I know nothing about him, except that he is the earl of Bedford, a British spy and that he ruthlessly deceived me when I was caring for him.*

She knew she must not allow herself to love him. She must not allow herself to trust him. "Good morning," she whispered, somehow tearing her gaze from his face. She glanced at one of the windows. Bright sunlight poured into the room, and she decided it was probably close to noon.

He laid the tray with his tablet and quill on a small, beautiful rosewood table, where a striking floral arrangement was. Then he glanced at her, his smile gone. "How are you feeling?"

She thought about it. "Weak. Hungry. Better."

He approached. "You were very ill."

"You took care of me." She studied him, almost disbelieving. Why had he nursed her? Had he merely wished to repay her for saving his life? Or had it meant more?

He hesitated, studying her in return. "Yes, I did. I was concerned."

"You must have a dozen servants who could tend me."

"I do not quite have a dozen servants." His smile came and went. "And frankly, I had a bit of help. Two housemaids were kind enough to help me attend you. You were with fever for most of the night." Suddenly he leaned over her and lay his palm on her forehead. His touch was terribly reassuring—but it also made her heart leap.

Would his touch always excite and arouse her? He was *not* her revolutionary war hero. There had been so many lies.

He gave her a very long look, as if he knew that he made her pulse race, and dropped his hand. "Your fever broke a few hours ago." His expression tightened. "I hope a lesson was learned."

She did not flinch. "Yes—to avoid ever being imprisoned in any way, again."

His elegant brows lifted. "I do believe we shall have a serious discussion soon."

"Why? Why do you care?"

He stared for a long moment. "I suppose I care for many reasons. I am going to get dressed. I will send breakfast up."

*He cared.* Charles had never told her he had cared, but he had acted as if he loved her, and at the time, she had believed that. When he had been exposed as a fraud and a liar, she hadn't known what to believe. Did she dare believe Paget now?

She wanted to believe him.

Julianne hugged herself and watched him leave. A part of her suddenly wished he would come back and take her into his arms. Another part of her—far saner—urged her to run from him. As far and as fast as possible.

When he was gone, a maid walked in without knocking, carrying a breakfast tray. Lady Paget was behind her, resplendent in rose silk trimmed with gold. "I see you are awake, Miss Greystone."

Julianne's heart sank. About to get up, she sat back in the bed, pulling the covers high, as if they might protect her from Dominic's mother. Her smile hadn't changed. It was blatantly false.

"Nancy, please put the tray on the bed so Miss Greystone can reach it," Lady Paget instructed.

Julianne was starving, but as the tray with its covered plates was laid down, she did not touch it. "Good morning," she said carefully.

"My son was very worried about you—but you already know that." She nodded at the bergère Dominic had vacated and the maid moved it closer to the bed. Lady Paget sat on it and stared.

"We are friends." She didn't know what to say, but knew no good was going to come of this encounter.

"He has told me all about you, Miss Greystone. I am very grateful that you nursed him back to health when he was so gravely injured."

Julianne did not like the innuendo hanging to her first words. Why did this woman look down upon her? Was she simply a vain, preening snob? Or did she have a reason to despise her—for she certainly seemed to dislike her. "I could hardly let him die."

"Even if you had known the truth? That he was an earl and a patriot?"

She bit her lip. "Even had I known the truth, I would have helped him. He told you that I mistook him for a Frenchman?"

"He told me that you mistook him for an officer in the French army." Her gaze was frightening in its intensity now.

*She knows,* Julianne thought anxiously, *that we are on opposite sides of the war.* "I am very grateful to Dominic for what he has done, and for being allowed to recover in this house—" she began, but Catherine cut her off.

"I owe you for taking care of my son when he was seriously injured, so I allowed you to recover from your incarceration and illness here." Her green eyes flashed with anger. "But you are well now. This is my house, too. I have no tolerance for Jacobins, Miss Greystone. None."

Julianne inhaled. "I am sure you don't," she said, and then wisely decided not to point out that this was a free country.

Catherine stood. "You are certainly entitled to your politics—but you are not entitled to a room in this house. You are the enemy."

Julianne stared, stiff with tension. "I support the revolution," she tried, "but I am not your enemy."

"You most certainly are the enemy," Catherine cried. "I am a Frenchwoman, a countess, a royalist! My son is an Englishman, a Tory and a patriot! You meet with your radical associates, espousing the great cause of *l'egalité, la liberté,* for all! Where is that freedom, Miss Greystone? It is not to be found in Paris, where my home was vandalized and destroyed deliberately by a mob. I fled Paris, fearing for my life. Is that freedom?" she cried. "Is that the revolution you condone?"

Julianne did not try to answer.

"I am afraid to go to my country home, which has been in my family for centuries! Is that freedom?"

She somehow said, "I do not condone vandalism, violence or other means of intimidation. But serfs, laborers and peasants deserve freedom, too."

"In this house, you may keep your opinions to yourself. As for your radical activities, my son bears great burdens—and now he must worry about you? Rescue you? Shelter you? Because he is taken with that reddish hair, a fine figure, a pretty face?"

"We are friends," she managed.

"I know a pair of lovers when I see one," she said harshly. "If you think my son will ever make a serious commitment to a woman like yourself, a radical, Jacobin *bohème,* you are wrong! This is a passing inclination on his part. I know my son!" Flushed, she turned and stormed toward the door. But before leaving, she paused. "I want you out of my home as soon as you are fully recovered, Miss Greystone. I am hoping that will be today. Dominic is blinded by your charms. I am not."

Julianne collapsed against the pillows. The countess would be intimidating even without being on the receiving end of her fury. And how could she even think Dominic blinded by her charms? He was the coolest, most rational man she had ever met!

*Are you in love with her?*

*That is highly impertinent...*

Why would Lady Paget even ask such a question? Julianne stared up at the ceiling, so tense now, her fists were clenched. She was drawn to a man she didn't even know, when a war stood between them and she was only a passing interest. God, what was she doing?

She sat up and flung the covers aside. A wave of dizziness took her.

She sat back down. She needed to eat something, and then she would leave.

JULIANNE ASKED FOR HER clothes, but the maid told her that the dress had been tossed into the rubbish, and her undergarments were hanging to dry. Her interview with Lady Paget remained foremost in her mind. She wanted to leave immediately, before having another unpleasant encounter. The prospect of never seeing Dominic again hurt terribly, which was even more reason to leave.

After pleading with her, Nancy brought her clothes, and now Julianne stood in a chemise and under petticoat as they attached a bustle to each hip. "Thank you so much for lending me your things," she whispered. She was still somewhat light-headed from her illness and her ordeal.

Nancy was petite, dark haired and French, and probably Julianne's own age. "His lordship instructed us to meet your every command, my lady." Her French accent was thick. She smiled slyly now. "I would not refuse, not when His Lordship is so fond of you."

Julianne did not smile back. She knew exactly what

the pretty housemaid was thinking. "We are friends," she tried.

Nancy laughed. It was a happy sound. *"Bien sur!"* Then, as slyly, "He sat up all night with you, my lady."

Julianne reverted to French. "It is simply Miss Greystone, Nancy. I do not have a title." But her heart hammered now. "Did he really sit up all night with me?"

Before Nancy could answer, Dominic said, "Why don't you ask me?"

She whirled. He leaned negligently against the door, wearing a magnificent chocolate-brown frock coat with gold embroidery. A bronze waistcoat was beneath and French lace gushed from his cuffs and at his collar. His breeches were cream colored, his stockings white. His gaze was very languid and trained steadily upon her.

Julianne felt as if he could see through her chemise and petticoat.

"Why are you out of bed?" he asked.

Nancy had frozen behind her, her head down. Julianne could feel her delighted and wicked thoughts. "I am getting dressed. I am leaving."

"Really? Since when?" He sauntered forward now.

"I must go, Paget."

He reached her and touched her chin, tilting up her face. Julianne trembled, slammed with desire. "You are going nowhere today."

Her trembling increased. She would never tell him about the horrid interview with Lady Paget. "I can't possibly impose upon you any longer."

He was amused. "I imposed upon you for an entire month."

"Dominic," she tried.

He moved some of her hair back behind her shoulder—a lover's casual gesture. "Nancy, would you leave us for a moment." It was not a question.

Nancy fled, fighting a knowing smile.

"She knows—everyone knows," Julianne said.

"She suspects, which is an entirely different matter. But no one can prove anything. I will deny any rumors—if anyone dares to gossip." He was calm. "Why are you running away from me?"

"Because I would be ten times the fool to stay!" she cried.

He stared. "So I take it that I am not forgiven for my deception during my stay at Greystone?"

"No."

He paced away and said, "You need rest. You cannot leave yet." His gaze lifted to hers.

His look was making her resolve crumble. "Lucas is probably home. He will be frantic when he realizes that I am missing."

"Lucas is not back in town. I left a letter for him this morning."

She stared, with some dread. "What did you tell him?"

He slowly smiled at her. "Oh, have no fear. I did not tell him in a letter that you were dragged from your bed by the authorities and imprisoned in the Tower, with charges of sedition pending. I prefer to tell him that in person."

She cried out. "Please, we must never tell him what happened!"

He gave her a sharp look. "You crossed many lines, Julianne. You could have been hurt, beaten, raped in that prison—and charged. And no one might have ever known anything about it."

She hugged herself. "But none of those things happened, and I intend to be much more circumspect in the future."

"None of those things happened, because I rescued you. Are you suggesting that you will continue to agitate for your radical causes?" He was incredulous.

"I can hardly change how I think."

"People change their minds all of the time."

"So you wish for me to become a Tory—a reactionary, like you?" she cried.

He flushed. "I am a Tory, but I am not a reactionary, Julianne." His tone had filled with warning.

"I am sorry. I don't even know you. I have no right to assume what you are thinking, or what you believe."

"No, you do not." He stared, unsmiling. "I do not expect you to change how you think. I know you very well. Your beliefs are ingrained. They are in your heart."

He knew her well because she had always been honest with him. But she didn't know him at all.

"I do expect you to change your behavior. I asked you to promise me to refrain from carrying on your radical activities when we were in my coach, and you did not make the promise."

She didn't know what to say. She had no wish to ever be arrested again—yet the cause she fought for was greater than herself.

He made a sound—a harsh, mirthless laugh. "Oh, I can feel how you are scheming now—you have no intention of backing off. Julianne, next time, you might be hurt. Next time, you might be charged with sedition, or worse! I heard that Butler spoke at your assembly."

She was taken aback. "I don't agree with him."

"Thank God!"

"Pitt is a tyrant."

He choked. "Believe what you will. But let us consider

the facts. This is war, and those supporting France will no longer be tolerated, Julianne. The government has declared war on radicals like yourself. You may hold to your beliefs, but you cannot espouse them and you cannot act on them. It is insane to do so! Please," he added harshly.

"It is almost as if," she said slowly, "you care about me."

His gaze narrowed. And he reached out and drew her forward directly against his body. "I already told you that I care. How often must I repeat myself?"

She was acutely aware of being in his arms. "You deceived me once, entirely."

"Yes, I did, and I regret it entirely."

Julianne went still as his mouth claimed hers, fiercely. And then as her heart leapt, desire fisted and she was incapable of even wanting to resist. He deepened the kiss.

And the desire made her dizzy and faint. She kissed him back, wondering if she dared to believe him, to trust him, shaken to the core of her being. He tore his mouth from hers, kissing her throat and then her breasts. Only two thin layers of fabric covered her body and Julianne whimpered. It was impossible to think coherently.

But he seized her shoulders, anchored her and kissed her very thoroughly again. Julianne gave up trying to think. There was only the whirl of growing sensation and pleasure, of building pressure, of anticipation and need.

He ended the kiss, breathing hard, his green gaze on fire. "I want you very much."

She stared into his gaze, too breathless to speak, her mind beginning to function. Did she dare start over with him now?

And her heart screamed "Yes!" at her.

He touched her cheek with his knuckles. "I don't ever

want to go through the horror of finding you in prison again."

"I don't ever want to be in prison again."

"Good." He was firm. "We are agreed. And I want you to stay here with me until you are fully recovered."

She knew that if she stayed, she would wind up becoming his lover again.

"I am not letting you leave," he said softly.

Their gazes locked. "That is tyrannical."

He smiled. "I suppose so."

"I don't think Lady Paget will allow me to stay."

He merely raised a brow, amused. "This is my home," he said, "and she will do as I wish."

And Julianne knew she had lost the argument.

JULIANNE WAS CURLED UP in her bed when a knock sounded on her door. She had been so exhausted that she had slept on and off for most of the day. She had just awoken and it was early evening now. Her heart leapt. She hoped Dominic was at the door.

Nancy came inside, a pile of clothes in her arms. "You have a caller. Can I help you to dress?"

The only person who would call on her was Lucas, she thought. She prayed Dominic was out. As she got up, she asked, "Is Lord Paget at home?"

"He is downstairs with your caller," Nancy said, holding up a beautiful silk chemise trimmed with lace.

Julianne walked over to her and looked at the beribboned linen stays, the dimity under petticoat, and then at the pale blue silk ensemble—a corded and draped skirt and fitted jacket. "Whose clothes are these?" She had never worn such fine garments in her life.

"I don't know. I believe his lordship sent someone to Lady Paget's seamstress. Perhaps these garments were ordered by someone else and he found a way to acquire them?"

"I don't think I should wear them."

"I was instructed to bring them to you," Nancy said, looking worried. "You will be beautiful, Miss Greystone, in that shade of pale blue."

Julianne surrendered. Just then, she did not care what she wore—if Paget were filling Lucas's ears with details of her misadventures, he was going to be furious with her.

Fifteen minutes later, her hair simply brushed, with a few sections pulled and tied back, the rest hanging loose, Julianne followed Nancy downstairs. As she descended the last few steps, she could see into the larger salon, as the mahogany doors were wide open. She saw both men before they saw her. Dominic faced the door, still clad in his dark brown coat. He held a drink in his hand. Lucas had his back to her, wearing an unadorned tan frock coat, breeches and boots. She faltered as Dom's gaze moved slowly over her, widening with stark appreciation.

Lucas turned and stared coldly.

Her heart drummed. She didn't even try to smile, coming down the rest of the stairs, and crossing the threshold of the salon with vast trepidation. "Hello, Lucas."

He did not mince words. "I am very angry with you."

She looked past him at Dominic. "Did you spare me at all?"

"No, I did not."

She went to her brother and kissed his cheek but he seized her arm. "You were incarcerated."

"Yes, I was. But as you can see, I am fine."

"Only because Paget managed to free you!" His gray gaze flashed.

"You are engaged in your own clandestine activities. Surely there is not a double standard here?"

Lucas choked on disbelief. "I am not engaged in sedition—in treason! And do not bother to defend yourself. I am tired of hearing about your rights. Clearly, I have indulged you when I shouldn't have."

She said carefully, "Whatever Paget told you, I am sure he exaggerated."

Dominic said flatly, "I told him everything, Julianne."

She bit her lip. "Then Lucas knows I am no worse for the wear!"

Lucas was looking back and forth between them now. "I know that you lied to me, Julianne. That you attended an assembly filled with seditious speech, that you were struck and knocked down. Your jaw is black-and-blue! I understand you were very ill. But the moment you are well enough to travel, you are returning to Greystone Manor. At least there, no one will pay attention to what you say or do."

"I am not sure of that anymore," Dominic said to Lucas, his gaze still locked with Julianne's. He finally looked at him. "What has just happened in London will be happening all over the country. I have had my suspicions confirmed. The Alien Office will hunt down British radicals—everywhere in the country."

Lucas turned to Julianne. "I have heard the same thing. I have much to worry about. And now I must worry about you."

She felt guilty then. "I am not a fool, Lucas. I have no intention of openly advocating my causes, or of inciting or attracting the authorities and their agents." Both men regarded her at once. "I mean it. And I am glad you are back in town." She finally smiled at him.

"I have to leave again, first thing in the morning. I

hate to admit this, but I am afraid to leave you to your own devices in Warlock's flat."

"She can stay here." Dom was final. "I owe her, and I intend to repay her now."

She turned to him. Not looking at Lucas, he said to him, "She can stay here, and I will make certain she rests until she is recovered."

"So you will be my keeper?" she asked, her heart thundering.

"Yes," he said flatly. "Someone needs to protect you—from yourself."

Lucas said sharply, "What is going on here?"

"Your sister saved my life. I feel that I must now save hers." Dominic was firm.

"You already have, Bedford, when you got her out of the Tower. Your debt is undoubtedly repaid," Lucas said, glancing with some suspicion between them now.

"I do not feel that it is repaid. What if Pitt's men decide to question her? She is now undoubtedly on a watch list."

Lucas gave Julianne a dark look. "You are right. I'd like a moment with my sister, if you do not mind."

Dominic nodded, set his brandy down and strode out of the room.

Julianne sank down in a chair. Exhaustion—most of it emotional, she thought—claimed her. Lucas pulled over an ottoman and sat facing her. "Why are you near tears?"

She somehow shook her head. "I am exhausted."

"Yes, being imprisoned is very exhausting."

"Lucas!"

"He isn't Maurice, Julianne—he is *Bedford*."

She tensed. "I know."

"Do you? I believe that you are falling for him."

She looked into his searching, worried eyes. "I should

go home," she said, referring to Warlock's Cavendish Square flat.

"You haven't answered me." He took her hand.

Julianne clung to it. "I pray that I am not falling in love with him, against all common sense. But sometimes it feels as if he is my hero after all."

He pulled her close and held her. "He is not for you, Julianne. Trust me on that. Of course he feels like a hero to you—he just got you out of the Tower. But one day, he will marry some wealthy debutante. It is what nobles do. As witty and wonderful and as beautiful as you are, you will never be that woman. He is the earl of Bedford, Julianne, and you only have to look around you now to see that you cannot overcome the gulf of class and economy that separate you. I hate that he has affected you so."

Julianne was afraid that Lucas was right.

"Has he made advances?" Lucas asked.

Julianne felt herself blanch. It was a moment before she could speak. "How could you ask such a thing?"

He studied her carefully. "Thank God you are in one piece." Lucas embraced her briefly. "I have to go, Julianne. I have traveled all day, and it is getting late. But I believe it is best for you to stay here, for a while."

"You won't tell me what you are up to, will you?" When he simply smiled, not answering, she hugged him, hard. "Please be careful, Lucas."

"I am always careful."

He was so confident! Julianne walked him to the door. Dominic stood in the hall outside. Julianne paused on the threshold as her brother and Dominic walked into the adjacent tower room. She watched them exchange handshakes at the front door, aware of the fact that in a moment she and Paget would be alone in the house. Tension swept over her.

When Lucas was gone, the liveried doormen closed the door and Dominic turned. Her heart lurched as their gazes met from across the entry tower.

He strode across the tower room. Her tension escalated. It was dark out now. She knew she must somehow forget that they had been lovers; she must ignore the attraction that continued to smolder between them.

And he would not make advances now, would he? She had been so ill yesterday!

He took her arm and steered her back into the salon. Julianne did not balk.

He poured brandy into a snifter and handed it to her. "It has been a very long day."

She accepted the drink. "Yes, it has." Her heart had begun to pulse more swiftly now.

"Are you reconciled to staying here?"

"I suppose so."

"You do not look happy about it."

She set the untouched drink down. "I am damned if I do and damned if I don't."

His expression was dark. "Apparently, we feel the same way."

"What does that mean?" she whispered.

"It means that I have missed you, Julianne."

Just then, she believed his every word. "Dominic. I miss you so much, too."

He pulled her close and claimed her mouth with his.

# CHAPTER TWELVE

DOMINIC HELD JULIANNE as she slept, early morning sunlight creeping into his bedchamber. He felt as if a huge burden had been lifted from his shoulders. There was no denying that he had missed her. When in her arms, he slept heavily, without nightmares.

She stirred.

"Shh," he murmured. "Stay in bed. You should rest."

Reluctantly, he released her and sat up. No longer smiling, he admitted that he had become fond of her, very fond. During the past few weeks, he had told himself that it simply did not matter. The events of the past days had changed everything.

He had been sick with fear when he had learned that she was in the Tower, and overcome with horror when he had seen her in that rat cell. And he was furious whenever he thought of her getting caught up in that Reeves attack upon the assembly she had been attending.

He was grim now as he quietly slid from the bed, reaching for a dressing gown and draping it over his nude body. He was a Tory and she was a Jacobin. They were passionate about their beliefs. But they were lovers now. Surely he could trust her.

And did it even matter? This could hardly be a new beginning. How could it be, when he would soon return to France?

And then there was Nadine.

So much had obviously changed between them. He no longer felt connected to his fiancée; he could no longer look into her eyes and ascertain what she was thinking. She had admitted that she felt the same distance now. Yet he would always defend, admire and care for her. He had planned to end the engagement for political reasons, but now he was keeping his mistress under his roof and that made it all the more necessary—and urgent—to speak with her.

Nadine had always understood him. They had never argued. He had always wanted what was best for her, and she had always wanted what was best for him. Nadine had indicated that she had lost interest in their union, as well, but he did not relish telling her that it was over. He couldn't imagine any woman being happy about the fact that her fiancé had become attached to someone else.

He hoped that, one day, Nadine would find herself as interested in another man as he was by Julianne.

Dom walked quickly across his bedroom, but paused at the door to his sitting room to glance back at Julianne. The bed had navy blue covers and a quilted navy blue canopy. The top of the canopy was gold, as were the draperies, the sheets and pillows. Julianne was pale and small as she lay alone in his massively sized bed. His heart skipped, but he was stirred with foreboding.

If only he could trust her completely. He wished he could tell her every horrific detail of the past two years. It would feel good to unburden himself. But he would never do such a thing.

He turned away, walked into his sitting room and crossed to his *secrétaire*.

No one was allowed in his suite except for his valet, Jean. The housemaids who cleaned it did so under Jean's supervision. He was dressing and going out. Julianne would be alone in his private chambers.

The past few years had taught him to be suspicious and circumspect. He had learned to trust no one. He glanced at his desk carefully now, even though it was not in his nature to leave any incriminating signs about. The letter he was in the midst of writing was harmless. Only some parchment, a quill and inkwell were beside it. The letter he had received from Michel yesterday was under lock and key.

Dominic went to his massive bookcase and withdrew one book from a shelf that was eye level. He opened it and took the key from the small pocket which had been carved in its cover, then replaced the book.

He returned to his desk, unlocked the desk's third right-hand drawer and withdrew the letter. He had already read it, and the news wasn't good. The Committee of Public Safety had ordered General Carrier to undertake a "pacification" of La Vendée, through the complete destruction of the region. Michel needed that convoy well before mid-October.

He would write Michel later and convey the current plan, but also advise him that he would not cease his efforts to move up the scheduled rendezvous. He hoped to send the missive by courier at dawn tomorrow.

Dominic took up a box of flint from another drawer and lit one. He then burned Michel's letter.

Because he also had some maps he had sketched within the drawer, and some notes, he relocked it.

Dominic went back to the bookcase, took out the volume of poetry and replaced the key. He sighed. He wasn't sure he really believed that Julianne would spy amongst his affects. He was merely exercising caution.

IF SHE HAD BEEN falling in love with Paget before, it was certainly worse now.

Julianne stared at the quilted navy blue canopy over her head. She had just opened her eyes and she did not know whether to be thrilled or dismayed. There was nowhere she would rather be than in Dominic's arms.

She suddenly heard him moving in the adjacent sitting room, and she leaned up on one elbow. He was putting a book into the bookcase, his back to her. Then he crossed the room, disappearing from her view. She heard a door open.

Her heart turned over, hard, as she lay back against the pillows. She might be inexperienced but she was no fool. He wanted her and he had admitted that he needed her—but that hardly meant that he loved her. However, the smallest gestures had the biggest impact on her. When he planted a brief, chaste kiss on her shoulder or cheek, she had the oddest notion that he was falling in love, too.

She knew it was dangerous to begin to think that he shared her powerful feelings. She knew she should not trust his word, not after his deception in Cornwall. And even if he did care, a huge gulf remained, separating them. It was the gulf of class and politics. One day he would marry someone as rich and titled as he was.

She was so afraid. She was afraid of the feelings in her heart. She must not allow herself to fall in love. And not because he had deceived her, not because he was a stranger, or a spy and a Tory, but because he was the earl of Bedford. She was only his mistress.

She sat up slowly, against a dozen blue-and-gold pillows, hugging the silk covers to her chest. She had never been in his private rooms before. She felt as if she were in a royal bedchamber. The lower parts of the walls were paneled in gilded wood, the upper half, flocked in navy fabric threaded with gold. The ceilings were gold-and-white, boasting two large crystal chandeliers. There were two seating areas in the room, one in front of a hearth with a gold-and-white marble mantel. There was also a beautiful rosewood breakfast table by a tall window, out of which she could see spectacular gardens. The floral arrangement there was yellow and purple. She felt certain that the flowers had come from his gardens.

She should leave him. She should get up, get dressed and go back to Cavendish Square. And then she would find the first traveler returning to Cornwall and beg a ride home. There, she could go back to her ordinary, political life. There, she could try to forget him.

But she wasn't going to do that, because she wanted to see Paget another time. She wanted to look into his eyes after this last night. She knew she was hoping to see a reflection of her own feelings mirrored there.

The dressing gown she had worn the day before had been laid out on the back of a chair for her. She slipped it on and thought she heard a door closing. She hurried to close the door to his chamber, rushing into the adjacent parlor, but Dominic was not there.

She was certain he had just left, as the door to his dressing room was open, as was the door to the hall outside the sitting room. This parlor was gold, with pale blue accents, and as such, was much more cheerful—and less majestic    than the bedchamber. A small sofa was in front of the fireplace, while a dining table was set before the windows overlooking the gardens outside. One wall boasted the bookcase, another, his *secrétaire*.

She walked over to his dressing room and knocked politely. When there was no answer, she called his name softly and glanced inside. She saw his caftan on the floor,

and knew he had already dressed and left. Absurdly, she
was disappointed.

It was midmorning, and she was ready for breakfast,
but Julianne saw the parchment and quill on the desk and
paused. She should write to Tom. It would only take a
few moments and she wanted to apprise him of the recent
events. She went to the desk, ignoring the letter he had
been writing. She reached for a page of vellum. As she
pulled it forward and sat, her gaze skipped over the bold
script on the letter's page, and she saw the date and opening line.

It had been begun a week ago, and the salutation was,
"My dear Edmund."

Hardly interested, Julianne reached for the quill when
she saw the envelope beside the inkwell. It was impossible not to read it.

It was addressed to the renowned—no, infamous—
reactionary, Edmund Burke!

Julianne was shocked. She despised Burke's views!
She despised Burke, the turncoat! How despicable he
was! Once a longtime friend and follower of Charles
James Fox, whom Julianne so admired, Burke had recently announced his formal separation from the Whigs
and had become, almost overnight, one of the nation's
leading Tories. Burke was renowned for having written
numerous tracts on the ills and evils of the French Revolution, which he considered nothing more than sheer anarchy. He was a proponent of stopping the revolution in
its tracks!

Filled with dread, she seized Dominic's letter and
began to read, so agitated she could not breathe properly.

And she became confused.

Dominic had begun by writing, "You know, my good

friend, that I stand with you on the principles that unite us—and that I stand behind the dire necessity to prevent the revolution from ever reaching the shores of this great, free land. However, I have grave reservations about using the Alien Office to repress dissent throughout the country. In a nation like ours, a healthy discussion of opposing ideas strengthens freedom. It does not weaken it." He added, "Obviously outright and bold sedition must be oppressed, but there is a line between allowing free speech and condemning seditious speech."

He went on to say that England's social and political fabric should be strengthened through gentle, gradual, much-needed reform—such as widening the franchise, such as mandating a standard minimum wage. He even found the notion of an income tax upon the wealthy worth considering.

"I pray you will consider my suggestions," he ended. "And have no doubt that I remain staunchly loyal to Prime Minister Pitt and the Tory Party, and that I will continue to do everything in my power to prevent radicals and republicans from importing the revolution to our shores."

Julianne was stunned. Yes, he was against the revolution, and he meant to fight it, but he wasn't the absolute reactionary she had assumed he was. She was hardly opposed to gradual and gentle reforms in her own country. She felt certain that such reforms would never be made— the ruling parties had too much to lose. Still, his views weren't intolerable to her—not at all!

*He is not for you, Julianne. Trust me on that... One day, he will marry some wealthy debutante....*

She shivered, although she wasn't cold. Did it really matter if he favored reform in Great Britain? She had better never forget that he would always be the earl of Bedford, and so far above her that he might as well have been a prince to her Cinderella. Caring was not love, and men in his position did not marry for love, anyway!

Julianne put the letter back down, shaken. *Did she secretly wish to marry Paget?*

Her heart was thundering.

She had lost all desire to write Tom. Maybe she would write Amelia, she thought, suddenly miserable.

The quill was no longer on top of the desk, and she looked at the floor. Sure enough, it had fallen. As she retrieved it, she saw that the tip was broken and useless. She reached for a drawer to find another quill, not that she really cared about writing anyone now.

It was locked.

She tried the lower right-hand drawer again. It was most definitely locked. She stared. What was he keeping inside? She didn't even have to think about it—war memos and war secrets were probably hidden there.

She was glad it was locked. She did not want to spy on him. Julianne tried the drawer above it and it opened immediately. She saw several quills—as well as a stack of envelopes tied with a black ribbon.

The delicate script on the topmost envelope was definitely feminine.

She froze. She knew she was staring at a pile of love letters.

Instantly she closed the drawer. She knew she should not look at the letters. But her mind was oddly blank. Did she have a rival? Surely those were ancient letters!

She continued to stare. She was sharing Paget's bed. Damn it—she had to know who those letters were from—and if they were recent or not.

She took the pile of bound envelopes out, trembling.

Julianne untied the ribbon and turned over the top letter. It was from Nadine D'Archand.

Surprise immobilized her. *D'Archand*. Was she one of the émigrés Marcel wished to locate? Was it even possible? Was D'Archand a common name—or an uncommon one? She could hardly believe the coincidence.

But this letter was from his fiancée. Now, she wondered if Nadine was even dead. After all, when he had told her about his fiancée, he had been in the midst of his deception.

Trembling, she glanced over her shoulder, but the parlor door remained shut. She opened the envelope and withdrew the letter and read it.

April 15, 1791
My dearest Dominic, I know we said our good-byes last night. But I could not help myself. Last night was wonderful. What a perfect evening to have spent together before my trip to France with your mother. I could have danced with you until dawn. You do know, of course, that you are a superb dancer, and we made every other couple there green with envy?

Julianne was sick. She could almost hear Nadine's soft, warm laughter now. She could almost see her in a ball gown, pretty and glowing and so in love. With moisture gathering in her eyes, she read on.

I know you are a bit anxious about our vacation in France, but I miss home, and so does Catherine. I so miss Paris! My dear, we will be fine and we will be home before you even know we have been gone! Thank you for the flowers, for the beautiful brace-

let. Thank you, Dom, for such a perfect evening. I
already miss you.
With all my love,
Nadine

Julianne stared at the letter in her hand, unable to
see the delicate cursive clearly. Nadine had been in love
with Dominic. Of course she had. She had no doubt that
Nadine had been a beautiful, kind, warm woman. Had
Dominic loved her in return?

*Do you still love her?*

*No.*

Suddenly Julianne did not believe him. He had been
masquerading as Charles Maurice at the time. And now,
damn it, she was afraid. Was Nadine's family in Cornwall? Was *Nadine* in Cornwall?

Julianne refolded the letter, her hands shaking. She reminded herself that the letter was two years old. She tried
to reassure herself—why go so far as to claim Nadine
was dead if she were not? And it was horrid, hoping that
someone was truly dead, but she would have never allowed Paget a single liberty if he were betrothed to someone else. She slid it back into the envelope and began to
retie the ribbon. Tears blurred her vision. There was so
much dread. And she heard footsteps outside the door.

She jammed the pile of letters in the drawer and
slammed it shut. As she shot to her feet, Dominic opened
the door and saw her. His gaze widened.

She inhaled, very distressed.

His gaze narrowed.

Julianne said, "I was going to write Tom." The
moment she spoke, she knew she shouldn't have said
anything at all.

"I see." His tone was flat, his expression impossible to read.

She wet her lips. "I was looking for a quill." She stopped, realizing her mistake. But she had never been so flustered.

"The quill is right there, on top of the desk."

His face was a mask of indifference, yet she knew he suspected that she had been prying into his private things. "It is broken."

Very quietly, he said, "I see."

She stared and he stared back. If she asked him about his fiancée, he would know she had been reading his letters, yet she longed to blurt out her questions.

He finally asked, "Were you spying upon me?"

"No!" she cried.

A terrible paused ensued. "I thought you might want breakfast. Unfortunately, I cannot join you. It is in your room."

She edged away from the desk. He did not move toward her. He did not attempt to embrace her. There was no exchange of happy greetings, no reference to the passionate night they had shared. His regard was intent and searching—it was mistrustful.

Julianne wished she had never gone through his desk or seen those letters.

JULIANNE WAS VERY SURPRISED as she approached the salon where Sebastian Warlock was waiting for her. She couldn't even recall when she had last seen her uncle— possibly she had been a child of ten or eleven. But Amelia had said that he and Lucas were close; Lucas must have mentioned that she was staying at Bedford House. She supposed it was fortunate to have a chance to get to know her mother's brother. But as she hurried down the hall, following Gerard, she thought about the fact that he never came to visit Momma.

Sebastian Warlock was standing by the sofa in the small blue salon with white accents. She faltered. He was a dark, handsome man and somehow formidable. He appeared rather impatient now. He was dressed in drab brown, without a wig, indicating either indifference to fashion or unfortunate circumstances. Having seen his London home, Julianne suspected the case to be the former. She did not recognize him at all.

For one moment he stared at her, his regard going over her from head to toe, quite clearly inspecting her. Julianne was taken aback.

He finally smiled, briefly, and came forward to greet her, taking her hand. "It has been a very long time, Julianne." He bowed over her hand and released it.

"Yes, it has," she said, feeling oddly tense. She reminded herself that this man allowed Lucas the use of his home, and Lucas liked him. "This is a surprise, but a pleasant one."

He studied her for another moment. "You are the surprise, my dear. You are beautiful and you so remind me of your mother."

Julianne's tension increased, even though she knew that Momma had been a beauty in her day. "I hope you are flattering me."

"I just remarked on how pleasing to the eye you are." His brow lifted.

"You surely know Momma is addled."

"Ah, yes, I do, just as I know that you are an intellectual bohemian."

She didn't know what to say. Was that last a compliment? Had Lucas said anything else? He would never reveal her radical politics to anyone outside the immediate family, she thought. "A great many subjects interest me. I am an avid reader, but I can hardly keep up with my interests."

His expression was bland. "I believe Lucas mentioned some such thing."

She was beginning to feel a bit of alarm, although that was surely absurd. Why had Lucas been discussing her? Had he mentioned Amelia? "My sister also reads avidly, although she has a fondness for novels, not journals."

"I am not here to see Amelia," he said.

"It is kind of you to call," she said, awkwardly. "I would offer refreshments, but I am a guest here."

"I don't need refreshments. How are you feeling, after your ordeal?"

What, exactly, was he referring to? Did he enjoy keeping her uncertain and puzzled? For she was beginning to sense that he was hardly making a social call. "Did Lucas tell you that I was ill?"

"Lucas is very worried about you."

She felt considerable trepidation, then.

"I am also worried." He gestured at the sofa.

Julianne sat, fearing the worst. Surely Lucas hadn't told their uncle about her brush with the authorities, for by doing so, he would have exposed her radical orientation. "Lucas manages the estate and the family—he always worries, often needlessly." She smiled firmly, hoping to close the subject.

He slowly smiled, but it was not warm or kind. "Julianne, I have little time to spare. I have called for two reasons. The obvious one being my familial concern for you."

She smiled again. Lucas had told Warlock that she was ill, she decided. "I was somewhat ill recently, but I am well on my way to a full recovery. It is kind of you to inquire about me."

"I am speaking about your radical associations, my dear."

She froze.

"I am speaking about your Society of the Friends of Man in Cornwall, the Rue de la Seine Club in Paris, and of course, about your attendance at the Newgate Convention earlier in the week—and your arrest and imprisonment in the Tower."

She stood; he took her arm and pulled her back to sit. "You need not fear me. I am your uncle, after all."

"How could Lucas tell you all of this?" she cried.

"First, I want you to listen to me—and listen well." He wasn't smiling now. "I haven't called on you in years, Julianne, but that doesn't mean I don't care about your fortunes. And you were very fortunate this time, to have a great peer like Bedford come rushing to your aid."

She inhaled. He suspected the affair—she was certain.

"Do you truly think to triumph over the British government? This is not France. We are not ready for—or ripe for—a revolution here. Only one of three possible outcomes can meet radicals like you, Julianne—incarceration, transportation or execution."

She cried out. "You are trying to frighten me. I cannot fathom why Lucas told you all of my secrets."

"Can you admit defeat and give up your causes?" His stare was hard and direct.

She trembled in fear. "No, I cannot. I cannot—will not—admit defeat. And I am not giving up anything, sir!" She stood again.

He stood, as well. "Then heed me very well. You are not playing a game of cards. You are playing a game that affects men's lives and causes their deaths."

It took her a moment to absorb such a dire statement. She gasped. "I am hardly playing a game."

"Oh, you are playing a game—a dangerous game, my dear. It is a game of us against them. It is a game of life and death. The stakes are so very high, and if you insist upon playing, then you must do so with great care."

She wanted to end the conversation but she stared, almost mesmerized.

"You have promise," he said softly. "You are brave."

"What do you want?"

"This game is akin to chess. We make a move, they counter. I retrieve Paget. You write the Parisian Jacobins. I seek to locate a traitor. You seek to locate a family. It is a game, a very dangerous one, and we are all players in it."

Did he know that she had been asked to locate the D'Archand family in Cornwall? Julianne was stupefied. Did he consider her a *traitor?*

And what was he, exactly? Because she did not think Warlock the mere lord of a small estate.

"Were you frightened when Rob Lawton broke up the convention? When you were thrown in the Tower?" He spoke mildly.

"Of course I was!" she cried.

"Good. If you are going to play, then you should be afraid—fear makes one cautious."

"What does that mean?" She looked up at him.

For a moment, he stared. "The British Convention of the Delegates of the People was ended before it ever began. Tom Treyton was arrested in Edinburgh along with three hundred other attendees."

Julianne cried out in disbelief!

His expression was hard. "They will be tried for high treason, Julianne."

She could hardly assimilate what he was saying. How had this happened? And then she realized the dire jeopardy Tom was in. "That is a hanging offense."

"Yes, it is."

"I must free Tom!"

He slowly smiled. "I had hoped for just such a response."

As she met his gaze, she felt nothing but dread.

"I can help Treyton," Warlock said.

Hope surged. "Then please, do so!"

He nodded slightly. "I will have him released, all charges dropped—if you do something for me in return."

The dread returned, instantly. "What do you want of me?"

"I want you to continue your radical associations, Julianne. And then you will report back to me."

It took her a moment to comprehend him. "You want me to spy on my friends and associates?"

"Yes, I do."

For one moment, she stared, shocked. And then outrage began. "There is nothing familial about this call. You want to use me. You are despicable!" she cried. "Does Lucas know what you are asking of me?"

"He most certainly does not, and I suggest you keep this conversation to yourself."

"I intend to tell Lucas how horrid you are immediately!"

"That is not wise, Julianne. Remember, I have what you want—the ability to have Tom released." His gaze hardened. "I have a few uses for radicals like Treyton, my dear. None of them are pleasant, should you fail to comply, should you speak to your brother, should Treyton remain behind bars."

She slowly realized what he was saying—he would hurt Tom if she defied him. "You are ruthless!"

"I am. This is *war,* Julianne."

She began shaking her head. But even as she wanted to refuse him, she wondered how far he would go. Would he truly torture Tom if she refused to help him?

"I must leave," he said pleasantly. Julianne wanted to spit at him. Instead, she stared as he picked up his bicorne hat. "I suggest you think carefully about poor Treyton, alone in a cell, at the mercy of his gaolers." He started for the salon door.

"Better yet, think of Treyton swinging from the gallows, as he will surely be found guilty if I do not intervene."

Speechlessly, Julianne stared at him. How she hated her uncle.

"I am not all bad, Julianne. Actually, I am a patriot, and I will do whatever I have to do to keep this country safe." He settled his hat on his head and nodded politely at her. "I expect your answer by the end of the week."

Julianne watched him leave. Then she ran to the door and slammed it closed, collapsing against it.

# CHAPTER THIRTEEN

DOMINIC FOLLOWED the D'Archand's servant into the salon to await Nadine, remembering the sight of Julianne closing the right-hand drawer of his *secrétaire* when he had paused on the threshold of the room. His gut churned. *She had gone through his desk.*

Surely she was not spying on him for her radical friends. But she had told him already that her Jacobin friends in Paris had asked her to locate an émigré family that had settled in Cornwall; what else had they asked her?

He did not want to believe it.

Nadine appeared on the room's threshold, interrupting his dark thoughts. She was wearing pale pink, a color that suited her olive complexion, and her smile was reflected in her eyes. In that moment, she reminded him of the woman he had known since childhood. But his mood did not lighten. Nadine was a friend and an ally; he trusted her implicitly; he would trust her with his life. But he could not trust Julianne, the woman who was his lover—the woman he cared for.

"I was wondering when you would call again," she said, a question in her eyes.

He came forward, taking both of her hands and kissing each cheek in turn. "All you had to do was ask."

"I thought we both needed some time to adjust to being reunited, after such a long separation."

He guided her to the sofa. Nadine had always been a thoughtful and deliberate person. Her comment did not surprise him. "We have always thought alike. I also needed some time to adjust to our circumstances."

She studied him as she settled comfortably on the sofa, taking his hand and clasping it warmly—a habit he had forgotten. "I can see that you are worried, Dom. It is mirrored in your eyes."

He hesitated. He meant to tell her about Julianne, but he needed to carefully segue into the topic. "I have a great deal on my mind, relating to the war and the revolution."

"Is there news?"

"There is always news." To divert her, he said, "The Duke of York has decided to besiege Dunkirk, which would be a great prize for London. But I believe York should be marching on Paris."

"I agree, the road to Paris will not remain open indefinitely, but I am hardly a general." She shrugged, quiet for a moment. "What is wrong?"

He finally smiled. "I have come into the habit of brooding, Nadine."

She didn't smile back at him. "We have both changed so much, haven't we, Dom? After all we have gone through, it feels as if I danced all those nights away with a someone else—someone without real cares, without any comprehension of war and death."

"It does feel that way," he said. "We were so innocent, weren't we? To think that I used to consider a crisis the failure of a tenant to pay his rents…. I never thought of you as young or naive when we became engaged, but you are so much worldlier now, it is almost as if you are an entirely different woman."

She shook her head. "I can barely recognize that

young girl. She did not have a clue as to the misery and brutality that exists in the world. She had no worries, no real concerns—she was happy, all of the time! Who is happy all of the time, Dominic?" She added, "I have a habit of brooding now, too."

He said carefully, "You seem happy enough today."

"I am happy to be with you." She said softly, "You changed the subject, cleverly, but not cleverly enough. So what is truly bothering you?"

There was no getting past the discussion, he realized. He studied her for another moment, and her gaze was serious and searching. "We have to discuss our affairs, Nadine, but I don't want to distress you—that is not my intention. You have been through enough."

She lay her hand on his forearm. "We have always been honest with one another. I refuse to be any other way with you. If there is something you wish to say, even if you feel it might be distressing, you must say so anyway." She added, "You might be surprised, Dominic. Very little distresses me these days—outside of death and anarchy, war and revolution."

She was right. They had always been honest with one another, and he had come to tell her about Julianne. He owed her that—he owed Julianne. "I was not truthful when I told your family that I had spent the past months in the country."

She smiled. "I know." She stood, moved swiftly to the salon door, and glanced into the hall. Then she shut it and returned to the sofa, saying, "Have you been in France this entire time?"

But he was alarmed. "Do you think you are being spied upon?"

She hesitated. "We have so much to discuss."

His eyes widened. She was leery of spies—in her own home! "Why would anyone spy on you?"

"Tell me why you felt that you needed to deceive my family, first." She smiled fleetingly. "And I want to know what you were doing in France, and how long you were there." She sat back down beside him.

"I have spent over a year and a half in France," Dominic said. Vague, hazy, horrific images began to form. He would not allow them "When I found Catherine in Paris and we could not find you, I escorted her home—it was late November." His mother and Nadine had gone to France in the spring of 1791. "I then returned to continue searching for you. I gave up after several months, but by then, I was already Jean Carre, a print shop owner and a Jacobin. I had learned so much about the Jacobins, including those in the National Assembly, that I realized I should stay, continue my charade and send what intelligence I could gather home." He paused, thinking about his neighbors, whom he had had to deceive on a daily basis. He had taken tea with the baker, reveling in one republican triumph after another, but it had been a facade. He would return to his shop, close up for the evening and become Dominic Paget again.

"Go on," she whispered.

"But in the spring, there were rumors of an uprising in le Loire. You can imagine how that affected—and excited—me. Those rumors included the name of the rebel leader—Jacquelyn."

Her eyes widened. "Michel?" she gasped. "Michel—our Michel—leads the La Vendée rebels?"

"Yes. Michel is alive and well and courageously fighting the French army at every turn. I joined him last May."

"You were there at Saumur?" she cried, aghast.

"We captured an entire division in early May, then

consolidated control of the river and town in June." He
knew he must hold the memories at bay, but they had
begun to become focused in his mind. The dead and
dying in the bloody river, Father Pierre, lifeless in his
arms, Michel screaming that they must retreat.

"Dominic." Nadine clasped his cheek, her gaze worried.

He jerked back to the present. "I am sorry. We were
defeated outside Nantes at the end of June."

"I heard. I cannot believe you were there—thousands
died! How is Michel?"

"The last time I saw him, alive and well and determined."

"Is there a way I can get a letter to him?"

He started.

"He is my friend—I have known him for years."

"Yes, there is a way to reach him," Dominic said. He
hesitated.

She took his hand in both of hers. "There is bad news,
isn't there?"

"Do you remember Father Pierre?"

"Of course I do. He married my cousin Lucien—he
buried my mother."

"He died in that last battle."

She choked. "He was an old man! He was fighting the
French army?"

Dominic nodded, putting his arm around her.

She trembled, but did not move into his arms as she
would have done two years ago. He reached into his coat
pocket and handed her a kerchief, which she dabbed
against her eyes. She was, he saw, determined not to
cry. "When will this bloody war end?" she asked tersely.

"I don't know."

She pulled away and he let her go, but she looked at

him. "The war has changed me, Nadine," Dominic said. "And it has also changed my life."

"Of course it has. No one can be the same. Not if you have lived through a single battle, a single riot." She inhaled. "I am not the same."

"But you remain a beautiful and intelligent woman—more so than ever. You remain extraordinary."

Her eyes were wide and riveted upon him. "Why am I certain that you are about to let me down, somehow?"

He found it hard to speak now. "My feelings for you have not changed. I am your most ardent admirer, your most loyal friend. But I have changed, Nadine, greatly, and I will never be able to go from ball to ball with you again."

She stared, hands clasped. "I would dearly love to go to a ball. But it would feel a bit absurd. What are you trying to say?"

"I cannot marry right now. In fact, I don't know if I will ever think of marriage again."

She stared, clearly surprised, but otherwise, he could not tell what she was thinking. Once, she had been so transparent! "I know there are contracts. I know I gave my word. But marriage has become an impossibility."

"I see," she said. And then, very softly, "You are going back, aren't you? You will return to your print shop and your life as Jean Carre."

A lie formed, on the tip of his tongue. But he had known her for too long, and he trusted her with this secret. "I will take up a new alias, actually."

She breathed hard. "I want to go back with you."

"Absolutely not!" He was aghast. He had expected her to, perhaps, make a plea to continue the engagement—not this. "Why would you want to go back to France? This isn't about our engagement, is it?"

She stood, her dark eyes flashing. "No, it's not. I have my own story to tell, Dom. I suffered grave injuries in the riot, but broken bones heal in months—not a year and a half."

He stared up at her. He had wondered what had taken her so long to return to Britain.

"I was rescued from the mob by a kindly shopkeeper," Nadine said. She was pale now. "He witnessed the riot, and after the mob left, he found me unconscious in the street. He thought I was dead, but I was very much alive and he took me in. His wife and daughter cared for me until I healed. They are wonderful, good, simple people, who live in fear that their treason to the state will one day be found out."

He stood and took her hand, aware of the anguish she was fighting. "Do you remain in contact with them?"

"No, it would put them in jeopardy."

His mind turned that over. "What kept you from coming home immediately?"

She shrugged free of his grasp and slowly paced. "I discovered a mother and her daughter, hiding in a vacated shop, terrified for their lives," she said, pausing before a window and staring at the gardens outside. "They were from a titled family. That was their crime. Her husband had been dragged from his bed in their home in Marseilles, and clubbed to death—in front of their daughter. Both women were raped. Marianne and Jeanine were then left as rubbish. They fled to Paris, hoping to find relatives. They did not—their family was gone. I hid them in an empty cellar for several months while I endeavored to find the means to transport them to Le Havre and then on to Britain. Eventually I made the right contact. I met a Frenchman in the gendarmerie who is actually a royalist—I believe he might still be in the police, actively aiding and abetting people like Marianne and Jeanine. Or, he could have been found out. And he could be dead." She turned to face him now.

"You could have been found out," he said quietly.

"Yes. Once I had my contact, Marianne and Jeanine were on their way to safety. And I had learned that I could help people like them, like me, escape the horrors of the Cordeliers, the Brissotins, the Girondins— the Jacobins. Marianne and Jeanine were the first of a dozen men, women and sometimes children that I helped smuggle through France."

"What you did was courageous, Nadine—and dangerous. Thank God you got out of France safely."

"I have no regrets."

"I won't allow you to return to France. You can help us here, in Britain, instead of returning to France where you will surely, eventually, be uncovered and executed."

She trembled. "A part of me dreads going back. I lived in constant fear, and I am hardly deluded! In fact, the reason I went home was not just because I missed my father and sisters. A haut gendarme was terribly interested in me. I believed he had learned the truth and that it was no longer safe for me to stay in Paris."

"Then I am grateful you left when you did," he said. Now he understood her fears of spies—perhaps, she was being hunted by French agents. "Stay here in Britain, Nadine, and I will put you in touch with the right men— men who are in need of your talents and skills."

She hugged herself, as if her bare arms were cold. "You shouldn't go back, either."

"I am going back." He was firm.

And then he saw the tears that had arisen in her eyes. "You never cry."

She brushed at them. "I have learned how to cry,

Dominic." She hesitated. "You said your feelings for me haven't changed, but I am sensing that they have changed. And if they have, I understand. I am not the same woman you left at a ball two years ago, just as you are not the same man. Neither one of us has time for romance now."

He tensed, instantly thinking of Julianne. He wondered if he should conceal the fact that he was involved with her. Carefully, he said, "You are not arguing for our marriage."

"No, I am not. Like you, I have lost interest in our marriage, but not because of you—because of the revolution." She trailed off. Her gaze was suddenly distant. "I cannot marry now. As you said, marriage is an impossibility."

"So I have not hurt you?"

"No, you haven't hurt me." She smiled and walked back to him. "I still love you. I will always love you. I could wait for you, if that is what you want—or, when this terrible time is over, we could decide then if we wish to finally make a union."

He knew he had to tell her about Julianne. Very carefully, he said, "I was wounded before I left France." He did not like dissembling but he would do so now, to protect her from worrying about him. "I spent the month of July recovering in Cornwall."

"You tell me this now? How badly were you hurt?"

He hesitated. "I almost died."

She stared, aghast.

"But I survived. I was nursed night and day through a terrible infection and a fever by a single woman— Julianne Greystone."

Nadine started. "Is she related to Lucas and Jack Greystone?"

"How do you know the Greystone brothers?"

"They helped me escape France, Dominic." She added, "Jack Greystone saved my life."

He started. "By getting you out of the country?"

"The gendarmerie attacked us on the beach, just before we could make it to his ship. Several men were shot. I was almost shot."

"What happened?" he demanded.

"Someone betrayed us. The gendarmerie were hiding at the cove when we arrived, and they ambushed us. It was a terrible battle. I am indebted to Greystone, who shielded me from the fire with his own body. He got me off the beach and onto the ship and he was wounded instead of me—although he never said a word."

He owed Jack Greystone doubly, Dominic thought, grim. He stared more closely at her, certain that she was recalling that night in bitter detail. "Julianne is one of his sisters, Nadine. I happen to know them both, somewhat. Lucas and Jack got me out of France together."

She was incredulous. "It is such a small world! You said they took you to Cornwall? Our new home is outside the village of St. Just. Do you know it?"

"Yes, I do. The earl is a friend of mine and I was at Greystone Manor, which is a short ride away."

She smiled oddly at him. "How ironic this is—his sister saved you and he saved me."

"Yes, it is very ironic." He cleared his voice. She glanced at him and he said, "Julianne is currently at Bedford House. She is my guest."

"Good. I want to meet her."

He almost winced. "Nadine—there is no easy way to say this. I hope you will understand. I have come to care for her—and not just as a friend."

For a moment, she stared blankly at him. Then her eyes widened.

When she simply stared, in abject surprise, he said, "So when you asked me if my feelings for you have changed, my answer remains no, they have not. However, I have been—" he hesitated "—pursuing Julianne."

She continued to stare, now incredulous. "Are you in love?" she finally asked.

He became uncomfortable. "Why would you ask me such a thing?"

"You just told me that you are pursuing someone else, when we remain officially betrothed. Are you jilting me because of her?" Nadine asked, rather calmly.

He flushed. "I am going back to France. I refuse to do so and abandon my bride," he said flatly. "You know the risks as well as I do of being an agent in that country. And I am not in love."

Her gaze narrowed. "Is she your mistress?"

He choked. He knew he must deny it, for many reasons—including that Lucas Greystone must never find out. "Nadine, she is a gentlewoman."

"Yes, she is—which means that, if you seduced her, you are a complete cad. Not to mention that you owe her brothers for saving your life. I happen to know that you are not without morals, so that leads me back to my first question—are you in love?"

He wondered if he flushed. "Hardly," he snapped. "I do not like being interrogated. In any case, she is my guest right now, and you will undoubtedly meet."

"Oh, you are riled! This subject—this *woman*—has you in a snarl." Nadine frowned. "I don't know what to make of this…this…circumstance. I have lost you not to the war, but to another woman—to a mistress!"

"You have not lost me—you will never lose me," he said, meaning it.

"I have lost you if you are pursuing her, and not me."

He stared. Perhaps, in a way, she was right. "You are distressed—but not as distressed as a jilted fiancée should be."

She grimaced. "I don't want to marry, but I *am* distressed. I am confused. We have been apart for two years—still, we have known one another since childhood!"

"Which is why I will always be your most loyal friend," he tried.

She didn't hear him, blinking back a tear. "I happen to want you to be happy. But she is only your mistress. Unless, of course, you are actually in love. Are you considering marrying her?"

It was his turn to be taken aback. And he wondered how he would feel about marriage to Julianne if Britain and France were not at war, if a constitutional monarchy were restored in France. There was more than the gulf of their political differences and the war between them. He thought about his place in society. It would be a difficult and challenging match, but not impossible—in ordinary times.

"Are you considering marriage to her?" Nadine asked again, surprised.

He frankly didn't know. And hadn't he suspected her of treachery, just that morning? "I am very fond of her, but our relationship is fraught with conflict."

"What on earth does that mean? Is she demanding marriage?"

"No, she is not."

"So what could possibly cause conflict between you and your paramour?"

He hesitated. She was going to find out about Julianne's politics sooner or later, as Catherine would never hide the facts from Nadine. "There is something you should know. She has Jacobin sympathies."

Nadine stared in disbelief.

He felt defensive. "She saved my life, Nadine, and she simply doesn't understand the realities of the revolution. She has no clue of the anarchy in France. Her desire to serve the common man is admirable, actually. She would give the coat off her own back to a passing stranger— even if it is the only coat she owns."

Nadine choked. "Listen to yourself! You are defending a Jacobin?" She was incredulous.

"I feel certain that—"

Nadine cut him off. "There is nothing to admire about the Jacobins!" She stared closely at him. "She must be very beautiful."

He decided not to answer.

"You don't have to answer," Nadine cried. "I know she is gorgeous. I know she is sharing your bed. You are in bed with the enemy!"

WHEN WARLOCK LEFT, Julianne sank back down on the sofa, shaking. She covered her face with her hands.

Tom was in dire jeopardy. He was far more radical than she was. He might even approve of Butler's ideas. He certainly despised the English aristocracy—he had spoken of dispossessing the entire class in one fell swoop, no matter what it took! He had even spoken about over-throwing the king, and having a government like the one in France—run by elected representatives of the population. But Julianne had never really debated him on the merits of such revolutionary ideas, as it was so far-fetched. As Warlock had said, England was not France, and they were not ripe for revolution here.

But Tom's beliefs were actually treason.

If Tom were charged with treason, she had every reason to believe he would be found guilty.

How could she not do as her despicable uncle had asked? If only there was another way to obtain Tom's release!

"Julianne?"

She leapt off the sofa at the sound of Dominic's voice. He stood upon the threshold of the salon, regarding her intently. "You are close to tears. Gerard told me Warlock was here. What has happened?"

Did Dominic have the power to obtain Tom's release? She hurried forward. "I have never despised anyone more." Julianne slammed the door closed behind him as his eyes widened. "Tom has been arrested. He is going to be tried for high treason."

Dominic clasped her shoulders. "Calm down if you can."

"How can I be calm? The authorities broke up the convention in Edinburgh. Three hundred delegates were arrested. One was Tom!"

He released her. "I had heard of the arrests last night. It never occurred to me that Treyton would be one of those arrested."

"I am so worried—and you are not worried at all."

He appeared grim. "Treyton is rabidly Jacobin. I think he might be dangerous to men like myself, to men like your brother."

She froze. Somehow she had forgotten about Tom writing to Marcel and identifying Dominic as a British agent. She trembled, aware that she now had an obligation to tell Dominic the truth. He might be in jeopardy. There could be spies near Bedford House, or even within it.

But she would never forget the look in his eyes when

he had caught her at his desk that morning. If she told him what she had done, he would never trust her—and he would hardly help Tom.

She did not know what to do.

"Why are you wringing your hands?"

She released them. "He cannot be tried for treason. What if he is hanged? He is my friend—I have known him since childhood."

"What else did Warlock say?" He spoke calmly—too calmly.

She inhaled. Warlock hadn't forbidden her from revealing their conversation to Dominic, but she was fairly certain she was supposed to keep it secret from everyone.

"Julianne? You are ashen."

"I am afraid of him."

Dominic's stare sharpened. "I assume you are referring to Warlock?"

"You must not confront him."

Dominic took her arm rather forcefully. "What did he want?"

"He wants me to spy for him."

Dominic seemed shocked. "He said such a thing, directly?"

She nodded and cried, "He wants me to betray my own friends. He wants me to maintain my radical associations and report every plot and activity to him." She was so sickened. "If I do so, he will have Tom released without being charged. Otherwise, he will hurt Tom—he said so! Dominic, he is my *uncle*."

"What did you tell him?" Dominic asked sharply, releasing her.

She stepped back. "I would never spy on my friends. I would never betray the revolution."

Dominic stared at her, his green gaze hard and almost

frightening. Julianne's tension soared. If only she hadn't told Tom the truth about Dominic. "Why are you looking at me that way?"

"Because I am reminded of how passionately Jacobin you are," he said.

He was looking at her with some wariness. She had betrayed him—but he did not know it. He must never know, she thought desperately.

"What aren't you telling me?" he asked.

She shook her head, horrified by her own duplicity. "I have told you everything."

"You are a poor liar." Abruptly he strode to the sideboard. Julianne stared, uncertainly, as he poured two brandies and turned back to her. He handed her one.

She trembled. "You betrayed me in Cornwall, but I don't ever want to betray you."

"Good. Then don't." He sipped.

She was so distressed. "What will you do about Warlock?"

"For the moment, nothing. As long as you stay out of his games."

"That is exactly how he described spying, Dominic, as a terrible, dangerous, deadly game. Is Warlock a spymaster? He must be! Is Lucas a spy?"

"You are not drinking your brandy."

He wasn't going to answer her. "How can you be so calm?"

"Hysteria will not solve anything."

She had to focus on the immediate matter at hand, she thought. Warlock was spymaster, Lucas was involved, somehow, and she had to think about Marcel and what he might be doing. But just then, Tom's life hung in the balance. "I am terrified that Tom will hang. You helped me. You had me released from the Tower before I was even charged. Surely you can do the same for Tom."

He took a sip of his brandy. "Why should I help Treyton?"

She gasped and set her snifter down, untouched, on a side table. "For all the reasons I have said!"

"I am sorry, Julianne, but I don't care that he is your friend. I think he should be imprisoned, where he can do no harm." He was final.

She saw that he meant his every word. She was aghast. "I can't let him hang, Dominic. I simply can't—I won't. Dominic, I am begging you, if I mean anything to you, you will go out of your way, and against your principles, to help him."

"That is a low blow. You mean a great deal to me, and my answer remains. No."

She saw from his expression how set against Tom he was. "My God, my only option might be to do as Warlock has asked."

"Like hell," he said, but so dispassionately that she flinched. "You are not playing these spy games, Julianne." His stare was searching.

She knew he was thinking about finding her at his desk that morning. He suddenly put his snifter down and approached. She tensed as he reached for her, pulling her close. He said, very softly, his breath feathering her cheek, "Do you want to tell me anything else, Julianne?"

She looked up at him fearfully, thinking about Tom and Marcel, and Nadine's letters.

"I want to trust you," he murmured. He lifted her chin with his forefinger. "You are sharing my bed."

With the distress and fear, there was so much desire. "We made love last night," she said softly. "As we made love in Cornwall."

He waited.

"We made love this morning," she said helplessly. She wanted to confess the extent of her feelings to him. "You rescued me from the Tower, when I was in dark despair."

"So you are making love to me because you now owe me."

"No. I am making love to you because I care about you."

"About me—or Charles Maurice?"

She felt herself flush. "I care about you, Dominic."

He stared intently. "You have never before admitted that you care for me."

"You know that you are my first lover. I couldn't have made love if I didn't care."

"But that was then—when I was a revolutionary. I am a Tory now. How can you care for a conservative like me?" His stare was unwavering now. It was hard. It was demanding.

"Do you think that I am playing with your affections?" she cried.

"I want to believe you. What were you doing at my *secrétaire* this morning?"

She stiffened. "I meant to write Tom." She wet her lips, feeling desperate. "I read your letter to Burke, Dom, and I am sorry!" Her heart thundered now as he considered her. "I despise him! When I saw his name on the envelope, I could not help myself."

"I appreciate the confession."

"It was such a surprise, to find that our views aren't completely incompatible, and to realize you aren't a reactionary, after all."

He studied her for a long moment. "No, our views are not entirely incompatible."

She touched his arm. "There is more. Please don't be

angry…I pried into your privy affairs. I also read one of Nadine's letters."

His expression did not change. "I see. Weren't those letters tied together in a ribbon, and secluded inside a drawer?"

"Yes. But I was not spying—I was looking for a quill."

"I genuinely want to believe you, Julianne. I was not pleased to find you at my desk."

"It will never happen again!"

He seemed to want to smile, but he did not; he touched her cheek, fleetingly. And he was very grave. "There is something I have to tell you. It is about Nadine."

She froze. Dread arose, instantly. Hadn't she known it would come to this? "She isn't dead, is she?"

"No, she is not."

*His fiancée was alive.*

And the knowledge felt like another impossible betrayal, stabbing through her heart. She sagged against him. "That was another lie?" She was desperately trying to understand—she could not withstand another lie.

"No. It was not a deception on my part." He was firm. He slid his hands over her back. "Everyone thought that she had died in a riot in France in 1791. I thought she had died in that riot, because I went to France to look for her and I never found her. Witnesses saw her vanish in the mob. My mother believed she had been trampled to death. Until I returned to London last week, I genuinely believed that she was dead."

*His fiancée was alive. Nadine was alive. Nadine, who loved him.* How could this be happening? How could she be standing in Dominic's arms while Nadine was alive?

But even as her thoughts raced wildly, she heard his every word and she was horrified for the other woman. "Thank God she did not die—and not that way."

"That is generous of you."

"Do you love her?" she cried.

He pulled her even closer. "Not the way that you are thinking. I love her as a sister."

She could barely breathe. And tears were rising, but they were tears of relief. "Are you certain?"

"I am very certain." He took her face in both hands but he did not kiss her. "We are ending our engagement."

Julianne stared, shocked all over again.

"I am very fond of her. I have known her for most of my life. She is as affectionate of me as I am of her. I will always care for her and look out for her. But we have both changed and neither one of us has any interest in marriage now. She is in agreement with me."

Her mind whirled.

"I told her about you."

Her shock was complete. "You did what?"

"What kind of man would I be if I took you to bed while engaged to her? I owed her a part of the truth. I would never tell her the extent of our relationship, but I warn you, she is astute, and she has assumed you are my mistress. I did not confirm it, obviously."

She remained stunned. "I cannot quite believe you told her about me."

"It was important for me to do so, because you have become important to me."

Julianne gasped, still reeling, and finally he kissed her.

## CHAPTER FOURTEEN

JULIANNE SLOWLY WENT downstairs. It was close to noon the next day, and she was just leaving her room. Although Dominic had made love to her last night, she hadn't been able to sleep afterward. All she could think about was Tom being incarcerated in Edinburgh, Warlock's terrible proposition and the stunning news that Nadine was alive. And now, she was beginning to worry about having told Tom the truth about Dominic. She feared Dom's ever learning of what she had done.

Hope warred with fear. Dominic cared about her. It was obvious. He had ended his engagement, and he had told Nadine about her. It was also obvious with his every touch and caress. But caring about her and loving her were two different things. Was there any chance that their relationship might progress and become legitimate? Julianne wanted far more than being a mere mistress. But yearning to be courted—yearning to become his wife—was indeed dangerous. She understood the odds and the etiquette—as Lucas had said, she was too far beneath him on the social scale for him to ever consider marriage to her. On the other hand, Bedford could do whatever he wished.

She knew she had to be patient. Only time would tell where her journey with Dominic would end. But Tom did not have time on his side. He was going to be charged with treason, and once that happened, he would be on his way to a trial. She knew she would never be able to obtain a royal pardon for him. Therefore, she had to find someone to help her get him released now, before he was ever charged—either that, or she must play Warlock's game. She did not know if Lucas was back in town, but she prayed he was. She was on her way to see him to plead for his help.

As she approached the ground floor, she heard voices coming from a nearby salon. She faltered, glancing down the winding staircase, certain that one of the voices belonged to the Dowager Countess. She had no wish to engage Catherine now. Julianne decided to retreat rather than make a mad dash for the front door. But before she could turn and go back upstairs, Catherine appeared in the doorway of an adjacent salon.

"Someone is here to see you, Miss Greystone."

Julianne tensed. The Dowager Countess's smile was as cold as ever. She thought of her uncle, and feared that he would be her visitor. But then a dark-haired woman appeared by Catherine's side.

And Julianne knew who she was. She felt her heart drop with sheer dismay. The young woman was strikingly beautiful and exquisitely dressed. She was so obviously an aristocrat, so elegant and genteel—so clearly everything that Julianne was not. Somehow Julianne knew she had come face-to-face with Nadine.

The other woman seemed perfect for Dominic. Why had he ended things with her?

Julianne realized they were staring at one another. She forced a smile. It felt miserable.

"Do come forward, Miss Greystone." Lady Paget smiled. "Have you meet Lady D'Archand, my son's fiancée?"

Julianne glanced at Lady Paget. Dominic hadn't told

his mother about his engagement. And while she wanted to reassure herself that he would soon do so, she wasn't comforted. Nadine was too elegant, too wealthy and too beautiful. She was exactly the kind of woman Dominic should be with. And suddenly Julianne lost all confidence—how could she compete with her for Dominic's affections? Why had he decided that he would not marry her? What if he changed his mind? Dominic had said he would always care for Nadine!

And how could she make this woman's acquaintance, when Nadine had been his fiancée, and Julianne was now warming his bed?

"Hello, Miss Greystone. Dominic has told me about you." Nadine came forward, extending her hand. Her smile was small and tight, but her tone was polite.

And that made Julianne feel ever worse. She realized she wasn't breathing. *What, exactly, had Dominic said about her?* "I am very pleased to meet you, Lady D'Archand." She didn't know how she got the words out. All she wanted to do was end the encounter before it ever began.

"I have been eager to meet you. I understand you nursed Dominic back to health in Cornwall. I am very grateful."

Nadine's stare was searching, as if she wished to know all of her secrets. Julianne felt like an adulteress, except she was no such thing. Hadn't both she and Dom believed Nadine to be dead when they had become lovers? Yet she did not wish the other woman ill, not even now!

Nadine continued, "We have been friends since we learned how to walk. As children, we rode our ponies together, took our luncheons together and explored together. Before the war, there were so many teas and soirées. There were wonderful, fairy-tale balls." She smiled, but her gaze remained direct. "I would do anything for him and he would do anything for me. I couldn't bear to live in a world without him, so thank you for saving his life."

She meant her every word, Julianne thought. And she had very adeptly made her point. She and Dominic had everything in common, while all she had was his current attentions.

For hadn't Dominic said that Nadine had assumed they were lovers? She prayed she was not recalling his words correctly. "He was very ill, and I would have taken care of anyone in such a state."

"You are kind and compassionate," she said. "I understand he was in your care for an entire month."

What tack was this? Julianne wondered uncomfortably. "I could hardly turn my back on him. I would do the same for anyone."

Nadine studied her. "A month is a long time to spend together in a place like Cornwall. And now you are in London, and you are his houseguest."

She was certain that she flushed. Had Nadine emphasized that last word? "I suppose that we have become friends, due to the ordeal we shared."

Nadine stared for a moment. "And which ordeal is that?" she asked softly. "The ordeal of his almost dying while at your home, or the ordeal of your being imprisoned in the Tower as a political prisoner?"

Julianne started. "He told you that?"

"No, he did not," Nadine said, as softly. Her gaze was unwavering upon Julianne.

"I told her," Catherine said sharply. "Nadine is the daughter I have never had. I have told her *everything,* Miss Greystone."

Julianne was certain Lady Paget had told Nadine that

she and Dominic were lovers, as well. Nadine might suspect the truth, but Lady Paget had only to ask a servant where Julianne had slept. How she wanted to flee!

"You must be very grateful to Dominic. I cannot imagine being incarcerated anywhere, much less in the Tower of London," Nadine said tersely. "No one should have to suffer like that, Miss Greystone, and certainly not a woman. But you seem to have recovered."

The last thing Julianne wished to discuss with Nadine was her confinement—or being a guest in Dominic's home. But Nadine was being very generous. "I will always be grateful." It was time to make a quick exit, she decided. "I am running late," she began, but Nadine cut her off.

"And Dominic must be very fond of you, in return."

What could she say? She felt frozen. "We have become friends."

"Yes, of course you have. I can see how you and Dominic would have become close, while he was convalescing. Dominic can be utterly charming and very persuasive when he wishes to be. He is also very handsome. I can see how you would have become close, even though you are a Jacobin and he was merely pretending to be a republican. But the two of you are no longer nurse and invalid. You are no longer in the isolation of Cornwall. You remain a Jacobin, and he is hardly an officer in the French army. Yet you are in London—and his guest here at Bedford House."

She stared at Nadine, who stared back at her. "Yes," Julianne finally said, "I have Jacobin sympathies and he has invited me to stay here anyway, because of our friendship."

There was a pause. It was as if Nadine struggled to maintain her dignity. "How can a Jacobin and a Tory be friends, in a time of war?" Nadine asked with undue calm. "It seems an impossible feat."

"We have agreed to put our political differences aside," Julianne said tersely.

"How is that possible? I know Dominic well. His life is under siege—by your allies. France is in the midst of a civil war and you are on the side of his enemies." Her tone rose slightly.

Julianne did not know how to respond. "I am sympathetic to the revolution, but I am sorry for your losses and I do not condone chaos and anarchy, or the dispossession of an entire class of society."

"Has he ever told you about his life in France? Has he ever told you about the many relations he has there? He has a dozen cousins in the Loire Valley, Miss Greystone, most of them married with children! Has he told you what it is like at Christmas? With holly in the halls, and pine in the air, when we share our Christmas dinner with our cousins and our neighbors? When we cannot even seat everyone in three entire rooms! Or has he mentioned how we harvest the grapes in the fall? Did you know that he actually rolls up his sleeves and takes off his shoes and stockings, and picks the grapes with the peasants and children? And that he loves doing so?" Her eyes were moist now. "We played hide-and-seek as children in his vineyards, Miss Greystone, with my sisters and his cousins."

She was making her point yet again, Julianne thought in sheer dismay. Dominic was half French, she was a Frenchwoman, and they had everything in common, including a long, intimate past.

"You are as beautiful as I suspected you would be," Nadine said, a tear sliding down her cheek.

Julianne felt terrible, and she wanted to escape.

"He hasn't told me any of those things," she managed hoarsely.

Nadine struggled for composure. She finally smiled. "No, he hasn't—because he cannot talk about his life with you, not really." She inhaled. Another tear slid free. "How long will you stay in town, Miss Greystone?"

She hesitated, attempting to find her own composure, admiring the other woman in spite of herself. "I don't know."

"I would like to get to know you better." She managed another smile. "Dominic has made you his guest, so we must become acquainted. You must call on me. I am around the block. And then there is Cornwall. You do know that we are neighbors."

Julianne started, with dread. "No, I knew no such thing."

Nadine nodded grimly. "Yes, we have relocated to a manor not far from the village of St. Just. My father felt that the solitude of Cornwall would be a safe haven for us. Apparently we are a short carriage ride from one another."

Nadine's family had to be the branch of the family she had been asked to locate. Nadine's father was in trouble—he was being hunted by the Jacobins. Julianne was stricken.

"You seem surprised—no, distraught."

"I am happy to have new neighbors." She managed a smile, her mind spinning. She would tell Dominic immediately.

"Or perhaps I will call." Nadine seemed thoughtful. "If you do not mind?"

Julianne could think of nothing worse, but she somehow smiled. "That would be lovely." Clearly, Nadine meant to pry into her relationship with Dominic. Julianne wished she could defend herself and explain that she loved Dominic—that she had thought Nadine dead—but of course, she would never offer up any such defense. Somehow she said, "I am glad we had a chance to meet. But I am sorry, I must go. I am meeting my brother, Lucas, and I am very late."

"Mr. Greystone is in town?" Nadine asked with some surprise.

Julianne started. "Yes, he is. Do you know him?"

"I know him," Nadine said. "But not well. However, he and Jack Greystone saved my life on a beach not far from Brest."

Julianne stared, stunned. "Lucas and Jack helped you flee France?"

"Yes."

Julianne's mind was racing. Lucas had brought Dominic from France on Jack's sloop; he had done the same for Nadine. Was Jack also involved in the war, or was he just a smuggler as he and Lucas claimed?

Julianne realized that they were staring at one another, and she wondered what Nadine was thinking. "I am glad you got out of the country safely," she finally said.

"You sound as if you mean it," Nadine returned slowly.

"I do mean it."

Nadine's stare was piercing. "You are not, precisely, what I was expecting," she finally said. "Have you fallen in love with him?"

Julianne stiffened.

"I asked him the same question. He also refused to answer."

Julianne felt ill. Why hadn't Dominic answered?

"As impolitic as it is, I must be forthright now." Nadine's gaze had sharpened. "You are either smitten, or you are using him, Miss Greystone. I cannot decide which is the case."

Julianne paled. She refused to look at Lady Paget now. "I would not betray Dominic."

"I hope not," Nadine said.


JULIANNE POUNDED on the door of Warlock's Cavendish Square house, praying Lucas had returned to town. She was expecting a servant to open the door, and was stunned when Jack did so.

His gray gaze widened in surprise when he saw her— clearly, he hadn't known she was in town. "Julianne!" Then he grinned and pulled her into his embrace.

Julianne was distraught, but thrilled to see him. She clung to him briefly. Then she pulled away as they stepped inside; Jack was disheveled, his clothing stained, quite possibly with dried blood and gun powder.

"What are you doing in London, Julianne?"

"I have been taking a holiday," she said quickly. "Jack! Where on earth have you been all summer? And what has happened?"

"I have been making my fortune on this war," he said cheerfully. He closed the front door. "And it isn't an easy task, outrunning two navies. But what is upsetting you? You are very distressed."

She replayed the recent encounter with Nadine in her mind. But she had come to Cavendish Square to beg Lucas to help Tom escape a certain hanging.

"And why are you calling? If you are in town, aren't you staying here?" His gaze narrowed.

She refused to flush. "I am staying at Bedford House, where I am a guest."

"Since when do you move in such crowds?"

"Since I saved Bedford's life."

"Oh, ho. I smell a rat. What aren't you telling me?"

"Where is Lucas?" she cried. "I am desperate for his help—but you will do!"

"Thank you very much." Jack put his arm around her and steered her into the salon. "You know I will always help you."

"Thank God. Something terrible has happened, Jack. The convention in Edinburgh was raided and Tom was amongst those arrested."

"I actually heard about it. So Treyton was one of those arrested?" He did not seem disturbed by the news.

Julianne cried, "He will soon be charged with high treason! We have to help him. You have always liked Tom."

"No, actually, I have liked the fact that he is besotted with you, but I find him rather rabidly and boringly political."

"I am rabidly and boringly political!"

"You manage to be radical with charm. And you are my little sister." He winked.

"Will you help him?"

"Julianne, even if I agreed to help him, I do not have the power to get him freed." He was serious now, a rare moment.

She breathed hard. "Warlock does."

He started. "What makes you think that?"

"Isn't he your spymaster? Yours and Lucas's?"

"I beg your pardon?"

And she wondered if she should tell him about Warlock's awful attempt at blackmail. And she was afraid to do so. Jack would be furious, and he would tell Lucas. One or the other would confront Warlock. Jack would probably assault him. Warlock would, in the end, hurt

Tom. "I don't like Warlock and I don't think either of you should trust him."

"Lucas trusts him—therefore, so do I. But he isn't a spymaster!" He was amused. "He is a down-and-out gentleman with rotten manners and an equally rotten estate."

She bit her lip, giving that tangent up. "Very well. But I know what you are up to, Jack! So do not claim you are not involved in the war. First, you helped Dominic flee France, and you have also helped Nadine. I wonder how many other Frenchmen and women you have helped flee to this country. Do not claim that you are a mere smuggler now! You do have means!"

"How do you know about Lady D'Archand?"

"I just met her, moments ago. She mentioned that you saved her life."

"I could hardly allow her to be shot, Julianne."

They were off topic. "Will you help Tom or not?"

"I already told you, I do not have the means to help him."

"You and Lucas can do anything when you put your minds to it!"

Jack rolled his eyes. "So you are still fond of Tom?" he finally said.

He misunderstood. She didn't care. "Yes. Please, Jack, I am begging you."

He stared closely. "Why do I feel as if I am being played?"

"Promise me you will help Tom."

He studied her for a moment, then walked over to the sideboard with that rolling deck swagger he had. He poured a glass of Scotch whiskey and saluted her. "I am not promising any such thing. So, tell me about Bedford."

She felt like stomping her foot. "Bedford has nothing to do with this."

His stare hardened. "Tom is a leveler, Julianne."

She hadn't realized that Jack knew anything about those radicals. Clearly, he knew more about politics than he claimed. "He doesn't deserve to die."

"Probably not."

"So you will help him?"

He was serious now. "My instinct tells me to leave him exactly where he belongs, Julianne. But I will discuss the matter with Lucas."

She shuddered. Jack had changed. He was hard now, under the surface, as never before. But hadn't the war changed them all? And she knew Lucas would have little inclination to help Tom. "Fine," she said furiously. "But if you let him hang, I will never forgive you."

"Never is a very long time."

JULIANNE SLIPPED PAST the two liveried doormen, wondering if Dominic was home. It was the late afternoon, and she was ready to leap into his arms for comfort. Lucas would never agree to help Tom and Jack seemed as determinedly set against him. Could she simply let him hang? She did not think so.

If she were the one in jeopardy, Tom would do everything in his power to help her.

The house was quiet as the doormen let her inside. She hurried upstairs, heading directly to Dominic's rooms.

His suite was at the far end of the hall, past her bedchamber. As she approached, she heard voices coming from his rooms. She hesitated outside the sitting-room door, which was ajar, not wanting to intrude.

"That will be all, François," Lady Paget said pleasantly.

About to knock, she jerked back against the wall.

She so wanted to avoid the Dowager Countess! Was

Catherine telling Dominic about her horrid encounter with Nadine? Julianne did not move as the servant hurried out of the suite, wondering if she should knock anyway, or simply retreat. François glanced at her impassively. She smiled politely in return as Catherine's tone became strident.

"You are my son and you are being taken advantage of!"

Julianne inhaled—they were arguing about her.

"You are being unfair," Dominic said calmly. "And I do not appreciate your meddling in my private affairs."

"Surely you knew that Nadine would meet her sooner or later?"

"I was hoping to be present when introductions were made," he said, sounding annoyed.

"You can hardly introduce your mistress to your fiancée!" Catherine cried.

Julianne held her breath, afraid of what he might say. And he said, "Nadine and I are in agreement, as always. Neither one of us wishes to proceed with our engagement, much less a marriage."

Lady Paget gasped.

"I know you are disappointed. But I have no time for a wife now." He was final.

"Nadine is one of the most beautiful and intelligent women you know. You have been friends since childhood and you care deeply for one another—"

"I am not changing my mind."

"Julianne Greystone is a Jacobin! Yet you have ended it with Nadine because of her?"

"She is not the enemy. I am asking you to respect my affections, and give her a chance at obtaining yours."

There was absolute silence now. Julianne dared to peek into the chamber. Catherine was ashen, while Dominic wore a determined and authoritarian expression she knew well.

"What if she is a spy, sent here to destroy you?"

"I know what you have been through, so I cannot blame you for being afraid of Julianne. I also know you are worried about me. If you ever got past Julianne's politics, you would like her, very much. I am asking you to make such an attempt."

"But I can't get past her politics!"

"I know you will do as I have asked." He was firm. "Where is Jean? Who is François?"

His tone was so sharp that Julianne looked into the room again. Dominic's expression was one of displeasure.

"There was a death in his family," Lady Paget said. "Jean had to leave—he is returning to France as we speak. I was fortunate to find a new valet immediately. He comes highly recommended from Lord and Lady Frasier."

Dominic's reply was immediate. "Jean's mother died two years ago and he did not go home. The Frasiers are from the north, are they not? From the borders with Scotland?"

"Yes, they are," Lady Paget said, sounding puzzled.

"Get rid of him. He could be an agent, sent to spy upon us."

Julianne was aghast.

"But the Frasiers—"

He cut her off. "His recommendation could be fabricated and it would take weeks, or more, to find that out."

Lady Paget cried out. "God, Dominic, has it really come to this? We must fear spies in our own home? What were you really doing in France? Why did you leave?"

"You know I am not answering any of those questions. Simply get rid of François."

There was a silence and Julianne leaned her back against the wall, tears arising. This was her fault. She had not a doubt. If François was a French agent, sent to spy on Dominic, it was because she had betrayed him to Tom. She had never regretted anything she had ever done more. And now, she would have to make a confession. He had to know.

Footsteps sounded. Julianne cringed.

Lady Paget passed through the doorway, her face pale and pinched, and then she saw her. "You! How long have you been standing there?"

She trembled. "I came to see Dominic. I did not mean to eavesdrop but I did not want to intrude."

"I am praying you will not destroy my son!" Her green eyes flashing, Catherine lifted her skirts and strode down the corridor.

Dominic emerged from the room and he stared. "I take it you are looking for me?"

"Yes." She bit her lip and said, "I did not want to over-hear you. But I was even more afraid to encounter Lady Paget, so I hid."

He studied her, softening. "She has been a terrible ogre to you, hasn't she?"

Some relief arose. "I understand why she dislikes me."

He gestured and she walked into the blue-and-gold parlor. "But you are not spying on me."

She tensed. "No, I would never do such a thing."

He smiled briefly. "You met Nadine. How did it go?"

She inhaled. "She is a lovely woman, but it was hor-rible!"

He pulled her close. "I am sorry you are distraught."

"I feel as if we are cuckolding her."

"No. We are not betraying her. She is neither my fiancée nor my wife."

She searched his gaze, which was becoming warm. She dreaded telling him about Tom.

"Julianne?"

"Dominic, I am worried that the Comte D'Archand is in danger."

His expression changed. "How so?"

"I didn't realize Nadine's last name was D'Archand until I read her letter. I should have realized then that her family was the one Tom and I were asked to locate. But I thought it a common name. This morning I learned that her family settled in Cornwall and I knew that they must be those émigrés that Marcel is hunting for."

His eyes had widened. "I will warn them immediately." He released her, turning for the door.

There was some dismay. But of course he would rush out to warn the Comte of the danger he was in. She did not want to see any harm come to Nadine or her father. And what about her confession? Her heart was thundering now.

At the door, he paused. "Is there more?"

He was already suspicious of spies, so why did she have to really say anything? She somehow smiled. "Just… hurry home, Dominic."

His eyes darkened. "A command I can hardly disobey."

JULIANNE AWOKE, SMILING.

She sighed, aware that she was alone. Perhaps an hour ago, Dom had kissed her cheek and told her that he had to go. She sighed again. She was impossibly sated and she had slept deeply and dreamlessly, as if she had no worries. But as she opened her eyes, anxiety instantly stole over her.

She so hoped that she had not made a drastic mistake in not telling Dominic about her betraying him to Tom earlier in the summer. She prayed that there weren't any spies in his household. And now, she was going to have to do as Warlock had asked—she was going to have to spy on her friends for him.

The draperies in his bedroom were drawn, but some bright sunlight was slipping through the cracks. Julianne threw the covers aside and got up. As she did, she knocked something from the pillow beside her to the floor.

There was an envelope on the spare pillow, with her name boldly written upon it. She would recognize Dominic's handwriting anywhere. Her heart leapt and she glanced at the beautiful rug on the floor below the bed. She had knocked a blue velvet jeweler's box off the pillow!

What on earth…?

She jumped to the floor and retrieved the box, her heart racing wildly as she opened it.

She froze in disbelief. A stunning diamond bracelet glittered up at her.

*Dominic had given her diamonds.*

Tears arose.

She set it down on the bed and opened the envelope. A card was within. It read "Wear it well. Yours, Dominic."

IT WAS A BEAUTIFUL DAY to be out and about, Julianne thought as she sat in the back of a small curricle driven by one of Dominic's coachmen. She smiled and admired the bracelet on her right wrist. It glinted with fire as she held it up to the sun. Dominic had given her diamonds, and now, her worries seemed inconsequential. She was in love, her heart soaring impossibly, and maybe, just maybe, he felt as she did.

She was on her way to Hyde Park. Dominic had not been in when she had finally finished dressing and gone downstairs. She would have to thank him later.

Hyde Park was ahead. She had sent a note to Warlock requesting a meeting, but she had yet to hear back from him—giving her some relief and a small respite. She had impulsively decided to enjoy the day while she could. She had intended to walk, but Lady Paget had been on her way out at the same time as Julianne. She had insisted that she use the curricle.

Julianne's smile faded. When Lady Paget had walked into the entry tower, Julianne had been at the door. She hadn't even had to think about it—she had pulled her sleeve down over her bracelet, to hide it from the Dowager Countess. She could imagine how caustic Lady Paget would be when she realized what Dominic had done.

And then the Dowager Countess had mentioned that there would be guests for supper and the usual evening attire was required. Julianne had been stupefied. She had just been invited to Catherine's dinner party.

The curricle was moving through the imposing iron gates of the park's Knightsbridge entrance and Julianne leaned forward. "I am going to walk for a bit, Eddie."

The young coachman pulled the curricle over, as several carriages and gigs were on the path, halting it so she could alight. Julianne walked up to her driver. "You don't have to wait. It is a lovely afternoon and I am going to enjoy every moment of it."

"The Dowager Countess told me to wait, Miss Greystone," Eddie returned.

And Julianne found that odd, as well, but perhaps

Lady Paget was doing as her son had asked—perhaps she was trying to give Julianne a chance. She smiled at him and started down a nearby walking path. She was hardly alone. Several pairs of ladies were strolling, as were two couples and a gentleman.

It felt as if it were the most beautiful day she had ever witnessed.

She was smiling when she bumped into the gentleman. "Oh, I beg your pardon," Julianne cried, meeting a pair of pale blue eyes. She had been so distracted, and in such a reverie, that she had walked right into him.

"Are you all right…Miss Greystone?" he asked. He was tall, lanky, with almost white-blond hair and a large, crooked nose.

Perplexed, she met the gentleman's light blue gaze. "I am fine. Do I know you, sir?"

He slowly smiled, and it sent a chill down her spine. "No, but I know you and I thought you would you like to know how Tom Treyton is faring."

Her heart lurched. The force was sickening.

"There, there." He took her arm and wrapped it in his. "I did not mean to startle you, Miss Greystone."

"Who are you? We have not met, I am certain." She tried to tug her arm free but he would not allow her to do so, and she was truly alarmed.

"You may call me Marcel."

She inhaled, seized with fear. *Marcel was Tom's Jacobin contact in Paris.* But this man was English. Still, surely this was not a coincidence. "What do you want?"

His smile was cold. "I want to help you. And you want to help Tom."

An Englishman in the heart of London was working for the French government. "Of course I want to help Tom. How is he? Has he been charged yet?"

"He will be charged with treason by the end of the week, Miss Greystone."

Her heart now sank with equally sickening force. Was this even true? Warlock had never said any such thing. "What do you want of me?"

"I am someone who can help your friend—if you help me."

With dread, she asked, "How can I possibly help you?"

His smile vanished. "There are plans to resupply the La Vendée royalists. I must know them."

"I can hardly help you!"

"Bedford has those plans, my dear. And we both know you have the best chance of discovering them."

Horror began. He wanted her to spy on Dominic?

"Bedford is returning to France shortly," Marcel said bluntly. "I must know the date of the convoy's rendezvous with the royalists, and the exact location before he leaves and takes that information with him."

Julianne was in more shock. Dominic was returning to France? She did not believe it!

He added, "I believe he is leaving within the week, so you must work swiftly. And of course, you may feel free to convey any other useful information you come across that will help us in our efforts to win this war against the revolution."

She would never spy on Dominic! She knew her cheeks were red, for they were burning. "I don't know what you are talking about."

He slowly smiled. "We both know that he is a British agent, Miss Greystone, and that you are a Jacobin— an active one. We both know you are sharing his bed. It shouldn't be terribly difficult for you to go through his desk and his personal effects, to find what we are looking for. And if that search does not yield the information we need, I am sure you can cajole the information directly from him."

She could not breathe now. "I will not spy on him."

"Then Treyton will hang—and I will make sure he is the first of the three hundred to swing." His pale blue gaze burned.

She cried out. Her frenzied mind raced. She would work for Warlock to avoid spying on Dominic. She would tell her uncle everything. Surely, he would protect Tom.

As if he could read her very thoughts, the man said, "You will not tell anyone of this conversation, Miss Greystone. Not your lover, not your brother and not your uncle. I can make your life very difficult—and I can easily do the same for Treyton."

She stared at him, thinking. If she learned who he really was, Warlock or Lucas or Dominic could arrest him.

"Think of it this way, Miss Greystone. We are already watching Bedford night and day, thanks to you. What is one more betrayal?"

"You bastard," she said.

"You are aiding a great cause, which you are devoted to, and you will prevent your dear friend from hanging. Well? Have I convinced you to aid *La Republique?*"

She nodded, praying he would not discern that she was lying.

His eyes narrowed. "Time is not on our side. I will contact you again in two days. Make sure you have something for me."

She did not move. She had to find out where he could be reached. "What if I can obtain the information sooner? How can I reach you?"

He slowly smiled. "You can't."

She inhaled, stricken. How could she turn him in to

Dominic, if they couldn't find him to arrest him? "If you hurt Tom in any way, I will not help you."

"Oh, you will do exactly as I have said. Aren't there two helpless women living at Greystone Manor?"

She froze.

"Isn't your mother an invalid? And your dear sister—what is her name? Oh, yes, it is Amelia. She is the older one, is she not? A committed spinster? It amazes me that two women would reside by themselves in such a remote location. If there were a problem, oh, say a fire in the house, or the advent of outlaws and thieves, or even an abduction, there isn't a single neighbor for them to turn to. I cannot comprehend leaving two women alone to fend for themselves in such a dangerous time."

"Are you threatening my sister and my mother?" Julianne managed.

"Yes, I am. If you do not do exactly as I say, one or both women will suffer the consequences. And if you need proof, I can dispatch my men to make an example of your mother. Just so you know that I am very serious, indeed."

Julianne cried out. She said hoarsely, "Do not hurt them. I will do what you want."

"Have a good day, Miss Greystone," he said. He bowed and walked away.

Julianne watched him go, beyond fear.

# CHAPTER FIFTEEN

JULIANNE STARED AT THE dark, empty hearth in the fireplace, seated upon a chaise in her bedchamber. It was several hours later, and Julianne had spent the afternoon in a state of horror. There was a French agent in Britain, and he wanted her to spy on Dominic. And now, Tom's fate did not hang alone in the balance. If she did not obey, he would hurt her mother or Amelia.

This was far worse than what Warlock had demanded of her. She did not know what to do. Her first impulse had been to write Amelia and warn her of the danger, but she was certain she was being watched—after all, Marcel was spying on Dominic. Such an exercise would be futile; her letter would be intercepted. And she did not want to anger Marcel.

She didn't dare go to Warlock, Lucas, Jack or Dom. They wouldn't be able to act decisively against him because she had no way of directing them to him.

She felt the tears arise. She was in over her head and she knew it!

She was going to have to spy on Dominic, she thought with a shrinking sensation, to protect her mother and her sister.

"Good afternoon."

Julianne flinched, not having heard Dominic open the door to her bedroom. She quickly rearranged her expression and smiled at him, getting to her feet.

"Is something wrong?" he asked, his smile fading.

Her instinct was to tell Dominic everything—because Marcel was Dominic's enemy, he meant him harm, and Dominic was unaware of it.

But she couldn't say anything. And while she might hurt the rebellion in La Vendée, she wasn't directly hurting Dominic, while she was protecting Amelia and her mother. She was even helping Tom.

"I love my bracelet," she whispered.

"Is that why you are crying?" Perplexed, he walked over to her.

She nodded, the tears swiftly rising. She was ready to weep in his arms.

"You are so upset," Dominic exclaimed, taking her into his embrace.

Julianne clung to him. "I love you," she whispered, against his chest.

He drew back, surprised.

She stared up at him, having no intention of retracting her words.

"What happened, Julianne?" he asked quietly.

"You gave me diamonds!" she cried, smiling through her tears. "I am undone."

He smiled back, but she saw that he remained confused. "You have asked me if I care, and I wanted to make an unequivocal statement."

She slipped free of his embrace and walked away to find her composure. If she did not, he would realize something was truly amiss.

He said softly, "I just spoke with D'Archand."

She whirled in surprise.

He smiled a little. "It actually went very well. He was not surprised, and as Nadine and I have mutually agreed to end things, he was amicable."

*His engagement was officially over.* But did it even matter now? For suddenly she realized that if Dominic ever found out what she was about to do, he would never speak with her again. And then there was the terrible fact that he was returning to France—to the war and revolution there. "Did you warn him last night about Marcel?"

"Yes, I did. What is really bothering you, Julianne?"

He was so astute, she thought nervously, she had to be careful. He must never learn that she had spied upon him, if she managed to succeed in such an attempt. So she smiled at him, sliding her hands up to his shoulders. "I want to thank you for the diamond bracelet," she murmured, and she kissed him.

He started as she feathered his mouth with her own, and then he kissed her back. Within moments, their mouths were fused, and his hands were roaming down her back. Julianne let her mind go blank. God, she had never needed him more. She had never loved him more.

He broke the heated kiss. "If I did not know better, I'd think you were attempting to distract me."

She breathed, "Make love to me."

His eyes widened. "We are due downstairs in two hours—"

"I don't care."

His eyes blazed, and suddenly she was in his arms, and he was carrying her to the canopied bed. As he laid her down, he said, "There is something I must say first."

She clasped his jaw. "Then hurry and speak your mind."

"Eager wench!" But his smile faded. He sat down by her hip. "Julianne...I love you, too."

JULIANNE HESITATED on the bottom of the stairs. She could hear animated conversation, the strains of a harp and the tinkling of glass. Her heart was thundering now.

A mirror was across the hall and she was reflected in it. She didn't even recognize the woman reflected there. She was staring at a pale, elegant stranger.

Dominic had sent her a stunning ensemble for the occasion: a silver silk evening gown, with cap sleeves, a low-cut bodice and full, draped skirts. It was lavishly embroidered and intricately beaded, the underskirts darker, and beaded with ebony stones. She also wore a magnificent ruby-red wig adorned with lace and pearls. She had never been so exquisitely and expensively dressed before, and she doubted she would ever be as well dressed again.

He loved her and he trusted her. She was about to violate that love, that trust.

Julianne could see into the grand salon. It was exactly as she had imagined, with its gilded furniture, its crystal chandeliers and its masterpieces. Now, it was filled with guests as elegantly dressed as she was. She saw Lady Paget, who was wearing crimson, and a dozen other ladies in their jewels and evening gowns. The gentlemen were all wearing their finest evening coats, satin breeches, silk stockings and buckled shoes. Most of the men wore white, powdered wigs.

She saw Dominic.

Her heart lurched hard, first with love and then with dread. If he ever learned of her actions, he would never forgive her.

He was wearing an embroidered navy blue velvet coat, French lace cuffs spilling from its sleeves and cascading from its collar. He also wore tan satin breeches and beige stockings. His wig matched his own hair color exactly. He had never seemed as elegant, as noble or as magnificent. She loved him so completely, exactly as he was, and she could not imagine him as anyone other than Bedford or anything other than a Tory.

*He is not for you... Trust me on that....*

She did not want to recall Lucas's words, but he was right, even more so than he had imagined. She started forward. Then she faltered. Nadine stood with Dominic and they were chatting.

Dismay arose. She did not fight it. Nadine was a warm, generous and beautiful woman, and she was an aristocrat. They cared deeply for one another, and they were perfect for one another— Nadine would never spy on him. In that moment, Julianne felt as if she had a crystal ball and could see directly into it.

Dominic would learn of her treachery one day—and he would turn to the other woman. He would marry Nadine after all, and live happily ever after....

Dominic had seen her. His eyes widened and he started across the salon, smiling. Somehow, Julianne managed to smile back.

Dominic surprised her by taking her hand and kissing it warmly. "Why are you standing out here? I didn't see you."

He had never openly displayed his affection before. "I am sorry that I am late."

"I'm not. You have never been lovelier. I must take you to more supper parties."

She met his warm gaze and realized she wished for nothing more. How she wished there was no damn war, how she wished for an ordinary life. "I am certain that can be arranged," she managed, an impossible lie.

"You aren't wearing the bracelet," he said.

"How can I? If anyone sees it, he or she will know it was a gift from you, and there will be one conclusion to draw."

"That I am smitten?" He smiled.

She felt her heart racing. "That I am ruined."

"You happen to be right. I will get you something more discreet," he said, taking her arm in his.

He meant it, she realized with more dismay.

"Shall I introduce you around? It is my pleasure to do so." His smile faded. "We are being remarked."

Julianne felt her heart slam. Warlock stood with a dark, attractive, resplendently dressed man, and both men were staring at her. "Warlock is here." Terrible tension arose, but then, he had said in his note that he would speak to her that night. "And who is that?"

"He is with Nadine's father, the Comte D'Archand," he said. "Are you all right? You seem on edge."

"I am fine." And as she spoke, she saw Nadine detaching herself from her group to approach, a pleasant smile on her face. Julianne could not imagine a conversation with her now, but Nadine paused before them.

"Good evening, Miss Greystone. You are certainly the most beautiful woman here tonight."

Surprised, Julianne started. The compliment seemed genuine. "Thank you, but I doubt that. It is a splendid assembly, is it not?" she tried, desperate to make small talk.

Nadine lay her gloved hand on Julianne's arm. "I did not come over to distress you."

"I am fine," she said, for the second time. If she did not find her composure, she would have to plead a migraine and leave. As if sensing her vulnerability, Dominic lay his hand on her shoulder. She leaned back, against him.

"Nor did I come over to casually converse. I want to thank you for warning my family of the danger we are in," Nadine said, her gaze direct and searching.

Julianne glanced at Dominic. "You told her?"

"Yes, I did."

Nadine took her hand. "I owe you, Miss Greystone, and apparently, I have misjudged you."

Feeling ill, she said, "You hardly owe me."

Nadine said simply, "I always pay my debts." She smiled at them both and moved on.

"I knew you would both, eventually, begin to like one another," Dominic said, sounding pleased.

Before she could respond, she realized that Lady Paget was approaching. Julianne fixed a smile on her face.

The Dowager Countess smiled back. "Good evening, Miss Greystone. I am so delighted you have joined us. Your gown is simply stunning—it suits you."

Julianne was incredulous.

"I MUST SAY, JULIANNE, I am intrigued." Sebastian Warlock sauntered into the music room, where Julianne was waiting for him.

It was half past eleven in the evening now. Supper had been interminable, as it consisted of a dozen courses. Tension filled her now as Julianne followed him inside. "Maybe we should close the door, so no one notices us?"

"That is not a good idea," he said casually. "If we were found behind closed doors, people would jump to the wrong conclusions."

"They would think we are carrying on? You are my uncle!"

"I doubt they would think we are carrying on—but they might wonder at what business we are concluding. Play for me," he said, smiling.

He was so very clever, she thought, staring at him.

"Your feelings are written all over your face, my sweet little niece."

Then he knew she despised him, she thought, sitting

down on the piano bench. "I have warned Jack about you."

A dark brow arose. "Really? I like Jack and I am very fond of Lucas. They both like me. I imagine he dismissed your warnings as mere ranting."

"One day, they will both realize that you are an amoral, self-serving bastard."

"Oh, ho! You have a way with words, which I admire. And what a temper! But I am not surprised. Your mother had a temper, too."

She stared in surprise. "My mother?" Her mother was the mildest mannered person she knew.

"Yes, she did, but that was long ago, when she was a spoiled debutante, accustomed to always having her way." He pulled a music chair over and sat on it. "Do you play?"

"I haven't played in years." She posed her hands over the keyboard, her heart racing. How dare he speak of her mother that way. "You never visit her."

"She doesn't remember me."

Julianne struck a chord, rather rudely. He winced. "You should visit her—you should visit Amelia. She is your *other* niece." She began playing a sonata by Handel, surprised that she still knew it by heart.

She was so worried, but the music swept her away. It flooded every part of her being, filling her as water did an urn. It had been so long....

As the rich chords vibrated, he said, "I take it you have agreed to my proposal?"

"I am still considering it." She swept her hands up and down the keys, breathless now, as he started in displeasure. Feeling a sense of satisfaction, she ended with a series of deeper, powerful chords, which resonated through the room.

Warlock seized her right wrist abruptly. "I beg your pardon?"

She slowly looked up at him. "You must do something for me first."

"What courageous ploy is this?"

She shook off his hand and stood. "Free Tom and I will then spy on whomever you want."

She was lying through her teeth. She doubted he would agree. But if he did, she would have one less pawn to worry about.

"Like hell," he said softly, staring coldly now.

She felt some alarm, then.

"What is going on in here?" Dominic strode into the room, his expression as dark as a thundercloud. Then he turned back and slammed the door closed.

"Julianne is playing for me," Warlock said amiably.

Dominic's dark stare was murderous. If looks could kill, Warlock would keel over. "Leave us, Warlock. And I will deal with you in another moment."

Warlock was amused. "Such an attachment."

Dominic gestured at the closed door. Warlock smiled at Julianne. "I look forward to seeing you again, Julianne. It has been a pleasure."

She watched him leave, filled with relief that the encounter was over.

Dominic strode to her. "What were you discussing?"

There was no point in lying. "We were discussing Tom."

"Treyton has gotten what he deserves."

"Prisons are dangerous places," Julianne said, returning his stare.

"I am not intervening on his behalf." He was firm. "You are not becoming involved in these spy games, Julianne. I won't have it. I want your word."

She bit her lip and nodded. "I don't want to play spy games," she said, and it was the truth.

"Good." He pulled her close. "The last guests are leaving," he said softly.

Julianne could not wait to leap into his arms.

BRIGHT SUNLIGHT POUNDED at her eyelids. Julianne awoke and realized that a maid was opening the draperies in Dominic's bedroom. For one sleepy moment, she smiled, thinking about Dominic's lovemaking—and his love. Then she recalled what she had to do.

Tugging the covers up, she sat, her stomach churning with dread. She reminded herself that there was no choice. Momma's and Amelia's safety—perhaps even their lives—were at stake.

Her stomach roiled.

She fought the nausea.

The last of the draperies were now open. Bright sunlight filled the room. "I have brought you *le petit déjeuner, mademoiselle*." Nancy smiled at her. "His lordship left at nine this morning, and he told me to do so at ten."

Julianne couldn't smile back at her.

"*Mademoiselle?* Are you unwell?"

Julianne cried out, leaping from the bed and racing for the chamber pot. There, she vomited violently.

When she was finished, Nancy slid her caftan over her naked body. Julianne trembled, the nausea gone. She slowly stood up, with Nancy's help. Her gaze met the concerned housemaid's.

"Are you better now?" Nancy asked softly.

What explanation could she make for having been so sick? Julianne wondered. She smiled at Nancy. "I haven't been feeling well, these past few days," she said, and as she spoke, she realized it was the truth. She had been sleeping late frequently and awaking still tired, if not exhausted. At times, she was ravenous. At other times, she was queasy. And her fear and anxiety were now truly making her ill. Her head ached constantly.

"I think I have a bit of the flux," she said. But she knew that was not why she had vomited.

Nancy hid an odd smile, looking away. "Some toast will help."

And Julianne wondered if the French maid had realized that she was carrying Dominic's child. "Yes, I am sure it will."

Julianne smiled at her and went to brush her teeth. How much worse could it be? she wondered. She was thrilled to be pregnant—if she was, indeed, with child. But bringing Dominic's child into the world now, when she had to betray him, seemed like a travesty.

She finished her morning ablutions and lingered in the bathing room, listening to the maid as she made up the bed. Finally, Nancy departed.

Her heart thundering, Julianne left the closet. Hating what she was about to do, she walked over to his bedroom door, wishing she could lock it and knowing she must not. Instead, she listened to any sounds that might be coming from the hallway. There were none.

Fairly confident that no one was outside, she opened the door very slightly and peeked into the hall. It was empty.

Moving swiftly now, she shut the door and hurried over to Dominic's *secrétaire*. The lower right-hand drawer remained locked. Where would he hide the key?

She sat down at the desk and rapidly went through the other drawers. She found many items, but not a key.

So she sat in his chair, turned to face the door and began thinking.

Her mind leapt to life. Hadn't she seen him at his bookcase several times, first thing in the morning, when she first awoke? And it was always in the same place. Didn't he often go to his desk to make notes or write letters after lovemaking, while she fell asleep? And now, she thought she recalled seeing him at his bookcase—in that identical location, not far from the catty-corner window.

She looked at the wall of books. What better place to hide a key?

She got up and went to the area she had seen him standing at and began going through books on the uppermost shelves, certain she had seen him returning a book to the second or third topmost one.

Ten minutes later, a small brass key fell out of a volume of poetry.

Julianne stared down at the floor, her heart thundering so loudly. She could hear it and it sounded like a drum. She laid the book horizontally on top of several vertically stacked books, and slowly bent and retrieved the key.

She was going to be ill again, she thought.

Glancing at the closed door, she hurried to the *secrétaire*. She unlocked the drawer and opened it and sat down.

There were some scribbled notes within. His cursive was indecipherable —and she was relieved. But there was also a sketch and an unfinished letter.

Julianne cursed.

The sketch was of a coastline. There were several marks, but no place names. It didn't matter. She was fairly certain she recognized the coastline with its jutting left-and right-hand peninsulas. He had drawn the coasts of Brittany and Normandy. The starred area looked to be in the middle of the two.

She was sicker now, but she committed the sketch to memory. Then she picked up the letter. He was writing to someone she did not know.

My dear Henri
Thank you for your letter. I am always glad to be kept abreast of all affairs at the Chateau. Please begin the harvest on the second week of October, as I have determined that is the best time to pick the grapes, assuring us of the best fruit. My agents will arrive in Granville to inspect the season's yield, and discuss various prices with you, once its quality is assured. Should there be any delay due to the difficulties inherent in these conflicted times, I will inform you posthaste.
Sincerely,
Dominic Paget

Was he writing his agent at a vineyard on one of his estates, or was the entire letter in code? Would he really care about a harvest now—about the price of wine? On the one hand, she dearly hoped she had found nothing but strange sketches. On the other, she prayed Marcel would be pleased.

Julianne replaced the notes, the sketch and letter, locked the drawer and put the key back in the book.

And in despair, she thought, how easy that had been.

"YOU SEEM DISTRAUGHT." Warlock slowly stood up from the club chair he was seated in.

It was five in the afternoon and Dominic was on time for their meeting. This particular gentleman's club was dark and dreary, the wood-paneled walls almost black, the rugs dark red, the furnishings as grim. Various groups of gentlemen were seated about the room, some reading, others with drinks or in muted conversation. It was the first time they had met here. No one looked at Warlock, but several gentlemen saw Dominic and tried to catch his eye.

He ignored everyone. Julianne had been acting oddly for the past few days and he could not imagine what was bothering her. He felt that it had to be far more than the jeopardy Tom Treyton was in.

Their relationship was progressing so swiftly now and he was stunned by the extent of his feelings for her, and the new nature of the intimacy they were sharing. Even their lovemaking had changed. But she was upset, and so was he, but for his own reasons. He hated the notion of returning to France, yet knew he had to do so. But it was almost as if he was suddenly torn between staying with her and fighting for his country.

Warlock had been alone with a brandy and a news-paper. He gestured at an adjacent leather chair, the arms terribly worn. "If you remain angry with me for speaking with Julianne last night, you should be pleased to know that she hasn't agreed to anything."

Dominic sat abruptly. "Leave her out of your damned spy games—if you want my help."

Warlock started. "You are in love!"

"Perhaps I am. Either way, I suggest you leave Julianne alone." He snapped his fingers at a passing servant, vastly annoyed now. Dominic ordered a scotch.

"You are threatening me?" Warlock was amused. "I know you better than you know yourself. No matter how attached you have become, you would never turn your back on La Vendée."

Warlock was right. He was in love but he had no intention of reneging on his commitments, or failing in his patriotic duty. He leaned forward. "Just leave her out of this damned war. Have you heard anything new from Windham?"

Warlock said, very softly, "There is a mole in the Admiralty."

That hadn't been what he had been asking. Dominic stiffened, shocked. "You must know who it is—or be on the verge of finding out. Otherwise, you would not be in such good spirits."

"It is one of Windham's clerks," Warlock said, now grinning.

Dominic almost choked. A French agent was inside the War Office, clerking for the war secretary? He was in disbelief.

"I do not yet know who he is—but I am on his trail, and I will soon find out."

Dominic knew Warlock well, too. "Now I see why you are in such good humor. You will leave him in place and play cat-and-mouse with him."

Warlock saluted him with his glass. "Oh, yes. When the time is right, we will feed him false information. Eventually, I will uncover and unravel his entire network."

He loved this war, Dominic thought grimly. But someone had to do what Warlock did.

Sebastian reached into his breast pocket and handed Dominic a sealed letter.

He instantly recognized Michel's handwriting. Warlock said, "I also received a missive from Jacquelyn. The French soldiers who were defeated and imprisoned at Mainz have been released. They have been redeployed—and are marching on the La Vendée rebels in le Loire."

His heart lurched hard. The focus of operations on the Rhine front had been the city of Mainz, which had been besieged by the allies last March.

Dominic ripped open Michel's letter and began reading it. As he had thought, the rebels were starving and severely lacking in munitions and arms. And Jacquelyn knew that the troops released from Mainz were marching toward them—he was begging for immediate aid.

And as he read Michel's letter, his insides roiled. He was going back to war, anarchy and revolution... He wasn't sure if he would survive this time. And for the first time, he was thinking not of his life, but of his sanity. "Is Windham considering moving up the dates for the supply convoy?" he finally asked.

"No."

He would send the letter he had just written by courier tomorrow at dawn, he thought grimly. Michel would not be pleased to learn that the rendezvous with the supply convoy would not take place for another six weeks—in mid-October.

"I have arranged passage for you on the seventh at dawn," Warlock said.

Dominic started. He would return to France in four more days! His respite was *over*.

"You will go directly to Nantes, meet with Jacquelyn and assess the situation. Stay out of combat. Report back to me immediately. Maybe your firsthand account of the situation will change Windham's mind."

He was suddenly furious and he threw the letter at Warlock's chest. "It is all in there. They are starving. They have few arms. There are no munitions. *That* is my report!"

"We estimate that the French troops will be within striking range in another week," Warlock said calmly, taking the letter and laying it aside. "And I mean it, Paget. You are too valuable—do not even think of joining in any battle."

He knew he would never stand back on the sidelines, like a coward, while his people went to war. But now it truly began to sink in. He was leaving in days.

What about Julianne?

And something within his heart twisted. It hurt. Strangely, he did not want to leave her.

In that moment, he knew he must make provisions for her. She could hardly return to Cornwall, and live at Greystone manor in the impoverished straits she was accustomed to. He would instruct Catherine to allow her to reside at Bedford House; he could even bring her sister and mother to town for companionship, if Julianne wished. But then what? He could not ask her to wait for him. It wasn't fair.

He stood abruptly. He wasn't going to linger with War- lock. He would take Julianne to the opera tonight, or the theatre or anything that he could find that would enter- tain her. Tomorrow he would send for a modiste. He had been meaning to do so for some time. And he would buy her some bauble that she could wear on a daily basis, some small pendant or cameo that was discreet.

"I have to go," he said. In fact, he would stop at the jeweler's on his way home.

Warlock shook his head.

HYDE PARK WAS DESERTED at this early evening hour. It was 6:00 p.m.

The past hours had been agonizing, as she waited to hear from Marcel. Dominic had taken her to Vauxhall last night, and then they had dined in his rooms by can- dlelight. That morning he had summoned a modiste to

her chamber—and ordered her an entire wardrobe! Then
he had taken her to the British Museum, where they had
spent the afternoon. Julianne had been torn between joy
and despair; his affection had never been more obvious but she had remained sick with worry over what she
must do.

She did not know why Dominic had become so intent.
She suspected he had become as aware of the ticking
clock as she was. He had not yet mentioned that he would
return to France, but he was behaving as if their time
were running out.

Now Julianne paced, not far from a carriage path,
filled with fear, anxiety and dread.

How could she betray Dominic this way? How could
she not? Even if Dominic hadn't warned her how dangerous playing spy games were, she would be afraid. Marcel
seemed ruthless.

Julianne continued to pace. Images of the wonderful
evening they had shared last night haunted her: Dom's
smile as he watched her watching the musicians on the
stage, his warm gaze as he regarded her across the supper
table, his smoldering regard and tender smile as he moved
over her, later, in bed. Dom, tossing aside swatches of
fabric and pieces of fur, accepting this and refusing that
in her chamber, as she simply gaped helplessly at him
and the modiste. Strolling though the museum, hand in
hand, with other museum-goers turning to stare at them.

Julianne could hardly think at all. Her life was in a
shambles.

A curricle was coming up the path from Park Lane.
She became still, clutching a small reticule tightly, her
heart thundering within her chest. She was almost certain
that Marcel would be inside. She was filled with dread.

It slowed as it approached. Julianne walked toward

the carriage path and halted beside it. The curricle finally came up to her, and the bay in its traces was halted. Marcel smiled at her, touching the brim of his top hat.

Julianne did not smile back. "You are despicable."

"What do you have for me?"

She reached into her pocket and handed him the sketch of Dominic's map, which she had made from memory, and the notes she had made from his letter.

He looked at both pieces of vellum. His eyes widened. "Where did you get these?"

"The original sketch is locked in his drawer, as is the letter. I memorized both. I have done my part. I want your word that you will leave my sister and my mother alone."

"And why would I do that, when you have just proven how very useful you can be to me? Your brother Lucas is on his way to France. I believe he is on his way to Le Havre. Find out exactly when he is leaving—the time and place of departure—and where he intends to disembark."

She gasped. Now he wanted her to spy on Lucas? "You bastard! You lied! I won't do it!"

"If you do not, I imagine your poor mother might fall down the stairs and break her neck." He smiled, but his pale eyes remained cold. "You belong to me now, Julianne."

IT WAS ALMOST EIGHT O'CLOCK and Dominic was not yet home. Julianne paced in the salon just off the entry tower, as the soft gray shadows of twilight filtered into the room. She was so sickened by what had happened that she had actually vomited upon coming home. This time, she knew her illness had nothing to do with the pregnancy.

Did she dare tell Dominic about Marcel? She could

hardly continue on this way. But if she told him, she would have to tell him *everything*.

She heard a movement by the salon's threshold and she paused, whirling. Lady Paget stood there, appearing cautiously concerned. "Is everything all right?"

Julianne hugged herself. Catherine had been polite and even pleasant to her since the day of her supper party. Was she in the other woman's good graces? If she told Dominic about Marcel, she had little doubt Catherine would learn of her treachery and hate her all over again.

It occurred to her that Catherine did not know that Dominic meant to soon return to France. She knew Lady Paget well enough now to know that she was fiery and temperamental—not one to hide her feelings. If she knew, she would be distraught.

"It's late. I am waiting for Dominic."

"I am holding supper for all of us," Catherine said, surprising Julianne. They had yet to dine together as a threesome. "He sent word he would be a bit late."

Suddenly she glimpsed movement outside the windows, which looked onto the front drive. Julianne turned and saw Dominic's huge black-lacquer coach in the driveway. A liveried footman was preparing to open the door.

Oddly relieved, Julianne smiled at Lady Paget and went from the salon and into the entry tower. Catherine followed. The front door was already open, and she hurried across the hall. Outside, the skies were growing darker, and were stained red.

Dominic stepped down from the coach.

Julianne paused by the front door, Catherine beside her, biting her lip. Approaching the wide stone front steps, Dominic smiled up at her.

And then she saw, from the corner of her eye, someone crossing the drive, as if coming from the stables. He was not far behind Dominic. He must have heard the man, because Dominic glanced behind him and he started. Catherine said, "What is François doing here?"

Puzzled, Julianne looked back at the approaching servant—and saw him raise a pistol and point it at Dominic.

Dominic dove to the ground as the pistol was fired, the sound of the ball's explosion deafening.

Julianne screamed.

François dropped the pistol and turned and ran.

Dominic leapt up and began running after him. His coachmen and footmen also set chase.

Julianne lifted her skirts and rushed down the steps, Catherine ahead of her. François was ahead of Dom and his men, already on the lawns, and she didn't know if they could catch up. But even as she watched the chase, he tripped and fell.

An instant later, Dominic leapt upon him.

Julianne ran up to them. Straddling François, Dominic demanded, "Who sent you?"

Panting, Julianne stumbled and stopped.

*Marcel had done this.*

François spit at him. "Pig! You feed upon the poor. You get fat and we suffer. I will never tell you who sent me. Swine!"

Dominic smiled savagely and slammed his fist into the man's nose. Blood spurted. "Who sent you? Tell me, or I will take a club to your knees."

François spit in his face again.

Dominic dragged him to his feet, his eyes ablaze with fury. "Get me a club, Eddie. Iron will do."

Julianne inhaled. "Dominic."

He turned to look at her. "Go into the house, Julianne. You, too, Mother."

Julianne didn't move. Her ears rang. She felt faint. In

fact, she felt as if she had stepped outside herself, and was about to observe a terrible scene. "I know who sent him. It was Marcel."

Dominic released François and stared incredulously at her.

"What did she say?" Catherine cried as Eddie and one of the footmen seized François.

Julianne stared in dread at Dominic as he stared back at her, his expression stark. He stepped over to her and spoke. His voice was calm. "Marcel is the Jacobin who wrote to you and Treyton."

She wet her lips. "Yes."

"And why do you think Marcel sent this assassin?"

She trembled. "Because I told Tom just after you left Greystone Manor who you were—and he told Marcel."

Dominic did not move.

"Oh my God, I was right," Catherine whispered in horror.

He said slowly, his gaze unwavering upon her, "That was well over a month ago."

"Yes," Julianne said. She had to tell him the rest, but she was paralyzed.

"She has met with a man twice this week, in the park!" Catherine cried.

Now Julianne knew why the coachman had been told to drive her, and wait for her. He had been spying on her.

Dominic never glanced at his mother. "Who did you meet in the park?"

The tears came swiftly then. "Marcel."

His eyes widened.

"He threatened Amelia and my mother. He meant it! I had no choice, Dominic. Please try to understand!" But even as she begged him, she knew her pleas would fall on deaf ears.

His face had hardened, but a look of anguish and revulsion was in his eyes. "What did you do?" He never raised or changed his tone.

"I went through the locked drawer in your desk."

He slowly nodded. "And you gave Marcel my notes, my map, the letter?"

"No." She wet her lips. "I memorized the map and the letter and conveyed the contents to him."

He shook with emotion.

"I love you," Julianne cried desperately, "but I had no choice!"

"Where is Marcel now?"

"I don't know—he contacts me," she exclaimed.

A terrible silence fell.

Dominic stared at the lawn beneath his feet, as if thinking. Julianne watched him and could not breathe. Then he looked up and said, "Mother, send for Warlock." He turned. "Eddie, bind François, put him in the library and have him guarded. Arm yourself." Then he looked at Julianne.

She cringed.

"You are no longer welcome here."

# *CHAPTER SIXTEEN*

JULIANNE FOLLOWED DOMINIC, his mother and the servants into the house, trailing behind them in a state of shock. It was over, she somehow thought. A doorman closed the front door behind her, she halted. Now what? She did not have a clue as to what to do or where to go.

Catherine hurried away, obviously intending to summon Warlock. Eddie and the footman were dragging François down the corridor, toward the library. Dominic never broke stride, and he vanished into the grand salon, closing both doors behind him. He hadn't looked back, and Julianne was left standing alone in the tower room.

She realized she was shaking like a leaf. She felt as if she had ceased to exist for everyone in the house.

She stared at the closed doors of the salon. That morning, she had been in Dominic's arms. Now, she was afraid to attempt to speak with him.

How would she manage to live without him?

But hadn't she known that this was the price that she would pay for her treachery?

She closed her eyes tightly, recalling his impassive expression a moment ago. He had to be hurt now—he had to be enraged.

And it was entirely her fault that he had almost been murdered. She almost despised herself.

She fought for courage and walked over to the salon, and opened one door.

He was standing by the sideboard, a drink in hand. His tone remained impossibly emotionless. "I would not come in, if I were you."

"I had to protect them," she said.

He turned his back to her, drinking from his glass.

Julianne shut the door and fled up the stairs to her room. There, she collapsed on the bed, weeping. She knew how disciplined he was. Once his mind was made up, it could not be changed. He had cut her out of his heart and his life, she was certain.

She did not know for how long she cried, but eventually she lay still and stared up at the mauve-and-white ceiling. She had never felt as drained.

So many memories whirled, and in all of them, she was with Dom, and he was as in love with her as she was with him.

Helplessly—hopelessly—she indulged herself in them.

A knock sounded on her door.

Julianne sat up, and was disappointed when Nancy walked into the room. "I do not wish to be disturbed," she said hoarsely.

The little maid was grim. "I am sorry, *mademoiselle,* but I have been told to help you pack your things. His lordship has a coach waiting." But she handed her a handkerchief.

Julianne trembled. He was sending her away that very night. Of course he was. Her shattered heart broke all over again.

Nancy shrugged helplessly, and then she whispered, "What could you have done, to make him send you away? He was so in love with you, *mademoiselle!*"

She hugged herself. "I betrayed him, Nancy."

The maid's eyes widened.

Julianne sat on the edge of the bed, trying to think,

when she was dazed and exhausted and grief stricken. He had a coach waiting. She did not have the strength, the will or the courage to attempt to stay in his house, if he was intent on tossing her out. And why would she stay? It was over now. She suddenly wondered if her brothers were at Cavendish Square. She would tell them everything! She so needed Lucas or Jack, so she could cry on their strong shoulders.

She felt as if she were in a nightmare. That morning, he had loved her; now, he despised her and wanted her gone.

"We should start packing," Julianne said, the decision to leave made. But the moment she stood up, the floor shifted and the walls turned and she knew she was so exhausted she was about to faint. Nancy cried out and caught her, helping her back onto the bed.

"Have you told him you are with child? He will forgive you your betrayal, *mademoiselle*. I have no doubt— he loves you and he has no heir!"

Julianne took a deep breath. She was not deluded, as Nancy was. She did not think Dominic would ever forgive her, child or not. And she would never use their child to get him back. She hadn't even thought about what to do in regard to this child. She didn't have the strength to do so now. "Please, don't say anything. Not yet. I am feeling better now. After a sip of tea, I can help you pack."

"You should tell him about the child," Nancy said, appearing stubborn. "He will forgive you in time, *mademoiselle*, for he loves you."

Julianne did not believe her—and she wasn't sure she wanted to. Hope now felt like a dangerous emotion, one she could not afford. But hadn't their entire affair been like a fairy tale? Two lovers torn apart by both politics and war. He a prince, she a dreary country girl....

Had she been a fool to believe in that love?

"I don't think he will ever love me again." She sent Nancy a quelling look; she did not wish to argue now. Julianne and Nancy began to pack up her things. As they did, Julianne felt the web of despair and despondency stealing over her. She felt herself sinking deeper and deeper into its sticky mire. She finally paused, staring at the items on her bed. It was over. She was leaving. But every garment she owned had been given to her by Dominic. Each item had a dozen memories. And that was all she would have now. But did she even have the right to take any of her things?

Another knock sounded on her door. In the act of woodenly folding a chemise, Julianne froze. She had no doubt that Catherine had come to berate and disparage her for her treachery.

Nancy looked questioningly at her.

Julianne knew she could not take any more conflict now. "Send her away," she began tersely.

But the door opened, revealing Dominic. Warlock stood slightly behind him.

Her heart leapt. Hope arose. "Dom?"

His expression hard, he walked inside. As if coldly assessing the state of their activities, he looked at the bags and garments on the bed. Then he looked at her. "You will not be leaving here tonight, after all." Revulsion was reflected in his eyes.

Julianne felt her knees buckle. *He hated her.*

And Dominic did not move; Warlock rushed to catch her. "Are you ill?"

"I am sick with heartache," she said, but she was looking at Dom.

His hard stare never wavered. His expression of distaste did not change. He dismissed Nancy, who fled the room. Dominic also closed the door, alarming Julianne.

"You could have come to me, Julianne. I want Marcel," Warlock said, encouraging her to sit on the bed.

"I would have done so—if I knew who he was and where you could find him. But he is too clever. He contacts me. Not the other way around," she said harshly. "He has threatened Momma and Amelia, Sebastian! Please, send for them, so we can keep them safe!"

"Absolutely not. If I send for them, he will know you have been uncovered."

She cried out in disbelief. "You would sacrifice your own sister to your own ends?"

He smiled. "Hardly, Julianne. I will send one of my men to Cornwall tonight as your new houseboy. He is an expert marksman and has often served me as a bodyguard. He will protect Amelia and Elizabeth."

Relief caused her tears to rise. *Her mother and Amelia would be safe.* Then she looked at Dominic.

He was staring. He glanced away.

He couldn't even make eye contact with her now, she thought, stricken. He hated her that much. Nancy was so wrong—he would never forgive her. "What about Tom?"

"I said it before and I will repeat myself. If you help me, I will help Tom." Warlock smiled pleasantly, as if they were discussing the races. "We need Marcel. When will he contact you again?"

She started. "I don't know. He now wants me to spy on Lucas."

"That must be because he assumed I would be dead tonight." Dominic was harsh.

Oh God, he was right, Julianne thought. Marcel had received the information he needed—which meant he could get rid of Dom. She was as responsible for this assassin's attempt on his life as Marcel, she thought in horror.

Warlock studied her. "You will stay here. You and Paget will continue on as if nothing has happened. We cannot allow Marcel to think you have been compromised."

She was confused—surely she had misheard. She looked at Dominic. "What is he saying?"

"He is saying that we will pretend we are happy lovers, still," Dominic said tersely. "You will return to my rooms. You will sleep there. In public, in front of the servants, we will smile at one another with affection." He suddenly reached into his breast pocket and threw an object onto the bed, beside her hip. It was a small royal blue, velvet jeweler's box. "You will even wear that, because I bought it for you this afternoon. We will play this game perfectly."

She did not touch the box. She could not be more devastated.

"He is correct, Julianne. You must play the part of lovers perfectly. Marcel must not suspect that we will have you lead him to us." Warlock raised a brow. "You look absolutely devastated. You are going to have to engage in theatrics."

And total comprehension began. She wasn't being thrown out of Bedford House. Not yet, anyway. But only because the men intended to locate and arrest Marcel. And now, she must pretend that all was well with Dominic—when he despised her.

She trembled. She hated Marcel. She wanted him thrown in the Tower and hanged. "Of course I will help," she said, looking back and forth between Sebastian and Dominic. "And what happens when you have found Marcel?"

Warlock did not answer; Dominic did.

"We will give up all pretense," Dominic said coldly, "and you can go back to where you belong."

JULIANNE SLOWLY CAME out of the dressing room in Dominic's suite, clad in a rose-colored nightgown and a small white cap, her hair in a braid. She had never been more uncertain, or in as much despair. Dominic despised her and she did not blame him. But how was she going to share his rooms now?

And when she went out, even if just downstairs, how was she going to pretend that nothing terrible had happened?

She could not stop trembling. Nancy had brought her a supper tray, but she hadn't been able to eat or drink anything. Instead, she kept reliving François's assassination attempt, and Dominic's reaction to her confession.

It was difficult enough withstanding his cold anger, and she was so afraid of him now. Not that he would ever hurt her, but she was afraid to receive another scathing, revolted look. Just then, she wanted to curl up in her own bed, and be left alone with her misery.

At least Momma and Amelia were safe now, from that Jacobin monster.

She wondered if she should climb into bed, pull up the covers and pretend to be asleep when he returned. Her stomach lurched with sickening force. Would they really share his bed? Should she take a blanket and retire to the sofa? Could she really survive in these circumstances? How long would it be before Marcel contacted her and she was sent posthaste from Bedford House?

She flinched when she heard the sitting-room door open and close. Slowly, as rigid as a block of ice and as chilled, she turned. Dominic entered the room, his jacket over one arm. He did not appear to even notice her standing by the bookcase as he walked past her. Not looking at her, he strode across the salon and into the bedchamber. There, she heard him undressing.

It was as if she were invisible to him now.

She sank onto an ottoman. What should she do—wait for him to fall asleep and then decide upon a chair in which to collapse? But he always went to bed late, just as he was always up early. She was exhausted—she doubted she could outwait him.

She slowly stood and walked toward the bedroom. She saw him within and she inhaled. He was stark naked, broad shouldered and narrow hipped, his buttocks high and hard, his back to her. He reached for a crimson caftan and shrugged it on.

Her heart thundered. She knew every inch of his body even better than she did her own.

How could this be happening?

He turned to face her, his expression hard.

She had been in his arms that morning, she thought, caressing every inch of him, just as he had touched every hidden part of her body. Unbelievably, she warmed.

"Don't even think it," he warned. "I wouldn't touch you if I were a dying man and this were my last night on this earth."

She shuddered. "What do you want me to do?"

His gaze raked over her. He turned and yanked the topmost blanket from the bed and strode toward her, shoving it at her. She quickly caught it, only to find a pillow being hurled her way. She couldn't catch that and it fell to the floor. Stunned by his outburst, she backed up.

Flushed, he said, "I don't care what you do. Sleep on the sofa, the chair or the floor, for all I care."

She fought herself and did not cry out, for his words caused more pain to stab through her.

Then he whirled past her, striding into the sitting room. Julianne hugged the blanket in acute agony to her chest. She watched him go to the bookcase, take down the volume of poetry and remove the key within. She whimpered.

He ignored her, moving to his desk and sitting down there. He unlocked the drawer, took out the letter he had been composing to Henri and began slashing out the sentences already there. Then he tore the parchment into a dozen pieces and tossed them aside. His expression was one of rage.

Julianne did not move. Silently, she cried.

He opened another drawer, took up a fresh page of vellum and dipped his quill in the inkwell. He thought for a moment, then began to write furiously.

Blinking rapidly but unable to stop the tears, Julianne picked up the pillow on the floor. She walked over to the sofa, feeling old—no, ancient. She wasn't going to survive this pretense, she thought in anguish. The sooner Marcel was caught, the better.

The quill loudly scratching, he continued to scribble furiously upon the vellum.

Julianne lay down on the sofa, curling up under the covers, facing away from him.

THREE DAYS LATER, Julianne clung to the safety strap in Lady Paget's curricle as it traveled up Oxford Street. It was a beautiful September afternoon, with the summer still lingering, and quite a few carriages were present. Several noblewomen were also strolling arm in arm in all their tony finery, gazing into various shop windows.

Marcel had contacted her that morning, requesting a

3:00 p.m. rendezvous. Julianne had never wanted anything to be over as she wanted her charade at Bedford House to end. Pretending to be Dominic's happy lover was beyond agony; she could not sleep or eat and she was constantly fighting nausea and dizziness.

But mostly, she was in terrible pain. When he held her hand, or lifted it to his lips, or smiled at her—all for the sake of whatever caller or servant was present—she was ready to burst into tears. But she would remind herself that she hated Marcel and that she would do anything to help capture him. Somehow, she would smile back at Dominic.

The evenings spent behind closed doors were the worst. He ignored her now, his anger unceasing. Clearly, for him, she had ceased to exist.

She had never felt more alone, especially as her brothers were out of town and did not have a clue as to what she was going through. She began to write Amelia, but knowing she would be going home soon and unable to even begin to express herself, she had torn up the parchment and thrown the letter away.

Now Julianne realized they were approaching the Pantheon, where she would meet Marcel. She began to perspire, fear tightening every fiber of her being. Thank God this terrible interlude would soon end, she thought. She wanted nothing more than to go home and escape Dominic's utter indifference.

Eddie slowed the carriage. A moment later, he was helping her to alight. "I doubt I will be more than a half an hour," she said.

She entered the Pantheon, clutching her reticule tightly. The main hall was vast, the size of most of Bedford House, with a high, domed ceiling. She knew there were several different rooms within, but Marcel had told her he would find her in the main hall. There were perhaps a dozen groups present; clusters of bewigged gentlemen were in deep conversation, gentlewomen were strolling, as were several couples. The hall was flanked on both sides by double-storied aisles behind dozens of magnificent columns. She could not see into the shadows of those side halls.

As she glanced across the main hall, she did not see Marcel. He was undoubtedly hiding by a pillar or in a far aisle, she thought. Was that where Dominic and Warlock were, as well? She had been told that they would go to the Pantheon and take up their positions before she arrived.

She watched a couple flirting by one of the columns, not far from where she stood. He wore green velvet, she wore dark blue. His back was to her, but she could glimpse the pretty woman's face. They were lovers, she thought with a pang, for the woman kept touching his arm, smiling, and he held her hand. She watched as he kissed it ardently. Or if they were not lovers yet, they soon would be.

She was a woman of experience now.

Suddenly the young man detached himself from the woman and turned. Julianne froze as she recognized Marcel, who was wearing a long curly white wig. He approached, his strides languid. "Good afternoon, Julianne. My, you look ghastly." He was sharp. "What is wrong?"

"Spying does not agree with me."

He studied her. "And?"

Julianne fought not to glance past Marcel. So far, neither Dominic nor Marcel were in her line of vision. "Lucas leaves for France tomorrow on the first tide, and he will disembark at St. Malo."

Marcel started. Then he smiled. "That is very good, Julianne. Do you have anything else for me?"

"Isn't that enough?" she asked, but she heard the tension in her tone. Where was Dominic? Warlock? Julianne realized she had glanced around the hall.

"Who are you looking for?"

"No one." She trembled, dismayed. *Where were they?*

"I hope you are not considering betraying me."

She wanted to spit at him. "One day, you will get your just deserts."

He laughed and walked off.

Julianne stood alone in the midst of the great hall, in absolute disbelief. What had just happened? Why hadn't Dominic seized Marcel?

She turned to watch Marcel leave the hall, through the front entrance that would take him out onto Oxford Street. She clenched her fists in frustration and despair. Then she looked around the Pantheon again, but she saw neither man.

Very angry, she lifted her skirts and rushed outside, where Eddie was waiting besides the curricle. "Take me home, please," she said tightly, climbing inside. This terrible interlude wasn't over after all, she thought desperately. She could not survive another night behind closed doors with Dominic.

She hugged herself and fought the need to succumb to self-pity. Her mind went around in circles as she tried to decide what had happened to Dominic. She began to worry. Surely, only a terrible accident or incident would have kept him from seizing Marcel in the Pantheon.

A half an hour later, the gig turned into the drive at Bedford House. Julianne was incredulous. Warlock's closed carriage was in the drive, parked before the front steps, not far from Dominic's larger lacquer coach.

She practically leapt from the curricle, without help, and was about to fly up those steps, when the front door opened and two servants came out—carrying bags that were suspiciously familiar. They looked like the bags that Nancy had brought to her bedchamber for her to use that first night after Dominic had learned of her betrayal. She froze.

The servants did not look at her. They took the bags to Dominic's coach and placed them on the roof, where they were lashed into place.

"Well done."

She whirled at the sound of Warlock's voice. He and Dominic had just come out of the house and stood above the front steps. Warlock was pleased; Dominic was grim. "You did not seize him!"

"I never said we meant to capture him, Julianne. But now I know the identity of our man."

*She had been played.* "You were at the Pantheon?"

"Of course we were there," Warlock said pleasantly.

She turned to Dominic and knew that whoever Marcel was, it was not good news. And for the first time in days, his gaze met hers. "What is it?" she whispered, frightened.

He did not speak.

"Marcel is, unfortunately, highly placed," Warlock said.

More dread began.

Warlock came down the steps and took her hand and actually kissed it. "I know you dislike me, but if you ever need my services, send word."

She withdrew her hand as if burned. Was he telling her goodbye?

And somehow, as she turned to Dominic, she knew.

Her heart lurched with frightening force as their stares locked.

He came down the steps. "You may take my coach to Cornwall."

She inhaled. "I can't leave like this."

"I am not giving you a choice." He took her arm and began to guide her toward the vehicle.

Panic began. How could she leave like this? What if Nancy was right, after all? What if, one day, he might be able to forgive her? But he would never do so if she left now, without a genuine chance to explain her actions to him! "Please let me speak with you before I go. Please— if I ever meant anything to you."

They had reached the coach, and a footman opened the door for her. "There is nothing left to say." He did not look at her.

"I am sorry! I love you!"

His face set, he pushed her forward and upward. Julianne found herself thrust into the coach and she fell onto the seats. The door slammed closed.

She jerked upright and moved to the window and flung it open. Dominic stared; she stared back. And then he nodded, without removing his eyes from her. She heard the brake being released. She cried, "Are you going to France?"

He stepped back from the carriage, as it began to move.

He was sending her away and returning to France. It was over.

Julianne hung on to the window, looking out, until she could no longer see him.

# CHAPTER SEVENTEEN

*September, 1793—Cornwall, England*

JULIANNE PULLED HER WOOL cloak closer to her body as the stark outline of Greystone Manor came into view. Seated within Dominic's coach, she stared miserably ahead. How desolate, gray and lonely the manor now seemed, silhouetted as it was against the pale blue, cloud-swept skies, the vast Atlantic ocean, the near-white cliffs. Rain was in the air, she thought helplessly, and she felt as desolate, as isolated, as alone as that manor seemed to be.

She hugged herself, but not because of the cold.

The journey from London had been endless. Nancy had been sent to keep her company, and she sat across from Julianne now. She had done her best to cheer Julianne, but of course, her efforts had been in vain. Julianne could barely keep up her end of the conversation. After their first day on the roads, Nancy immersed herself in a novel, realizing that Julianne had no interest in chatting. How could she make small talk? She was in too much heartache. She had traveled in this coach with Dominic so many times, and she could recall each and every single one of them. Her memories both consoled and devastated her. They were a flood tide. She had never missed Dominic more.

Her future felt as gray as that autumn day in Cornwall. She stared at the manor as their coach halted. It was truly over, and she must somehow accept that. Her memories would be her only companion. Instead of being crushed by them, she must be comforted. She had their child to think about now.

Eventually, she would have to tell Dominic about the child—if he survived.

She remained so afraid for him, so afraid of what he would face in France. By now, he was in the Republic. Was he in the midst of a battle in le Loire, even as she sat safely in his coach? Or was he in the midst of some dangerous assignment, playing spy games in Nantes or Paris?

His enemies were everywhere! They were the republican soldiers; they were the Jacobins on the street. She had heard about the *"représentants en mission"*—the citizens in tricolor sashes, who scoured the country for traitors to the revolution. These agents could accuse generals of treason and take over their command. They could so easily accuse Dominic of treason. How could Warlock allow him to go back there?

Would another assassination attempt be made upon him? Or would he be arrested and sent to prison to await the guillotine? she wondered, shivering, and was made sicker by the thought.

She needed to know that he was well. She had already decided to write Nadine, for surely his lifelong friend would be kept abreast of his fortunes. But she was afraid Nadine would not reply to her. Catherine had probably told her everything by now.

"We are here, *mademoiselle*," Nancy said, touching her hand softly.

Julianne managed a grim smile.

A footman had opened the door for them. As he did,

the front door of the manor opened, and Amelia rushed out, followed by a tall, muscular man. "Julianne!" She was beaming, her dove-gray skirts flying as she raced toward them.

And suddenly Julianne began to cry. She had never seen a more welcome sight. She rushed from the carriage and into her sister's arms. They clung.

"Are you all right?" Amelia cried, her gaze searching, her smile gone. "Is this Bedford's coach?" Wide-eyed, she stared at Julianne.

Julianne had written her twice while in London. She had not told Amelia about the affair, even though she had desperately wanted to confide in her sister. But Amelia would not approve, as she hadn't approved of their affair in July. She had told her that Dominic felt that he owed her and that she was his houseguest. She had assured her sister that Lucas approved, and then distracted her with tales of society and the events she had been attending.

"Yes, the coach is Dominic's." As she spoke, her tone quavered. She could not dissemble with Amelia any longer; she had never needed her sister more.

Amelia clasped her cheek with worry. "I am so glad you are back. I have missed you terribly. Come inside, Julianne." She was firm.

Amelia knew that something was terribly wrong, Julianne thought. "Nancy, do come in. You will spend the night."

Nancy curtsied. *"Merci, mademoiselle."*

Amelia turned to the stranger who was standing by the front door, watching them all. "Garret, please show Nancy to the kitchens."

Arm in arm, the sisters walked into the house. Momma was seated in one of the big burgundy chairs before the hearth, where a fire blazed—it was already quite cold inside the house. She turned her head, saw them, and her eyes brightened. "Julianne!" she cried warmly.

*Momma had recognized her.* For one moment, Julianne was in disbelief. Then she ran forward and fell onto her knees as her mother embraced her.

"How are you, my dear?" Momma asked, stroking her hair. "And why are you so distraught?"

She looked up at her mother, crying. Momma had not recognized her in months. "I have been in town, Momma, in London. I am merely tired from the journey home." She managed to smile.

"I hope there were a great many balls." Momma smiled. "I cannot recall—do you have a suitor?"

Julianne tensed, but kept smiling. "Of course I do."

Momma nodded, and looked at Amelia. "I am suddenly tired…" She trailed off.

Amelia looked at Julianne, her own gray eyes bright with unshed tears. "I will take her upstairs and be right back."

Julianne nodded and stood up as Amelia and their mother left. She hugged herself as Nancy came inside. "Can I make you and your sister tea?"

She somehow nodded, trying to smile. Then she heard her sister returning downstairs. Amelia approached quickly, taking Julianne's hand.

"She remembered me," Julianne whispered.

"It was her most lucid moment in months, or maybe even years." Amelia's gaze was searching. "Your heart is broken, and this time, it is even worse than before."

"Yes, my heart is broken."

Amelia held out her arms and Julianne went into them. She had thought that she had no tears left, but perhaps because of the child, she felt them trickling down her face yet again. Then she stepped back. "I love Dominic so much, and he loved me—until recently."

"Oh, Julianne," Amelia said, but with some pity.

She was comparing Dominic to St. Just, Julianne knew. "No, he fell in love with me, Amelia. He broke it off with his fiancée and he gave me this." She held up her hand and pulled back her long sleeve to reveal the diamond bracelet. Amelia gasped. She did not show her sister the cameo he had given her in a state of anger—she would not, could not, wear it.

Amelia stared closely now. "If he is in love with you, then why are you brokenhearted?"

Julianne trembled. "I was threatened by a radical, Amelia, and I had no choice but to spy on him."

Amelia turned white.

She would tell her sister all about Marcel eventually, as Amelia needed to have her wits about her, never mind that they now had a guard. "Because of my actions, Dominic was almost murdered," she said. "And I had to confess to my treachery." Feeling unbearably weak, Julianne collapsed in one of the burgundy chairs. "He was furious, of course, and unforgiving."

Amelia knelt beside her and took her hand.

"He has thrown me out, Amelia, and turned his back on me—as if we never loved one another!" Julianne cried. "But I could accept losing him, if only I knew he were safe. He has gone back to France, Amelia, to spy on his enemies. Even as we speak, I do not know if he is alive."

"Oh, Julianne. I don't know what to say." Amelia's gaze was searching. "Certainly there would be news if some terrible fate had befallen him. Are you sure he loved you? He was so ruthless last summer... Please tell me you didn't resume your affair."

"Amelia, there is so much you don't know. I was thrown in the Tower for my radical opinions, but he rescued me. I fell ill, and he nursed me, and being in his arms was the most perfect place!" Julianne cried, clinging to both of her sister's hands. "I will always love him and there will never be anyone else for me. But he despises me now, and worse—far, far worse—he is in France, where he might die." Amelia would have to know, sooner or later. "I am having his child, Amelia." She touched her belly, which was just beginning to swell.

Amelia stared in shock. She was starkly pale. "Are you certain you are with child?"

"Yes. I haven't had my monthly since June." There was simply no doubt now.

Amelia put her arm around her. "I am reeling. He must marry you, Julianne."

She laughed, the sound hysterical and mirthless. "If he survives the war, I will be happy—that is all I am asking God in my prayers. But he will never be forced to the altar, Amelia, and I would never marry him under these circumstances."

"You are carrying his *heir*," Amelia said, straightening to stand. "He might be a cad, but I am fairly certain he will act with honor."

Would he decide to marry her—if he ever returned? Even while despising her? Julianne shuddered. She had already experienced living with him under that circumstance. She could never do it again. "He doesn't know."

"Then you must tell him."

"I wasn't sure before, and then he learned of my treachery." She shrugged helplessly. "Of course he must know, when he returns." She trembled, thinking *if* he returns.

Amelia put her arm around her. "There is time. And you are right. We must worry about his fate first. And we must take care of you and the child."

And suddenly Julianne was so glad to be home. "Thank you, Amelia."

"There is nothing to thank me for."

MY DEAR SISTER,

*You can imagine my shock when I received Amelia's letter stating that you are carrying Bedford's child. Julianne, I trusted you. I would have never let you reside at Bedford House otherwise. My impulse was to rush to Cornwall to berate you for your betrayal of that trust, for my shock so quickly turned to anger. But then I remembered, too well, your confession of your feelings for Paget.*

*I can never remain angry with you for very long, Julianne. I care for you far too much. However, I am disappointed and dismayed. No matter your naïveté and inexperience, I would have expected you to withstand Paget's attempt at seduction.*

*But I must also blame myself for failing to see what was transpiring before my very eyes. I must blame myself for leaving you in his care as his houseguest. I must blame myself for putting the demands of the war ahead of my duty to my own sister.*

*And I blame Paget for his inexcusable behavior.*

*What is done is done. Now I must consider your welfare and that of my nephew's or niece's. Marriage has not been mentioned. I intend to speak*

*with Paget as soon as possible and make certain
his intentions are now honorable ones.*

    *I hope this missive finds you in good health.*

*Your loving brother,
Lucas*

Julianne inhaled, having just reread Lucas's letter. It
had not come as a surprise. Amelia had told her a day or
two after her arrival at the manor that she would write
both Lucas and Jack immediately. Lucas's response was
exactly as she might have expected—calm, rational and
forgiving.

Had Lucas meant that he would speak with Dominic
in France? Was it even possible?

Her heart lurched. She had written Nadine a lovely
note, inviting her to the manor when she returned to
Cornwall, without mentioning the affair with Marcel.
She had asked after Dominic, but had yet to receive any
reply.

If she did not hear from her, she intended to write
again in another week or so. A silence would signify
that her suspicions were right, and Lady Paget had poi-
soned Nadine against Julianne. The next time, she would
explain her actions and justify them—to the best of her
ability.

But if Lucas did meet with Dominic, then she would
know he was still alive!

As for Lucas believing he could force Dominic to the
altar, his resolve worried her. Everyone who knew of the
child now seemed to think that Dominic would marry her
once he learned of his or her existence. Worse, Lucas was
a very determined man. He had never failed in anything
he truly wished to achieve.

Julianne's feelings had changed. She did not want to force Dominic to marry her, but she had begun to become acutely aware of the child growing within her. That child deserved a father and he or she also deserved the life that Dominic could give him. In the end, she knew she would have to put the child's future ahead of her own needs. If Dominic returned and decided to marry Julianne, she would have to comply and somehow manage in a loveless marriage.

Jack had also sent a note.

*Julianne—Do you want me to find him and kill him? Because if he does not return and marry you, that is exactly what I mean to do. J.*

Because Jack meant every furious word, Julianne was not amused. She could imagine Jack confronting Dominic.

"Julianne," Amelia said tersely, poking her head into the bedroom they still shared. "Tom is downstairs."

Julianne froze. Tom had been released?

And then she cried out, delighted. Finally, there was good news! Amelia smiled. "I thought you would be pleased. But…will you tell him about the child? Eventually he will find out."

Her smile vanished. She wasn't showing yet. But Cornwall was a small place, and in another month her condition would be noticeable, if she did not try to hide it. And eventually, there would be no hiding her pregnancy at all. "I don't know." She followed Amelia downstairs, aware that Tom would be horrified, and found him standing before the hearth. He whirled to face her, unsmiling.

Her smile vanished. "I am so glad you have been released!"

His gaze was hard and searching. "Hello, Julianne."

She recoiled. Tension filled her. He had changed, she saw that immediately. But prison was a terrible place, and he had been incarcerated without protection for far longer than she had been. "I am happy to see you, Tom."

He came forward, his eyes flashing. "Bedford arranged my release."

She was shocked. *Dominic had done this?*

"I can only assume that you asked him to help me. After all, you were his houseguest for most of the summer." His eyes darkened impossibly.

He suspected the nature of her relationship with Dom, she thought. But why had Dominic arranged for Tom's release? Surely he had done that after he had discovered her treachery? It made no sense!

"You seem very surprised."

She stiffened, now wary. "I did reside at Bedford House thus summer. I was incarcerated, too, Tom. The convention in London was attacked by Reeves men. Dominic rescued me and invited me to stay. He felt that he owed me for his life."

"And you convinced him to save my life."

"Are you angry with me?" She was in shock.

"Yes, I am angry. Do you think I would not learn the truth?" He cast an utterly disparaging glance across her figure. "You are sharing his bed!"

Julianne gasped.

"Don't try to deny it. Marcel told me. You are his mistress!" His eyes blazed.

Julianne trembled. "Yes, I am. I love him."

He cried out. "He is a damned Tory!"

"And I don't care!" she cried back.

He paled. "What has happened to your principles?"

"My priorities have changed."

"Your priorities have changed?" he echoed in disbelief.

"Marcel used me and then tried to assassinate Dom."

"Good," Tom cried. "I am simply sorry that he failed."

She felt as if she had been shot. "You must leave this property now," she said.

He did not move. "So you are a damned Tory, too?"

She would not dignify his last comment with a reply. "I am asking you to leave." As she spoke, from the corner of her eye, she saw Garrett step into the hall, protectively.

"So we are enemies now?" Tom asked bitterly.

He wanted Dom dead. As bitterly, she said, "Yes, Tom, we are enemies."

Tom did not speak for a moment. "I loved you!"

Julianne did not respond. She was too furious to do so.

His expression hard and tight with anger, Tom turned and left.

*October, 1793—The Loire Valley, France*

DOMINIC STARED DOWN at a series of rolling hills, all blackened and burned. His heart lurched and he could not breathe.

For as far as the eye could see, those lands belonged to him.

They had destroyed the vineyards, he thought. They had burned them to the ground.

He could not believe the destruction he was witnessing as he sat his black charger atop a blackened hill. He had grown up in those vineyards, and he fought not to recall playing there as a child with Nadine and their cousins. He inhaled, fighting for composure. Was the chateau still standing? Or had they taken that from them, too?

They had not been able to break the La Vendée rebellion, he thought, so instead, they would destroy their
land. It was far more than a military tactic, far more than
the intention to starve the rebels to death. The French
government meant to punish the royalists—they wanted
to break their spirit.

And Dominic decided he would fight to the bitter end,
to his last dying breath. *"À la victoire,"* he breathed. And
he felt the tears sliding down his face.

He swatted at them, annoyed. He had left Michel after
the Battle of Cholet—a battle they had lost. But it was far
worse than that. Michel's army had been split apart. He
had taken some twenty-five thousand men to Granville,
where he would meet with the British supply convoy.
The rest of his men were cut off and behind enemy lines.
The rendezvous had been rescheduled for the third week
of the month. Michel's troops were in danger of being
picked off—or slaughtered.

Michel needed him back. He was second in command.
He hadn't heeded Warlock's orders. He had been in the
midst of the battle, and on its front lines. Women and
children had followed them into battle, just as they followed Michel now. A young mother had died in his arms,
her little girl clinging to her. A relative had taken the
child; he had another memory of this damned war now.

No, he thought grimly, he had been back in France for
six weeks or so, and he had a hundred goddamned new
memories, each one worse than the one before.

Dominic had been desperate to visit Chateau Fortescue, as it was but a half a day's ride from Cholet, yet
he hadn't wanted to leave Jacquelyn or his command.
Michel had urged him to go.

He began to trot past the blackened and burned vines.
The stench was overpowering. Of course his lands had

been chosen for reprisal. Marcel had known he was returning to France and his place in Jacquelyn's command was undoubtedly well known to his enemies.

His gut tightened. *Had he been followed to France?* After all, Marcel remained free, and no one, not even Warlock, could track all of his activities.

He had never lived as cautiously. He did not blink without looking over his shoulder, to make certain no sniper stood there.

*Julianne had spied upon him for Marcel.*

It was a devastating truth that vibrated within his being with every breath he took. Dominic began to descend the steep slope, thinking of Julianne. It felt as if his heart were on fire inside of his chest. How could she have betrayed him? That refrain haunted him night and day. It was as if the answer was out there, somewhere, if only he could reach through the shadows to grasp it. And once he found that answer, he would understand....

He no longer slept at night. He was haunted by nightmares. In them, the innocent died in bloody battles and Julianne was there, ready to betray him. He preferred to stay awake, staring up at the ceiling, haunted by a single word. *Why?*

In her arms, he had slept like a baby.

She was safely in Cornwall by now. For that, he was relieved. Was she still engaged in her radical activities? Her radical associations? God, if only she could see what was happening to this country! As angry as he was, he did not want her involved in this war—and he wanted her securely out of Marcel's reach. Warlock had assured him that Garret Ferguson was one of his most skilled men. He had sworn that Julianne and her family would be safe from the likes of Marcel and his friends.

She had betrayed him—but he would always protect

her. She had betrayed La Vendée—but he would always love her. But he would never return to her. He would never forgive her for her treachery. He would never understand.

His heart burned again. It almost felt as if more tears wished to arise. He would not allow it. He did not want to think about her. He did not want to recall her shining eyes, filled with love, or her warm smile or teasing glances. He did not want to think about how beautiful she had been in that silver evening gown, or how passionate she was in his bed. He must not remember her utter naïveté, and how it frustrated him at times and how, at other times, it enchanted him. He must not think of the time they had spent together—but he thought about her every day, helplessly, and she haunted his nights.

An hour later, he spurred his charger into a canter and up the road that had emerged from the blackened hills, the chateau and all its outbuildings clearly ahead. It was still standing. But he wasn't relieved—he was afraid.

He was closer now. He saw that the stables, the various living quarters and the winery had been gutted. The stone buildings were blackened shells.

Two stories tall, the house was flanked by two higher towers. The pale stone walls were scorched in places. Some of the windows were broken. The front door was wide open.

Dominic halted his gelding and dismounted. He walked slowly up the stone path to the house and paused before the open door, looking inside.

Once, the front hall had boasted immaculate marble floors, crimson furnishings and masterpieces. Nothing remained, not even the piano-size crystal chandeliers.

He looked into the adjacent salon. Even the gold damask draperies were gone.

They had taken everything.

Even Julianne.

TWO DAYS LATER, Dominic handed his tired mount to a young camp follower, smiling at the lad and telling him to feed the horse well. As the boy eagerly led the horse away, Dominic sobered, walking past several groups of men, women and children, all around small cook fires. Michel was eating his supper with his officers at another larger campfire.

His horse would not be well fed. There was no grain, and the horse would graze wherever it could.

It was a dark starless night, with drifting black clouds hiding most of the moon. But the fire was intense, and as he moved into the circle of its light, he saw Michel, a short, dark man in breeches, boots and a shabby jacket. Michel set his soup aside—a soup that Dominic knew consisted of potatoes, carrots and, if fortunate, a piece of meat. Everywhere they went, the local farmers and citizenry offered their assistance, but locals could not feed an entire army.

Dominic went to sit beside Michel on a folded blanket. Jacquelyn clasped his shoulder, his gaze piercing. He did not say a word.

He was too choked up to speak for a moment, thinking of what he had seen. "It is gone. They burned the land. They took everything from the house."

Michel's grasp briefly tightened before he released Dominic. "Houses can be refurnished. The vineyards can be seeded."

He could not force a smile. Yes, he thought grimly, but only if the damned French republican government was overturned.

Michel went to the pot, and ladled some soup into

a bowl. He returned and handed the bowl to Dom, sitting back down beside him. "There is still no sign of the convoy. We have been here for two days."

Dominic put the bowl down, hard. A part of him was not surprised, but he was furious. "They will come."

"Will they? We are starving, and we have no arms. We cannot go on much longer." Michel's eyes flashed.

"Wait a few more days," he advised.

"Oh, I intend to." He rocked backed slightly, clearly thinking. "The garrison at Granville does not know we are here...yet. We have the element of surprise."

Dominic tensed. He did not think an attack on the garrison a good idea, as they were too poorly armed and missing a third of their soldiers. On the other hand, Michel had proven himself to be a great military commander. He did not reply, picking up his bowl, beginning to eat. The soup was tasteless. He was starving and he did not care.

Michel did not speak, either, until Dom had finished the bowl's entire contents. Then he said, very seriously, "You must return to London."

Dom froze. "I can hardly leave now."

"You are more valuable to me in London, at the War Office, as my emissary. You must make sure that damned convoy comes!"

He was right, Dominic thought grimly. But he hated leaving Michel now. Jacquelyn needed every man.

Slowly, Michel smiled, a sparkle in his eyes. "Besides, aren't you tired of a cold, empty bed?"

He jerked, instantly thinking of Julianne.

"Dom, you had a different woman in your bed almost every night before you returned to Britain. You haven't even looked at a woman since you got here last month.

I am wondering who she is!" He was laughing. "It must be love."

Julianne's image searing his mind, he said tersely, "It is not love and it is not a laughing matter."

Michel's amusement vanished. "What is wrong? You should see your face, *mon ami*. So you have chosen to be faithful to this woman?"

The decision had not been a conscious one, although he had turned away many women in the past few weeks. Suddenly he wanted to unburden himself, desperately. "She saved my life, Michel, when I first returned to Britain. And yes, I fell in love with her—even knowing that she was a Jacobin sympathizer."

Michel's eyes widened.

"She doesn't understand the revolution or the war," he said quickly, defending Julianne. "She is impossibly naive, impossibly romantic. Julianne would give her last penny to a homeless man. And she is beautiful, and warm and so generous…" He realized he couldn't speak. Suddenly he felt an overwhelming urge to be in Julianne's arms. In her arms, there was no war. In her arms, there was no anguish, no desperation, no fear. In her arms, there was only relief, comfort and love.

"You are genuinely in love," Michel remarked. "What happened? Why are you upset—no, angry with her? Is that why you never smile anymore?"

He met his friend's gaze. "She betrayed me. A Jacobin agent in London threatened to hurt her mother and her sister. They both live alone in Cornwall, and the mother is dim-witted. Julianne went through my things. She gave Marcel the information he wished for her to find."

"Why didn't she go to you for help?"

"She did not know how to reach Marcel. He made sure of that. So I wouldn't be able to stop him from attacking her family." In that moment, Dominic realized his anger had prevented him from fully considering and empathizing with her predicament. Marcel would have hurt or even murdered either Amelia or her mother. Of that, he had no doubt.

And he had been so angry he hadn't given a damn.

Michel said softly, "You should forgive her, my friend. She was in a terrible dilemma. Of course she would protect her innocent sister and her addled mother. You should forgive her and hunt down Marcel and destroy him for daring to use your woman against you. He is the one you must hate."

Dominic began to tremble. He could never hate Julianne!

She had to have been so afraid. Hadn't he seen how nervous and anxious she had been in the days before he had discovered her treachery? Was it even treachery? She loved him. He knew it. He hadn't doubted her love before she had gone through the locked drawer, and he hadn't doubted it after discovering what she had done. What he had done was retreat into cold fury, seeing only her betrayal, refusing to see anything else, refusing to listen to any excuse or explanation.

And suddenly he imagined the extent of what she had been living through, being threatened and blackmailed by Marcel, being forced to betray him in order to protect her sister and mother. Suddenly he had an answer to the question, *Why?*

She had *needed* him. But he had not been there for her....

"I still love her," he said. "I miss her."

"Good," Michel cried, smiling as he slapped his shoulder. "Then you will go to London, speak to Windham and reconcile with the beautiful Julianne. You are as French as I am, in your soul, Dominic. You must know as well as I that love should never be denied."

JULIANNE STOOD BESIDE the open front door of the house, facing Nadine, stunned. She had written Nadine again, explaining why she had betrayed Dom. But she had posted that last letter over a month ago. "I am glad to see you," she tried, somehow smiling.

Nadine hesitated. "I received both of your letters, Julianne. May I come inside? It is bitterly cold today." She smiled impersonally.

Julianne stepped aside so Nadine could come in. She shut the door, aware that Nadine wasn't warm—but she didn't seem hateful, either. On the other hand, she could not imagine Nadine behaving in any way other than an exemplary one, no matter the circumstance.

Garret had followed her to the front door, and Julianne turned. "Would you please put on tea?"

He went to do her bidding. Momma was napping and Amelia was in town.

Julianne could not contain herself. "Have you heard from Dominic? How is he? Is he alive?" she cried, trembling.

"I haven't heard from him, Julianne, not since he said goodbye when he was leaving London."

Tears arose. She had been worrying about Dominic ceaselessly and she cried so easily now. It was the child, of course. "Do you know if he is alive?" she managed.

Nadine slowly said, "Of course he is alive. If he were dead, we would certainly learn of the terrible news."

Was she right? Julianne hugged herself. Because it was so cold, even in the house, no matter how many fires, she wore a shawl. She was beginning to show, just a little bit, but the shawl concealed her full bosom and protruding abdomen.

Nadine wasn't looking, though, as she took off her gloves and coat, the hood fur-lined. Julianne took the coat and hung it on a wall peg by the front door as Nadine said quietly, "You really do love him."

Julianne whirled. "I am so afraid for his life!"

Nadine inhaled. "I didn't know what to think, Julianne, when Catherine told me about what you had done. I asked Dominic, but he wouldn't discuss it with me. In fact, his reaction to my questions merely affirmed what I had already learned—that he genuinely loved you."

"He hates me now."

"I am not sure about that," Nadine said softly. "But he is hurt and he feels betrayed. He *was* betrayed."

Julianne did not intend to defend herself another time. She gestured at the chairs before the roaring fire. Nadine smiled briefly and walked ahead of her. Julianne followed. "So it is a good sign, that at least we haven't heard bad news?"

"Yes, it is a good sign. It isn't safe for him to correspond with anyone here." Nadine faced her.

"Is there any more war news? I heard about the battle at Cholet."

Nadine shrugged, and she was grim now. "It was a terrible defeat, but even worse, Jacquelyn laid siege to Granville and failed. During the retreat, his columns became severely extended. The stragglers were attacked by the republicans. Thousands more died."

Julianne cried out and her shawl slipped from her shoulders. "I am sure Dom was in that battle!"

Nadine's eyes went wide as she stared at her round belly.

Julianne stroked the hard contour. "It will soon be

common knowledge. I am carrying Dom's child," she said proudly.

Nadine looked up and met her gaze, shocked. "Does he know?"

"No."

"He must know—Catherine must know." She began to cry. "Oh, Julianne, this is the best news I have received since Dominic left. It is wonderful!" And she hugged her, hard.

Julianne felt relief flood her. "I don't know if Dom will be pleased—"

Nadine cut her off. "He will be thrilled. He loves you, in spite of what happened, and he will love this child." She smiled. "My mind is made up. I am staying in Cornwall for the rest of the winter, so we will be neighbors. I will write Catherine immediately, inviting her to visit."

Julianne tensed.

Nadine patted her hand. "She has to know, Julianne. Trust me, she will be pleased. This is the most precious gift you could give her." Her smile faded.

And Julianne realized what she meant. If Dominic did not come home, he had a child to carry on for him.


JULIANNE STOOD AT THE kitchen window, staring outside. The day was gray and blustery, the trees wind-whipped. Beyond the barren front lawns and the pale drive, she glimpsed the frothing ocean. Yet she really didn't see any of the gray day; instead, she saw Dominic, standing in the front hall of Bedford House in all his splendid finery. His eyes were warm as they met hers and she was holding their newborn baby....

"Julianne? You will catch a chill at that window," Lady Paget said, taking her elbow. And her green eyes were filled with concern.

Lady Paget had arrived a week ago, with several bags. True to her word, Nadine had written to her, telling her about the child. Catherine hadn't minced words when Julianne had first let her into the house.

"I am aware of your condition, Miss Greystone," she had said, "and in spite of all that has happened, it is a blessing. I am here to mend fences with you."

Julianne had been in some shock, enough so that she had been speechless. Amelia had rushed to the rescue, greeting Catherine, apologizing for the state of the manor, offering her tea and having her bags removed to their single guest chamber.

Catherine had brought Nancy and her own ladies' maid with her, while Nadine called every day, often with her sisters. And the manor's halls were suddenly filled with feminine chatter, warmth and laughter....

A routine emerged. The women would take walks together, then read to one another in the salon. The Dowager Countess would take up her embroidery when Julianne sat down to read the weekly journals or retired for a nap. And then there was the new piano.

When Catherine realized that there were no musical instruments in the house, and that Julianne had once played the piano, she had a beautiful instrument delivered to the house. It had been put in the great room, not far from the hearth. Julianne played every afternoon.

Her audience quickly expanded. The six women would crowd her as she played, while Garret, Nancy, Jeanne and their stable boy would stop their chores to steal into the house and listen. Soon, the Comte D'Archand began to appear in the later afternoons for tea, bringing his violin to play with her....

But there was no news from Dom.

Winter had arrived. She knew that the La Vendée royalists had never been resupplied by the British. Nadine and Catherine discussed the dire straits Jacquelyn was in constantly. They always did so behind closed doors, not wanting to worry Julianne, but Julianne eavesdropped shamelessly. Like her, they were worried about Dom.

It was so cold in Cornwall. Was it snowing in France? Was Dom on a frozen battlefield somewhere? Did he spend his night shivering in a canvas tent? Or was he immersed in espionage in Nantes or Paris, eluding the Jacobins and their agents on every street corner? Why didn't he write!

"Julianne, I think it is time for an outing," Catherine said firmly, interrupting her dismal thoughts. "We will go into Penzance for lunch and shopping."

Julianne faced her. She had begun daydreaming almost constantly. Worry over Dom's safety vied with her dreams of a future with him and their child. "I am not sure that is a good idea," Julianne began, but she was suddenly intrigued. She had been in hiding at the manor, for what felt like an eternity, and she was eager to get out.

Catherine knew, for she smiled. "You cannot hide from society for much longer, my dear. And I will protect you."

Tears filled her eyes. Once, Catherine had been her enemy. In the past week, she had become both a friend and an ally.

Catherine smiled and said, "I am going to go upstairs and change my gown. Why don't you do so, as well? It will be a lovely outing, but we must dress warmly. Some social intercourse will be good for you."

She knew that she had been standing at the window, thinking of Dom—and dreaming of him. Julianne nodded. When Catherine had left, she reached for the counter and leaned against it. She desperately needed to get out of the house, but what she really needed was word from Dom.

And an image flashed of her and Dominic, sitting together in the great salon at Bedford House, smiling warmly at one another, a little boy toddling about the room.

Catherine had forgiven her, and she couldn't help hoping that Dominic would one day return and do the same. Still, she knew it was so dangerous to have such dreams.

She could hear Amelia and Nadine conversing in the hall. She was about to go upstairs and change into something far warmer, when she heard a horse whinny outside.

It was too early for the Comte to call. Julianne suddenly felt a chill tingle from the nape of her neck all the way down to the base of her spine. *Dominic.*

She felt him so strongly. Afraid she was losing her mind, she whirled. It had started to flurry outside. A big bay hack was there, the rider dismounting, his cloak swinging. His back was to her. All she could see was his dark hair, pulled into a queue beneath a bicorne hat, but she froze.

*Dominic had come home.* The rider turned and she saw him clearly through the window. It was Dominic.

Julianne seized her skirts and ran into the hall, then threw open the front door. Dominic was striding toward the house and their gazes met. He faltered.

She froze. But her heart thundered. "You're alive."

He had paused. "Julianne."

And her mind came to life. She had betrayed him. He

had left her. But he had returned from France and he was standing just outside her front door!

And then he started to run to her, his face a mask of anguish and determination. In that instant, Julianne knew she was forgiven. She rushed into his arms and he lifted her high and whirled her, then set her down and held her, hard. "Julianne!" he cried, crushing her in his arms.

"You survived!" she wept.

"I survived," he said, rocking her. He kissed her temple, her hair. "Julianne, I have missed you so much. I am so sorry I sent you away!"

She clung to the lapels of his cloak and looked up into his eyes. She was shocked because they were filled with unshed tears. She saw so many shadows there, a darkness left by the war. "I have missed you, too. Betraying you almost killed me. I hated doing so, Dom, but I was so afraid for Momma and Amelia!"

"I know." He took her chin, tilted it up and kissed her, hard and desperately.

And Julianne felt the depth and extent of his anguish then. She let him kiss her for a long, long time, so afraid of what he had suffered. She held his broad shoulders, while tears streamed down his face. But he did not make a sound.

She clasped his cheek. What horrors had he lived through? How could she help him heal? "I love you."

"I need you," he said hoarsely, in return.

"I will always be here for you."

He smiled grimly. "So I am forgiven for behaving like an utterly selfish and self-absorbed aristocrat?"

"There is nothing to forgive."

More tears arose. "Thank you."

"Don't thank me. I am so glad you are safe and home! Dom, please, I beg you—never go back!"

He searched her eyes. "I am needed in London, Julianne."

Silently, she thanked God and any other powers responsible for such a decision.

"Will you come back to London with me? So I can court you properly?" He almost smiled.

She trembled. "Of course I will. But what, exactly, do you mean?" Had her brothers already spoken to him? Did he know about the child?

He smiled through his tears at her. "I love you and I must make an honest woman out of you." He hesitated. Dominic was never uncertain, but he was uncertain now. "Will you marry me, Julianne?"

Her heart leapt. She had never wanted to hear anything more! "Have my brothers forced you to ask such a question?"

He started in confusion. "What are you speaking about?"

He didn't know, she thought, stunned. Her heart racing, she pulled her shawl apart. He glanced briefly at her exposed bodice—and then his eyes widened and he glanced lower. Julianne took his hand and swept it over her hard, rounded belly.

"You're with child," he gasped.

She held his hand against their son or daughter. "Yes, Dom, I am carrying our child. I pray that my news is pleasing."

He looked up, his green gaze glistening. "I have come home in utter despair. So many have died. They razed the vineyards…" And his gaze moved to their clasped hands, atop her slightly swollen abdomen.

No one should have to suffer as he had—as all of France was suffering.

"Julianne, in this time of dark despair, you are bringing me joy and happiness!"

She smiled as he pulled her back into his arms. He looked at her, his eyes still brimming with tears, but they were also shining with love. He said, "We are going to have to elope."

She laughed. "I do not mind eloping, Dom, but everyone else might."

He smiled. "Everyone else?"

Julianne took his hand and they turned. Crowded in the doorway were Catherine, Nadine and Amelia, with Nancy, Jeanne and Garret behind them. Everyone was beaming, even Catherine, who wept silently with a mother's joy.

Dominic turned and took her back into his arms. "So I am the last to know?" he asked softly.

"You are the last to know," she said as softly, her heart skipping.

He tilted up her face and kissed her again, but this time, slowly, deeply, with purpose. "Shall we elope before or after I take you upstairs?" he asked, smiling.

"After," she managed breathlessly, new visions dancing in her head.

His grin was wicked. "Temptress," he said softly.

"Rogue," she returned.

Julianne smiled as he took her hand, holding it tightly, as if afraid to ever let her go. And as they returned to the house, Dominic was descended upon with hugs, kisses and a great many declarations and questions. Julianne stepped back, to allow him his reunion with his family. Her heart was filled with joy. Her body was filled with desire. And there was so much love.

He was alive, he was home—and he had come back to her.

He glanced at her and mouthed, "Thank you."

And she knew she had given him the greatest gift of all—the gift of new beginnings—the gift of hope.

\* \* \* \* \*

Dear Reader,

It wasn't all that long ago that my publisher asked me to start a new historical series. My muse led me to the fascinating period of the French Revolution and the revolutionary wars. I was instantly intrigued by the politics and dynamics of the era. Spying on both sides was endemic! The British spent a fortune on their spy networks in France, they infiltrated the local police forces, and even tried to rig elections! The small radical movement in Britain was at first feared, and then repressed. And soon, the British began to truly fear a French invasion on their shores. What a great backdrop, I thought, to set a series of love stories! And so The Spymaster's Men series was born....

I have tried to accurately portray the events of the period, yet do so in such a way that my reader is neither overwhelmed nor bored. One quick note—the Pantheon, where Julianne meets Marcel, was actually destroyed by a fire the previous year, and while it was subsequently rebuilt, it would not have been standing in the summer of 1793 as I described.

The story of the La Vendée royalist rebellion in 1793 ensnared me from the start. I have very loosely based my fictional character Michel Jacquelyn on their leader, the nobleman Henri de La Rochejaquelein. The rebels were not just dispossessed noblemen, but peasants and Catholic clergy, too. The rebellion against the new French republican government began in the spring of '93 both as a protest against military conscription and secularization of the clergy, but there was also genuine outrage over the execution of the king—not to mention serious bread shortages and high unemployment. A series of surprising victories over the far greater French forces did follow, but as I described, the rebels were lacking in arms, food and other supplies. By the fall, this shortage was critical. The rebels were starving to death.

The British had begun to promise aid in the summer, but were distracted by the various war arenas in which they were engaged. Some sources claim that the convoy was supposed to rendezvous with Rochejaquelein and his men off Brittany (Granville) in mid-October, but it never came. Other sources claim no such plans were finalized, and Rochejaquelein besieged Granville in order to attain the port for a resupply effort. In any case, the siege of Granville was a disaster, and in retreat, his army was split. Thousands in the columns caught behind enemy lines died.

On December 2, twelve thousand British, German and émigré troops arrived off the coast of Brittany with supplies to join the starving rebels. But the rebels weren't there—so they sailed away.

Rochejaquelein and his army were defeated on December 12 at Le Mans. And on December 23, just north of Nantes, his men were annihilated. A few thousand escaped in small groups incapable of mustering up a strong resistance. Rochejaquelein was killed in January of 1794. "Final Pacification" of La Vendée was begun then. Farms and villages were burned and razed to the ground; the residents of La Vendée, regardless of age, gender of political affiliation, were hunted down and murdered. The very last rebel band of six thousand men was finally wiped out in April of 1796. And thus ended the La Vendée rebellion.

The Spymaster's Men live in dangerous times. Each hero faces death on a constant and daily basis, whether at home or abroad. As Dominic remarked, there is no honor in war. War changes everyone. But these wounded heroes can be salvaged, their souls saved—as you have just read.

I hope you have enjoyed Dom and Julianne's passionate romance. I am looking forward to writing the rest of the series and I hope you will enjoy the soon to be told tales of the rest of the Spymaster's Men.

*À l'amour,*

*Brenda Joyce*

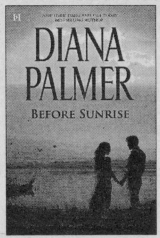

Life behind the palace walls has never been
this thrilling....

Classic tales of royal romance and intrigue from
**#1** *New York Times* bestselling author

# NORA ROBERTS

## THE PLAYBOY PRINCE

When it comes to women, Prince Bennett has always enjoyed
a challenge. So after meeting the quiet and beautiful
Lady Hannah Rothchild, the dashing playboy cannot rest until
he breaks through her careful reserve. Love had always been a game
to Bennett, but with this elusive, mysterious woman he discovers
his heart is on the line, and he's playing for keeps....

## CORDINA'S CROWN JEWEL

For a few precious weeks, Her Royal Highness Camilla de Cordina
could be just plain Camilla MacGee. Working in rural Vermont for
the devastatingly handsome and utterly cantankerous archaeologist
Delaney Caine is the perfect refuge. But Camilla's irritation with the
man soon turns into fascination, then desire, and the royal runaway
knows she'll have to confess. Would Del see her as a woman
to be loved, or dismiss her as a royal pain?

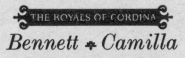

THE ROYALS OF CORDINA

*Bennett* ✦ *Camilla*

Available wherever books are sold.

*Silhouette*®
*Where love comes alive*™

**HARLEQUIN**®
www.Harlequin.com

# REQUEST YOUR FREE BOOKS!

## 2 FREE NOVELS
## FROM THE ROMANCE COLLECTION
## PLUS 2 FREE GIFTS!

**YES!** Please send me 2 FREE novels from the Romance Collection and my 2 FREE gifts (gifts are worth about $10). After receiving them, if I don't wish to receive any more books, I can return the shipping statement marked "cancel." If I don't cancel, I will receive 4 brand-new novels every month and be billed just $5.99 per book in the U.S. or $6.49 per book in Canada. That's a saving of at least 25% off the cover price. It's quite a bargain! Shipping and handling is just 50¢ per book in the U.S. and 75¢ per book in Canada.* I understand that accepting the 2 free books and gifts places me under no obligation to buy anything. I can always return a shipment and cancel at any time. Even if I never buy another book, the two free books and gifts are mine to keep forever.

194/394 MDN FELQ

| Name | (PLEASE PRINT) | |
|------|------|------|

| Address | | Apt. # |
|------|------|------|

| City | State/Prov. | Zip/Postal Code |
|------|------|------|

Signature (if under 18, a parent or guardian must sign)

### Mail to the **Reader Service**:
**IN U.S.A.:** P.O. Box 1867, Buffalo, NY 14240-1867
**IN CANADA:** P.O. Box 609, Fort Erie, Ontario L2A 5X3

Not valid for current subscribers to the Romance Collection
or the Romance/Suspense Collection.

**Want to try two free books from another line?**
**Call 1-800-873-8635 or visit www.ReaderService.com.**

* Terms and prices subject to change without notice. Prices do not include applicable taxes. Sales tax applicable in N.Y. Canadian residents will be charged applicable taxes. Offer not valid in Quebec. This offer is limited to one order per household. All orders subject to credit approval. Credit or debit balances in a customer's account(s) may be offset by any other outstanding balance owed by or to the customer. Please allow 4 to 6 weeks for delivery. Offer available while quantities last.

**Your Privacy**—The Reader Service is committed to protecting your privacy. Our Privacy Policy is available online at www.ReaderService.com or upon request from the Reader Service.

We make a portion of our mailing list available to reputable third parties that offer products we believe may interest you. If you prefer that we not exchange your name with third parties, or if you wish to clarify or modify your communication preferences, please visit us at www.ReaderService.com/consumerschoice or write to us at Reader Service Preference Service, P.O. Box 9062, Buffalo, NY 14269. Include your complete name and address.

A new generation of cowboys stake claims to their land—and the women they love....

Three classic tales from #1 *New York Times* bestselling author and *USA TODAY* bestselling author

# LINDA LAEL MILLER

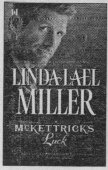

Available now!

Coming in March 2012.

Coming in May 2012.

"Linda Lael Miller creates vibrant characters and stories I defy you to forget."
—#1 *New York Times* bestselling author Debbie Macomber

# BRENDA JOYCE

| | | | |
|---|---|---|---|
| 77551 | DEADLY VOWS | __ $7.99 U.S. | __ $9.99 CAN. |
| 77547 | DEADLY KISSES | __ $7.99 U.S. | __ $9.99 CAN. |
| 77541 | DEADLY ILLUSIONS | __ $7.99 U.S. | __ $9.99 CAN. |
| 77507 | THE MASQUERADE | __ $7.99 U.S. | __ $9.99 CAN. |
| 77460 | AN IMPOSSIBLE ATTRACTION | __ $7.99 U.S. | __ $9.99 CAN. |
| 77442 | THE PROMISE | __ $7.99 U.S. | __ $9.99 CAN. |
| 77346 | DARK VICTORY | __ $7.99 U.S. | __ $7.99 CAN. |
| 77334 | DARK EMBRACE | __ $7.99 U.S. | __ $7.99 CAN. |
| 77275 | A DANGEROUS LOVE | __ $7.99 U.S. | __ $7.99 CAN. |
| 77219 | DARK RIVAL | __ $7.99 U.S. | __ $9.50 CAN. |

*(limited quantities available)*

| | |
|---|---|
| TOTAL AMOUNT | $ _____ |
| POSTAGE & HANDLING | $ _____ |
| ($1.00 FOR 1 BOOK, 50¢ for each additional) | |
| APPLICABLE TAXES* | $ _____ |
| TOTAL PAYABLE | $ _____ |

*(check or money order—please do not send cash)*

To order, complete this form and send it, along with a check or money order for the total above, payable to HQN Books, to: **In the U.S.:** 3010 Walden Avenue, P.O. Box 9077, Buffalo, NY 14269-9077; **In Canada:** P.O. Box 636, Fort Erie, Ontario, L2A 5X3.

Name: _____
Address: _____ City: _____
State/Prov.: _____ Zip/Postal Code: _____
Account Number (if applicable): _____

075 CSAS

*New York residents remit applicable sales taxes.
*Canadian residents remit applicable GST and provincial taxes.

HQN™ | HARLEQUIN®
www.Harlequin.com

PHBJ0212BL